Call Me Mommy

ALSO BY MARSHALL FRANK

BEYOND THE CALL

DIRE STRAITS

FRANKLY SPEAKING

ON MY FATHER'S GRAVE

Call Me Mommy

MARSHALL FRANK

HARLAN

PUBLISHING

Greensboro, North Carolina

Published by Harlan Publishing Company
P.O. Box 397
Summerfield, North Carolina 27358

Book and Cover Design by Jeff Pate
Cover Art by Fletch Brendan Good

First Edition

ISBN: 0-9747278-6-5

Library of Congress Control Number: 2005

ACKNOWLEDGMENTS

Though deviating from truth for obvious reasons, this novel would not have been possible had it not been for real events which affected my life and the life of my first born. I must extend acknowledgment to his mother, now deceased, for the core plot to this story.

I am wholly grateful for the input of friends and professionals who have reviewed all or parts of this manuscript. You know who you are.

Special thanks to Harlan Publishing for their faith and support.

And, as always, I accomplish nothing without the devoted partnership of my wife Suzanne, the most perfect human being on planet earth.

As the twig is bent, the tree inclines.

—Virgil

PART I

Miami, Florida, May, 1964

chapter one

It was a glorious day. Applause seemed to emanate from every corner of the campus as she made her way to the parking lot, beaming with pride. The announcements had just been released. Professors, friends, even students she had never met before offered congratulations for finishing with a perfect 4.0 grade point average, head of her class. After four long years, that sweet Bachelor's Degree was hers. Only one more paper to study, her valedictorian speech for the graduation ceremony. The long, arduous haul was over for this pert, wide-eyed country girl who, four years earlier, earned an academic scholarship at the University of Miami. It was time to celebrate. At twenty-two, Laura Jean Ramsey was the happiest woman alive.

She checked her watch. It was nearly four. She figured he would probably not be home by now. Normally, she'd phone him at the office but this called for a little surprise. First, a stop at a local deli for a pound of smoked sailfish, Swiss cheese and a box of sesame crackers, his favorite, then to the liquor store for a bottle...no, two bottles of champagne. She'd leave the baby at the sitter's an extra couple of hours, maybe even overnight so they could have this time alone. It had been so long. With all the school commitments, mounds of textbooks, countless term papers, the new baby and his law practice, it seemed they hardly knew each other. He would be so pleased.

She dropped a nickel in the pay phone and dialed. "Hi, Sally. It's Laura. I was wondering if you could keep the baby for a while..."

"Oh, Mrs. Ramsey. The baby is already gone. Mr. Ramsey picked him up a couple hours ago."

"Really? Oh, well. Never mind. Thanks."

Strange. Why would he...?

The forty-five minute ride from Coral Gables to North Miami Beach went by swiftly as she reflected on the year that changed her life forever, meeting the man of her dreams then toughing out a senior year through a pregnancy which was conceived in the back seat of a Sedan DeVille. He said he loved her and wanted to make it all right and proper. They were married barely a month before the baby was born. As she cruised north in her white four-door, '59 Chevy Impala, her thoughts drifted back to Ada, Oklahoma and how proud her parents would be when they got the news. *Oh Mom, Dad, I love you both so much. Please, be patient with me. I know you'll just love Lloyd when you meet him, I just know you will.* It was a sensitive topic.

She turned up the volume on the radio and listened to the news. President Lyndon Johnson was promising he'd never send any American combat troops to Viet Nam if elected. India announced the death of its Prime Minister, Jawaharlal Nehru, while another wave of Cuban refugees had made their way to the United States via Miami's International Airport. She changed the station and sang aloud to Louis Armstrong's, *Hello Dolly*, her frizzy brown hair swirling into her eyes from the open window. The warm, briny smell of the ocean invaded her car as she reached highway A1A where Sunny Isles Causeway terminated at the Atlantic shoreline. A turn to the left, then north through motel row, a gauntlet of two story resorts en route to the posh five bedroom home which had been his bachelor pad before they married. "Wheeee," she hooted, bouncing and singing, slapping the steering wheel in rhythm to the Supreme's *Baby Love.*

At the end of the two-mile stretch, the road narrowed into Golden Beach, an upscale community of elegant, custom-built manors sprinkled between the intracoastal waterway and the ocean front. She turned to the left and drove past several homes toward the intracoastal side of the island before arriving at a flamingo pink, two-story mansion with a barrel-tiled roof. As she pulled into the carport, she was surprised to see his little MG in the circular driveway and wondered who owned the blue Oldsmobile parked just behind it.

With a book bag in one hand, the sack of champagne bottles

in the other and a purse over her shoulder, she approached the side door and hollered, "Lloyd! Lloyd! Can you let me in? My arms are loaded." There was no answer, but she could hear music inside. She kicked at the door, but still there was no answer. Frustrated, she set the bags down, fumbled through her purse and inserted a key into the door. It wouldn't turn. *Strange,* she thought. *It worked fine yesterday.* She studied her key ring, then tried another. It didn't work either. *Oh, for cryin' out loud!* "Lloyd!" she shouted, louder this time. "Lloyd, open up honey. My key isn't working." Still no answer. She looked to the western sky and saw the bright golden sun hanging over the horizon. A warm bead of perspiration trickled from her temple.

My God, I hope he's okay. Hell, I'll just use the front door. Briskly, she stepped to the front of the house, passing the two cars in the driveway. A furry object was hanging from the mirror of the Oldsmobile. She could still hear the music from inside, a symphony playing *Autumn Leaves.* She took out another key and tried it into the front door, but it would not turn. *What the...? Hey, something's wrong here.* It was the right key but no matter how much she tried, it didn't work. Again she shouted, louder this time. "Lloyd. Are you all right? Let me in, please!"

No answer. Orchestral music continued to play. The salt taste of perspiration saturated her tongue as she licked her lips, then wiped her forehead. She peeked inside the awning windows but saw no movement, nothing out of place. A flickering glow from the console television set made her think he might be asleep in the Florida room. Confused, curious, she ambled over to the Oldsmobile but it was locked. Inside, she saw an open pack of Parliament cigarettes on the seat, Lloyd's brand. Several butts were crushed in the ash tray. A small Teddy bear hung from the mirror.

She returned to the side door, beating it one more time to no avail. Perplexed, mystified, she removed her shoe and used the heel to break a glass jalousie pane, pushed the screen and reached through to the knob. Drenched in perspiration, she stepped into the kitchen, relieved to set down the bags. The music from upstairs was louder now. *No wonder he couldn't hear me.*

In stocking feet she placed the champagne bottles in the refrigerator then strode across the tile floor into the living room expecting to see a new face, wondering all the while who owned the Oldsmobile. The Florida room was empty. A rerun of *Candid Camera* appeared on the black and white console with Allen Funt interviewing a group of children. In the front foyer, two suitcases were standing upright, but she would pay them no mind until she knew Lloyd was all right. *Maybe a friend of his is coming to stay?* It was all very strange, keys not working, the Oldsmobile, suitcases, loud music. Slowly, she ascended the curved staircase to the corridor then looked to the end. The door to the master bedroom was closed. Strains of the orchestra playing *Fascination* grew eerily louder as she approached. She glanced into the other rooms but they were empty. The baby's room was undisturbed, just as she left it that morning. *Where's Bowen? Where's my baby?* She remembered Sally saying that Lloyd had picked the baby up a couple hours ago. *Something is wrong here.*

Orchestral music crescendoed as she stepped cautiously toward the master bedroom door. A dark, ominous feeling came over her as she sensed all things in her life were about to change. She swallowed nervously and gave thought to running back down the stairs and out of the house. She was afraid of what she would find on the other side of that door. But there was no turning back. Her mouth was dry as talcum powder as she turned the knob and pushed.

The music grew louder the instant it opened. A stench of alcohol amid a pall of cigarette smoke blasted her nostrils. Shadows were moving against the far wall. The door swung wider, all the way, the music blaring, muffling sounds of grunts and groans. Her eyes nearly popped from her head. She stood watching in horror as he continued humping, thrusting, his bare buttocks pounding like a jackhammer between milky-white legs. The woman's knees were elevated, red toenails suspended, voices of sheer pleasure whining, moaning, rockin' and a rollin'. It was climax time as they howled together, embracing fervently, oblivious to innocent Laura standing in the doorway gasping in disbelief. As Mantovani reached maximum volume, she felt faint and stumbled toward the dresser, her heart pounding like sledge hammer, eyes riveted to the salacious scene before her. Shocked and quaking, she took several short panting breaths and then wailed at the top of her lungs, "No! No! No!" The unsuspecting couple halted abruptly, panting, then turned their heads to find Laura standing there crazed, teeth bared, spewing saliva. Out of control, she leaped upon the two of them, knocked over a bottle of scotch on the end table then beat her fists on his bare back, over and over.

At first he cowered, shielding his head. "Stop Laura.! Stop it!" The woman screamed, trying desperately to break away. Laura shouted again and again, unintelligible sounds as sheer pandemonium erupted in the room. Romantic strains of *Laura* continued to blare from the small record player on the dresser. The naked couple pulled and pushed, grunting, shouting expletives until the buxom blonde bounced from the bed, faced Laura for one fearful moment, then sprinted naked toward the bathroom. Reeking of alcohol, Lloyd grabbed Laura's arms to fend her off and shouted to his playmate, "Get dressed, Merrilee, and get the fuck out of here. Hurry." Hysterical, Laura let out a strident shrill, panting, biting at her husband, spewing phlegm, growling, hyperventilating like a crazed psychopath while he held her wrists.

"Laura. Stop it, Laura! Come on, you're crazy. You're crazy." He grabbed her hair, pushing her face down.

"I'll kill you, you son of a bitch! How could you? Why? Why? You bastard! I'll kill you!"

"Laura, stop it! Let me explain."

"Explain? Explain what? That you didn't mean to fuck her? You bastard!"

He was a head taller, sinewy and strong. He took control by holding her hair and twisting an arm behind her, then lifted her from the bed while she raved on. Finally, he pushed her into a small closet, slammed the door and wedged a vanity chair under the knob. From inside, Laura began pounding and ranting maniacally, "You bastard! I hate you! How could you? Let me outa here, you son of a bitch! I'll kill you!"

The blonde quickly dressed, rushed out of the bathroom and raced toward to the door. Lloyd shouted, "Merrilee, wait. Hold this door shut until I can get that dresser over here."

Laura heard the woman reply, gasping for breath, angry,

"Lloyd, god dammit, you didn't tell me, ...oh my God, I got to get out of here."

In the dark, cramped space amid racks of his suits and shirts, Laura continued to kick and pound the door, yelling at the top of her lungs. She stopped a moment, groping wildly, feeling his clothes hanging on the racks, then,...*oh no...* a wide, empty space where her clothes were,...once. *The suitcases? This was all planned?* It was all so surreal and bewildering, like she had crawled inside the skin of another woman. *This can't be happening. This couldn't be me.* No baby, no clothes, no house keys, her husband with another woman in her bed, her house.

He pulled a heavy dresser across the carpet and wedged it against the closet door. In a controlled tone now, she heard him say, "Okay, get outa here." A door slammed. The blonde was gone.

There was a lull in the shouting as Lloyd dressed, made up the bed and tidied the room. Laura's poundings had ebbed. She was exhausted, whimpering, her voice trailing off, hoarse from screaming. In the darkness, she slid to the floor, lowered her head into her hands and sobbed. "My God, what have I done? What did I do, God, what did I do?" Images of her three-month-old baby boy suddenly flashed through her brain. *Oh my God. Bowen. Where's my baby? Where's my baby?*

"Mr. Ramsey picked the baby up a couple hours ago."

Gathering her wits, trying to compose herself, she felt another surge of adrenalin, then shouted through the door, "Lloyd? Lloyd...where's the baby? Listen to me. I want to know, where's Bowen?" No answer . But she heard footsteps and the sounds of movement, like tumblers being rinsed, a flushing toilet, music being turned off. "Lloyd, answer me! I want to know, where is my baby? Let me out of here! Godammit, let me out of here!" Still, no response. Then she screamed at the top of her lungs, "Where is my baby?"

The harsh odor of moth balls in the stifling closet brought a burning sensation to her eyes. Totally defenseless, she found herself a victim of this monster who she called her husband. Her imagination began to soar. *Oh God. Oh God. What if he's a killer? What did he do with Bowen? Did he kill the baby? Is he going to kill me? Oh my God, my God. I've got to get out. I've got to find my baby.* She burst anew into a violent frenzy, screaming relentlessly, pounding and kicking on the door until she finally collapsed from the heat.

Meanwhile, Lloyd Bernard Ramsey had neatly arranged all the furnishings, showered, chewed a breath mint and telephoned the Golden Beach police. The cop was there in less than one minute.

"Yes, Mister Ramsey," asked the old timer at the door in his uniform regalia. "What's up?"

"Hello Harold, come on in. I have a terrible problem here."

As with the rest of the five man department, and its chief, Lloyd knew Officer Harold Plevnic well. He helped get him the job four years before. The Ramsey house was a regular coffee stop for local cops, especially when the MG was in the driveway.

They settled at the kitchen table, each with a glass of soda pop. "Laura and I,...well, we honestly should never have gotten married, Harold. I did it, you know, for the baby, because...."

"Because you're an honorable man, yes sir."

The conversation was interrupted by the muffled sounds of periodic outbursts from upstairs. Deferring to Lloyd, the officer paid no mind. "I think she just overdid it, completely stressed herself out with that school schedule and the baby and all, blinded by ambition, totally disregarding her responsibilities here at home."

"Yes sir, too bad."

"She even had the gall to accuse me of infidelity. Would you believe, Harold, she's saying she caught me with another woman?"

"That's absurd."

"Of course it's absurd. If I was going to...well, I certainly wouldn't in my own house."

"That would be crazy sir."

"Yes, well, Laura is not well, I'm afraid."

"What do you mean?" asked the greying cop.

Lloyd tapped the side of his forehead.

"Oh, I see. Delusions. Tch tch."

The dapper young lawyer lit a Parliament cigarette and exhaled a waft of smoke. "She's upstairs, ranting out of control. I locked her in a closet because I'm afraid she might hurt herself or hurt someone else. We were just talking, you know, about our situation and when I suggested a trial separation she agreed. She even packed her clothes. As she was about to leave, she went completely bonkers. Harold, I mean, I've never seen someone with such crazy eyes, screaming her lungs out, like something out of a horror show, beating on me, making false accusations. It's so sad."

"Yes sir. Very sad. May I ask, is the baby here?"

"He's over at my mother's. I took him there as a precaution, just in case there was any problem. Looks like I was right."

"Good thinking, sir."

"You know, I'm not that familiar with the mental health laws these days. What can I do to have her, you know, evaluated or something? Maybe placed somewhere for her own good?"

"Well, sir, if you're willing to sign the authorization as a close relative, I can have her transported to the psychiatric center at Jackson Memorial Hospital."

"How long would she be there?"

"'Bout three days."

"Then what?"

"Then you can petition the court to have her committed as incompetent for an undetermined period, until she's considered safe from hurting herself, or others."

"Do it."

"Yes sir."

"I want to help her."

The heat was oppressive, the air unbreathable, so she crouched to the floor of the closet and nudged her face at the sliver of light under the door to suck a gulp of fresh oxygen. In a matter of moments, Laura Ramsey's rosy life had plunged into a dark abyss, her world in total chaos. Weeping softly, hoarse, she muttered, "Lloyd, please. Please let me out. Where is my baby? I want my little boy." The wonderful evening she had planned briefly flashed through her mind until she visualized his grotesque, hairy ass humping between suspended sets of painted toe nails. *"Get dressed Merrilee and get the fuck out of here."* All this time his intentions had been a total sham. He had been fooling her, toying with her emotions, never loving her. Now she was discarded like unwanted trash. She realized he only married her to save his precious reputation.

Oh my God. What's he going to do to me? My baby! I've got to get out of here! She began kicking and pounding again, but to no avail. As she crouched to the floor to suck another breath of air, she saw shadows moving, shoes, voices, men's voices. Finally, freedom. She would find her baby and run far, far away, so far that he would never know where she was. There were people moving about in her bedroom and men's voices, so she composed herself. *Don't lose it, Laura. Stay calm. Get your baby and get out.*

The dresser moved away. Then the chair. As the door opened, a blast of fresh air cooled her face. Half sitting, half laying, twisted, flushed, contorted, she glistened from perspiration. Wiry brown hair stood out from her head like she had been zapped by ten thousand volts of electricity. First, she saw two sets of white pants, white shoes and white smocks. Two middle-aged men, one bald, the other with black wavy hair and a mustache stood over her. The bald one spoke first, "How are you, Mrs. Ramsey?"

Her eyes bulged like cue-balls as she strained to speak, her voice muted. "How would you be if you just caught your wife fucking a complete stranger, in *your* bed? Huh? Right here, in that bed, I walked in and..."

"Yes, of course. You'll have to come with us, Mrs. Ramsey."

"Come with you? What are you talking about? Who are you? Where is my husband? Where is my baby? What's going on?" She was more frightened now, shielding her body with outstretched hands.

They reached down, grabbed her flailing arms and wrestled her back to the floor. She writhed and squirmed, fighting, biting one on the arm. "Ouch!" "Ohhh!" "Yike!" They grunted and squealed, rolled and wrestled on the carpet for several minutes until sheer exhaustion set in. Finally, the bald one grabbed her in a choke hold and ordered his partner, "Phil. Get the jacket."

She felt rock-hard power in his arm and smartly relaxed before being strangled. "Okay. Okay," she grunted.

As the man returned with the straitjacket, she started resist-
ing again, pulling away, cursing, spitting, kicking until they tied
her into the jacket. Hysterical, her face scratched, Laura was
carted away with her arms wrapped across her chest, hair in
disarray, eyes flitting side to side. Her husband stood near to
Officer Harold Plevnic as she was ushered past, babbling, "Stop!
God damn you! Don't you see? He was screwing some broad.
Can't you see? Can't you see, you fools, it was him....not me
who..."

"Tch tch," muttered the police officer. "Too bad."

She babbled all the way to a waiting Nash Rambler. "My
baby, where's my baby? Just tell me where my baby...I have to
study for my speech, wait, let me get my speech. I'm valedictorian... My husband's a lawyer... wait... what's happening...
champagne...red toe nails...my baby, my baby...I want my baby.
Oh, Daddy help, please Daddy... I want my little baaaabeeee...
pleeeease."

A golden sun had settled into the western horizon produc-
ing a bright glow of pink and orange hues framed by a rich,
azure sky. Fading stratus clouds brushed across the distant sky.
The humid air left everyone soaked in perspiration, especially
Laura who had languished over an hour sobbing in a small,
airless closet. There were no inside handles to the rear doors of
the Nash. Wrapped like a hog on a spit, she struggled and managed to sit up as the car pulled from the driveway. She strained
to peer out the rear window where she saw the old policeman
stroll casually toward his car while her handsome twenty-six year
old husband stood at the front steps smiling at her and waving
goodbye.

chapter two

September - Four Months Later

The painted letters on the glass panel door read: *Smith, Oglethorp, Ramsey and Son.* Inside, Thurgood Spencer Ramsey swivelled behind his oak desk, puffing on a long stem pipe, sending a sweet aroma of imported tobacco out the open window which over-looked Miami's Bayfront Park and the sparkling bay beyond. A small oscillating fan on the bookcase offered a welcome breeze to the stifling September air. Thurgood was the quintessential big-city lawyer, silk Italian suits, office walls dripping with awards, accolades and photos of important people, an array of influential clients, a Lincoln Continental, membership at LaGorce Country club and a huge mansion on Miami Beach's exclusive Star Island. The youngest and the only lawyer among three sons sat dutifully before him, fiddling with his fingers before reaching for a Parliament.

"That was a nice settlement, my boy," remarked the elder Ramsey. "I'll bet old C.T. never expected his client to capitulate on the stand like that. You had him by the balls and he knew it."

"One point six million, Pop. I loved it. I can't tell you how much I love it. That's got to be my biggest divorce payoff yet. You shoulda seen the look on that asshole's face."

Thurgood snickered, puffing on his pipe. "Poor bastard, gets cleaned out over a lousy blow job."

"Yeah, well, it wouldn't have been so bad if he were the blowee and not the blower." First a chuckle, then a burp of laughter from Lloyd. Thurgood didn't find it as funny. "This is everything to me, Pop. I can't tell you how much I love this shit, putting on the squeeze then cleaning out some asshole. Riches to rags, from their pockets to ours, and it's all legal."

"Yeah, well you won't win 'em all, kid. Remember that."

"Someday, when I get tired of racking up those zeros, I'm gonna run for Governor, or something like that. Yeah. Maybe Senator. Someday. I can just hear it, *Governor* Lloyd B. Ramsey. Maybe, who knows? The White..."

"Ah, quit dreamin'," Thurgood interrupted, his mind obviously on other more important matters. "You've got a long way to go, boy. First you gotta grow into a man."

"What do you mean by that?"

The old man grinned. He knew he touched a nerve. "Never mind."

Lloyd lit another cigarette and changed the subject. "How 'bout that Whitey Ford, Pop? Another shutout. You see the Yankee-Red Sox game the other night?"

"Yeah, I saw it. What I could of it, between the antenna going on the fritz and the baby crying and your mother, where were you, anyway?"

"I watched it with a date."

"I see." The elder Ramsey turned pink in the face, then decided it was time to bring it up. "I've told you before, Lloyd, I'm not going to have it. I won't allow your mother to be saddled with your foolish mistakes. She's too old and troubled. That is final."

"What would you have me do, father, give the baby away? That's my son, you know."

"Oh really? What makes you so sure?"

"Come on Pop, she's just a hick. Guarantee ya, she ever had anyone else before me. Besides, I had the kid's blood type checked."

"And...?"

"He's got the curse. AB negative, just like his old man."

The barrel chested old man clenched the pipe in his teeth, stood and walked to the window where he peered over the gleaming marble library, then toward the open-air bandshell further south. "Muriel has been caring for that child day and night for three months, ever since you discharged that...that damsel from the sticks, while you go about living the life of a playboy, carousing all hours night after night. It's irresponsible."

"I can't very well care for him myself, father. I've got my practice here, clients..."

"What you've got, I gave you Lloyd. And what I give to you, I can take back. Is that clear?"

Lloyd loosened his tie in frustration and sat back in the chair. "Yeah, sure."

The distinguished attorney pointed the pipe stem at his son. "When your divorce is finally over, I want you to find a woman, Lloyd, a decent woman, not some bar fly, and get remarried, settle down. There's plenty of needy women out there. You've brought enough embarrassment to this firm..."

"Me. Married? Again? Are you...?"

"I am as serious as war, son. Either that, or give the child up for adoption."

The younger Ramsey leaped to his feet, incensed. "Never!"

"Why not? You're certainly not ready for fatherhood for God sakes."

"I beg to differ, dear father. That little kid is the most important thing in the world to me. I want to be to him what you've been to me. I want to be his guiding force, to make him into something special."

"Then have another kid down the road, after you've finished sowing your wild oats. You're in no condition to care for him and neither is his loony mother for that matter. I forbid Muriel to be burdened. That's that. The child's just a bastard anyway."

"Bastard? What do you mean by that? I married that broad. At least give me credit for that."

Thurgood pressed the tobacco into his pipe and relit the bowl. "You married her because you knocked her up. You knew damn well I wouldn't allow a paternity suit to cross this firm."

"I had sex with her one time. One lousy time."

"What for? You don't even like her."

"She was in one of my classes melting over me." Lloyd smirked and waffled his head. "What can I say? It's like fishing in a trout pond out there."

"Then you should have let her have the baby. That was stupid, what you did. Now it's too late."

"Pop, I don't want my son raised by some hick." Pacing the

floor, defiant, puffing a cigarette, Lloyd pondered his father's remarks, then smirked. "Since when are you so concerned about Mom, anyway? You know she'll do anything you want. Shit, I've never seen her stand up to you. If you told her to take care of the baby, she'd take care of the baby. Face it, Father. It's not Mom you're concerned with. You just don't want the inconvenience of a baby."

"You don't talk about your mother like..."

Lloyd chuckled. "Oh come on, Pop. Since when do you defend mother?" It was a bold statement to his father's face. Stunned, Thurgood sat back in his swivel chair, puffed his pipe and turned toward the book shelves. Lloyd seized the moment. "Mom has been nothing but a loyal vassal since, since forever..."

"Lloyd, you're out of line..."

"You know something? I don't ever remember you and Mom showing each other affection."

"Enough, Lloyd, you're digressing from the issue here."

"The entire office knows about you and..."

Pounding his fist on the desk, Thurgood rose indignantly, "That is enough! Do you hear me?"

Lloyd knew he had dangerously overstepped. After a short, tenuous silence, he asked, "Why can't I just hire a nanny or something?"

"Out of the question. This situation needs to be legitimized." Thurgood paced a moment, then turned. "Sit down, Lloyd. Let me explain something to you." He squinted, puffing. "Jim Oglethorp and I started this practice from bare bones when..."

"Father, I've heard all this before. Please spare me."

"You listen up, dammit. This concerns you, very deeply. Very, very deeply. We boast one of the most respected firms in this state. Never, I mean never has there been a blemish on our record or our reputation until..."

"Until...?"

"Until I made the grievous error believing you were worthy of a future partnership. I've made very few mistakes in my life, but this may have been the biggest. Now, either you get your act together, find a suitable wife and mother for that kid or start filling out applications for a county job. I will not have this firm stained." Uncustomarily speechless, Lloyd gazed into space with hostile eyes. "You've got six months. Can I be any clearer than that?"

Shrugging his shoulders, he replied, "Guess so."

"What the hell did you ever see in that...that...?"

With a wave of the hand, Lloyd responded, "She had nice tits. What the hell. They can't all be beautiful."

"Uh huh."

Lloyd cocked his head with another thought. "Who knows? Maybe the judge will give Laura the baby after all. After all, she is the natural mother."

"Sam Burlington is not going to turn an infant child over to a woman who's been confined to a mental institution for the last four months. There's another one of your stupid blunders. Had you handled that right....aw, never mind. It's all arranged anyway."

"How do you mean?"

"Sam doesn't forget those who contribute five thousand dollars to his election campaign."

* * *

Just as she had the day before and the week before that, and for four long months, she sat languidly on the edge of her cot, gazing out the window at palm fronds swaying in the soft breeze and dark afternoon clouds drifting in from the north, portending a stormy afternoon. The wall clock read four fifteen, time for another of those South Florida thunderboomers which would leave streets flooded and rooftops steaming. A pair of nurses strode briskly along a macadam path toward the administration building while another, perhaps an aide, wheeled a slumped young woman across the courtyard. A strident shriek sounded from another room, a woman in distress. At first such outbursts gave her chills, but now it was just an ordinary sound from the netherworld. Nothing could compare to the interminable boredom, endless hours idling within blank walls with no stimulation, no one to talk with, nothing to read other than movie magazines and outdated newspapers. Meal times were special only because eating was something to do. She thought constantly about her baby, imagining his sweet smile, his wandering eyes, wondering if he was being fed properly, cleaned, nurtured and loved. She yearned to be a mother, Bowen's mother. She missed him so.

An aide entered. She figured it was time for another pill. Instead, he motioned for her to come outside. "What's going on?" she asked.

"Come with me."

Minutes later, she was waiting in a carpeted room lined with bookshelves, a long table in the center and a slow rotating ceiling fan above. Anticipating a new acquaintance, she ran her fingers through matted hair, checked out her appearance as best she could and tried pressing out wrinkles in her cotton robe. Footsteps approached. The door opened. He entered abruptly holding a stack of file folders. She stood, her heart racing, wondering.

"Mrs. Ramsey. Pleased to meet you. Please sit."

He was a gentle, seemly man, mid-forties, with dark, wavy hair, a thin mustache and wire glasses. His eyes looked directly into hers with deep concentration. She figured he was Jewish.

"My name is Dr. Rosenthal. Paul Rosenthal. Your parents have hired me..."

"Oh yes, you're the psychiatrist."

"That's right."

"They told me I was going to be evaluated."

"That's right. That's what I'm here to do."

He sat at the far end of the table, studied an open folder, then looked directly into Laura's eyes. Shivering, she locked into a staredown, knowing he was her only hope for a return to the living world. "Doctor," she muttered, wiping a tear from the corner of her eye. "I am not crazy. I know I must look horrible, but please believe me, I do not belong here."

"Of course. Of course."

"They took my baby away, my little boy. He's only seven months old."

"I see."

"I want my baby. Please, Doctor. I want my baby!"

They spoke for forty-five minutes while he took notes chronicling her warm and loving family life growing up in Ada, her array of academic achievements including the presidency of the high school sorority, a brief but wholesome relationship with a high school senior, then her scholarship to Miami. She spoke of dating the handsome guest lecturer at her constitutional law class who would later become the father of her child. "He dripped in sincerity," she exclaimed. "At least I thought so. He was only the second man I'd ever been with. I thought he really loved me.

"I know I lost it that day. After all, wouldn't anyone? Wouldn't you? Coming home finding your spouse, the man you loved...with another woman, you know... being locked out of your own house, your suitcases packed for you, your baby gone, your identity erased. How cruel can you get?

"I suppose it was too good to be true. So stupid. I should have realized, all those nights he came home after midnight, smelling of alcohol, telling me about this client and that client. I thought it was true. Between the baby and my studies, I never caught the signals. Such a liar."

"Mrs. Ramsey, do you feel ready and capable to raise your child as a single parent?"

She answered without hesitation. "Absolutely, Doctor. I can go back to Ada, my parents could help out, at least for a while. I love my baby. I always dreamed of having a baby. He's a beautiful little boy, Doctor. Oh, I wish I had a picture... I love him so much..." Her eyes formed into liquid pools as a gush of tears streamed down her face.

He offered a handkerchief then looked into her deep, brown eyes. "I believe you do, Laura."

"My poor parents, I feel so terrible. They had to mortgage their house to hire an attorney, now you... plus traveling to Miami. Mama's a dress maker, Papa's retired from the Postal Service." She watched as he buried his head into his notes. Then she asked, "What do you think, doctor?"

"About what?"

"Am I sane? Can I get out of here? Can this horrible nightmare come to an end"

He removed his glasses and laid them on the table. "Laura, file documents reflect you have some serious psychiatric problems which I honestly do not detect. Not in this one session anyway. You are alert, sensitive, aware of your surroundings, you seem rational and focused, though a bit depressed which is understandable considering the circumstances. Counseling therapy, I think, would do you a lot of good, as an out-patient of course. I think you should have been released at the first hearing."

"Oh, thank you. Thank you, Doctor."

"You have two court appearances pending. The first is your divorce proceeding. The second, your competency hearing. I'll be there at both of them. It's too bad your divorce can't be postponed until after your release."

"My attorney has tried to delay it, but the judge, well...he insists on getting it over with."

* * *

The judge's chambers filled up quickly. It looked like any executive conference room with a long, high-polished redwood table surrounded by twelve chairs and wall shelves crammed with law books. Sounds of auto horns and busses from outside clamored through the open windows. The plain-clothes deputy who had transported Laura from the state hospital was seated against the wall directly behind her. She felt better about herself today, dressed like a proper woman, wearing make-up, her spirits lifted by Dr. Rosenthal seated two chairs away. Beside her sat the young attorney named Larry Vardell. To her left, Calvin and Zaidee Perrigo, her parents. For the first time since the ordeal began she felt protected. Her mother held her hand as she glanced with disdain across the table at her cavalier ex-husband, then toward his distinguished father representing him. *Look at that*, she thought to herself. *He gets off cheap. I had to hire a lawyer.* Minutes ticked by like hours as she waited for the judge to arrive, while wishing she could just ask one question, *Where is Bowen? Why didn't you bring my baby?* Larry Vardell had cautioned her to say nothing.

Judge Sam Burlington stepped boldly through the door, wearing a grey suit instead of a robe. He was a heavy man with a full, well-trimmed grey beard and horn rimmed glasses. "Please remain seated," he grumbled, clearing his throat as he took the end chair. He laid a file on the table then looked to the elder attorney to his right, nodding, "How's Muriel doing these days, Thurgood?"

"Doin' just fine Judge."

The hearing lasted thirty minutes. A Florida divorce in 1964 required specific grounds which required Lloyd Ramsey to offer a dissertation about the long days and nights in which Laura obsessed on her school studies, neglected the child and him, failed to care for the house as a good wife and mother should and caused enough stress to be labeled *mental cruelty*. In countering, Larry Vardell elicited strong testimony from Dr. Rosenthal who stated that Laura Ramsey was, in fact, competent and should be released from the hospital as soon as possible, that she was a loving mother who could and should be taking care of her child. Her parents offered their support and assistance as well. Laura fielded a brief interrogatory, controlling herself, careful not to accuse Lloyd of infidelity for fear of being deemed delusional again. All she wanted was the divorce, her freedom and most of all, her child. Her testimony was calm and intelligent.

"This marriage is hereby dissolved on the grounds of mental cruelty by the defendant, Laura Ramsey, who, the record shall reflect, remains confined to the state hospital for an indeterminate period. Further, it is the decision of this court that full custody of the child, Bowen Arthur Ramsey, is awarded to the father, Lloyd Ramsey. Mrs. Ramsey is not required to pay child support. Should Mrs. Ramsey be adjudicated competent and released from custody, she may visit with the child when and if deemed reasonable by the plaintiff, Mr. Ramsey. That is all."

Stunned, Laura sat frozen in disbelief, numbed to the deputy tapping her on the shoulder. Her baby Bowen was taken from her. *My baby...my baby...my baby...NO,...NO,....NO.* A somber Larry Vardell apologized. Her mother put her arm around her. Dr. Rosenthal saw an expression in her eyes that worried him greatly. Again, the deputy tapped her. She stood disoriented, turned to walk, then collapsed.

chapter three

The Following Month - October 1964

I t was a bright Sunday morning. In the corner of a dilapidated recreation room, a black and white television picture
turned to snow as an elderly man reached to adjust the
rabbit ears. Waiting for the orderly with her suitcase packed,
Laura glanced at the news anchorman announcing the replace-
ment of Russian Premier Nikita Khrushchev with Leonid
Brezhnev. The old man changed the channel again to find President Johnson haranguing his campaign opponent, Senator
Barry Goldwater. All meant little to Laura Ramsey who was about
to breathe freedom for the first time since that horrible afternoon in May. Doctor Rosenthal's brilliant and poignant testimony at the competency hearing contradicted his colleagues at
the state hospital and convinced the sitting judge that Laura
was sane and posed no harm to herself nor anyone else.

"It is my professional opinion," testified the good psychiatrist, "after many hours of examination and testing and review-
ing her behavior patterns at the hospital, this patient is not, nor
has been delusionary, nor is she manic-depressive or paranoid
schizophrenic. Her present state of mild depression can be
treated with counseling as an out patient. She is a danger to no
one, certainly not herself." After nearly five months of confinement, she could restart her life.

Her parents had secured a small, first-floor apartment for
her in Miami Beach's Normandy Isle, fifteen miles south of the
Ramsey mansion in Golden Beach. Her first and only priority
now was to gain custody of her baby Bowen and re-establish
herself as the child's mother. It surprised no one, including her

parents, that she did not even stop to inspect the apartment but headed directly for the telephone instead. Anxious, she dialed Lloyd's number. An operator answered. "I'm sorry, but this is no longer a working number."

"Please, can you give me the number for a Lloyd Ramsey? It's in Golden Beach."

After a pause, the operator returned. "I'm sorry, but that is an unlisted number."

"That son of a bitch!"

Hunched and rail-thin from years of back ailments, Cal Perrigo chewed his cigar and addressed his daughter, "Look, Laura honey, you gotta go at this slow and careful. Remember what Dr. Rosenthal said. Don't let yourself fall into another trap."

"You're right, Dad."

He continued, "Make sure you do everything the right way, Laura honey...simply go through the courts."

She sighed and took a seat on the sofa. "Sure Daddy, I'm going to go up against the all- powerful Ramsey law firm. Give me a break. Thurgood Ramsey is in bed with every politician, lawyer *and* psychiatrist in Dade County, except for Paul Rosenthal. Lloyd used to tell me how his father had all the cops and judges in his hip pocket. They're all golfing buddies, fellow alumni or political allies, or something. It's so exasperating. There must be a way to get my baby back. There must!" She breathed deeply, then looked to the ceiling. "Why does he hate me so? Why?"

Her mother patted her hand. "We'll get you another lawyer, dear. Then you can sue Lloyd."

"Sue him? Mother... how..."

"They accused you of hallucinating that... um... affair, with that girl, but you did see it. Right dear?"

"Of course I saw it mother, but I could never prove it. They'll always believe him. He's a God around this town."

"What about the girl he was with? Maybe you can find her."

"I don't care. She can go to hell, whoever she is. Besides, I'd have no way of identifying her. I just want my little boy. You know something, Ma? Maybe we could just take Bowen and whisk him off to Oklahoma. If I could only see him, we could be in Ada in two days."

Cal chewed his unlit cigar and replied sternly, "Laura, don't think like that. That man will hunt you down and have you back in a mental hospital. Don't think such foolish things."

"I suppose you're right, Daddy. I won't..." Laura suddenly sat straight up and blurted, "Listen to me, Mom, Dad, this is the big day I've been waiting for. What are we doing here? I want to see my baby. If I can't phone him, we'll go up there. Right now."

"No, darling listen..."

"I want to see my baby, Mama! It's been five months. Bowen is almost eight months old. Enough already. Are you coming with me or staying here?"

Laura took the wheel of her old Impala as they headed north along motel row, reminiscent of that fateful day, her last day of happiness, graduating, singing, preparing for celebration, unaware of the darkness lurking ahead. Thirty minutes later they arrived at the Ramsey house where the little MG was parked in the brick-lined carport. "My, what a lovely home," remarked Zaidee Perrigo. "You actually lived here?"

"That's his car, Mama."

While her parents remained in the car, she preened and tidied herself, excited at the idea of seeing her baby Bowen, wondering how he had grown, what he looked like, how he would react when he saw her. Moments after she rang the door bell, she noticed a slight movement from the window curtain. Anticipating confrontation, her heart began pounding, harder, stronger, faster. *Be cool, Laura. Don't start anything up with him. Just see your baby.* She rang again. Footsteps clicked along the tiles from the side of the house. Lloyd Ramsey appeared, ambling toward her in a white tennis outfit and a cynical smile on his face.

"My my, so they let you out," he said with a sly snicker.

She stiffened, trembling, hating him so. For those few seconds, she couldn't utter a word.

"What are you doing here, Laura?"

She stood a safe distance and after a deep breath replied. "Lloyd ..." sigh..."I want to see my baby."

"You didn't call first."

Bastard. "I didn't have your new number. How could I call?"

He leaned against the house, hands in pockets. "He's not here right now. Sorry."

"Oh? Where is he?"

"That's not your business, I'm afraid."

"Not my bus...? I'm his mother!" She choked, holding back the tears, peering into his handsome eyes. "Why?"

"Why what, Laura?"

She could barely speak. "Why are you doing this to me? What did I do, Lloyd...what did I do to make you hate me so?"

"I don't hate you Laura," he replied glibly. "Whatever gave you that idea?"

Don't argue. No conflict. "Look, I am Bowen's mother. He needs me, you understand that? A baby needs his mother. And I miss him so much. Please, Lloyd, please..."

"Now, now Laura, no whimpering. The court order said visitations will be reasonable, as deemed appropriate by myself. This is inappropriate, dropping in unexpected like this. Sorry."

She folded her arms across her chest, answering, "Very well then. You tell me. Can I see him tomorrow? The day after? You tell me, Lloyd. I'll abide by whatever you say." *You son of a bitch.*

"I don't know. You'll have to call."

Her voice started to elevate. "Lloyd, godammit, you know I don't have your number."

"Hmm. That's a shame, isn't it?"

"Oh for God's sake, Lloyd!"

"You have my office number."

"Oh sure. If I remember Miss Rappaport's standard line...'I'll see if he's in his office'. Strange, how you always had just stepped out. You were there every time, weren't you? You were always there. You just didn't want to..."

"Come on now, Laura, easy..."

"If you love your son, Lloyd, why wouldn't you want him to be with his own mother? Can you tell me that?"

"Well,...I have to make decisions that are in the best interest of the baby, and..."

"And, what?"

He looked toward the intracoastal riverway where two skiffs passed by in the placid waters, then back into her eyes. Beads of perspiration formed on her brow. He shook his head, "I'm not so sure you're a good mother, quite frankly Laura."

"What?"

"You always had him with baby sitters, almost all the time..."

She gasped, outraged, in disbelief.

"...day and night, while you tended to your school priorities, then spent another five months in a funny farm..."

"You bastard..."

"...where you were diagnosed as schizophrenic...among other things, delusional and all that. How do I know you're not still crazy? What if you lost control of yourself when he was in your care? I don't know. I'm very concerned." She leaned back against a column, hands to her face, trembling. "Laura, are you all right?"

Doctor Rosenthal's words echoed through her mind. *Be aware of your emotions, Laura. Don't allow him to bait you or else you'll just fall into his trap. Take control.* "Who's been caring for my baby? I want to know."

"Me, and others. He's doing just fine, Laura. Just fine. You have nothing to worry about."

"Then why can't I just see him?"

"Well, frankly, I'd like to see the psychiatrist's report and the hospital records before I let you take him. It's my responsibility..."

Suddenly, through an open window, a baby wailed from inside. Laura alerted and ran to the house, shouting back to Lloyd, "You said he wasn't here. You BASTARD!"

From the driveway, Cal Perrigo saw his daughter's reaction, exited the car and started toward her.

Frenzied now, Laura leaned to the window, shouting, "Bowen, ..my baby, Bowen, it's Mommy honey, it's your Mommy!" She jerked away angrily when Lloyd grabbed her arm. "Bowen, honey! Mommy's here!" She raced to the side, hoping for another open window nearer to the baby. She could still hear him crying.

From behind, her father pleaded with her, "Come on Laura, honey. We'd better go now."

She flitted window to window, then to the kitchen window where she screamed, "Bowen, baby...it's Mommy! I love you!"

Lloyd wrapped his arm around her waist and pulled her away, demanding, "Laura, get out of here. Get out I said."

"Come on, Laura honey, we must go now ," insisted her father, groping for her hand. He turned to Lloyd with a baleful expression. "You...you let go of my daughter." Lloyd recoiled, yielding smartly.

"Bowen baby. It's your Mommy! Remember Mommy?" The baby's wailing cries roiled on as Laura's father pulled her away.

Lloyd steeled himself and glanced condescendingly at his former father-in-law, then to his ex-wife. "Laura, if you continue this behavior, I'll have to call the police. And...you know what that will mean."

Her frizzled hair stood out like an Afro. Those horrible emotions of rage and fury that landed her in a mental hospital for five months had reignited so she paused, reflected and succumbed to her father's pleadings. She stared at Lloyd Ramsey with dagger eyes, knowing she could lose all hope of seeing Bowen again. He had the power, she had none. "I hate you." she growled as her father pulled her back to the car.

* * *

Laura was secure in her apartment, emotionally stabilized and prepared to take a steady job so the Perrigos returned to their remortgaged house in Ada where poor Cal would have to go back to work after all. Begging their daughter to join them was fruitless. She was adamant. Her baby was here and she was not leaving.

The clock ticked slowly as minutes turned into hours, hours into days and days into six long weeks. All efforts to see Bowen had failed. She had resorted to surveilling the Ramsey house, binoculars in hand, in hopes of catching a glimpse of her child until she was ushered off by an angry Officer Harold Plevnic threatening to have her incarcerated again. Images of being dragged off in a straitjacket loomed over her like a dark cloud. Each time Laura called Lloyd's law office, Miss Rappaport repeated the same mundane lies. "Out of the office, sorry."

She penned two heart breaking letters to Judge Sam Burlington pleading for an audience, for justice, to allow her baby to be with his mother. They went unanswered. On four occasions, she called Larry Vardell, her young lawyer who would give no more of his time without payment of services. He stopped taking her calls. She was penniless. Her parents were broke. She made application to social service agencies for financial assistance or legal representation, but the paperwork always seemed to get mired in bureaucratic red tape.

She looked forward to her weekly sessions with Doctor Rosenthal to bathe in sympathy and rejuvenate her waning morale. When she explained her parents could no longer afford to pay, he insisted therapy be continued. "Put it on the tab," he said. "This is too important. You'll pay me someday. Right now, you can't afford not to come." He was a compassionate man. But compassion by appointment for thirty short minutes a week was like giving a grain of rice to a starving woman.

Despair and loneliness plunged her into an abyss of depression. Her only friends were a handful of fellow classmates from the university who had since returned to their home towns far from Miami. Riddled with guilt over their financial status, she would no longer burden her parents. Whenever they called she lied, saying everything was all right, that she had seen Bowen and that he was fine.

She had scanned classified ads for jobs but could not muster the initiative to apply for any teacher's positions. *How can I apply for a teaching job when I've just been let out of a nut house?* Her career was doomed before she ever had her first job. Life had turned ugly and hopeless. She had failed somehow.

"I'm not so sure you're a good mother, quite frankly, Laura."

Constant weeping had drained her of strength and will. There was nothing else for her unless she could be a mother, which was out of her hands. She had been relegated to insignificance, utterly destroyed.

She went for long drives on highway A1A where the Atlantic met the shore, sometimes stopping to sit on the coarse sandy beach and gaze with dulled eyes over the horizon, wondering why... always wondering... reliving that fateful day, wracking her mind, wishing she could turn the clock back, hoping against all hope, craving just a single moment with her baby. She fantasized about little Bowen, imagining how he had grown by now, sitting and standing, perhaps taking those first baby steps she would never witness. It all snapped one day when she returned to the parking lot to find her Impala had been stolen.

It was a cool, starlit Friday night on Miami Beach. Alone in her apartment, she tried one more time to find the number for Lloyd Ramsey. She called his father's house, but they hung up the instant she spoke. The new television sit-com, *Bewitched,* was playing but her eyes remained fixed on the ceiling. She hadn't watched television for weeks but left it on to serve as her only companion. A group of kids passed by outside singing Christmas carols. It was December the 24th, the first Christmas for Bowen Arthur Ramsey. Her son. Her baby. She scanned the phone directory looking for the number for Doctor Paul Rosenthal. No answer. She dialed South Florida State Hospital, hoping they would have his number, but it was to no avail. *I'll never see my baby. My baby, my baby...*

Two gifts wrapped in red Santa Claus paper, one a stuffed animal, the other a wind-up toy, lay under the small unadorned tree. They'd been there for three weeks. She stared, imagining his bright eyes as he ripped them open, his baby sounds, his awe of all the lights and colors. She would never hear his first words, *Ma ma, Ma ma.* Not this year, not next year, not ever. She was a non-entity, without purpose, in total despair, nothing but a useless blip in the world. Choking on her tears, she tore open the wind-up toy and smashed it against the wall.

The telephone rang. Her mind drifted. Because it was Christmas eve, she crazily thought it might be Lloyd calling to give her the baby. She picked up the receiver. "Hello?"

"Hello, darling. Merry Christmas. Your Dad and I were wondering how..."

"Hello Mother. Yeah. Merry..." She sighed, deeply. "Goodbye Mother. I love you." She replaced the receiver on the carriage. Minutes later, the phone rang again. This time she ignored it. She ambled listlessly into the bedroom and picked up a small framed black and white photo of baby Bowen at six weeks old clad in an Easter Bunny outfit. She smiled, kissed the frame and broke down sobbing again.

The phone rang incessantly, five times, ten times, fifteen

times, on and on. She held the picture close to her bosom, cra-
dling, rocking, sensing his sweet breath, touching his soft skin,
smiling when he smiled at her, singing *Silent Night* as though
he were in her arms, caressing his image until she realized, ...*it's
all over. Nothing else matters now. Mommy loves you. My baby...
I love you, Bowen.*

Thirty-five minutes later, after a worried mother telephoned
from Ada, Oklahoma, two Miami Beach police officers broke
through the front door of the apartment and found Laura Jean
Ramsey near death in a bathtub full of crimson water, her left
wrist slashed in three places. Torn Christmas paper and a sop-
ping stuffed lion were floating in the water.

chapter four

Bowen was a lucky boy. He wore the finest clothes, rode in fancy cars, ate lots of ice cream and cake, had expensive toys, went to all the circus shows and carnivals and had his own television set across from his bed. At three years old, he lacked for nothing. Well, almost nothing.

The big tall man he called Daddy came home sometimes and would stop in Bowen's room for a minute, tussle his fine blond hair and say, "How're ya doin' there champ?" The bright-eyed youngster would give him a wide smile, thinking that Daddy might stay and play but he never did. Before walking out the room, he would always say "Be a good boy now. See ya later."

Each time he saw Daddy's picture on the living room table, he would point to it, look up with a smile to whoever was there and repeat, "How am I doing champ?" Daddy never held him, played with him or took him anywhere. Neither did he attend any of his three birthday parties. But he often brought gifts home, stuffed animals, toy trains, miniature houses and garages, pistols and a tiny pedal car. He had been a good Daddy because he made sure Bowen had everything. After all, he was a Ramsey. It was just that, well...Daddy was such a busy guy.

During the day, Bowen usually stayed with a part-time nanny, a greying, middle-aged woman who had three grown children of her own. She was efficient and neat, attended to his daily needs and installed manners and discipline.

Everyone always said he was a good boy because he rarely cried and played so well by himself, amused by all his toys and stuffed animals, and the new color television set. He liked cartoons and the *Gomer Pyle Show* best.

He liked it more when the other lady was there, because she was prettier and she smiled more than the nanny, showed him lots of attention, gave him baths and even held his hand when they went to the store or the playground. She had yellow hair all bunched atop her head which he liked to pat with his hands and then giggle when the curls bounced. She called it her carrot top. A funny white stick with smoke burning at its end always dangled from her sticky red lips. It hurt his eyes sometimes, but that was okay because he liked feeling her touch during his bath and when she held his hand in stores and playgrounds. Sometimes she would even come into his room at bedtime to make sure he was asleep. That made him feel important. He liked her best. Her name was *Mommy*.

*   *   *

Not one to relinquish the good life, Lloyd Ramsey found him a *"decent woman"* with whom he reluctantly exchanged vows at the altar six months to the day after his father's ultimatum. Incapable of love or the practice of monogamy, it made sense to select a woman who had established a track record of reliability, so he proposed a surprise business arrangement to Miss Yvonne Rappaport, the office receptionist. She was a hopeless chain smoker with small breasts, a thin body and bleached blonde hair which she wore in curls piled atop her head and reeked of the same perfume every day. But she was articulate and trustworthy, and presented herself in a simple but stylish fashion. Born in Queens, New York, one of three daughters of a long-shoreman father and a crippled mother, Yvonne wanted nothing more than a life of independence, good friends and to further her education in hopes of becoming a professional writer or an editor. It was on a Friday afternoon three years past when he shocked her with an invitation to a bayfront cafe for lunch.

"There's this, well, I guess you can call it, ...a problem."

Already bewildered by the unexpected date with her boss, Yvonne listened curiously.

"You know my situation with the baby and all...?"

"Yes, Mr. Ramsey. I heard."

"And the baby's mother...?" he tapped his forehead.

"Yes Mr. Ramsey."

"Call me Lloyd, please."

"Yes Mr. Ramsey, ...uh, yes. Okay...Lloyd." She thought it very strange, indeed.

"I'll be very honest. I'm in a situation where I need to correct the family arrangement. At least give it the appearance of legitimacy."

Perplexed, she said, "Excuse me, Mr...I mean, Lloyd, but why are you telling me...?"

"I'll get to that in a moment. First, let me ask... do you like children?"

"Well ..." she chuckled, puffing on an unfiltered Chesterfield. "How do you mean? I like other people's kids, sometimes, but I'm not big on kids, if that's what you mean."

"I'll get right to the point."

"Yes?"

"I would like you to, uh, marry me."

He popped the question just as she sucked a drag. Coughing, she grabbed her throat and went into convulsions. Lloyd offered water and patted her gently on the back until she recovered.

Furtively, she scanned the dining room and whispered, "Excuse me sir. But, I don't..."

"Wait a minute, let me explain what..."

"Mr. Ramsey. I'm sorry, I mean I'm flattered, I didn't realize you felt, uh... but I don't even know you."

"Yvonne, let me be perfectly honest. I'm not in love with you. I don't even want to go to bed with you."

It was a sobering revelation. Composing herself, she lit another cigarette and took a swallow of ginger ale. "I see. Look, I'm only, I'm sorry Mr. Ramsey, but I'm not about to be anyone's nursemaid, if that's what you're looking for."

"Marry me and I'll put a quarter of a million dollars in your account in your name the day of the wedding. All I ask is that you help take care of the baby, present yourself as my wife in the public forum, conduct yourself with dignity and make no other demands of me."

A quarter of a million dollars. Wow! The mere thought was

frightening as she imagined being tethered to the rich and pomp-
ous lawyer for the rest of her life. He was good looking enough,
athletic and preppy with that blond crew cut and dark brown
almond eyes. But he was also reckless and conceited, a lady's
man known for his string of conquests, certainly not a devoted
husband she had always dreamed of.

"Mr. Ramsey, I mean... Lloyd, I'm only twenty-three. You're
asking me to give up all the best years of my life. I do like boys,
you know. I mean, the offer is very nice, but, um,... I think I
want a life of my own."

"Look, we'll sleep in different bedrooms. You'll live in a mansion, with servants, prestige, a fancy car. I wouldn't care if you
had a boyfriend, so long as it was discreet with no embarrass-
ments and your household obligations were met. I'll even hire
a nanny part-time, if that's what it takes. But I need someone to
mother the child." He peered at her over a waft of smoke. He
thought she was hooked. "Think about it, Yvonne. A quarter of
a million dollars."

"I don't think so, Lloyd, sir. Not for the rest of my life,
through all the good years."

He took a swig of port wine, pondered, and replied, "Okay
then, make it a half million."

My God. A half million? "What good is it if I have to sacrifice
my whole life? I want marriage and children someday, you know.
The conventional way."

He thought of a compromise. "Okay. How about ten years?
That's all. Guarantee me ten years. If you insist on a divorce
after that, I won't hold you back. But you must agree to sign a
pre-nuptial. While you are my wife, you'll have all the money
you'll ever need. You can invest the half million for ten years."

She took another drag. *Yvonne Ramsey. Hmmmm. Five hundred thousand dollars.. Ten years I'll be thirty-three.* "Can I
think about it?"

"I haven't much time. Tomorrow?"

"Okay."

The next morning, Lloyd Ramsey found a sealed hand-written note on his office desk. It read: *I'll do it. Yvonne.*

* * *

It was a big day for Laura, like breaking through a long, dismal fog into bright sunshine, alive again, hopeful and spirited. This time she walked out the gates of South Florida State Hospital a free woman with a new outlook on life and great hopes for reuniting with the son she hadn't seen in three years. No more out-bursts, no more surveillances, no more attempts on her own life. She was going to follow the guidance of Doctor Rosenthal who still offered unpaid bi-weekly counseling sessions with her during his routine hospital rounds. She would get a job, save money and fight Lloyd Ramsey through the court system or the media if she had to.

Many changes had occurred in the outside world. An undeclared war raged in Southeast Asia, a war in which a boxing champion named Ali would refuse to engage, no matter the consequence. A movie actor named Ronald Reagan had just been elected Governor of California. Self-styled rebels known as hippies spawned a strange generation of boys wearing long hair while half-bare girls pranced about in a new rage called mini-skirts. The top rated television show was set in a sprawling ranch called the Ponderosa and Elvis Presley shattered a million dreams by marrying a young beauty named Priscilla Beaulieu.

Two and a half years of incarceration had been a nightmare. She vowed never to return. Dementia surrounded her night and day, unescapable sights and sounds she would never forget, drooling idiots, stupefied men and women gazing into space, outbursts of hideous laughter and the night howls like poor wounded animals suffering in the cold. For six months following her suicide attempt, she was catatonic, gazing hopelessly into space, monosyllabic, speaking in single word replies to simple questions. She had lost touch with reality, mired in a deep depression from which it took nearly two years to recover. She had nothing but time to reflect. One day, she looked into the mirror and saw that someone was there. It was her, a new Laura, a bright and loving woman with much to offer the world and it was going to waste because she had allowed *him* to take control. No more. A child was out there who needed her. A child named Bowen.

She moved into another apartment on Normandy Isle and bought a green 1961 stick shift Ford Falcon with four hundred dollars borrowed from her father. Landing a job in the public school system would be difficult because of her mental history, she thought, so she worked as a cocktail waitress at the Dream Lounge on Miami Beach where the mob boys were plentiful and tips were good. Two weeks later, she installed a telephone with a two-party line.

She tried searching the number for the Ramsey mansion but, as expected, it was unavailable. Then she called the law office. Surprised to hear the voice of a new receptionist, she asked to speak to Lloyd Ramsey.

"Who may I say is calling?" asked the woman.

"Oh, just say it's an old friend." Laura knew he wouldn't turn down a call from a mystery woman.

Moments later, he answered, "Lloyd Ramsey here. May I help..."

"Hello, Lloyd."

There was a long pause. She expected him to hang up, but instead he answered, "Oh, it's you. You're out, are you?"

"Yes, thank you. I'm out... for good this time. I see you have a new receptionist. What happened to Miss Rappaport?"

"That's not your business..."

"Tell me, how is Bowen?"

"My son is doing fine. He has everything he needs..."

"Except his mother."

"What do you want Laura? I don't have a lot of time."

"I want to see my son."

"I'm afraid that's impossible."

She had expected that. "Very well, Lloyd. We'll see. Good-bye." *Well, it was worth a try.*

Laura worked until she had saved over five hundred dollars in three months, enough to hire a good domestic lawyer, one with as many connections as the Ramsey firm. She had to be smart and certain of her approach this time.

Meanwhile, the sessions with Doctor Rosenthal at his office on Arthur Godfrey Road were taking on a new dimension. Three years of therapy with one counselor had mellowed into a comfortable rapport as she arrived like clockwork each week with great anticipation. He had become a part of her life's schedule. Now that she was *cured*, they would often digress, share stories, laugh and barter politics. It was on a June morning when he changed the course of her life for all time.

As always, classical music played from a small radio on his bookshelf. Sipping a cup of tea in the maroon, leather chair, she mused, "I don't know. I do enjoy some television, good dramas mostly, like *Mission Impossible* and comedians like Red Skelton. God, I love him. When he does that Gertrude and Ecliff routine, I crack up, I swear." She caught a glimpse of a smile on the doctor's lips. "How about you? Do you ever...?"

The doctor grinned embarrassingly. "I wish I could agree or disagree, but I'm afraid I don't watch very much television. Some news, maybe."

"Then what is it that you do like? You must enjoy some form of..."

"Me? I read. I read a lot. Love opera. I'm a big fan of the opera. Ever been to an opera, Laura?"

"No. I'm afraid Ada doesn't have much of an opera house."

"It's the ultimate in all of music. It is drama and power, comedy and tragedy, with strings and horns and voice all in one, the tenors, sopranos, choruses and arias ...oh my, you don't know what you've missed. You must see Verdi's Aida, Mozart's Magic Flute, and Rossini, Puccini... you've never heard Madame Butterfly?" He caught himself leaning back with his hands behind his head, rambling, until he spotted Laura looking at him with a curious grin.

She reflected for a second, and asked, "Would you repeat all that, Doctor?"

"I said you must see Madame Butterfly sometime, and Moz.....uh, why did you ask me to repeat?"

She smiled and looked into his deep, dark, intense eyes. "It just occurred to me. In three years, I've never heard you talk about yourself."

"Well, you don't come here to talk about me."

"I know." For the first time, a mortal man sat in that swivel chair across from her, a man vulnerable and sensitive. She studied the way he looked at her and saw there was something more than a doctor attending a patient. "Can I ask a question?"

"Yes. Of course."

"I don't pay you. Why?"

"Because you can't afford it."

"That's true. But I see your office here and the Cadillac you drive, and the tailored suits. You don't succeed, Doctor, by donating your services." They locked eyes again, until he looked away. She had never given it a thought and now she knew. "Why? I'd just like to know. If you wouldn't mind..."

It was an uncomfortable switch to be on defense. He would have taken control with any other patient, but this was not any patient. The hint of a smile glimmered in her eyes, making him feel naked, like she was peering into the windows of his heart. He began wiping his glasses, baring his dark, bushy eyebrows. He smiled sheepishly. "I've never done this before."

"Done what, doctor?"

"I don't know how to go about this."

"Yes?"

"Would you...uh, mind having dinner with me one night? At a restaurant, of course." She smiled, he smiled. A long silence followed his question. "Just dinner, that's all."

"Doctor Rosenthal, ...um, why...?"

"No therapy, no clinical evaluation, just a personal thing, you know. You don't have to. You can just, um, forget I ever..."

"I'm, uh, flattered. Flabbergasted would be more like it. What about Mrs. Rosenthal?"

A little chuckle, then he turned somber. "Thelma died a year ago. Pancreatic cancer. It only took four months. I have a daughter, Cynthia, she's six."

"I'm so sorry to hear..." *A year ago? I never knew.* He was honest and gentle, so trusting and humble. "I'd be happy to join you... Paul."

chapter five

Paul Rosenthal made no bones about religious leanings. Though proud of his Jewish heritage and a staunch contributor to the State of Israel, he was a die-hard agnostic. Laura was a non-practicing Presbyterian who hadn't attended a church in over five years and cared only about fulfilling her new status as Mrs. Paul Rosenthal. Thus, when the August wedding was performed by an aging Justice of the Peace, the doctor insisted that any mention of God be omitted from the ceremony. It only cost a bottle of Chivas Regal.

For Laura, her need for lust or romance was a thing of the past. Blind passion rendered her totally incapacitated once and she no longer trusted those kinds of feelings. He was twenty-one years her senior but it didn't matter. He was gentle and kind and needy, though not inclined toward physical gestures of affection. But he genuinely loved her. It was as though she had been rescued from a pit of quicksand, no longer having to struggle and scrimp, pinch pennies and cater to the drooling wolves at a hoodlum bar. She reveled in a new sense of pride, of standing in the community and the challenge to share her heart with the motherless little Cynthia.

It was only natural that Laura would think of having another child as soon as nature would allow, a child to supplant the long-standing void created by her tragic misfortune. But Paul was more conservative. He thought it best that she settle into the new family, to get her career going, earn her acceptance with Cynthia and wait a few years until she was rooted in as a Rosenthal. She never argued the point.

With Cynthia, it was love at first sight for Laura, a woman craving motherhood as much as an eagle craves the currents of warm air. But she was careful not to assume a surrogate role as Cynthia had yet to resolve the finality of her mother's demise. She was a well-mannered child, with dark hair and deep blue eyes, and a healthy curiosity, always delving and asking questions. Laura liked that. She often wondered how it might have been with her own son.

The marriage also ignited her quest for a reunion with Bowen. Though not enormously rich, Paul was comfortable enough to afford the finest attorneys in Miami. Forthright and candid, she said, "I want to hire the best. And I want detectives to follow him around and to see what's happening to my baby. For God sakes Paul, I don't even have a picture of Bowen."

He had anticipated this. "Very well, dear. We can do all of that. But, I have a better idea for winning your battle."

"Yes? What?"

He knew elections were to be held the coming year. He also knew that money wielded far more influence than any eloquent courtroom oratory. "I'm sending Judge Burlington a campaign contribution," he announced with a gleam in his eye.

"You're kidding. That miserable old..."

"Listen to me, my pet. Trust me. I know the way things work in Dade County politics."

"Isn't that almost like bribery?"

"Well, I guess you could say that. It sure would put the old geezer between a rock and a hard place. Wouldn't it now?"

So, after sending a six thousand dollar check to the judge's coffer, a grateful campaign manager by the name of Charlie High showed up at the good doctor's office to personally extend invitations to attend an exclusive affair on a chartered boat where Sam Burlington could offer his deep gratitude in person. Only those who belonged to the inner circle, the major donors, would be in attendance.

"What if Lloyd and his father are there?" Laura asked Paul.

"So what if he is? It would certainly send a message, wouldn't it?"

It was a gala affair indeed. On a warm and humid Saturday evening, the sixty-eight foot yacht was brimming with rich and important people hovering around the judge and several other prominent notables. To Laura's delight, the Ramseys were not present. Champagne flowed from cascading fountains while ice sculptures adorned both decks. Tuxedoed waiters served hors d'oeuvres from sterling platters while a pianist played cocktail music from inside the main cabin. The boat slowly cruised the length of Biscayne Bay from Miami to Ft. Lauderdale under a magnificent spray of twinkling stars. Laura was dazzled by the array of ladies' fashions, each festooned with more jewelry than she had ever seen out of a display case. As she and Paul stood near the bow sipping champagne, Charlie High approached. "Please, come with me," he asked.

Minutes later they were in the reception cabin standing before the old judge. He bared a forced, politician's smile and speared Paul's hand, shaking it vigorously. "Ahem, can't tell you what a pleasure it is to meet you Doctor Rosenberg. It surely is."

"Rosenthal, sir."

"Yes, Rosenthal, that's right. Ahem. Yes, sir. I've heard a great deal about your work, Paul. You will allow me to call you Paul, won't you? Just call me Sam." As he rambled on, the judge kept glancing back to Laura, twice, three times. He continued blustering, "I really appreciate your generosity, sir, and I assure you I will win this next election. I've got two opponents that I know of, both of whom are young whippersnappers barely out of law school. But they've got money." He glanced at her once more. She was not the prettiest woman on the boat, but Laura looked elegant in her new, strapless chiffon dress. He changed the subject and asked Paul, "I'm sorry, what did you say your wife's name was?"

"Laura, Sam. This is Laura."

"Yes. Hmmm." He leaned toward her, narrowing his bushy eyebrows. "Don't I know you from somewhere?"

Laura perked up, offered a bright, toothy smile and replied, "Yes, your honor. You presided over a court matter I was involved in once. A long time ago."

"Oh, I see." He looked at her curiously and took a swig from his martini. "What was that again, you'll have to freshen the memory. Ha ha."

"It was a divorce, sir. I was married to Lloyd Ramsey."

* * *

The court date was set for November twenty-second, the day before Thanksgiving. Her new attorney was a slick former chief prosecutor from the State Attorney's Office. A glib Lloyd Ramsey, his blond hair still worn in a flat-top, arrived alone, prepared to represent himself. There was a gleam in Laura's eye, seeing his reaction when the judge referred to her as *Mrs. Laura Rosenthal.* He was less amused when he heard the judge's ruling.

"Mr. Ramsey, ahem... you may, in fact, have lawful custody, but I'm afraid the law provides that Mrs. Rosenthal is entitled to visit with her child. According to all reports, her mental health has been restored, she is a competent and caring woman and should not be deprived of seeing her son. Neither should her son be deprived of knowing his mother. Apparently, the court's prior language allowing for *reasonable* visitation privileges has been taken too liberally. I will be more specific. The mother, Mrs. Laura Rosenthal, will be permitted to spend at least one full day with her son at least twice a month, or more, as deemed appropriate or convenient by the parties. This court is adjourned."

Thank God.

* * *

It was not often little Bowen received attention from Daddy and even more rare to see Mommy and Daddy together at the same time. On Sunday mornings, he would usually eat his Rice Krispies and banana while playing war games with miniature green soldiers. Mommy would smoke cigarettes and read the newspaper or talk on the phone to someone she called *sweetheart.* After that, he'd play alone in his room or watch television programs. If he was a good boy, Mommy would take him to the beach or a movie theater to see cartoons, or maybe the pony rides. A long time ago she took him to the zoo where he saw lots of animals. He liked the lions and tigers best.

This day was different than any other Sunday. Instead of romping around the house barefoot wearing a tee shirt and shorts, Mommy made him dress in stiff clothing that didn't feel good, then combed his hair with water and put tight leather shoes on his feet. Socks too. But he had fun playing with her bouncy, curly hair. That day she gave him a big hug. It made him feel kinda funny, but he liked it anyway.

Right after breakfast, he and Daddy went for a long ride on Collins Avenue, passing all the beaches and big hotels along the way, not saying a word until they crossed a narrow bridge and pulled into the driveway of the giant house where Grandma and Grandpa lived. It seemed really strange when Daddy knelt down and talked so near to his face, he could smell the stale cigarettes. Mommy smelled like that also.

"Listen to me, Bowen, my boy," said his father, holding his little shoulders while he toyed with an empty water pistol. "There is a lady coming this morning to take you for a ride. She's going to be real nice to you and buy you things."

"What's her name?" asked the child.

"Her name is Miss Laura."

"Is she real old?"

"No son, she's not an old lady. She's like your mommy's age. She likes you very much."

"How can she like me if she doesn't even know me?"

"Because you're a good boy and everybody always likes you. Now listen to me, she is probably going to say that she's a mommy, like your mommy. That's all right, okay? A lot of people say they are mommy. Just remember, you only have one mommy, even if the other lady says she's a mommy too. Be nice to her and mind your manners. Okay? No crying."

"Is she pretty?"

"Not as pretty as your mommy."

* * *

She donned a pale yellow sun dress, a pair of high-heeled wedgies and a wide-brimmed straw hat banded by a bright yellow bow. One might have thought she was setting out to meet Paul Newman, or President Johnson himself. "How do I look?" she asked, primping at the mirror.

"Laura, my dear, it's not the dress or the hat, or the hairdo. It's the glow in your eyes. I haven't seen you so happy in all the time I've known you. You truly look magnificent."

"Paul, it's been three and a half years. Do you think he'll...you know, accept me?"

"Well, he probably won't know you, but there's no reason he shouldn't accept you.."

"Lloyd's having me pick him up at his parent's house on Star Island. I was there only once. You should see it, walkways of Italian tile, seven bedroom suites overlooking the bay, two swimming pools, a forty-foot yacht docked in the back, it's magnificent."

"You better get a move on."

"Oh Paul, I wonder if he knows anything about his mother, if Lloyd ever talks about me."

"Well, you'll find out in about forty-five minutes. Go on now. It's after eight."

Nervous as a greyhound at the starting gate, she turned the ignition of her gleaming white El Dorado, sucked a deep breath and headed south to meet her son, to touch her baby boy for the first time since he was an infant. Her heart bellowed with anxiety, wondering how he would react, if he knew about her at all.

She stopped at a toy store and bought the biggest stuffed lion on the shelf, smaller version of the toy animal that sank in a bathtub that fateful Christmas Eve nearly four years before.

Star Island was an exclusive gated community consisting of a half dozen bayfront mansions located where McArthur Causeway meets the southern tip of Miami Beach and where only the rich and famous could afford properties valued as much as one million of 1967's dollars. Once across the water and permitted entry by a station guard, visitors reach a single one-way elliptical road traveling no more than a quarter mile until turning back toward the bridge. A row of tall royal palms lined the grassy median. Spanish and Italian style mansions dotted the waterfront, with Cadillacs, Lincolns, Rolls Royces and Mercedes Benzes parked in their massive driveways.

No longer intimidated by power and wealth, the respectable but apprehensive Mrs. Laura Rosenthal crossed the bridge in her sleek Cadillac, her heart rising to her throat. As she expected, a crusty old guard met her at the gate. She checked her watch. Five minutes to nine, on time. Lloyd's cryptic admonition on the phone rang through her head. *"Nine a.m. sharp. He'll be ready. Don't be late, Laura."*

"Yes Ma'am, can I help you?" asked the guard.

"Yes, I'm Mrs. Rosenthal, Laura Rosenthal, here to visit the Ramseys."

The guard checked his clipboard, looked up and squinted his eyes. "I don't have no Mrs. Rosenthal on the list here."

A bloodrush filled her head. "There must be some mistake. Lloyd Ramsey is expecting me, at nine a.m. He must have notified..."

"Sorry ma'am, can't let anyone in who hasn't got clearance. You'll have to back up and turn around."

He'll be ready. Don't be late, Laura

It was three minutes to nine. "Please, sir, I have to pick up my little boy for a visit. Can't you call the house and verify?"

"Ain't got a phone ma'am. It's up to the residents here to let me know. So you just back up and turn..."

Two minutes to nine. "No no, you don't understand..." *.Be calm, Laura. Easy.* "I can get the verification, if you'll just..."

"Sorry, lady. Now don't argue with me..."

"...let me through. Please!" she pleaded, shaking. The day she had dreamed of was being shattered. She couldn't bear the thought of a long drive home without ever seeing Bowen.

Don't be late, Laura.

One minute to nine. A Buick station wagon pulled behind and blocked her from backing. She looked ahead and thought about crashing through the gate, but that was all they needed to slap her back into a nuthouse. Lloyd had shrewdly complied with the court order but deliberately failed to give her clearance into Star Island. *That son of a bitch did it to me again. My God, I don't believe this.* Tears started to fill her eyes.

Behind her, a handsome, middle-aged gentleman had exited his car and walked up to inquire about the delay. "Oh, Mrs. Rosenthal, it's you."

"I'm sorry, but... I..."

"I'm Ben Shepard. We met on Judge Burlington's charter boat," he said, leaning over.

"Oh yes, how are you?" She looked at her watch. It was nine

a.m. sharp. "Can you help me please. I'm scheduled to see Mr. Ramsey, but, uh...they forgot to list me at the security gate. I'm supposed to ..."

"Oh, is that it? No problem." He turned to the crusty old guard and said, "It's all right, Gus. She's my guest as well."

It was like being freed from a bear trap. "Thank God," she murmured under her breath. At two minutes past nine, she accelerated through the open gate, sped the short distance toward the Ramsey mansion and spotted the tail lights of his MG backing from the driveway. She gunned the engine, then slammed on her brakes to block him. His trunk nearly rammed into the passenger door of the Cadillac as he leaped from the car and stepped angrily toward her.

"I have a good mind to send you away, Laura. I told you not to be late."

Careful. Easy does it. "You didn't tell the guard I was coming," she replied, seething.

He animated an *aw shucks* charade and snapped his finger. "Doggone, I guess I just forgot."

"Where is my little boy?" she asked, somberly.

Lloyd turned toward his car and called, "Okay Champ, come on now!"

The urge to weep with joy nearly burst from her heart. She stepped from her car, lips quivering, trying to break a smile. It was the moment she had dreamed of for three and a half long years. As she watched the child emerge from the MG, she exclaimed, "Oh God, he's so beautiful." Bowen toddled to his father then looked bashfully up to Laura, finger in nose. He wore a white dress shirt, with blue shorts and suspenders, and brown leather shoes, his silken blond hair parted perfectly on his left side.

Her heart raced a million miles per hour. Kneeling, smiling, she gently took his arms, studied his features and saw that he resembled his father. The boy looked at her quizzically, then up to his father. "Hello, Bowen," she said, taking his hands. She yearned to kiss and squeeze him, but Lloyd was standing by. She had to leave quickly before something, anything, screwed it up.

"Hello, Miss Laura," answered the child, properly tutored.

"Daddy said you're going to take me for a ride."

"That's right honey." *Huh?...Miss.. Laura?...* "Come, Bowen, let's get in the car, shall we?"

As he walked back to the house, Lloyd barked, "Five o'clock sharp, Laura. Right here. Don't be late." He turned and saw that she was staring at him. "What's the matter Laura?" he asked.

Her voice was low and filled with contempt. But not so low that he couldn't hear. "Someday, Lloyd. Someday...it will all come around."

Laura could barely tear her eyes from the beautiful child, her boy. *This is my son. My baby.* She drove euphorically onto the causeway, glancing repeatedly from the road to him, beaming. She had her boy, finally. For a few hours anyway. Before crossing the bridge into Miami, she turned into a park and stopped. "Look Bowen, I've got a present for you."

"Look, it's a blimp!" he exclaimed, pointing to the sky, ignoring her.

"See what I've got for you?" From the back seat, she pulled up a furry lion almost as big as he was.

"Wow, thank you Miss Laura. I like lions."

Miss Laura? Miss Laura? The words felt like daggers in her heart. She paused, pondered carefully then decided to lay the ground rules. "Listen Bowen, " she said, as they sat watching boats pass by. "You call me Mommy, okay, because I am you're mother, see? Didn't your daddy tell you that I'm your mother?"

He held the lion, poked at its eye and replied, "You're not my mommy. My mommy is at my house. Her name is Yvonne."

"What? Oh, my God!" She searched her mind, then remembered the name...*Yvonne? Yvonne Rappaport? So that's why she's no longer there. Lloyd married Yvonne Rappaport?* It struck like a sledge hammer, her son claiming another woman as his mother, and of all people, the office secretary. She walked away from the car leaving Bowen alone with his lion, corralling her emotions and thinking of what was best for Bowen, not herself. *Poor Bowen. My poor baby. What would Paul say to do. Oh, I wish he were here. That son-of-a-bitch, how could he do this?* She stepped to the edge of the coral rocks as a seaplane took-off, reflecting on all the conversations about child psychology she had shared with her husband, remembering his advice,

"Laura, remember, nothing is his fault. He can only know what he's been programmed to know. You have to be strong and loving by example and never enter into dispute with him. He'll come to you when he's ready. Just show him love."

Moments later, she started the car, took a deep breath and gave her child another broad smile. "You like animals? How would you like to go to the zoo?"

"Really? Yippee!"

It was a good day. Laura was as happy as she could be until five o'clock sharp when she was compelled to watch her little boy walk off and toddle back into the Ramsey world.

* * *

With the stuffed lion so large, Little Bowen could barely manage. He stepped to the rear of the Star Island house and saw the Ramsey family sitting around, smoking, drinking and chatting by the pool, then showed his father what *Miss Laura* had given him.

"Yeah, that's nice, Bowen. I'll tell you what, we'll leave it here at Grandpa's house, so you can have a toy to play with when you visit."

That was the last time Bowen ever saw the lion.

chapter six

S adly, the reunion with her little boy did not blossom into the bond that Laura had fantasized. Bowen had been well cared for, healthy, obedient and mannered, but he was distant and cold and unreceptive to gestures of love. He stood limp to her embrace, distracted and politely tolerant as his father had instructed him. Paul said it was not unusual for a child of that age considering his background. But his words were no consolation. Her offerings of love and affection simply went unreciprocated. Years of dreams fostered hopes that had been set too high.

She tried visiting with Bowen every two weeks for trips to the zoo, swimming at Venetian Pool or fun romps in the park unless, of course, Lloyd conveniently made *special* plans for the child. Laura would often call ahead only to find that her son was away somewhere, Hawaii, The Bahamas, boys camp, always in conflict with her week-end visits. Though Laura was rendered insignificant in Bowen's life, she was determined. Persistence, she thought, would pay off. One day she would have her child back where he belonged.

Gentle prodding to have Bowen acknowledge her as his mother proved fruitless. Everyone else in his life still referred to her as *Miss Laura*. The term was locked in his brain and he seemed confused whenever Laura raised the issue. Paul said the title was not important for now, that he would eventually recognize her as a mother when he matured. For now, she could enjoy what times she had with him and make the best of it.

Dragging Lloyd back to court was an expensive and futile endeavor, for little would be changed so long as he complied with the judge's order. Her attorney ruefully advised that a counter suit was ludicrous. Lloyd had ostensibly established a stable home environment with a capable wife, nannies and private schools. And he had money, influence and most of all... possession, which in the eyes of law was ninety-nine percent of the struggle. A judge would never uproot the child for Laura unless she could prove neglect or mistreatment, and that was nearly impossible.

Lloyd's marriage was dumbfounding. Laura could not imagine what Lloyd Ramsey ever saw in Yvonne, a poor office girl from Queens with no high level education and small breasts, no less. She knew all his turn-ons and that definitely was not one of them. It could not have been her status in the community or her money, because she had neither. She was pretty, but not beautiful nor was she particularly bright. Then again, that might be the answer.

Laura went about setting her priorities as a dutiful wife to Paul Rosenthal, a warm and caring stepmother to Cynthia and, finally, pursuing the teaching career she had sought since she entered college in 1960. Paul said her convalescence at South Florida State Hospital was not a criminal record and saw no reason that some early bout with depression would hold her back from the teaching profession she had aspired to for so long. He suggested a private school where her records would not be open to public scrutiny.

When she made her application to the Stanton School in Coconut Grove, the administrators were delighted to hire a past valedictorian from the University of Miami. When asked about her lack of employment since graduation, she fibbed saying she had toured foreign countries to enhance her education. There was no reason to reveal her three year incarceration.

Laura found her niche. She was a natural born educator. Within months, staff administrators were calling her the best teacher they had ever seen. She had a special way with kids, driving them to excellence yet showing compassion and individuality in her style, giving each kid special attention and bringing out the best in them. Junior high students, often the toughest, admired her for the manner in which she showed *them* respect, having each of them participate in the learning process. She held discussions, and solicited dialogue and encouraged students to be teachers as well, a welcome departure from customary droning lectures. Laura was a hit with her kids, with the faculty, with Paul and with Cynthia. Everyone, except the distant son she loved so much.

She also made a new friend in Wilma Ashenbrenner, guidance counselor and speech therapist at the Stanton School who was married to a psychiatrist as well. Homely but eccentric and very outgoing, Wilma had a biting sense of humor, always light and happy, refreshing for Laura who had seen enough of serious people in her life. She and Wilma would share lunch times together in the school garden, eating their sandwiches and comparing notes about their egghead husbands. She shared very little about Bowen's story, careful to ration information about her past.

During her bi-weekly *visits*, Laura coached Bowen to memorize her phone number, telling him to call any time he wished. It was intended as a subtle message that her love was accessible whenever he wanted it. She would always be there for him.

It was a Monday evening in February of 1970, two weeks after Bowen's sixth birthday when Cynthia answered the phone.

"Laura, it's for you! It's Bowen."

"Bowen? My goodness. What a surprise. Thank you darling. I'll get it." She rose from the easy chair and took the phone in the parlor. Paul was engrossed in a news story about the arrest of Marines in connection to the My Lai massacre.

"Hello?"

"Hello, Miss Laura. I mean..." Then he whispered, "I can call you Mother if you want."

Shocked yet delighted, she answered "Of course, darling. I told you, I am your true mother."

"It's just that, well...you know, I don't want Mommy to hear. Daddy might get mad."

Mommy. "That's okay darling. I understand. So what are you doing?"

"I'm in the hospital, laying in bed watching TV. You said I could call you."

"Of course. I'm so happy you called." She thought he was visiting another patient. "Who is in the hospital, Bowen?"

"No one, just me."

"Why are *you* in the hospital?"

"My operation is tomorrow morning. Daddy says..."

"Operation? What operation honey?"

"My heart operation."

Oh my Lord. "I'm sorry Bowen, but I don't understand. Your father never talks to me."

"It's okay. They're going to sew up a hole between the venicals..."

"You mean, the ventricles?"

"Yeah, the venicals...and I get to stay home from school. They said it wouldn't hurt."

My God! Bowen has a heart problem? Why wasn't I told? "Oh, darling, I didn't know. What time tomorrow? Who is your doctor? Where is your Dad? Oh, dear, I'm so surprised."

"Real early tomorrow. The doctor said I'm going to wake up, then go right back to sleep again." There was a painful pause as Laura collected her thoughts. "Miss Laura...?"

"Yes honey?"

"I mean..." He lowered his voice to a whisper. "...Mother?"

The filial reference shrouded her in glee and sadness at the same time. She whispered as well. "Yes, darling, what is it?"

"If you come here to visit me, will you bring me another lion?"

"Of course, darling. Where's that big one I gave you a long time ago?"

"Daddy says I lost it."

"Lost a giant lion? Well, never mind. Of course I'll bring you a lion. What's the name of your hospital?"

"Mercy Hospital."

What can there be that is below insignificant?

* * *

She searched everywhere until she stopped at a Rexall Drug Store where she found a small, amber lion made of cross-patch material and a mane of rabbit fur around the neck. She promptly rushed to Mercy hospital where Bowen was already asleep in room 228 of the children's ward. So she set up camp, settled into a vinyl covered chair next to his bed and spent the night.

Early the next morning, slumped and snoring, she was startled by a little boy's voice, "Hi, Miss Laura!"

She awakened and checked her watch. It was five forty-five. A broad smile crossed her face. "Hey there sweetheart. I told you I'd be here. Look what I've got for you."

She handed him the lion and basked in the glow from his face. "Oh, thank you."

She doted over him for thirty minutes until two nurses came in the room followed by one of the staff doctors. Activity was stirring throughout the floor as hospital workers scurried to and fro. Bowen's surgery was scheduled for seven o'clock, so it was time to prepare. "I'm hungry," he said. "They told me I'm not allowed to have my cereal this morning."

Lloyd and Yvonne Ramsey suddenly appeared and stopped abruptly in the doorway when they saw Laura. Clearly irritated, but cautious, Lloyd glanced at Bowen who was holding his new lion. "Hi Mommy, hi Daddy," he said. "Is it time now?"

Mommy?

It was awkward for everyone, particularly Laura, for she was not supposed to have known about any of this. Greetings were stiff and unfriendly. Yvonne started toward Bowen but deferred to his natural mother who was nearer to him. With a contemptuous expression aimed at Laura, Lloyd tussled his son's hair, muttering, "How're ya doin' champ?"

Moments later, after the nurse gave the ready sign, the cardiologist entered the room clad in his green operating-room garb. He had not previously met any of the family in person so he introduced himself, then asked the boy, "Well, young man, are we ready for some more dreams?"

"I guess."

"And who are all these nice people?"

Before Laura had a chance to speak, Lloyd interrupted and extended his hand, "We're Bowen's father and mother."

Lloyd curled his lip in a victory smirk, knowing he had just metaphorically knifed Laura through the heart.

"And you are...?" the doctor asked, turning to Laura.

How do I answer? She looked at Bowen, then Lloyd, Yvonne, the doctor and back to Bowen again. Her response could have been simple. *"I am Bowen's mother".* But she had to think carefully and edit her words. She might place little Bowen in a precarious situation of fending off his father's wrath, worrying that *Mommy's* feelings had been hurt and suffer emotional anxiety when he was about to undergo the scalpel. If she acquiesced and introduced herself as *Miss Laura,* a friend, she would be making an identity statement to Bowen from which she might not recover. She turned to her son and grabbed his little hand with both of hers, looked at him with the most loving eyes in the world and said, "I'm just...I'm Laura Rosenthal. And this little fella, well, he's pretty special to me." She dropped a tear and left the room.

chapter seven

The operation was a success and Bowen returned to conva-
lesce in his Golden Beach home under the care of the
nanny or his Mommy, depending on the time of day or
day of the week. The toy lion that Laura had brought to the
hospital mysteriously disappeared. When he cried, Daddy
bought another one, much furrier, bigger and with a life-like
mane. He named it Harry, homophone for *hairy*.

Lloyd refused Bowen for overnight stays at Laura's house,
or to join her for family travel excursions. It wasn't specified in
the judge's order. *"You're welcome to take me back to court. If
you dare."* Thus, the only way the Perrigos of Ada, Oklahoma
could see their grandchild was to be in Miami when Laura was
permitted one of her visits. That was impossible for Cal who
now held a full time job as a motel night clerk to pay for the
home mortgage. So Zaidee came alone not only to meet Paul
and Cynthia, but in hopes of seeing little Bowen while he recovered from surgery. It was three weeks since the operation and
Laura was due for one of her visits.

"He's not fully recovered, Laura, I'm sorry," Lloyd barked,
tersely.

Accustomed to begging, Laura held the phone from her ear
and took an exasperated breath. Zaidee listened nearby. "Lloyd,
I know he is up and around and playing. I promise I will not let
him exert himself. We'll go to the movies."

"The doctor says he won't be fully recovered until another
two or three weeks. Until then, I'm responsible for seeing that
he is...."

"Lloyd, for God sakes,..."

"...taken care of properly and as long as he is under my

control..."

"Lloyd, my mother is here. *His* grandmother. It would be nice if Bowen had a chance to meet his grandmother."

"Well that will have to wait, I'm afraid. Give it a couple weeks."

"She doesn't have two weeks, Lloyd. She has to go back to Ada. My Dad can't stay alone that long."

"Well that's too bad."

"At least let her in the house to see him. I'll stay outside. Honest, I won't say a word."

"That would be very disruptive. I can't allow that."

"Lloyd, she's sixty-six years old and she has a right to know her grandson." Her voice rose sharply as she sensed the familiar onset of those horrible emotions. "What the hell is wrong with you?" She saw her mother turn her head, concealing her tears. "You son of a..."

Dial tone.

* * *

As the years passed, Laura immersed herself at the Stanton School, relishing the successes with *her kids*, as she called them, and the respect she garnered from fellow faculty members. Meanwhile, she and Wilma deepened their friendship, socializing often as foursomes with their intellectual husbands, playing tennis, attending operas and enjoying the finer restaurants of Miami. With the exception of the fissured relationship with Bowen, which seemed irreversible, life was good.

Her cravings for motherhood found a worthy substitute as the bond with Cynthia grew closer. Maturing now, she took ballet and piano, excelled in her school and accepted Laura with all the love she would have given her own mother. When she was nine, Cynthia approached with a weighty question. "I talked to my dad and he said it was all right to ask."

"Sure, sweetheart, what is it?" She stepped tentatively to Laura who was sitting at the kitchen table and slipped into her arms. "Okay, tell Laura what's on your mind."

"Well, you know I loved my mom," she said, somewhat apologetically. "But I love you too, and you're, well...just like a mom.

I mean, you do everything a mom does and all. So can I call you Mom?"

There was a warm embrace as Laura bathed in the fulfillment of her yearnings. A flow of tears formed as she held the child like she would never let go. "I love you, Cynthia."

"I love you too...*Mom.*"

* * *

It was February the fifth, four days away from Bowen's eighth birthday. Laura phoned Lloyd to arrange her bi-monthly visit when she was startled by a message from the operator. "I'm sorry, this is no longer a working number."

"Excuse me?"

"That number has been disconnected."

She dialed the Miami law office where a secretary announced Lloyd Ramsey was no longer there but had set up a branch office in West Palm Beach. When she dialed information for the city sixty miles to the north, no Ramsey law firm existed. Not yet, anyway. Frustrated and angry, she drove to the Golden Beach house in hopes of confronting him or Yvonne to see what was going on. She couldn't miss Bowen's birthday. She had already missed too many.

When she pulled into the circular driveway that once was hers, she saw a "sold" real estate sign impaled in the front yard. No cars were there but she tried ringing the doorbell anyway. No response. An eerie deja vu crept over her as she peered through the awning window, remembering that awful day when the locks had been changed. The house was empty. All furniture was gone. She had no idea where to find her son.

Calling the elder Ramsey home at Star Island never did her any good, but she tried it anyway only to suffer the same response as always. A hang-up.

Three days passed. Through a private investigator, Laura learned that Lloyd Ramsey had purchased a new home facing the Atlantic Ocean on A1A in West Palm Beach, not far from the world famous Breakers Hotel. She dialed the new phone number. No answer. She finally connected with him that following Monday morning after Bowen was in school.

"I was supposed to pick up Bowen this week, Lloyd," she barked angrily.

"So, who was stopping you?"

"You never told me you were moving."

"Oh, was that required by the judge?"

Bastard!

The incident triggered enough courage to finally go to the courts and seek legal custody. It was time. Laura hired a well known domestic attorney who filed two suits, the first of which asserted it was in the best interest of the child to be turned over to his mother for full care and custody alleging:

1) That the child had wrongfully and deliberately been withheld from his natural mother and;

2) That the child had been wrongly taught that another person was his mother, and;

3) That the foregoing had been detrimental to the health and psychological welfare of the child, and;

4) That Mrs. Laura Rosenthal was a loving, attentive and capable parent who had been denied her rightful role as mother of the child, and;

5) That Mrs. Rosenthal had a good and proper home in which to care for and nurture the child, and;

6) That Lloyd Ramsey was an absentee father who rarely spent time with the child and;

7) That the child would be better cared for by the natural mother, and;

8) That Mr. Ramsey should be required to pay Laura Rosenthal two thousand dollars a month child support.

The second suit ambitiously demanded Mr. Ramsey to pay one million dollars in compensatory damages to Rosenthal for pain and suffering caused her since May of 1964.

The attorney was optimistic about the custody suit, figuring the second suit was intimidating enough for him to cede the child to his mother. It was a shot in the dark but worth the try. There was also new reason to be encouraged. Judge Burlington had suffered a stroke and was compelled to remove himself from the bench, thus turning Laura's case over to a newly appointed judge with no ties to the Ramsey firm.

One week before the court hearing, after months of preparation, Laura received a letter at her school office by registered mail. The return address was that of Lloyd B. Ramsey in West Palm Beach. As she opened it, she saw a hand written note attached to a carbon copy onion-skin letter. The handwritten note read;

Hello, Laura. This hasn't been sent. <u>Yet</u>. It's up to you. Lloyd.

The unmailed letter was addressed to the president of Stanton School and signed by Lloyd Ramsey himself.

Dear Mr. Stanton,

It has come to my attention that my former wife is now working in your employ as a teacher and counselor for junior high school aged children. While Laura Rosenthal is no doubt intelligent, personable, and a capable teacher, it may disturb some of the parents to learn that Mrs. Rosenthal spent nearly three years incarcerated as a mental patient in South Florida State Hospital, in Broward County, between September of 1964 and March of 1967. She was diagnosed as extremely schizophrenic and manic depressive, with suicidal tendencies and episodes of delusionary paranoia. I am sure Mrs. Rosenthal is feeling better these days and has been adjudicated competent and cured of her illness. However, I feel it is incumbent upon the school administration to have this information as it is undoubtedly missing from her original application for employment. If you have any questions, you can reach me at my office anytime.

Best Regards,
Lloyd B. Ramsey, Esquire.

The letter was never sent.

chapter eight

Three Years Later - 1975

Until Bowen reached the age of eleven, he led a relatively happy life considering he was the product of a broken home. But something always seemed to be missing. He had everything a kid could ask for, games, sports equipment, bicycles, a pony, two dogs, television, swimming pool and his own movie camera. What he didn't have was a union of two loving parents.

The routine never changed. Up in the mornings with *Mommy* who fixed his breakfast and made sure he got off to school. After school, a sitter was usually at the house until *Mommy* arrived around six to make dinner. His father was home some evenings but rarely spent time with him other than a perfunctory tussle of the hair and one of those *champ* remarks. Promises to take Bowen fishing were never fulfilled. Something always came up. He learned to expect nothing from his father. *Mommy*, on the other hand, was always there to answer his questions, help with his homework, make sure he was clothed and fed and kept busy with activities. She was his rock. Though she wasn't prone toward gestures of affection, she always tucked him in bed at night, called him pet names, touched his face and kissed him on the forehead. In his heart, he knew she loved him, so all that mushy stuff wasn't necessary. He looked forward to bedtimes just to feel her warmth.

He knew Miss Laura was his real mother, but it never really felt that way. She simply made no difference in his life, while *Mommy* did. She was there, Miss Laura wasn't. When Miss Laura called him and no one was looking, he'd cup the receiver with his hand and whisper, "Hi, Mother..." Bowen knew she liked that. "... Shhhh. My dad is in the living room, so if he comes in, I have to call you `Miss Laura'."

"I understand, darling."

It always went that way.

One Friday afternoon when he was eleven, he came home from school and *Mommy* was already there. That was strange, he thought, until she said, "Come on Bobo. Change into your old shorts and pack a bag. I'm taking you to the Keys. We're goin' fishin' for the weekend."

"Fishing? Oh boy!" he exclaimed, elated beyond description.

Three hours later, armed with an array of brand new rods, reels, lures and tackle boxes, she and Bowen arrived at Islamorada on Plantation Key and rented a small cottage where they retired early in order to meet the sunrise the next morning.

It was spectacular, indeed, as they settled at the end of a small pier watching the bright, orange glow gradually rise in the east over a placid ocean horizon until it fully appeared and gave light to the new day. It was so quiet and tranquil. Bowen was the happiest eleven year-old boy alive standing next to *Mommy* with his fishing rod extended over the rail and a piece of mullet attached to the hook drifting five feet below the surface of the water. He knew nothing about fishing and neither did she, but it was a long standing promise that his father never kept. For her, it was as unnatural as Sister Teresa packing a pistol.

Another boy and his father settled in a few yards to their left. A man on the other side cast his line. A lighthouse replica, white with a red roof, stood twenty feet high at the point of a small peninsula jutting west from the island. All Bowen could hear beside the sounds of an occasional boat were seagulls squawking and fluttering in the dawn as they foraged the beach for nature's morning yield. Bowen marveled at the pelicans perched atop wooden posts, aiming their sights on a school of needlefish below the surface then taking off like a low flying airplane, zooming inches above the water. One pelican reached a high altitude, then...

"Look, *Mommy*, the bird is dive bombing. Wow!"

In the blink of an eye, the large bird impaled the water and emerged soaring with a wriggling fish in its beak. Seagulls clamored near the bridge, flying and hovering, waiting for someone to land a fish, cut it and donate the scraps. Bowen took a deep breath, enjoying the smell of salt air and dead fish. Yvonne saw the glee in his eyes and turned away sadly.

"What's the matter, *Mommy,* aren't you having fun?"

She puffed her cigarette and smiled warmly, her curly bleached blonde hair blowing in her face. "Oh yes. This is great."

"When are you going to quit smoking? Don't you know those things are bad for you?"

It brought a little chuckle. "Not to worry, Bobo. These are Kents. They got a micronite filter, or somethin' like that. So, ya see, it's lot safer than other kinds." She reached into her purse, then, "Hey. Whadaya say, I take a picture, huh?"

"Sure, okay."

He never saw her with a camera in her hand before. She stepped away, held it to her eye, told Bowen to smile and then clicked. She asked a nearby fisherman to take a picture of her and Bowen. It was the first picture of the two together, in ten years.

"Wow, I got one!" exclaimed the child, his rod wavering and bending violently. With his face a mass of confusion, he stood looking for help, cranking the reel until the nearby man saw he was in distress and came to assist. Three minutes later, Bowen had a seven pound kingfish on deck and a gigantic smile on his face.

"This calls for another picture," she said, snapping away.

Minutes later, they were back into their lawn chairs with another piece of bait on his hook. Feeling sloppy and unpretentious, dressed in old, loose clothing that looked like they came from the Salvation Army, Bowen could have remained there for the rest of his life. Later that day, they stopped at an old dockside tavern where they enjoyed oysters and clams, conch chowder and French fried potatoes, soaking up the warm breezes, seeing everyone so happy and casual. "Whadaya say, tomorrow morning we charter a boat?" she asked. "We'll do some real deep sea fishin' with a captain and a mate who can show us what to do."

"Oh yes, yes!"

That afternoon, they returned to the same pier across from the fake lighthouse, and cast their lines once more. No one else was there. Yvonne propped her pole against the rail and sat quietly on her folding chair smoking a cigarette, watching as Bowen eagerly stood at the edge, reeling in, casting out and reeling again. He caught a small mackerel and threw it back, giggling. After a while, she went off alone for a barefoot stroll along the beach where she could sort her thoughts, glancing back to the pier every so often to check on Bowen. She returned and resettled into her chair, lit another Kent and took a deep breath. It was time to complete her mission.

"Hey, Bobo, lookie here."

He stared out over the waters mesmerized, his back to her. "Yeah? What's that?"

"Come here. I'll show you."

Stirred from a trance, he shook his head, laid the rod against the rail and stepped toward her. "Yeah?"

She opened her hand. "I found this on the beach."

"Wow. It's pretty. It's the prettiest shell I've ever seen." He leaned over and took the conical relic into his hand.

She studied his face, thinking that she had never seen him so content and happy. "You like it?"

"Yeah. Look, it's got orange and blue, and..look there, a hole punched through the bottom."

"That's from the bird's beak. Take it. It's yours."

"Gee thanks."

"It can be, you know, like somethin' to remember your first fishin' trip by."

"Yeah."

"You know Bobo, I think it's time that, well, I want to talk about your mother." She was obviously nervous, puffing another cigarette.

"Sure. What's wrong with you?"

"I don't mean me."

He paused a second, afraid to bring up the sensitive subject. "Uh, oh,..you mean, Miss Laura?"

"Yes, darling. Your mother."

It was strange to hear *her* refer to another woman as his mother. It was never allowed. "Well, I know she's kinda like my natural mom, but you're my *real* mother, I know that."

She took another deep breath and watched a pair of sloops pass in the distance. Waters were getting rougher now as evening winds started to whip. "You know, Bowen, when a parent loves a kid, they only say and do things they think are in their best interest. Even though they make mistakes sometimes, they think they're doing the right thing at the time."

"What are you getting at?"

"Well look, you're a big boy now and there are things you should know. Your natural mother loves you very much. It was not her fault she didn't get to raise you. It's how your father wanted it. She really is a very good person."

"Yeah, so?" He oscillated the rod to and fro, thinking it would attract more fish. The topic was making him very uneasy.

"If anything...you know, ever happened to me, always remember, I was...uh, I mean, I'm actually nothing more than a good friend, a *real* good friend, but Laura...she's really the special one. She's your real mom, always was, always will be. I want for you to love her, hear?"

"Uh, ...I guess. But Dad doesn't want me to call anyone Mom except you."

"Well, .. Bobo, I disagree with your dad there. How do you think he would feel if you called him *Lloyd* all the time?"

"He'd be mad."

"Not mad, Bo. You'd be hurting his feelings."

"Yeah. I know. Why are you telling me all this?"

"Because...." He watched a tear form in her eye, her mouth turned downward, quivering. "Well, it's, well...I love you kid." She reached out and for the first time ever, extended her arms. "Come here, you fool." Bowen laid the rod on the deck and stepped over to the woman he had called *Mommy* all his life and slipped into a pair of arms he rarely felt before, not in that way. And it felt good. So good. He put his arms around her neck and felt her shivering.

The following Monday, he knew. When he came home from school, her clothes were missing from the closet, her make-up was gone from the vanity and she never came home to make dinner. It was ten years to the day that Yvonne Rappaport had married Lloyd Ramsey.

chapter nine

The monsoon came down in buckets that Monday evening as she met Paul at the door to take his raincoat. "Hello dear. Here give that to me." A peck, a smile, then a few pats on his lapel.

The distinguished psychiatrist ran fingers through his wet, speckled grey hair, removed his shoes and received a hug from thirteen year-old Cynthia. "Hi Dad. You look like you've been swimming with your clothes on."

"Feels like it too." As he stepped into the sunken living room, he removed a folded newspaper from his jacket and commented, "It's over, Laura."

"What's that, dear?"

"The war. Look here. The communists invaded Saigon. It's just a matter of time now," he said, shaking his head. "Fifty-eight thousand dead Americans and for what? I want to read more, especially Goldwater's interview. President Ford is supposed to address the nation later."

"Oh yeah, Goldwater, the Republican extremist. I remember when they called him the war monger."

The Rosenthal home was full of intellectual stimuli. Bookshelves were lined with all the classics, Voltaire, Shakespeare, Hemingway, Longfellow while strains of Mozart, Schubert and Verdi could be heard regularly from quadraphonic speakers throughout the house. Paul and Laura often included Cynthia in family discussions about current affairs not only because it helped her school work, it gave her a deeper understanding about the world around her. It was a forum for an expression of thoughts and opinions, an important element in parent-child relations, according to her father. After he changed into more comfortable attire, they grouped around the Florida room, he with his pipe, Laura a set of notebooks and Cynthia holding her calico cat named *Heidi*. Dinner had been prepared by a house-keeper.

"Too bad Bowen can't ever participate in our talks," said Laura.

"Yes, too bad," Paul answered, somewhat placatory. He turned his attention to Cynthia. "Tell me, have you been watching the developments on the busing issue?"

Eager to join in, Cynthia replied, "Yesterday, I read about a case in a Boston school district where they want to bus twenty thousand students out of their neighborhoods to integrate."

"And what do you make of it?" he asked.

"Well, I kinda feel sorry, I mean I think Negroes should be allowed to go to the good schools just like us and not just Negro schools, because they're people too and they should have as many rights as anyone, but I don't know about this busing stuff. I mean, I would hate to be forced to go twenty miles just to attend a Negro school. But on the other hand, it's the only way Negro kids can get a better education. It's a hard question."

"Okay, okay. Let's hear what your mom has to say."

With a pensive look, Laura hesitated then mused, "When I was a little girl in Oklahoma, I had a Negro friend named Lila. We played in the park and fed the ducks and I honestly never thought about her being different than me until one day, my father prohibited me to see her any more. He said it had nothing to do with her being a dark person, it was because other families would think that we were 'nigger lovers', as he put it. And that could have been big trouble. What really bothered me wasn't losing her as a friend, but thinking about the awful rejection she must have felt only because she was a certain race. So I can imagine how angry Negroes feel, especially in southern states where anti-segregation laws have not been effective in the schools."

It was Paul's turn. "I have mixed emotions, honestly. Uprooting kids from their neighborhoods is bound to create a proliferation of private schools and then white flight. Twenty years from now, Negroes will still be in inner city schools while whites run off to the suburbs. Busing then will have solved nothing, while..."

The phone rang, interrupting the thought pattern. "I'll get it," Laura said, stepping to the parlor. Paul continued chatting with his daughter.

"Hello," she said, holding the receiver to her ear. At first, she heard nothing, then the sound of a child whimpering. "Hello?" she called out again, bewildered. It sounded like he was holding back an explosion of tears. "Bowen? Is that you?"

"...Yeah."

"Bowen, what's wrong, darling?" She heard a burst of weeping. Laura knew it was serious. "Talk to me Bowen!" From the other room, Paul heard the intensity in Laura's voice and walked over to monitor.

"I came home..." he sniffled, then broke into another crying jag.

"My God, Bowen, stop crying a minute and tell me what's wrong."

"She's gone! She's gone! And she's never coming back!"

"Bowen, who's gone?"

"*Mommy.*"

She hesitated a moment, pondering. "Yvonne? She's gone?"

"She said you were my only mother,... that I should love you."

A chill came over her. "Oh my God." Her heart beat heavy as a tsunami of emotions swelled through her body. She placed her free hand to her face, her mouth agape. "Oh, Bowen, poor baby..." *Oh come to your Mother, my baby, my poor baby...I'll share your pain, I'll comfort you, my son, I love you so.*

His voice cracked, weeping. "I'm sorry, I know you're my mother, but I don't want to lose my *Mommy.* All her clothes, everything of hers is gone. Please don't feel bad. But I miss her. She left this note."

The wound in her child's heart brought tears to Laura's eyes. Her son was weeping over the loss of another woman who he saw as his genuine mother. Paul asked what was going on, but she shushed him. "It's all right, Bowen. I'm okay. Where's your father?"

"He's on the way home. I called him and told him what the note said."

"What did it say, honey?"

"It's right here. It says, uh... `A deal is a deal. Tell Bowen I'm sorry. Yvonne'.*" He broke into another fit of sobbing. "What does she mean, deal? I don't understand."

"Oh Bowen, poor Bowen. Look it'll take an hour, but I'm coming to pick you up. You need someone with you. Wait there."

"No, no, no. Please, my father, he'll kill me. He's on the way, don't come."

She held him on the line for another five minutes, until he whispered frenetically into the receiver, "...he's here, Miss Laura. Uh, I gotta go."

So... it was a deal.

* * *

Lloyd Ramsey was wrought with frustration. The sudden upheaval in his perfect life was more than he could deal with. Yvonne never let on. He never expected it. He wasn't even aware it had been ten years. Until now, his world had been arranged like a fine-tuned machine. He drove a Ferrari on week-ends and a Lincoln during the week, belonged to the Polo Club and traveled often to Las Vegas and the Bahamas. His son was healthy, bright and had anything he wanted. Yvonne had been true to her commitment, loyal and dutiful, never making demands and caring for Bowen day after day like clockwork. His law practice was thriving in West Palm Beach where he handled wills, probate and domestic affairs, mostly divorces. It was an ideal forum for meeting distressed damsels, a virtual reservoir of vulnerable sex partners. At thirty-seven, he no longer wore his hair in a flat-top but rather long, draped over the collar just as he thought women liked it. He hob-nobbed with politicians and power brokers daily as visions of an appointment to the Circuit Court and a future stint as Governor danced through his head like a sugar plum fairy. He had it made. No restraints. Until now.

He came home to find Bowen crying on the phone, angrily removed the receiver and slammed it to the carriage. "Don't be calling Laura every time you feel bad, you hear me kid?"

"*Mommy's* gone," he cried, showing his father the note. "And she's not coming back. What did she mean by a deal?" Faster than he could see, he felt the whip of his father's backhand across his cheek. "Ouch!" Then again. "Please, stop!" And again. "No, no," he screamed, cowering fetal-like on the floor. Finally, he stopped.

"Knock it off, you hear me? There's nothing about any deal." Lloyd contained himself, tempted to take another swing, even daring to kick the boy, but he mellowed. "Don't worry, Champ, everything's going to be all right."

It was as though someone pulled planet earth from under Bowen, leaving him suspended with nothing to hold. She was his Gibraltar, there day after day, listening, helping, seeing him through little trials and tribulations, the only person in the world he could truly rely on, who loved him and cared. Now, a huge void echoed in his heart. He pondered over the story-book week-end in Islamorada, and remembered the little talk on the pier and then realized what she meant by it all. Of course it had been planned, she knew she was leaving all the while. It was her way of saying goodbye without having to say goodbye. Later in his room, he took the small, blue and orange conical shell from his pocket and twiddled it in his fingers, reminiscing. When he heard his father turning the door knob, he quickly shoved it under the pillow.

"I'll find you another mommy, Bowen."

"I don't want another mommy. I want my *mommy.*"

chapter ten

1975 - 1977

It started a few months after Yvonne disappeared. Lloyd had problems keeping live-in housemaids to watch after Bowen, having fired two in a row for "poor attitudes". He had hoped for another reliability machine like Yvonne, but they couldn't match up. Finally, he brought on part-timers whose ancillary duties, besides tending to Bowen, were preparing meals, washing and ironing clothes and shopping, but they couldn't live in or spend evenings. That forced Lloyd into the undesirable position of staying home often unless he could find a sitter. At times, he allowed Bowen overnight stays with friends. Other times there was no one and Lloyd had to stay home and play the father role.

For Bowen, it was like there had been a death. All his life, he had relied on the devotion of one woman, a woman who tucked him in bed at night, helped him with homework, made him well when he was sick, cooked his meals, clothed him and took him fishing. Now she was gone. Time did not heal the wound. His entire outlook on life had deteriorated. His grades, which had been perfect throughout elementary school, sagged along with his morale, for there was no one at home who seemed to care whether he did well or not. His father would harangue him about *responsibility* and being a *Ramsey*, which counted for nothing in Bowen's eyes, other than trying to keep him off his back. "Get over it," his father once said. "She's nothing to you, anyway. Just another money-grubbing bitch. You either get your grades up or there won't be any trips to Hawaii next summer."

Bowen would have preferred a trip to the Florida Keys any-time.

Late one Saturday night, Bowen was having nightmares and awoke to see the illuminated dials reading five minutes to one. Voices from downstairs caused him to believe his father was with friends, as usual. Without exception, his friends were always women. Pretty women. He rarely entertained the same woman twice. This time, Bowen heard laughter and music and sounds of giggling, moaning and groaning, so he snuck out to the hall where he looked down from the staircase. He was careful to crawl quietly on his stomach lest he get into big trouble.

A strange, pungent odor permeated the darkened living room which was barely illuminated by a single blue lava lamp on an end table. Next to it, a bottle of liquor and two tumblers. Dissonant sounds of electric guitar music wailed softly from the record player. Bowen's eyes had adjusted to the dark so he could see his father was face up, sprawled naked on the big easy chair with a woman's head bobbing up and down as though kissing his private parts and another woman without clothes dancing about the floor with an invisible partner, singing, giggling, smoking a funny wrinkled little cigarette. His father said, "Gimme another hit, baby." The dancing girl dropped to her knees and placed the wrinkled cigarette in his mouth. He took a long deep drag and exhaled slowly, cooing. "That's good shit," mumbled his father, his long hair draped over his face. Then the room smelled worse.

As the days and weeks ensued, the odor permeated the house every night. His father openly smoked the odd cigarettes like it was a normal every day part of life. Bowen thought about telling someone, a teacher, perhaps Miss Laura during one of those Sunday visits, but changed his mind. He would be violating his father and subject to his wrath if he opened his mouth. He had heard about marijuana in school but never saw it before or knew its odor. Now it was a common presence in his home.

One afternoon, when school was out, he spotted a classmate on the vacant baseball field and ran up to him. He had a school-wide reputation as a marijuana user.

"Hey, Bruce, wait up."

"Hey Bowen. What do you want?"

"Got any marijuana on ya?"

"What? Hey, bug off. I don't know what you're talkin' about."

"I won't tell, honest. I just want to...you know, see what it's like."

Bruce was tall, too old for the sixth grade and had a face full of acne. "What do ya wanna know for?"

"I don't know. I saw someone smokin', and I was wonderin' if that's what it was."

"How do I know I can trust you?"

"You don't. But you've got my word and that's better than any guarantee."

Bruce studied his eyes, then said, "Come with me. And remember. You stool, and you're dead."

He looked right and left, saw that all the kids had long since departed school, then settled into the first base dugout. Bruce pulled a little sack from his pocket, rolled a smidgen of *grass*, licked it shut and toked up. Bowen watched with fascination.

"Here, Bowen, take a hit."

"Naw, no thanks."

"What do you mean, *no thanks*. You sure you're not a stooly?"

"No, I'm not. Honest."

"Then you'll smoke with me. Here."

Nervous, Bowen took the flimsy joint from Bruce's fingers, placed it to his lips, sucked and burst into a coughing fit. After he stopped hacking, a light-headedness came over him. Bruce chuckled. After another puff and feeling sick this time, Bowen passed it back. "I don't like it."

"That's all right. This ain't good weed, anyway. If you hear where I could get some better grass, let me know. I'll pay."

* * *

Laura phoned from her office during the afternoon break between classes. Every two weeks, it was a perfunctory matter, one she always dreaded. "Hello, Lloyd, this is Laura. I'll pick Bowen up Sunday, the usual, nine o'clock. I'll have him back at..."

Lloyd had a new tone to his voice. "Hey, listen Laura, I was thinking."

Oh God, what now? "Lloyd, don't be telling me you've got him on another camping trip somewhere, or traveling to the Bahamas, godammit..."

"Wait a minute."

"Or he's too busy with soccer practice. This has gone on long enough and I'm..."

"Laura, settle down. Listen to me. Look, uh, why don't you go ahead and keep him for the weekend?"

A long, tenuous silence prevailed as his words reverberated in her brain. She needed to listen again, unbelieving. "What did you say?" she asked, holding her breath.

"Well, maybe he needs to spend a little more time, you know, with his mother."

Should I pinch myself? "Stop right there, Lloyd. Say no more. Give me the day and the time. I'll be there."

"Come Friday evening. But bring him back Sunday night."

She was completely flabbergasted. The last time that Laura put her boy to bed was in May of 1964 when he was three months old. She didn't dare question the sudden change of heart. As soon as she hung up the phone, she called Wilma Ashenbrenner who, like her, was on break. They met in the canteen.

"Oh, Wilma, I'm so excited. Bowen's coming to stay for the weekend. I can't believe it. Lloyd's up to something, I know it. He's never been kind or thoughtful about Bowen this way."

She sipped coffee from a paper cup. "That's wonderful. I'm happy for you, Laura."

"I'm thrilled. And I'm nervous, too."

"I bet he'll be real happy."

Laura sipped through the straw pondering a moment, then... "Do you think I should tell him the news?"

"Why not, Laura? He'll probably be very excited."

"I'm not sure. Maybe I should wait a while."

"Take first things first. Spend a long, wholesome weekend with your boy and have a good time."

"I've got to think of something we all can do together like a family. A *real* family. Oh Wilma, all I've ever wanted was to have my son, to play a role in his life."

"Well, to be honest, I could never understand why you haven't before."

"It's a long story."
"Maybe someday you'll share it with me."
"Yeah. Maybe."

* * *

For all his years, Bowen knew Miss Laura, or *Mother,* as a pleasant woman who visited monthly, drove him around, bought him treats and took him to shows. But he was never included in her life as a family member. Since moving to West Palm Beach almost four years past, he had not stepped foot in her Surfside house because the seventy miles was too far considering her limited time restraints. It had been that long since Bowen saw Mr. Rosenthal, the beady-eyed psychiatrist who was always reading books.

Lloyd routinely addressed her as *Mother* now. *"Your Mother is on the phone, Bowen." "Ask your Mother, Bowen."* The sudden adjustment made him feel somewhat uneasy. The term, *Mother,* somehow seemed disloyal, like he was violating Yvonne, or... *Mommy,* wherever she was. He thought about her constantly.

Deep within, he knew his father's change of heart toward Laura was purely selfish as he wanted freedom to conduct his personal activities without the burden of a kid around all the time. Bowen was simply in the way, extra baggage, someone to throw food and gifts at then cast away like a house cat. He ranked near the bottom in his father's priority column, after work, women, cars, drugs and alcohol. Most of all, Bowen missed being special to someone, like he was special to *Mommy.* So maybe it was a good thing to spend more time with his natural mother. After all, his *Mommy* had told him how special he was to her, that his Miss Laura really did love him. *Mommy* never lied to him. So, maybe he should give it a try. It couldn't be so bad.

It was a long, scenic drive along A1A, with *Mother* at the wheel of her sleek '74 Cadillac El Dorado, smiling ear to ear, making small talk and singing together to the music on the radio to the Captain and Tennille's *Love Will Keep Us Together.* He couldn't ever remember seeing her so happy. While the mood was upbeat, he harbored great apprehensions about staying over at the house, wondering about his bed time, how strict they were, if there was a television in his room, if Mr. Rosenthal would accept him, if Cynthia would be his friend or if she would have nothing to do with him because he was too young.

"Come Bowen, you know this song? Sing with me."

Well, helloooo, Dolly, Well helloooo, Dolly, ...

"Bowen, one of the things we do at home, especially Friday nights with Cynthia is make time for little family meetings where we all can talk and express our thoughts and opinions..."

Weird.

"...about anything. It could be politics, music..."

Ugh.

"...or even sports..."

Sports? That's okay.

"It's really fun, and stimulating. Kids have important ideas too, you know, and we like to hear them. So, maybe you'd like to participate. Okay?"

"Yeah. Sure." *Participate? Strange.*

After a dinner of corned beef and cabbage and stiff conversation at the table, the foursome adjourned to the glass enclosed Florida room where Paul Rosenthal chaired the first family meeting which included Bowen Ramsey. Feeling like an outsider, he watched and listened in amazement as Cynthia raised a number of salient issues concerning crime, abortion, rock and roll music and current motion pictures. Bowen was asked for input but felt at a loss for he simply could not articulate on this level. He felt stupid. Sensing this, Paul changed the topic. He turned to Laura and said, "Maybe it's time to break the news."

"Should I?"

"Sure. Go ahead."

* * *

Bowen was barely listening, his mind adrift into televisionland, wondering if he was going to miss *The Six Million Dollar Man*

"Bowen?" she said, getting his attention.

"Yes?" A slight grin formed in her lips as she leaned forward, her hands folded, looking into Bowen's eyes. He knew this was something important, to her anyway.

"How would you like a little brother or sister?"

"Huh?"

"Bowen, I'm going to have a baby." She smiled broadly, hoping for a happy reaction from her son. There was nothing but silence. All eyes were on Bowen. "What do you think about that? A little brother, or sister? Won't that be nice?"

Nice? I don't know. Gee. What about me? I'm the one you said you wanted. Now that you have me coming over, you want a baby more. I thought I was going to be real special here, but now it's going to be a baby. Why a baby? I don't want a brother or sister. This isn't fair, it's not fair.... He couldn't be honest, and he couldn't be dishonest. He had nowhere to turn. He couldn't go home, his *Mommy* was out of his life, no one understood, or cared. All eyes were glued to him, Paul's, Mother's, Cynthia's, and he could see smiles disappearing into confusion, for he hadn't given them the reaction they wanted. Feeling the room closing in, he abruptly leaped from his chair, ran into the guest room and slammed the door.

* * *

"Oh, my Lord. I wonder what's wrong," she asked Paul.

"I'm not sure. Obviously, he's traumatized. This concerns me, very much," the gentle psychiatrist remarked, puffing his pipe. "There are some ghosts haunting that boy, more than I thought."

"What should I do? Oh, Paul, I don't want to mess this up. I never thought he'd react that way."

Cynthia excused herself. "Uh, I think I'll go on to my room now."

Paul crossed his legs, furrowed his brow and searched deep into that brilliant, eclectic mind. "This was a bit sudden for him, being immersed into the culture of an established family, with expectations he could not meet. It might have a been a bit too soon. We should have given him time to assimilate."

"I wonder why he took it so hard?"

"Well, Laura, you entertained him once or twice a month, but you've never come to know him, so..."

"I know, but it wasn't my..."

"I know, I know. Listen, right now, I think you should go in there and let him know you love him and that it's all right for him to feel that way. Don't make him afraid of you. Give him the freedom to have feelings without guilt."

She ambled down the hall and knocked on the bedroom door. "Come in," he said, in a near whisper.

She found Bowen sitting on the edge of the bed toying with a small seashell.

"Hi," she said, wistfully, then sat next to him.

"Hi."

"What's ya got there?"

"Seashell."

"It's pretty. Did you find it?"

"No. Someone gave it to me."

"Oh." She placed her arm around his shoulder. He shook her off, and kept fiddling with the shell, looking down and away. "Bowen, I'm sorry that bothered you in there. You want to tell me what you were thinking?"

"Nothin'."

"It's all right you know. No matter what you were thinking, it's all right. I just want to understand you, and I need for you to help me do that."

"I'm fine. Really."

She sighed with frustration. "I love you son. I love you very much." Words that could never express the depth of her feelings.

"Uh huh."

"Hey, we're going to Seaquarium tomorrow. Unless you'd rather the zoo. What do you think?"

"That's fine. Can I watch TV now?"

She sighed and studied his body language which clearly translated to; *leave me alone.* "Yeah. Sure, Bowen. You can watch TV."

chapter eleven

Later in the week, Bowen and his father were at the dinner table with a new auburn-haired woman named Betty Jo and another couple around the same age, all new faces. As usual, he was in his own distant world, insignificant within the group, gnawing an ear of corn, fantasizing a tarpon at the end of his line and paying little attention to conversation until he heard his father mention the word... *pot.* So he tuned in.

"Ah, it oughta be legalized for cryin' out loud," commented Lloyd after a guzzle of Chianti. He hoisted his stem glass. "It's no different than this."

"I don't agree, Lloyd," replied the man with the bushy mustache, nodding toward Bowen as if to say, *Hey, your kid is listening.* "It leads to other things. That's the big problem."

"It's not even addictive. That's been proven. Marijuana, by itself, is not an addictive drug. So, if people are stupid enough to use heroin, or whatever, then sure...they got a problem. Shit, alcohol is actually more harmful than pot because it is addictive. You can't get cirrhosis from smokin' weed. It's stupid. Hey, everyone's smokin', even judges and doctors, but it's the street slobs they put in jail."

Betty Jo nodded, "Oh yes. I agree with Lloyd."

Again, the mustachioed man nodded toward Bowen who was artfully pretending to be distracted. "Hey, Lloyd, maybe , uh, we should talk about this another time?"

Lloyd smiled and tussled Bowen's hair. "Oh, don't worry, Al. The champ here knows it isn't for kids. Right champ?"

"Right, Dad."

"Frankly, if he's gonna do it, I'd rather it be in front of me than behind my back."

"Uh, Lloyd, dinner was great, maybe we should...."

"I believe in being open, Al. No sir, no secrets in this house. You should always be open and honest with your kids. I won't be a hypocrite. He's old enough to understand, so I really don't care if Bowen knows I smoke a little once in a while. It's just recreational, nothing big time. It's harmless." All eyes turned to Bowen who felt like running from the table, but he dared not. "And when he gets older, he can make his own choices. Ain't that right, Champ?"

Bowen nodded, but his mind drifted to Islamorada and the lambent waters, warm breezes, diving pelicans and his mommy's voice, *"You know Bowen, when a parent loves a kid, they only say and do things that they think are in their best interest."*

"Sure."

* * *

Later that night, after company had long gone, Lloyd attended to the voluptuous redhead while his son dutifully remained in his room watching television, playing games, reading, trying to shut it all out. It was the familiar scenario, living room music, tumblers of scotch, the odor of marijuana. Only the guest was different. His father had become bolder with his habits, unconcerned about Bowen's presence as though he were a mere fixture in the house. Restless, unable to sleep, Bowen slipped out of the room three times to get a cold drink from the refrigerator passing by the *lovebirds* along the way, pretending to ignore them laying on the sofa listening to music, drinking, smoking, talking, giggling. It was the third visit to the kitchen when Bowen heard his father call out, slurring his words, "Hey kid, what's the story? You still hungry? Whazza matter? Not enough eats for dinner?"

"Uh, no Dad, just thirsty."

"Well, bring a couple of sodas back in your room and, uh stay there, okay?"

Turning his head away, Bowen sulked past the couple where the pungent aroma of pot pervaded the air. Then his father mumbled again, in a near whisper. "Hey champ. I think I know your problem, yeah."

Bowen stopped respectfully, but continued to face straight ahead.

As he watched Betty Jo stroking his father's golden mane, a flash image of *Mommy* passed through his brain and he was angry. He father never doted over her like he did these other women. Lloyd drew a sloppy grin and murmured, "That's what it is. You're curious, ain't ya?"

He stood, embarrassed, wishing he hadn't come out. "Naw, not really."

"Look kid, it's nothin', see? Just a little grass. All grown-ups do it. It's harmless, nothin' to worry about." Betty Jo sucked a drag, held it deep and exhaled, then giggled. Bowen turned and faced his father, glancing down at the tiny cigarette. "Heeeere," Lloyd said, gesturing, extending the burning little stick. "Now don't you do this on the outside, but if you wanna try, go ahead. Take a hit, kid." Frozen, Bowen was astonished at his father offering him drugs, perplexed at being so unloved. "Go ahead. If you're gonna do it, I'd rather you do it in front of me." Bowen stared, wondering, tempted, feeling compelled. "Go on, champ."

Forever yearning for approval, Bowen stepped toward his father and took the burning joint to his lips. She smiled. He smiled. They were pleased. Bowen had done well.

chapter twelve

December 1975

I t was surely different without *Mommy.* Christmas was a week off yet no tree and no decorations were anywhere in the house. He wondered if his father had bought presents because none could be found. Now that he was nearing twelve years-old, Bowen was staying alone after school until his father arrived, which was usually past seven. Curious about hidden gifts, he violated one of his father's fervent edicts and snuck into the master bedroom suite where he looked under the bed and then into the walk-in closet. It was there he smelled it. Behind the shoe rack, in the corner, he spotted a one gallon paint can with the lid lying to one side. It was three-quarters full of marijuana. He knelt to the floor and took a small handful, sniffing it and wondered why all the fascination with it, why his father defended it, why Bruce and the other kids seemed to worship it. They were such big shots in school. There had to be something.

If you hear where I can get some better grass, let me know. I'll pay.

Bowen's allowance of thirty dollars a week far exceeded that of any school chum his age. Besides, his father had established an investment account in his name which would set him up for life provided he went to college. He didn't really like smoking pot, so he didn't know why he felt the compulsion to steal the handful, lay it in a handkerchief and wrap it into the size of a ping-pong ball.

The following day, he met Bruce in the boy's bathroom between his physical education and reading classes.

"I've got some," said Bowen, his heart racing.

Bruce smirked, tilted his head back daringly. "Yeah? What?"

Two other boys came in and stood at the urinal. "I can't say. Uh, wanna meet in the dugout after school?"

"No, there's a practice today." Bruce leaned, and whispered, "Under the causeway bridge, on the east end."

"Okay."

Throughout the day, Bowen's heart thumped an extra beat each time a teacher called his name. He felt transparent, like they could smell it or see the lump in his pocket. When school let out, he ran from the playground to the bridge where he perched himself on the concrete embankment and waited. Bruce arrived in the company of two other boys, one a chubby eighth grader named Howard who he'd never seen before and the other a popular boy from his class who he thought was straight. His name was BeeGee, short for Billy George. Unlike the others, BeeGee was neat and tidy with a traditional, short haircut parted on the side. Until now, Bowen had always been perceived as a loner, a smart rich kid who didn't participate in school affairs nor hung out with the popular kids. He simply blended in a crowd unnoticed, insignificant, just like he was at home. Indeed, it was an ego rush spending off-campus time with BeeGee.

Bruce wore faded blue jeans and a dirty, grey tee shirt outside his pants and a pack of Marlboros rolled in the sleeve. He examined the weed crumpled in Bowen's handkerchief then arranged it in a paper roll and lit a match. Howard and BeeGee glued their eyes to Bowen as he looked on wondering if he should try it again, to be accepted, to see what he missed the first time. Bruce inhaled deeply, held his breath for what seemed like a full minute, then exhaled slowly. Bruce looked at the joint then took another hit. "Whoa, there baby doll. Man, where'd you get this shit?"

"You like it?"

"This must be Colombian gold. What'd ya pay for this? Huh?"

"I can't tell you."

Bruce gave it to Howard who took a long drag, then to BeeGee who did likewise. They were aloft in pleasure, their faces serene, without a care in the world.

"Here, take a drag," Bruce said to Bowen.

"It's just recreational, nothing big time. It's harmless."

He didn't want it, really. But he reveled in the embrace of this roguish group and needed to prove his trust. He took the flimsy joint, remembering not to suck too much and inhaled. He coughed once or twice as the boys looked on. The raucous sound of a ninety-five horse-power Evinrude echoed under the bridge as a pair of men in a small fishing boat passed by. The boys sat quietly, holding their knees. Bruce took the joint back, cupped it in one hand and waved to the boaters with the other.

Then Bruce took another hit from the joint. "You got any more of this?" asked the pimple-faced kid.

"A little. Not much, really."

"Whatever you can get, I'll pay you twenty-five dollars an ounce."

Twenty-five dollars an ounce? Bowen Ramsey's need for money paled by comparison to the cravings of belonging and acceptance, to be important to someone, anyone. Kids seemed to like him now. Before, BeeGee would never talk to him but now he was slapping hands, laughing, telling jokes, smoking dope together. It was glorious.

"Hey, man, you're okay, Bowen," said BeeGee, snorting with laughter. "We're gonna be good friends. I can see that."

Wow!

* * *

Without *Mommy* to please any more and having a father who didn't care, it was as though another personality had crawled under his skin. Once a quiet, pensive kid who tended to his studies, played alone and would never steal or do anything that would bring shame or embarrassment to the good Ramsey name, Bowen took on a new identity. He was *cool* now. Each day, he arrived at school greeted eagerly by a coterie of chums among the inner circle, stopping often for a brief smoke party under the bridge before heading home. He was always alone when he arrived home so no one would notice that he was high. But his father noticed one change in his behavior. "Hey Champ, how come you're always sleeping?"

"Just tired, I guess."

By his twelfth birthday, February 9th, he had become a discipline problem to teachers, skipping classes, ignoring projects, aligning himself with the more disruptive children, talking, chewing gum. When his next report card came out, his father was livid.

"What is the meaning of this? You damn near failed math and science."

"Sorry."

"I won't stand for it."

"I'll do better, Dad. I'll bring up my grades."

"Is that a promise?"

"Promise."

"Back when I was in school, I never had a bad grade because I put my mind to studying, because I wanted a future..." Lloyd prated on about the good family name, the future he had in store for Bowen, the money set aside for his Harvard education, while Bowen daydreamed about the kids in school, how much they really liked him now. "...so you better straighten up, okay Champ?"

"Okay, Dad."

"Say, I've got a friend who runs a stable. How would you like to go horseback riding this Saturday?"

"Do you think we can ever go fishin' in the Keys?"

Exasperated, Lloyd threw his hands in the air. "Jesus Christ, Bowen. Show some appreciation, okay? I arrange a great day on horses and all you can ever think about is stupid fish."

"You said..."

"I know what I said. Get your grades up."

"Then will we go?"

"You raise those grades, I'll take you fishin' in the Keys."

* * *

It was another one of those afternoons alone in the house when Bowen wandered into his father's bedroom and found the paint can gone. He looked all over, but it was nowhere to be found. Pungent odors continued to emanate from the living room during the late nights so he knew the marijuana had to be somewhere. Even if he only brought enough for one or two joints, the kids made him out as a big shot. He needed to maintain his new image.

The garage was a place he never entered because his father parked the Lincoln outside while storing the Ferrari inside. He never rode in the Ferrari. It also housed the washing machine and dryer, two hot water heaters, a rider lawn mower and a few unused tools which Lloyd kept inside the large cabinets. When he looked in one of the cabinets, he saw a twenty gallon aluminum garbage can sealed with a strip of electrical tape across the top. He carefully lifted one end of the tape, popped the lid and there it was. Full. *BeeGee and Bruce are going to love this.* Worried that the odor would reek from his handkerchief, he snatched a small plastic bag from the kitchen and returned to scoop enough to fill half, careful not to take too much to be noticeable.

When Bowen met Bruce in the hallway the next day, they agreed to meet under the bridge after school. Sure enough, Bruce arrived, this time with a seventeen year-old kid with very long, black hair who called himself *Power.*

"How much of this can you get?" asked Power.

"Uh, not too much, just, you know, now and then..."

"Is it your old man's weed?"

Bowen paused, thinking seriously about the answer. "No, uh uh."

The kid took out a small hand scale, weighed the dope, and said, "I'll pay you fifty bucks for this. There's more if you can deliver."

"Sure."

* * *

Laura and Paul had noticed a change in Bowen's personality during the bi-monthly weekends at the Surfside house. He seemed detached, nervous, shaking his feet nervously when sitting in a chair, grinning ear to ear for no reason. He rarely spoke unless spoken to. Answers to questions were abbreviated, short and terse. Paranoia seemed to have invaded his entire persona.

"Paul, it just feels like he's so distant from us. Finally, after twelve years, there's a chance to get close with him, but he pulls away."

"Laura, have you thought about drugs? His symptoms strike me that way. I've seen it a hundred times, children who are products of a divided family, no sense of attachment, reaching out to peers for acceptance. Perhaps marijuana. Maybe alcohol. He has no ambition, impassive about anything you suggest, tired and sleepy. His grades have dipped, right?"

"Yes. They have. God, I hope you're wrong."

"There's an awful lot of it out there and when you listen to the hippies and that rock and roll stuff, it practically encourages kids. It's a statement of rebellion, establishing new turf, giving themselves an identity not imposed on them by the establishment."

"His father would never stand for it."

"Don't be surprised. If Bowen's clever enough, his father would never know."

Her head rested on his shoulder as he relaxed on the sofa. He pecked her on the forehead and draped one arm over her shoulder. Open displays of affection were not the norm at the Rosenthal house. That was fine, Laura knew her limits. "Oh Paul, I hope we have a healthy baby."

"We will, Laura. We will."

She looked into his eyes as a melange of fleeting thoughts suddenly flashed through her brain. That moment, she nearly asked, *Paul...you'd never take my baby away from me, would you?*

"What's wrong, Laura?" he asked, seeing she was troubled.

"Oh,...nothing. Nothing really."

chapter thirteen

February 9th, 1976

Flight announcements blared from the public address as Bowen and Laura sat waiting to board at gate G-14. She had hoped that his birthday trip to St. Thomas for two days of deep sea fishing would have ignited his waning spirits, but there was no change. He was distant, ill-mannered, slumping in the chair flipping pages of a comic book and acting like he'd rather be anywhere else.

"Well, Bowen, how's it feel to be twelve?"

"Ain't nothin'"

"What's the matter, Bowen? Would you rather just skip the whole idea?"

"Naw."

"I thought you'd love the idea of a fishing weekend."

"Sure."

"Well, you don't act like it."

"Sorry. I guess I don't act right sometimes."

She looked at him, wishing he would look back, but his head remained mired in the book until she posed a direct question. She had a way of shunning ill feelings, to bury pain and see only goodness, especially in her son. Nothing would dissuade her tenacity or her zest for cultivating a relationship. As always, she would absolve Bowen of his foibles and place blame where it rightly belonged from the time he was three months old. Lloyd Ramsey.

"Attention passengers. Flight 1198 with direct service to St. Thomas of the Virgin Islands is now boarding through gate G-14. Please have tickets ready..."

"Come Bowen. Aren't you excited?"

"Sure."

The boy shuffled listlessly behind his mother as the attendant accepted the tickets. Slowly they followed the dense crowd toward the door of the Boeing 707. Just before stepping on, Bowen remembered something, "Oh, wait...I forgot..."

"Forgot what, Bowen?"

"I left my comics on the chair out there. Can you hold up? I'll be right back."

"Go on ahead, silly. I'll be right here. Bring your ticket stub with you."

* * *

Bowen rushed back to the concourse against the flow of boarding passengers until he reached the seat where they had waited, grabbed the comic books and turned. As he started back, his peripheral vision caught sight of a passing figure walking briskly down the concourse toward the main terminal. He paid no mind until it registered in his brain, the hair, the step, the posture. Images flashed, faces, events, feelings. Before handing his stub to the agent, he figured he'd look out to the concourse one more time. Unable to see over the hoards of travelers, he stood on one of the seats. *It can't be, it's my imagination.* There, a couple hundred yards away in a trot toward the main terminal, he spotted the back of her hair, blonde, curled atop her head. *It had to be...it's gotta be...her*!

"Mommy! Mommy! Mommy! Wait... Mommy!" He took off running.

* * *

From the door of the aircraft, Laura could hear Bowen outside, screaming "Mommy, Mommy" ebbing as he distanced himself down the concourse. Confused and exasperated, she raced out of the tunnel in pursuit. When she heard his screams again, she knew.

"Mommy, wait up! It's Bowen, Mommy!"

Laura dashed after, evading passengers, keeping her eyes

on Bowen through the dense crowds, trying to catch up. Every fifth or sixth step running, she saw Bowen hop like a Pogo stick trying to see over the crowds, dodging travelers, suitcases, trolleys, running as fast as his legs would carry him. Laura kept him in sight as Bowen darted into the main terminal searching for the curly blonde hair, but she was gone. He stopped and panned the terminal, left, right, left. Laura caught up and grabbed his arm. "What's wrong with you?" she asked, holding back anger.

"No, no, she's still here, somewhere. Where'd she go? Where'd she go?"

"Bowen, settle down, we're going to miss the plane!"

Ignoring her, he headed toward the automatic exit doors and out onto the street where he spotted the woman leaning into a Yellow Cab, then entering the back seat. Laura yelled, "Bowen, come back here!" He raced through, knocked over a small Haitian woman, stopped to utter a hurried apology, then ran into the street only to see the bunched blonde hair through the window of the taxi fade away at thirty miles per hour.

"Mommy...it's Bowen! Wait up! Please!"

With arms flailing over his head like a windmill, he hailed another taxi which came to a screeching halt to avoid hitting him. Bowen leaped in the back seat, huffing, panting and gasped an order, "Follow that cab. Please. It's my mother in there." That same moment, the door pulled open again as Laura took a seat next to Bowen.

The driver, a young black from Jamaica, looked into his rear view mirror a bit confused and asked, "Follow what cab?"

"The Yellow Cab that just left with the blonde lady in the back."

Beside herself, Laura tried catching her breath. "Bowen, we've missed the plane. What the heck are you doing?"

He ignored her question and addressed the driver, "Please sir, hurry, I have to catch up to her. Please." Moments later, they were going sixty toward Lejeune Road, searching.

"Bowen! I'm talking to you."

"It's...it's..."

"You think you saw Yvonne?"

"Uh huh."

"Are you sure it was her?"

"Yeah. Well, I think so." Then he raised his voice again, peering through the windshield. "Please driver, can't you find it?"

The driver asked, "Was it a Yellow Cab, like this one?"

"Uh huh."

Drenched in frustration and a sense of defeat, Laura leaned her head against the window and stared out at the city passing by, wishing she could simply burst into tears. It would be so easy. She glanced over to her son who sat at the edge of his seat steeled to the windshield, obsessed with finding the one woman in the world who he accepted as his mother.

Driver: "422 to Dispatch."

Dispatch: "422, go ahead."

Driver: "I have a young passenger looking for a Yellow Cab that just left MIA upper ramp about four minutes ago carrying a white female passenger..."

The driver looked into the rear view at Bowen and asked, "Got a description, boy?"

"Curly blonde hair bunched on top her head," replied Bowen. "Her name is Yvonne..." Before he could continue on, the driver was talking into the mike again.

Driver: "Blonde hair, bunched on top her head. Name's Yvonne."

There was a short pause. The dispatcher repeated the message to all taxis when another deep, male voice crackled over the radio.

Voice: "645 here. I just picked up at MIA upper ramp, blonde woman, matches that description. I'll ask her name ...hold on...."

Another pause. Laura could see Bowen's eyes sparkle, listening, hoping to hear her name, cocking his ear to the static-riddled radio.

Voice: "Says her name is Myrna Johnson...that who you want?"

The driver looked at Bowen again in the rear view. "Is that her, boy?"

He shook his head. Laura watched Bowen's heart sink to the floor, his expression shrouded in disappointment as he slumped back into his seat.

"Bring us back to the airport, please," Laura said to the

driver. She placed her hand on his leg trying to be comforting, but he jerked away. "I'm sorry, Bowen." She turned toward the window, shielded her face with her hand and let the tears flow.

* * *

It was a swift, quiet ride across Julia Tuttle Causeway as she lit a cigarette, peering out at the sparkling bay, gazing at the skiffs cutting across the waters, skiers coasting, skies a perfect blue. She could see the driver look curiously at her through the rear view mirror as he stopped at a traffic light on Miami Beach's Arthur Godfrey Road. She ignored him. Before reaching the Fountainbleu Hotel, they crossed a small bridge where a boy and his father had dropped a line into the water. For a moment, she thought about *him*. But that was then and this was now, and she would not wallow in the past nor allow herself the pain of reflection, or of guilt.

The taxi driver pulled up the driveway of the magnificent landmark hotel, lowered the meter flag and stopped. A doorman approached, then a tall, distinguished gentleman followed in a maroon Polo shirt and khaki shorts, wearing a huge smile. She bolted from the car and into his arms.

* * *

The driver heard him say... "Oh Yvonne, I missed you so."

chapter fourteen

June 1976 - Three Months Later

At the end of the school term, Bowen managed two A's, a B and three C's. His father gave him another one of those *Ramsey* speeches about excellence and success while Bowen daydreamed. He had it memorized. When it was over, Bowen asked, "Are we going fishin' in the Keys, like you said?"

"No."

"But I got my grades up. You promised."

"Your grades are not what they should be. And you watch your mouth with me, you understand that, Champ?"

* * *

Saturday morning was a warm, humid and sunny day with nary a cloud in the sky. Across the street from the mansion, the ocean seemed like a sheet of shimmering glass, quiet, placid, with barely a ripple in the surf. Squawking seagulls thrummed and foraged for tid-bits in the sand, a common symphony Bowen would fondly remember for all time. A hoard of shell hunters waded in a low-tide sandbar a hundred yards out, some frolicking, others holding hands. Lloyd had gone for a tennis game saying he would be back at noon. Meanwhile, Bowen had made up his mind.

He packed a small grocery sack with a change of underwear, socks, extra shirts, toothbrush and comb. He had over one hundred dollars, plenty, he figured, until he could get himself a job catching fish and selling them to restaurants. For extra insurance he grabbed a scoopful of pot from the garage, enough for another hundred bucks if he needed it. By the time Lloyd returned, Bowen was gone. A torn piece of yellow paper was left atop his bed with a note:

You never keep your promises.

* * *

Laura was in the baby's room feeding two-month old Grace, named after the Princess of Monaco. She was a delightful child, born of love into a happy stable home. She represented a dream repaired, a fulfillment wrongfully denied her for twelve long years. Finally, Laura was complete. Well, almost.

Cynthia answered the phone. "Mom, it's for you!" she shouted.

"Who is it?" she hollered back from upstairs.

"It's Mr. Ramsey!"

"Tell him I'll call him back in a few minutes."

"Uh, he says it's real important."

Thinking the worst, Laura laid the baby in her crib, rushed back into her bedroom and lifted the extension. "What's wrong with Bowen?" she asked tersely.

Through clenched teeth, he spouted a question, "Do you know anything about this?"

"About what, Lloyd?"

"About his running off?"

"Running off? What are you talking about?"

"You mean he's not with you?"

"Bowen? No, he's not...Lloyd, what's going on?"

"He's run away, godammit!"

"Run away? Oh God. Lloyd, did you call the police?"

"I'm not calling any goddam police, Laura. I don't need the publicity."

"How do you know he wasn't kidnaped or something?"

"Well..." There was a long, painful pause.

"Well, what?"

"He left a note."

"Oh? What did it say?"

Lloyd explained how Bowen had pressured him for a fishing trip to the Keys but he had to earn it by making straight A's, which he failed to do. The note was clear.

"So, he's probably headed for the Keys somewhere," she surmised. "We'll call the Monroe County Sheriff's Department as well and alert them."

"No, godammit. No cops. Laura, you'll make me sorry I called you. I just figured maybe you knew."

She could not hold back. Years of degradation exploded inside of her. "Listen to me, you son of a bitch! All you care about is your goddam image while your son...*MY SON,* has been on your back burner all his life. Don't you get it Lloyd, you've failed."

"Failed? How dare you. I give that kid everything,....."

"Give. Shmive. You failed as a father. There I said it! Do what you want, you miserable rotten piece of shit, I'm sick and tired of groveling to you. All that matters here is Bowen, nothing else. *MY SON* Bowen and not your fucking image. Now if you don't call the cops, I'm going to. Tough shit, asshole!"

Her face afire, heart racing, hands trembling, she slammed the phone down. Images of the men in white coats raged through her mind, red toenails, the struggle, the straitjacket... *"My baby, my baby. Where's my baby? I want my baby"*... months and years locked away in an institution, sensing the same, manic frenzy swelling inside like that horrible day in 1964.

But that was then.

* * *

It was six-thirty that humid evening when the famished twelve year-old boy stepped off the Greyhound bus in Islamorada, Florida. His first priority was finding a place to eat. As he entered the Conch Shell convenience store, the clerk's eyeballs popped from his head when the boy pulled out a wad of cash to pay for two candy bars, a bag of chips and a Coke. From there, he found a row of tiny white, flat-roofed stucco cottages set back from Highway One amid clusters of cabbage palms and tall pines. An old faded blue Desoto was parked in front. "Hey there Sonny, what's up?" asked the fat woman inside the dusty office.

"I'd like a room please." Bowen was tall and lanky for his age but with boyish features, unable to pass for any older than twelve. His hair was dark blond and shaggy, Beatles style. He winced from alcohol breath as she burst into laughter.

"Ha ha ha. That's good. You got any money?"

"Sure do." He removed the wad from his pocket to prove his point. Her laughter quickly changed to a curious smile.

"Where's your mom and dad?"

"Uh, they stopped at the bridge to go fishing. I'm supposed to get the room and they'll be here later."

"You sure about that?"

"Uh huh."

"That'll be fifteen dollars. Plus tax. Fill this form out."

Excited over his return to heaven on earth, he locked the door to his cottage and walked a mile and a half to his destination. The fishing pier across from the simulated lighthouse was the same as it was the year before. Ah, so good to be back. He figured he'd buy a cheap fishing pole in the morning. It was eight-thirty-five as he gazed out at the setting sun, leaning against the rail, thinking, reminiscing. The pier was full of anglers, young and old, tending to their rods hardly saying a word. A sense of relief came over him, tranquil and content, like he'd been freed from a cage. No pressures, no performing, no expectations, just he and his private thoughts, unencumbered, sucking in the ocean air, listening to the surf, fantasizing fish swimming below. No need for marijuana here. He had all the high he needed.

With barely enough cash to last a few days, he knew he would have to face his father eventually, but he didn't care. He was savoring the present as though there was no future. Perhaps it was a good thing to worry his father and make him angry. It would be a wake-up call, due notice that he, Bowen, was not a piece of property but a person who craved love and acceptance for who he was like anyone else. Except for his school grades, his father never showed concern for things important to him. This was all he wanted, nothing else. A day by the sea on Islamorada, content, soaking the sunshine and imagining what it was like to be a fish following its natural instincts, going where it wished with no expectations, answering to no law other than the law of nature. But no one understood that. He dared not speak about *her* to his father for he would say she was a no good *money grubbing bitch*. He couldn't talk to his natural mother

for he would surely hurt her feelings. His friends would think
he was a sissy. So it was good that he had his time here alone, to
share with *Mommy*.

* * *

Laura asked Wilma to come and sit for the baby while she,
Paul and Cynthia headed for the Keys to begin the search. To
Lloyd's chagrin, the Sheriff's departments from Palm Beach to
Monroe Counties were alerted though there was little they could
actively do to search for the boy. "There are thousands of run-
aways, Mrs. Rosenthal," one cop said. "If we sent out an investigator for every kid that ran away, we'd have no one left to handle
robberies and murders. Rest assured, we have him in the system."

They had photographs printed with Bowen's name at the
bottom of each. Close to panic, Laura fretted, babbling on about
weirdos out there, child molesters and drunkards. Paul had all
he could do to maintain her calm and alleviate her fears. "We'll
find him, Laura. He's an intelligent boy. He'll know how to take
care of himself."

"But what if he's not even in the Keys? What if…"

"Laura, there are a lot of *what ifs*. Right now, if everything you
say is true, it's likely he'll seek out the place he's been wanting to
go."

"My God, Paul. There are over a hundred miles of the these
islands…"

"Yes, but there's only one road in and out. So, that's the
good news."

When they reached the northern most island of the archi-
pelago, Key Largo, they stopped at a gas station and showed
Bowen's picture to the attendant. That was the beginning. By
eleven that night, they'd shown the photo to hundreds more
without making it to the next island down. They checked into a
motel and were up at five the next morning, out in the streets
showing pictures everywhere, restaurants, gas stations, motels,
tackle shops, all to no avail. They called hourly asking Wilma if
there was any news, but there was none. Paul was beside himself with exasperation. "Laura, this is worse than finding a needle

in a haystack. We must go home. We have the baby, and Cynthia." He patted her hand sympathetically, "Why don't you talk to some detective in missing persons here in Monroe County. They might be ably to steer you better."

"I suppose I should. But remember? They said they don't have enough manpower."

"You're here now. Try again. Bowen will show up, I'm sure. And he'll be fine, you'll see."

She broke down, exhausted from the eons of trials and tribulations, of suffering when it never should have been in the first place. If only she could have had her boy. If only he could have had her. But there was no turning back the clock. "Paul, I'd like to bring in a nurse to care for the baby, for just a day or two. I'll call the police again. I have to stay here. I have to find him."

"I understand. Of course, Laura. I'll rent a car and bring Cynthia home. You stay and do as you must. Be sure to call home every hour in case something has developed."

chapter fifteen

Bowen awoke at daybreak to the sounds of a squawking radio dispatcher outside his window. When he looked out, he saw a portly police officer standing near the office talking to the fat woman. Surely, he thought, she's telling him about a young kid who checked in room four all alone. Afraid of being caught, he dumped the entire stash of marijuana in the toilet and flushed. He didn't want it anyway. There was no rear exit so the only chance of escape was slipping out the door if the cop turned his back. Sure enough, the officer returned to his cruiser, faced the highway and lifted the microphone to his lips. Bowen grabbed his sack, snuck out and ran behind the cabin into the foliage. He made it.

After snaking his way through a mile of trees and mangroves, Bowen stopped at the Conch Shell convenience store and bought two donuts and a carton of milk, plus enough candy bars, crackers and Coke to last all day. Again, he bared a wad of cash and asked the dark-skinned clerk where he could buy a cheap fishing rod. "There's a small marina a half mile north of here," he answered with a smile. "Hey, what's your name kid?"

He thought a moment, then, "Bow...Uh,..it's Bob. Um, what's yours?"

"Bedrosian." He saw a quizzical look on Bowen's face, then smiled. "I'm Armenian."

"Okay, Bedrosian, see ya later."

A while later, Bowen had his rod, reel, line and bait and took a position at the pier where he could look out over the seascape dotted with boats, islands and the lighthouse. He was safe now, back where he fell in love with living. It never occurred to him where he would sleep that night. Neither was he aware of the bearded tramp watching him from the surf below, smoking cigarettes, sipping beer.

* * *

Lloyd Ramsey was wrought with embarrassment. He was sure he had been a good father, giving everything in the world to his kid, toys and games, activities, travel, the best clothing, food and entertainment money could buy. Bowen's investment account was more than most people would earn in a lifetime. He had freedom, friends and a mansion to live in. So what was it, he wondered, that upset him so? Fishing? The Keys? *What got into that ingrate?* He paced the floor as the elder Ramsey looked on, packing the same pipe he'd been using for fifteen years.

"If the boy wants to go fishing, for cryin' out loud, why didn't you take him fishing?" asked Thurgood.

"I hate fishing."

"So take him anyway, if it means that much to him."

Lloyd steamed with every step. "If that kid thinks he can pressure me with these tactics, he's got another thing comin'. I'm his father. Who the hell does he think he is?"

"So, have you heard from the cops?"

"No, but I've hired a private investigator. He's down in the Keys right now."

"What about his mother?"

"I called Laura, but she went into one of her ballistic frenzies with me and hung up. Bitch. I've got a good mind to...."

"Easy does it my boy. I've got a sneaking suspicion you'll be needing her more than you realize."

Ignoring his father's ominous remark, Lloyd lit a cigarette, blew a waft of smoke and muttered, "Where is that damn kid?"

* * *

He caught two small mackerel that day and threw them back in the water. There was nothing else he could do but give them away. It was getting late. Bowen dared not register in a motel again for they would surely call the cops just like the fat lady. He'd find a blanket to lay on and sleep under the stars, maybe near the pier. It was another one of those beautiful sunsets with glimmering, lambent waves, sailboats drifting and a touch of stratus clouds offering a blast of orange, pink and blue hues to the distant sky. One angler remained, a woman in a lawn chair just like *Mommy* had. A small grin crossed his face thinking about her carrot patch, toying with those bouncy curls, hearing her voice calling, *"Hey Bobo, time for your bath....Get your homework done first, Bobo..."* wondering where she went, wondering why she abandoned him.

He took his sack, rod and tackle box and started heading for land when the grubby derelict with the straggled beard called from below. "Hey, boah. Catch anything?"

"No, sir. Well, a couple small ones, nothing much."

"Where's your ma and pa?"

"Uh... well... They're around here somewhere."

The man looked up and smiled, biting on a burned out cigarette between his yellowed teeth. "No they ain't."

"Oh, uh, yes, they're up the street there."

"You're a runaway, ain't ya?"

A lump formed in his chest followed by a blood-surge to his head. Nervously, he replied, "No. Uh uh." He considered making a run for it but he was loaded down with all the new fishing equipment.

The man stepped onto the boarded walkway and confronted weary Bowen as he was about to disembark. "You hungry boah?"

"Well, uh, a little."

"What yer name?"

Gotta lie. "Bob. Bobby Johnson."

"Well, that's probably a lie, ain't it?" There was a brief stare-down, then, "I'm hungry too. Come, Bobby Johnson or who-ever you are, I'll let you buy me a dinner. You can tell me all 'bout why yer runnin' off."

"Buy you? Uh, I don't have any, uh..."

"Yeah ya do. I seen you in that store pullin' out the wad a cash. Come on boah, let's eat."

He may have been a bum, unkempt and hairy, but he was friendly enough and company for Bowen. After all, the man could have robbed him then taken off, but he was thoughtful enough to suggest eating together which wasn't such a bad idea considering his state of hunger. They hiked along the highway to a rustic marina with a dockside bar and grille, where leather-tanned people wore cut-offs, flip-flops, tee shirts and headbands to soak the perspiration. The bum exhibited the most obnoxious table manners Bowen had ever seen, slurping conch chowder, chomping shrimp and fried fish with mouth agape, guzzling beer, belching after every swallow. He tried imagining how he looked without the facial hair, but he couldn't see beyond the jaundice, rheumy eyes and the rotted teeth. He was near his father's age, he figured, a little older, maybe. Then it occurred to Bowen... *This guy was a kid once, just like me.*

"Name's Gabby. Just like Gabby Hayes. Ya know, like in the movies. Ever hear a him?"

"No."

"Ever hear a Roy Rogers?"

"Well, yeah."

"He was his podnah. Gabby. How much cash you got kid?"

Bowen took a long swallow from his Coke, trying to think of how to answer. "Not very much, I'm afraid."

"Got 'nough for a room? I'm gittin' tired a sleepin' in these ole boats."

Bowen figured the man hadn't seen a bed in days. What the heck, he needed a room too. This way, he could get registered. "Yeah, I think so."

"Good. Let's go. I know a place."

The tiny, mosquito-infested motel room had twin beds, but it was nearly impossible to sleep with the foul odor and body noises emitting from the bum. Nature finally prevailed and Bowen dozed off, his mind afloat into another day on the pier, caring nothing about his father or BeeGee or teachers or anyone else. He dreamt briefly of how life may have been with his real mother then wondered why he couldn't have gone with *Mommy,* where she was, why she left, if it was his fault, somehow. Soft lights flickered outside the window as the sounds of cars passed by on the highway, the fetid smell from the snoring bum, visions of fish bending his rod, waves slapping against the pilings, seagulls...

When he awakened, he could see the orange glow through

his window facing to the east. The bum named Gabby was sound asleep, a good time to collect his things and sneak out before he awakened.

Minutes later, he was at the Conch Shell selecting a carton of milk from the glass case when he heard a voice call out, "Hey there Bob, can I help you?"

He paid no attention. A second later, the Armenian was at his side asking, "Hey Bob, your name *is* Bob, isn't it?"

"Oh, yeah."

"I'm Bedrosian, remember? How's it going?"

"Fine."

"You staying in the Keys a few days with your parents, are you?"

"Yeah. Uh, can I buy a Three Musketeers also?"

Bedrosian smiled. "Hey, just pay me for the milk and donuts. Okay? The candy bar is on me."

"Gee, thanks."

Next stop was the bait and tackle shop a mile down the road. It was crowded early so he waited in line behind other customers before buying another pound of mullet. A teenage boy was behind him looking on, but he paid no mind. As he trekked along the side of highway U.S. One with his tackle box, bucket and rod in hand, he kept glancing back and side to side to make sure Gabby wasn't following. Before he reached the pier, a dirty black Rambler suddenly pulled off the road. The driver was the same gaunt teenager he saw in the bait shop, with an unfiltered cigarette burning in his mouth. He leaned to Bowen and asked, "Hey kid, want a ride?"

"No thanks. I'm at the pier now."

"Where's your folks?"

"I'm here by myself." He didn't stop to think. *Daggum it. Shouldn't a said that.*

"I know a great fishing spot, if you wanna come in."

Bowen reflected on the litany of warnings about accepting rides with strangers, but this was a teenager, not some old pervert or bum. Besides, he wasn't catching many fish at his pier so, he figured, what the heck. He loaded his gear and jumped in.

"What's your name?" asked the gangly teen.

"Bob. Bobby Johnson," he lied. The alias was getting easier.

They were instant friends. He said his name was Reggie from Oklawaha, Florida, the same town where Ma Barker and her boys were gunned down in 1935. Reggie had just turned eighteen years old, a drop-out and now a runaway also. He lived with his divorced mother, an alcoholic bar fly until he couldn't stand the embarrassment any more. His father was in prison for manslaughter and robbery. Bowen liked the idea that an older kid wanted to be his friend so they embarked on a long day of riding around, visiting other islands, chatting and smoking a little pot which Reggie had hidden under the seat. They stopped to fish from a bridge connecting Lower to Upper Matecumbe Key and caught several small yellowtails and threw them back. Reggie knew of a thatch Tiki hut where they would sleep the night, saving the money of a motel.

It felt really good to have a friend.

chapter sixteen

Laura had anticipated him showing up in a polyester suit, but he looked more like an oyster shucker in blue jeans and a Papa Hemingway tee shirt. He was tall and rugged with dark thinning hair and leathered skin like he'd been at sea for a lifetime. An aura of calm in his sky-blue eyes put her at ease and gave her a sense of hope. She liked that. Cops are usually cold, indifferent and detached, she thought, but Grady Culpepper sat at the restaurant booth talking to her as though she were a long lost friend.

"I didn't think runaway kids were enough of a priority to get such personalized attention from police," she said, in a questioning tone. "I honestly didn't expect a cop to respond."

"Depends," he replied, sucking an unlit wood-tipped cigar. "Not much goin' on today, got no open cases. I like kids, that why I work Juvenile. Got two of my own, twelve and ten. Don't want to see your boy get himself in any trouble out here. These Keys can be rough."

She passed him the photos while he took copious notes, rarely lifting his head as she prated on about Bowen's family history. Occasionally, she'd take a breath to let him finish writing a sentence. He was not particularly handsome, but there was a magnetic primal draw which she hadn't felt in a thousand years. Perhaps it was the honest face or his genuine concern about her boy, or those hairy, powerful arms that looked like they'd lift a station wagon. She took note of his simple wedding band and caught herself feeling guilty for entertaining such thoughts about another man. When he spotted her staring, she looked away quickly as Paul's image flashed though her mind.

"What makes you so sure he's in the Keys?" he asked, chewing on the cigar tip.

"It's his passion. I know him, I know why he ran away, to be here. There's no doubt in my mind."

"I see."

"Please, Sergeant, where should we go next? I'm so worried."

"It's Grady, ma'am. And if you like, you can come with me for this morning. We'll look 'round, ask some questions. Don't worry. We'll find 'im. A gold badge opens a lot of doors. But I've got to be in court later this afternoon."

"Thank you, Sergeant...I mean, Grady."

Overcome with worry, Laura's hunt was drawing blanks everywhere as she and Grady Culpepper roamed the northern Keys with Bowen's photo, interviewing every waitress, station attendant, bridge tender, boat captain or tourist they could find. She called home every hour on the hour to check on any news or phone messages. Nothing. Finally, the good detective went to his court assignment, assuring her he'd be back the next day if he could. Bar hopping and scanning restaurants, she was up until one a.m., finally falling asleep in her car next to a boathouse on Tavernier Key. By Monday, she again linked up with Grady Culpepper as they made their way to Islamorada. At ten-thirty, they were at a one-story motel on Plantation Key where a gaunt woman with straggled hair and bulging eyes gawked at Bowen's photo. She wore a dirty cotton dress and no shoes.

"Ne'er saw that kid. Uh huh."

Grady flashed his gold tin and looked deep into the dullness of her eyes. "You sure, lady, you ain't seen this kid?"

She shook head. Another disappointment.

Laura stepped from the office, sweat pouring from her brow, and bumped into an unkempt man with jaundice eyes and rotten teeth. She winced. "Excuse me," she muttered, recoiling from his body odor, sidestepping.

"Hey, lady. You guys lookin' fer a kid?"

She turned back, keeping her distance. "Yes." Grady stood tall, badge in hand.

"Got a pitcher?"

The detective stepped in and produced the photo. "Well?" Laura asked, apprehensive.

"That's him. Boy slept here last night."

Her heart skipped a beat. "Oh my God, where is he? Please tell me."

"Dunno. Snucked outa heah 'n the night. Nice boy, though. Name's Bob. Right?"

"No, it's Bowen."

"Tol' me Bob. Sorry, can't help ye any more 'n that."

"What was he doing? Where did you find him? Please help me."

Gabby described the fishing pier where he saw Bowen and how he reminded him of himself when he was a boy. "That boy jes' wanna fish. Look around piers and bridges, you'll find 'im."

* * *

By Wednesday afternoon, the boys had spent their combined monies on mullet, sodas and candy bars, but hadn't enough for food that evening. The Rambler was below a quarter tank and Reggie was getting worried. They were heading north on highway one, back toward Islamorada when Reggie asked, "How much money you got left, Bobby?"

"Uh, not much. A couple dollars maybe."

"Shit, I'm dead broke. How're we gonna eat?"

Then Bowen remembered Bedrosian, the friendly Armenian who had given him a free candy bar. "I've got enough to buy us a couple packs of crackers and some soda. I know someone at a convenience store down the road from here."

Checking his gauge, Reggie drove back into Islamorada where they stopped at the Conch Shell store. Two cars were parked in the lot. Inside, two young girls were paying for sodas while another man searched for a six-pack of beer in the rear. Bowen was surprised to see Bedrosian still there. A few minutes later, they were alone. The wall clock read seven twenty-three.

"Boy, you sure work long hours, Bedrosian," he said, standing eagerly at the counter, hoping for another free candy.

The Armenian smiled and shrugged his shoulders. "Hey there little Bob. Well, you know, I have to work to pay the bills. Catching any fish out there?"

"Not much. But that's okay."

"I hear dolphin are running about two miles out, the same

with..."

As they chatted, an expression of sheer fright suddenly gripped Bedrosian's's face as his cue-ball eyes gazed beyond Bowen's shoulder toward the coolers, his lips quivering.

"Gee, what's the matter Bedrosian? You okay?"

Trembling, the Armenian opened the cash register, sputtering, "Take it. Please!"

Bowen turned, gasped and froze. To his utter astonishment, Reggie was brandishing a small revolver, waving it crazily toward Bedrosian with a maniacal look in his eyes. "Bobby, take the money!" he shouted.

Bowen leaped backwards. "No. Uh, I can't."

"What? Whadaya mean, you can't. Take the fucking money! Now!"

"I've got money, Reggie, really."

"Don't fuck with me, Bobby! Take it!"

Overwhelmed with fear, his eyes were steeled to the little gun. *What if he shoots me? Oh my God.* He had no choice. Bedrosian was behind the counter, trembling, his hands aloft while Bowen, a kid with two hundred and fifty thousand dollars in an investment account was participating in an armed robbery. Frightened, confused, Bowen vaulted the counter, reached into the register and took out all the paper money, apologizing. "I'm really sorry, sir."

"Let's go. Hurry!" ordered Reggie.

Bowen sprinted from the counter past gun-waving Reggie and headed for the door. That's when he heard the sounds of firecrackers. *Pop Pop.* He twirled and saw Bedrosian holding his stomach, grimacing, falling against the counter, peering directly into Bowen's eyes before collapsing to the floor.

"He was reaching for a gun," exclaimed Reggie. "Asshole! Come on, let's haul ass before someone comes in here."

Bowen fixated on the man who had been so friendly, his smile, his good nature and then the grimacing face, dark eyes peering into his as he slumped to the floor. This wonderful serene paradise suddenly turned into chaos, robbery and murder. When he leaped into the car, he spotted a shadow coming from around the side of the building at the dumpster. There was Gabby, the hairy bum, standing there stunned, peering curiously into Bowen's eyes as they sped away. *Oh no. Oh no. He saw me. I know it.* Reggie hit the pavement and screeched north. Now petrified of this wild kid from Oklawaha, Bowen wondered what he really was, how many others he had shot or killed. Would he be killed as well? Reggie gunned down an innocent man without even flinching. He had to get away, far away.

They sped north until they reached Tavernier Key where a line of cars were waiting for a draw bridge to close. Perspiring profusely, Reggie puffed on a cigarette speaking not a word, worried about the old bum who could describe his car to the cops. Friendliness was gone. They shared a common bond now, a bond of desperation. Cars were lined at the bridge, behind and in front, jammed bumper to bumper. Bowen looked to his right and saw a vacant Deputy Sheriff's car parked at a marina restaurant. *No. Can't call a cop. I'm guilty too. I could go to jail. I gotta get away!* There was no better time if he was going to run. The bridge was high, Reggie was locked in. He couldn't chase after him now, because he would be too obvious. A cop was in the restaurant, somewhere. Reggie couldn't draw attention to himself. It was time. He flung the door open and bolted.

"Hey...wait, motherfucker! Bobby, get your ass back here!" He looked back for one second and saw Reggie standing outside the driver's door, shouting, waving his fist. "You son of a bitch. Asshole!" Reggie was trapped there. The shouting voice faded as he ran further and further until he could hear him no more. He ran toward the restaurant, then around it onto a service road leading to an old auto graveyard, afraid of looking back, afraid of hearing those God-awful popping gunshots, running like he would never stop. After what seemed like miles he fell into a thicket of brush and stopped to catch his breath. He remained there another hour until darkness settled in.

He'd had enough. He needed safe haven. It was time to return home and face the consequences for running away. *Better than murder.* The images of poor Bedrosian flashed through his brain, that grimacing stare into his eyes as he clutched his stomach. He wept for him, muttering aloud deep within the brush, "I'm sorry, Bedrosian, I'm really sorry."

* * *

Seeing that Laura was in a state of exhaustion, Grady insisted she take a rest and join his family for dinner. With reluctance, she accepted but felt it was a waste of precious time when she should be out there searching. The Culpeppers lived in a stilted frame house on Tavernier Key at the edge of a waterway leading to the Gulf where the golden sunset was a nightly attraction for residents of the street. Grady's wife, Ali, was a pleasant, petite woman who seemed to dote over her daughters too much, cutting their food for them while, in Laura's opinion, they were old enough to cut their own. The home was filled with love and contentment, sharing and open affection, the kind of home she had always yearned for but never quite attained. They seemed to know about her struggle as they greeted her with hugs, a strange but delightful feeling. Grady spoke proudly of his long career with the Monroe Sheriff's Department and his liaison with kids. Then the phone rang. He took it in the other room as Laura chatted with his wife and two daughters. Moments later, keys in hand, Grady was rushing out the door. "There's a call, honey. Some shooting at a convenience store. I'll call after I get there. Laura, anything you need, just ask Ali. Sorry. I'll get back with you."

Laura stayed at the Culpepper house another hour, then figured there was time to find a room for the night. She checked the clock and saw it was nearing nine, time for another check-in call at home. It would be her twentieth of the day.

"Hi Cynthia, it's me again, Mom. Any...?"

"Yes! Mom, so glad you called. Bowen just hung up."

It felt like an electric charge shot through her heart. "What?"

"He wants to come home. He says he's at a pay phone, next to a Cities Service station."

"Is he all right?"

"Sounds kinda shook up. Wants to know if you'll pick him up."

"Oh, thank God. Thank God."

Thirty minutes later, Laura found him quivering like a vibrator outside a phone booth near a gas station exactly where he said he'd be. She held him in her arms and kissed him all over his face. It was foreign to him but she didn't care. He was safe, that's all that mattered. "I'm hungry," he said.

She smiled. "Me too, Bowen. There's Royal Castle up the road. That sound okay?"

The radio news was broadcasting a robbery and shooting of a convenience store clerk in Islamorada. Bowen reached and turned the volume knob to the left. *Click.* The car was silent now until Laura smiled and said, "See, Bowen, there's lots of bad people out here. It's a good thing you called when you did."

* * *

Bowen would forever be haunted with the dark secret which he could never tell anyone, no matter who, no matter where or why. The consequences would be far reaching, banishment, trial, prison, perhaps the electric chair. The image of Bedrosian's face would flash through his mind day after day, awakening at night in cold sweats, wracked with guilt that he had played a part in this terrible crime. Often, he shook his head violently in an effort to flush the memory from his brain. He wished he knew more about Bedrosian, if he had a family, children, mother, father, what his hobbies were, his dreams, but he dared not pursue it any further. He had to act normal and avoid drawing attention to himself. Bowen had learned the art of camouflaging emotions so well that they no longer existed as his own.

Silence was deafening as he rode up the long, boring two-lane highway with his mother at the wheel. He pondered his father, wondering how was going to react after five days of being a runaway. He had never been so bold and insubordinate before. Bowen was glad, for now his father would surely see him as a person, a kid with feelings and needs just like him. In a sense, he had made a statement that he was not a mere possession. He pictured his father in a raging fit, blowing his top, ranting about the good Ramsey name. He might even get a beating. Then again, he might be overjoyed seeing that he was unharmed and healthy, and managed life alone for five days. Maybe he'd feel good that his son came home. Maybe, just maybe, his father would feel something for him. Anything.

* * *

Bowen spent the night at Laura's house where he could wind down and collect his feelings. On the phone, Lloyd argued and ranted, demanding Bowen be returned to West Palm Beach the next morning, "Without fail, no ifs, ands or buts."

During the long drives from Plantation Key to Miami and on to West Palm Beach the next morning, Bowen remained eerily reticent, rarely talking, staring out the car window. She was unable to extract anything of her son's feelings other than his craving to go fishing in the Keys, what his father always denied him. He simply decided to go on his own. But there had to be more, for he was a profoundly unhappy child, *her* unhappy child, with agony in his heart, yet she was powerless to probe any further. She thought of therapy for Bowen but that would be a slap to Lloyd's ego, an insult to the Ramsey name, out of the question.

It was a sad moment for Laura as she watched Bowen exit her car then amble listlessly up to the front door of the Ramsey mansion. "Goodbye, Mother," he murmured, unable to face her.

"I love you, Bowen," she choked, holding back tears. "See you two weekends from now."

She watched her slump-shouldered boy shuffle slowly toward the house. Then the front door opened and Bowen was swallowed by the loveless mansion.

* * *

His heart was beating like a bass drum, shaking uncontrollably as he stepped slowly into the Florida room where he could hear his father talking on the telephone. After five days of independence, the dreaded moment had arrived.

Sprawled on the cushy sofa, Lloyd glanced over at his young son timidly entering the room, then turned away without expression. It was as though he had never been missing at all. Bowen stood and waited, anxious, restraining the driving impulse to run somewhere, anywhere. He thought, perhaps, his father would hold up a finger or something, indicating... *I'll be with you in a moment.* But that wasn't the case. No acknowledgment. Lloyd was making small talk with some woman, discussing imported wines, comparing notes, paying no attention to the frightened twelve year-old standing there waiting to be chastised or hugged. Either would have been fine.

The conversation drifted into foreign travel, how fond Lloyd was of southern France and the Mediterranean coast. He, in turn, listened to whatever she was saying, laughing, exchanging kisses. More minutes passed. The shivering stopped, though his heart continued to pound until it sank to new depths. His father was paying him no mind, as though he had never even been out of the room. Feeling meaningless, like a fixture upon a shelf, Bowen went to his room, turned on the television and began shaking his head, hoping to cast away the suffering image of Bedrosian. Then he pulled the little seashell from his pocket, laid it on the night table, and stared.

chapter seventeen

Sunday, September 11th, 1977 - The Following Year

Afternoon skies were darkening as the wind whipped the ocean waters three miles out. One of those nuisance storms was starting to roll across the horizon causing a rocky ride aboard the forty-six foot yacht chartered by Lloyd Ramsey. But that didn't faze the dapper thirty-nine year old playboy as he humped and thrusted himself into the buxom redhead in the spacious state room below. They laughed and giggled, swaying to the inexorable movements of the sea as wine swished in plastic tumblers, marijuana joints burned in the weighted ash tray and bowls of cherries slid back and forth atop the counter. The bed was firm enough, but the boat rocked and swayed causing sensations of heavy, then light, heavy, light....rising, sinking, up and down, "Wheeee."

A knock came at the door. It could only have been the captain or the first mate. Otherwise they were alone.

"Shit," exclaimed Lloyd. Without missing a stroke, he craned his neck and shouted, "What is it, for cryin' out loud?"

The mate's voice replied, "Sir, I'm afraid you're wanted on the ship to shore."

"Take a message, will ya. I'm busy."

"Sorry, sir. It's the police. Something about your son."

Sex came to an unclimactic halt as he grimaced and clenched his teeth. "That fucking kid. I'll kill him."

"Go ahead baby," she said, kissing his ear. "I'll be here when you get back." She was the sexiest woman he'd ever known in his life. Well, that's what he told her.

He slipped on his pants and deck shoes and rushed to the

bridge where the weathered, old captain was at the helm. Dotted with three or four tall buildings, the Ft. Lauderdale shoreline was barely visible across the sea to the west. Through wind and radio static, his hair swirling violently, Lloyd was able to make out the five words he never thought he'd hear about a Ramsey. "Your son has been arrested."

"God damn him. That's it. I've had it! Quinn, turn the God damn boat around and head in. I'll take care of that little punk."

A lifelong sea addict, Quincy Eiland had been serving the Ramsey family for over twenty years providing discreet chartered voyages for prestigious clients, family affairs, or in the case of Lloyd, clandestine trysts with his most vulnerable and beautiful divorcees. With Quinn, Lloyd had developed a trust, someone on whom he could dump his troubles without fear of judgement. Quinn was wise and caring and rarely ever talked about himself. Lloyd liked that too. So, with this new dilemma, Lloyd opted to remain on deck during the entire hour and a half returning to West Palm Beach, leaving the redhead abandoned in the state room.

"How's your boy doin' there, Mr. Ramsey?"

"Jesus Christ. He's supposed to be at The Breakers today taking golf lessons."

"That so?"

"He's a pain in the ass. Give him everything in the world, but all he wants to do is hang out with dirt-bag friends, listen to that squealing rock and roll shit, ya know, Jimi Hendrix, Jim Morrison, and whatever, skipping school. I don't know, Quinn, it's a different age"

"Yes sir, sure is. How old is he now?"

"Be fourteen next February."

"It's a tough age, Lloyd." Quinn pushed the accelerator to twenty knots as the yacht rode the waves, winds whipping through their hair. They stood close to each other, shouting to hear.

"When I was a boy, I listened to my father. That's why I am where I'm at today. But these kids now, forget it. Then they watch all that flag burning shit on TV, and make heroes out of hippies, Jesus...what am I supposed to do as a father? Huh?"

"I never had any kids, but...."

"You oughta be glad, Quinn. I made a big mistake back when. Yes sir. I sure did. My father said I handled it wrong and ya know something, he was right. Fucking bastard."

"Yes sir."

"I got three hundred thousand dollars in an investment account for him. It's all his. All he had to do is go to college and it'll be worth double that. He's blowing it."

"What's he doing, if I might ask, sir?"

Lloyd turned his back to the wind and cupped his gold lighter, then took a deep, exhilarating inhale from his Parliament. "He don't listen. He's always tired, he skips school, doesn't do his homework, laughs and giggles when I catch him in a lie. Caught him sneaking into my booze, lies all the time. All the time. I'm beside myself."

"Yes sir, I can see that."

A half hour before mooring the yacht, the redhead came up to the bridge wearing a raincoat over her red bikini, her long, amber hair lank from the downpour. She could see frustration and anger in Lloyd's eyes, so she gave him a kiss and returned to the room to stay dry.

An hour later, Lloyd Ramsey was in the embarrassing predicament of appearing at the small Boynton Beach Police Department where he met with the chief, Ernie Bloom. The silver-haired cop knew Lloyd Ramsey by reputation and was not particularly impressed. Lloyd, likewise, knew Bloom as a straight, no-nonsense chief who could not be bought under any circumstance.

"Mr. Ramsey, your boy was caught with another kid selling a half ounce of marijuana to one of our young undercover cops. His friend had two LSD tablets in his pocket. They were pretty stoned at the time. We're going to turn him over to Youth Hall where he will be detained until tomorrow morning when there will be an arraignment before a juvenile court judge. You, or his mother, will be required to be there at nine o'clock."

"Uh, Chief, is there any chance we can talk?" Lloyd glanced to the lieutenant sitting across the table. "You know. Alone?"

"Not a chance, Mr. Ramsey."

The next morning, Lloyd showed up in the crowded courtroom, unaccustomed to a position of subservience, just one of a hundred parents milling about in the old sandstone building waiting for the most humiliating sound that could emanate from the deputy. "Next case! Bowen Ramsey! All parties please approach the bench!"

Lloyd looked like a British butler at a rock concert, the only parent there wearing a Gucci suit, Italian shoes and a Cartier watch. He stood awkwardly next to his son and listened to the matronly jurist read from a folder, glancing periodically over her granny glasses toward the two of them. Lloyd was powerless here. He knew no one of any importance in Boynton Beach and neither did his prestigious father. There were no favors on the menu.

"I will release the child in the custody of the father pending a hearing. Should there be any violations in the meanwhile, or should he fail to appear in court, you will be held in contempt. Is that understood, Mr. Ramsey?"

Lloyd gave his son a malevolent sneer and answered the judge through clenched teeth. "Yes, your honor."

* * *

Paul Rosenthal was in his easy chair, reading the Miami Herald's account of President Carter signing over the Panama Canal to its homeland. "This is not a good idea," he mumbled under his breath. "Never can predict what the next thirty years will bring." In the adjoining Florida room, Cynthia was in hair curlers watching *Happy Days* and munching potato chips when the phone rang. Laura picked it up in the kitchen. That's when she heard words she had dreamt of for thirteen and a half years.

"Laura. Okay, he's yours. Take 'im, godammit I've had it. You want Bowen? I can't deal with him any more."

I don't believe this. Thank you Lord. Oh God, thank you. Her eyes welled up as she choked out a question. "You're not messing with me, are you Lloyd?"

"No. He's yours. Little bastard's fucked up, and I haven't time for his shit."

"Oh, yes. Absolutely. I want him. Absolutely."

When she told her husband the news, there was a pensive, doubtful expression. She studied his face, then asked, "What's the matter Paul? Aren't you happy for me?"

"Yes, Laura. I'm happy for you. I hope you are prepared. It's not going to be easy, you know. On any of us. A lot of water has passed under his bridge."

* * *

Because Bowen was a first offender juvenile, the charges culminated in a warning from the judge and six months of non-reporting probation. The Rosenthals knew about the arrest but had no idea of the extent in which Bowen had plunged into the netherworld of drug abuse, thievery and deceit. Ever since the run-away debacle the year before, wrought with a melange of emotions over the Armenian's shooting, Bowen regressed further into his newfound subculture where he acquired many new and surly friends, learned the street jargon, modeled their body language and experimented with every drug available. He enjoyed acceptance within his netherworld while managing a facade for teachers, counselors and his father. Bowen had mastered the Jekyll-Hyde approach to daily survival, presenting himself sober whenever necessary, then cutting loose among his cronies. Each day before classes began, he would rendezvous under the bridge with BeeGee or Bruce, or others, then arrive at school high, but not too high. With his father's schedule memorized, he knew just when he could delve into more drugs or pull the string and straighten up. When the boys embarked on a shoplifting spree, Bowen participated despite having enough money in his pockets to buy whatever he was stealing. It wasn't the merchandise he needed, it was the camaraderie. Bowen belonged nowhere else.

He attended homeroom every day to be marked present, then skipped more classes than he attended. He paid other students to do his homework unless it was an oral report which he could handle extemporaneous, with little preparation. His grades were certainly not up to his innate abilities. That was a low priority.

At home, Bowen remained in his room virtually *all* of his time, listening to rock music with the door closed. On weekends, he was gone from morning until dinner time, *out playing with friends*, much to his father's delight for it gave him freedom as well. Bowen often phoned saying he was eating dinner with a friend. When he was home, he'd eat in his room. There was no interaction. Father and son wallowed in self-absorption, neither crossing paths until the day Bowen was arrested.

Visitations with Laura had become scarce, not of Lloyd's

doing, but of Bowen's deceit, always saying he was busy with school projects, sports practice or whatever. In truth, the real magnet was drugs and cronies. So when Bowen found out he was going off to live with his mother he went into a fit of rage, fearing a drastic adjustment with a new set of friends, teachers, rules and a doting mother who would surely pay more attention to his activity than his father ever did. Intellectually, he knew she was his mother but it never *felt* that way. If it were *Mommy* instead, he would have been thrilled, but she was long gone. He had no choices.

Memories of *Mommy* were fading though he often wondered where she was, what she was doing, if she ever married again, what her new name would be. Every time he saw a thin blonde woman with curls atop her head he looked twice, three times. He thought of asking his father to hire a detective to locate her, then dropped the idea. After all, she wanted nothing to do with him, so why bother. His father would refuse anyway.

He wondered whatever happened to Reggie, the boy who shot the Armenian, if he was caught, if he did it again somewhere else. He thought about grungy old Gabby who saw him leave the crime scene. Thank goodness he didn't know Bowen's real name. He never heard any more about the shooting, not from police, not from anyone, so he was home free and safe, his secret intact. It was like it a dream, a nightmare, almost surreal, like it never really happened until he'd visualize Bedrosian once more, cringing, those eyes asking...*why? Why?*

On Saturdays, Bowen would get up, check with his father who would be by the pool with a *friend*, then head out to meet with friends to decide the agenda for that day, shoplift, purse snatch, steal drugs, smoke, drop acid, listen to music. But this was not like any other Saturday. Laura arrived bright and early to pick him up, her face lit like a bulb smiling with pure happiness.

Ten minutes after he set foot into the Rosenthal house, when all the perfunctory greetings were over, he asked if could go to his room.

"Of course, darling," said his mother.

He laid the suitcases on the floor, closed the door, turned up the volume on the radio and laid face down on the bed. He didn't come out until dinner time, six hours later.

chapter eighteen

February, 1980 - Two and a half years later

Paul Rosenthal was a brilliant psychiatrist when it came to diagnosing and treating mental disorders like schizophrenia, depression, insanity and idiocy. He could pinpoint the psychosis, give it a name, find a pigeon hole and write the prescription, be it medication, counseling or both. That was his training. Each patient was a text-book character fitting some pattern or another with whom he could detach himself and leave the office every day with a clear mind. That was, until young Bowen Ramsey entered his otherwise tranquil world. Now it was a set of new rules. When Bowen came, it affected everyone and the cross relationships among them. It was a personal problem now, not a professional one and though Paul could render opinions, he could not always find the answers that came so easily to him at the office.

He had expected Bowen to be uneasy at first, distant and evasive. The teenager showed no interest in the new baby. He rarely spoke at the Friday night discussions and often found excuses to beg out of family outings. His brief flurry with the law was considered a minor setback, an outgrowth from the lack of supervision and love denied him by his father. Now, things were different. This was a loving home. It should have made a difference. Instead, he seemed to worsen with a lackadaisical approach to everything and everyone, always tired, secretive and distant.

Three months after Bowen moved in, there was a day burglary at the Rosenthal house. A rear glass sliding door had been jimmied and several jewelry items were gone from Laura's dresser. Little was thought of it until the second burglary a month later. This time, one of Laura's prized porcelain figurines was stolen along with Paul's cufflinks and tie clasps. Bowen denied stealing anything.

In mid December, a neighbor's daughter came banging at the Rosenthal door demanding Bowen return a gift he had stolen from under her Christmas tree. It was a wrist-watch for her mother. Bowen had been invited there after school. He shrugged his shoulders, widened his innocent eyes and denied, "I don't know what you're talking about." Later, the girl returned with a Surfside police officer and stood in the lanai accusing Bowen. There had been no one else in the house. "She's lying," replied Bowen to the officer.

To Laura's amazement, Paul stepped in and angrily confronted Bowen in the presence of the officer. He finally lost it. "Bowen, lead me to that gift, now!" Is that understood?"

He shrugged again. "Sorry, Mr. Rosenthal. She's lying. I didn't take anything."

Everyone stood by astonished as Paul turned bright pink, grabbed Bowen by his long, blond hair, yanked his head back and spoke with seething anger, "I said...take me to the watch, Bowen. Or I will beat you to a pulp here and now! You understand me you little asshole?" Laura was flabbergasted.

Bowen's expression shifted. "All right, all right. Let me go." Minutes later, the boy was in the corner of the yard digging up the gift from a shallow pit.

And so it went. For the next two and a half years, the Rosenthals either secured their belongings in a safe deposit box or bolted them to the floor. Liquor was missing from time to time, but it was impossible to prove Bowen was the culprit as he adamantly denied doing anything wrong. He never brought his friends home. When confronted about drugs, he had a standard reply. "No way. Not me. I never use drugs. They're bad for you."

The conflicts were leaving its toll on the marriage, not to speak of poor Cynthia whose treasured charm bracelet was long gone. She hid everything else. Laura and Paul argued constantly about how to handle the boy, what discipline to apply, what ultimatums to give him, but nothing seemed to help. Paul hoped

Bowen would be returned to his father, or anywhere else, but Laura would never agree to that. Despite everything, Laura defended her son, citing his convoluted childhood, the absence of love and affection and proper guidance growing up, telling her husband, "If anyone should understand, Paul, it ought to be you!"

"Sorry Laura. But the symptoms of sociopathy frighten me."

"What do you mean?"

"He feels no guilt."

"So what are we supposed to do?"

"He needs serious counseling, but it won't do any good unless he cooperates. Frankly, I'm beside myself. I never expected such upheavals."

"I love my son, Paul."

"I know you do, Laura. But, whatever the reason, he's a bad kid and he's bound to do more damage around here. We've got to do something. Let him go back to his father."

"Never!"

"I can't take much more of this. One more theft, one more..."

"Paul, wait...you listen to me. I love you very much, and I know how much you've done for me, but I cannot turn my back on Bowen. He needs me. He'll get over this phase. I know it."

"One more act of insolence, one more criminal act and he's got to go, Laura."

"Paul...I don't care if he rapes the pope. I will not abandon my son! Is that as clear as I can make it?"

" Hmmm."

* * *

It was a cool February Saturday morning as Laura and Bowen headed for the Keys. It was the best sixteenth birthday gift she could think of; two days of fishing in Islamorada. Paul was nearing sixty, too old for these kinds of things, so he and Cynthia stayed home to look after three year-old Grace.

As they reached Key Largo, Laura pulled into a Kwik Chek grocery store, handed Bowen five dollars and told him to pick up a six-pack of Coca Cola and some chips. Laura waited in the car. "Be sure they're cold, Bowen," she said.

Minutes later, as Bowen was paying the cashier, he heard a deep, raspy voice from behind. "Bobby?"

An older man in a Kwik Chek apron ambled over to bag his order. The employee stared at Bowen and repeated, "Ain't you that boy, Bobby Johnson?" He was weathered, mid-fifties with a Kwik Chek name tag pinned to his shirt.

Bowen realized the question was directed toward him. "Sorry, my name's not Bobby Johnson."

"It ain't. You shore? I mean you done grew some, but..." The man continued to stare.

Bowen looked twice at the employee I.D. tag. *"Gabby"* A hot flash surged through his head. The man's eyes were no longer yellow and rheumy, the hair was cut and trim, but the rotten teeth were a giveaway. Visions of the vagrant from four years earlier flashed through his brain, chomping food, slurping beer, body sounds as he slept, but no vision was clearer than the day he looked around the side of the convenience store and spotted Gabby stumbling from around the dumpster, looking straight at his eyes as they sped away.

Deny, deny. I'm taller now, older, he can't be sure. "Sorry, Mister," he answered nervously, running off. "My name's, uh, Matthew. Yes, it's Matthew. You're mistaken. Bye."

As Laura drove away, Bowen turned to look out the rear window. Sure enough, Gabby was outside the store, peering through cupped hands shading his brow.

* * *

The desk sergeant was buried in paperwork, chomping on a wood-tipped cigar. Between the incessant phone calls, stacks of reports, handling walk-in complaints and inquiries and a lieutenant breathing down his neck, he was ready to hang up the badge and return to plumbing. On Monday, there was a line from his desk all the way out the door leading to highway One, mostly people needing copies of accident reports or asking how to bail out a jail inmate. A timid and disheveled man in his fifties finally reached the first position. The sergeant never lifted his head from the typewriter. "Name?"

"Name's Gabriel Burrows. Gabby, to most folks."

"Address?"

"I live over at The Haven. It's a trailer park, 'bout mile marker..."

"I know where it is. Phone?"

"Ain't got no phone."

"What's your problem?" The crusty old sergeant glanced up at Gabby, puffed his cigar then locked his eyes to the manual typewriter. Sounds of a squawking police dispatcher could be heard in the background.

"Ain't got no problem, thank ye."

"Okay, mister. Then what are you doing here?"

"That reward still good?"

"What reward?"

"Ya know, the robbery and shootin' back when, down Islamorada way, at the grocery."

The sergeant recoiled his fingers, stuffed out a cigarette, and asked, "Mister, I don't know what you're talking about. You see that line behind you?"

"Yea. Shore do."

"Well, you either get to the point or you'll have to check with me another time."

"There was a reward Sarge, sir, 'bout this feller shot at that Conch Shell store on Islamorada, three, four years ago maybe. I knows who did it."

"You do, eh?"

"Yea. And I want the reward."

"How do you know who did it?"

"I got this here tag number. Come off a Caddy." Gabby opened his wallet and showed a brown piece of paper torn from a grocery bag with numbers scribbled in pencil: *1W515565.*

Come on in, Mr. Burrows. A detective will be with you in a minute."

* * *

Throughout the weekend, flashbacks stormed Bowen's memory fresh as the day it happened— Reggie's face, the waving gun, popping sounds, Bedrosian's pain, Gabby staggering at the dumpster, the race into the woods, trembling. He thought the old bum was either dead or in prison but there he was, alert, clean, employed and no longer pandering for handouts. Bowen now realized that old Gabby had been sober enough to remember his face, the phony name *Bobby Johnson* and that terrible day when Reggie went crazy, shooting an innocent man over a few dollars. What he didn't know was Gabby's intent.

He had tucked the shooting long behind him, a mistake of the past, a horrible secret he could share with no one. Four years past, after it happened, he would often talk into a mirror absolving his guilt, rehearsing his lines if ever faced by the cops. *I didn't shoot him. Honest, I didn't even know my friend had a gun until we were in the store. I never robbed anyone. I'm a rich kid. Bedrosian was a friend. I didn't know. I'm really innocent. Honest.*

When she drove past the Conch Shell, the *scene of the crime*, Bowen looked away, praying she wouldn't stop there. Finally, on Sunday morning, he feigned stomach cramps and asked his mother to go home.

* * *

Three days passed. It was an ordinary Wednesday, unseasonably humid, the threat of rain hovering all day under a grey sky. After school Bowen joined a boy named Greg with whom he smoked pot, settled at a parking area near Haulover Beach and listened to *The Rolling Stones.* Greg drove an old Chevrolet Impala which reeked from the stench of stale cigarettes. Playing basketball was the standard lie for coming home late so it wasn't unusual for Bowen to float in just before dinner time. As Greg drove up toward Bowen's house, they spotted a grey Plymouth with black wall tires parked in the driveway. "Hey man, looks like an unmarked pig."

"Keep on driving, don't pull in," Bowen said in a subdued tone. Immediately, visions of old Gabby blasted into his brain. *Oh God. He really took the tag number.* His eyes grew wide, his mouth dry. "Don't park here, keep driving," he ordered.

Greg smiled like there wasn't a care in the world. "Hey man, no sweat. You can handle the pig."

"Turn around. Now! Please, Greg, get out of here."

Seeing that Bowen was serious, Greg backed the car and drove off. "Hey what's with you, guy?" he asked, snickering. "You act like you killed someone."

* * *

Laura paced nervously as the two young white men in polyester suits sat patiently on the sofa. They looked like brothers cast from the same mold, short brown hair, long sideburns, bell bottom trousers, broad ties, each holding a yellow pad, each speaking in the same monotone as though they were auditioning for the role of Sergeant Joe Friday.

"I'm sorry officers. Bowen's usually home by now." She looked up to the mantel clock one more time. It was seven-fifteen, just three minutes since she last checked. In his study, Paul fumed angrily, embarrassed that police detectives were seeking out a suspect in his own house. Cynthia was in her room doing homework when the phone rang. She answered, then hollered to Laura, "Mom, it's for you."

Laura lifted the receiver in the parlor out of earshot from the detectives. "Hello?"

"Uh, hello Mother, I'm...."

She spun around and cupped the receiver with her hand. "Bowen, where are you?"

"Uh, I'm at a friend's. I'm invited here for dinner, okay? So, I'll be home later."

"Bowen, there are two detectives here asking questions. You must come home immediately."

There was a long, painful pause. Then Bowen asked, "Uh, what are they asking about?"

She turned her back and whispered into the phone, "It's about some shooting back in 1976, in the Keys. They think you were involved." Laura could hear him breathing, but there was no response. "Bowen, you were only twelve then." She listened to the quivering sounds of his breathing. "Is that when you ran away?" More sounds of nervous breathing. "Answer me, Bowen." Another long, arduous wait, listening breathing... "Bowen? Bowen?"

Dial tone. *Oh my Lord.*

* * *

The following night, Lloyd Ramsey was in his mansion entertaining a Playboy centerfold. He was standing at the bar to pour another glass of sherry when the phone rang. "Excuse me," he said as he picked it up in the den.

"Hello?"

Hearing no response, Lloyd looked quizzically at the receiver, then repeated, "Hello. Hello."

Still nothing.

"One more time, or I'm hanging up. Who is this?"

"Dad?" His voice was low, subdued.

"Bowen?" He paused and scratched his head. "Is that you?"

"Uh, I need some..."

"Where are you, kid? Your mother says you ran away again. What in the fuck is wrong with..."

"Dad, I need some help. Really bad."

"What? Help? You got to be kidding. First, you're out in the streets again, then I find out that you've been involved in some shooting, some robbery is it?"

"Please Dad. I can explain...I really need help, please...."

"You've brought nothing but shame and embarrassment to the Ramsey name. As far as I'm concerned Bowen...you don't exist."

Dial tone.

PART II

chapter nineteen

September 1988 - Eight Years Later

The office was full of rich mahogany and oak, shelves laden with books and periodicals, family photos encased in silver frames and the rich aroma of leather. A closed window overlooked a playground of slides, teeter-totters, monkey bars and kids of all ages romping. Central air-conditioning was set at seventy degrees, nice and cool just the way the good doctor liked it. The room was quiet, a time for reflection, thinking about that evaluation report but the pen simply twiddled between nimble fingers as the mind drifted into more personal matters, love, children, health, future. Suddenly, a knock.

"Come in."

"Doctor Rosenthal, you're wanted on line two," announced the bespectacled secretary standing at the door, pad in hand. "I think it's your husband, and, oh yes, there is a Mrs. Von Brauten waiting outside with her daughter. She has an appointment in regards to a late enrollment."

"Thank you, Maggie."

Still shapely as she was in her twenties and wearing chic, wide-rimmed glasses, Laura had aged well for her forty-six years, a bit of cosmetic surgery notwithstanding. Her smart style and dress were the envy of all the staff of Stanton School where she had risen to the position of Dean, thanks in part to having trudged through three arduous years earning her Ph.D. in education, working by day, studying by night. Her close alliance with the school president, Dr. Wilma Ashenbrenner, helped as well.

Though not without problems of family illness, this was a

fairly happy time for Laura with her career flourishing, her own health never better and her twelve year-old daughter an "A" student and editor of her school newspaper. Grace was a beautiful and active child though a bit precocious at times. She figured that was normal for a kid her age.

Paul had suffered a stroke in the summer of 1984, leaving him incapacitated on one side of his body. Hired nurses attended to his needs by day while Laura was there at night. Though he remained mentally sharp, he was forced to close his practice of forty years and work at home, writing articles for journals and serving as a consultant here and there. The stroke left him depressed, frail and aged far beyond his sixty-seven years but Laura remained upbeat, forever thankful for his presence during the dark times when she needed him most. Before Paul took sick, they had built a new five bedroom home in Gables By The Sea, an upscale development just minutes from the school.

The memory of her nightmare with Lloyd Ramsey had long dissipated into oblivion, a blip in her life, a chapter closed and never revisited. She had everything, money, family, travel, health, professional status and respect. Everything but the son she never had to begin with. She loved him so.

During the first two years of his disappearance, Laura searched coast to coast, hired investigators, made hundreds of heart-felt pleas via television and alerted no less than a hundred law enforcement agencies from Hawaii to Maine, all to no avail. Paul finally convinced her to go on living for herself and for her family and allow fate to take its course. She enrolled in night courses, immersing herself in study and advancement. As the eight years clicked away, Bowen became a distant but vexing memory, an unreachable son who had probably died somewhere and she was cheated the opportunity of closure, to say goodbye. An array of photographs adorned the office of a little boy from age four to a picture taken before his sixteenth birthday. He would be twenty-four now, a young man, she thought to herself as she lifted the phone.

"Hello, Paul?"

"Laura, my dear...."

"Paul, I just talked to you an hour ago. Are you all right?"

His voice trembled now, his words slurred. "Ah. Just your

decrepit old husband, still around 'til tomorrow, at least. Listen..."

"Darling, I have someone waiting outside, could I call you back?"

"Yes, well...all I wanted was to let you know I'll be watching the debates tonight, in case you want to make other plans."

"Honey, I'll be watching with you. We can argue together."

"Argue? Why?"

"Well you don't think for a minute that Dukakis is going to lose, do you?" A smirk crossed her face. She knew she tickled his ire.

"Bah.. Anyway, Grace is spending the night..."

"Don't worry Paul, I'll take her." She checked her watch. It was not uncommon to hear from him four or five times a day.

"Oh well, that's all..."

"Paul, I really have to go."

Laura made a stately appearance into the waiting room where a streaked-blonde woman roughly her own age was seated with a teenage girl a bit older than Grace. Greetings were cordial as she ushered them into her office and offered a chocolate from a box on an end table. The woman introduced herself as Mrs. Claude Von Brauten, the wife of a fashion designer and an artist in her own right with paintings displayed in a number of art emporiums around the country. Though a bit stuffy, she was quite attractive beneath layers of makeup with her hair swept back in a French twist. She wore a red silk pants outfit that formed a slightly pudgy shape. Laura was drawn instantly to her voice, her manner, her essence, as though she knew her.

"We just moved back from Monterey, California where Michelle here was enrolled in The Bridgeport Private School for girls. You've heard of it, I'm sure." Laura nodded. "She was an "A" student there, and I'm sure she would be here. I know it is generally not accepted for children to enroll in mid term, but I was hoping ..."

Laura interrupted, "You say you lived in Miami previously. What school was she in?"

"Oh, it's been eight years since we left here for California. Michelle went to public school then. Second grade, I believe," she said quizzically, turning to her daughter, "Isn't that right darling?"

"Yes, Mother. I've been in private schools ever since you remarried, since third grade."

The woman saw that Laura was eyeing her closely as though there was a special interest, then asked, "Well is there a chance, Mrs. Rosenthal? We have the money."

"Well, it just so happens that we had a dropout last week..."

"Lovely."

There was an aura about her, a manner, the nose so straight and pointed, high cheek bones, bright red thin lips. "May I ask, where are you from?" Laura asked in a more personal tone.

"Oh dear, I was raised in Miami and never left here until I married Claude eight years ago. Why do you ask?"

"Oh..." Laura was caught off guard. "I don't know. I came here for college thirty years ago and never left. We may have crossed paths somewhere." The woman seemed irritated with the small talk. Laura handed her an enrollment form. "Please fill this out, Mrs. Von Brauten and turn it in to my secretary. I'll need you to come back before the end of the week with all her records, medical information and such. You know the routine, I'm sure."

At five sharp, two hours later, Laura was making her exit for the parking lot when her brain flashed on Mrs. Claude Von Brauten once more, so she scurried back to the office, shuffled papers though her secretary's out-basket and found the application. There was her name; Merrilee Turner Von Brauten. *Merrilee?*

"Get dressed, Merrilee and get the fuck out of here. Lloyd, you didn't tell me...oh my God, I got to get out of here."

Red toenails suspended, teetering within his humping torso, the screaming, the loud music, the smells of liquor and cigarettes... all coming back...the stifling closet, straitjacket, hospital wards, night howls, her baby, " *Where is my baby? Where is my baby?",* banished from motherhood, Christmas without her child, without her dignity, lonely gifts, a crimson bath, three years of her life behind locked doors. Buried for eons, it all rocketed to the surface in a single moment.

* * *

"I just know that was her, Wilma. I can feel it. There was something about her."

"So what if it is, Laura. What can you do? You certainly can't hold animosity...."

"It's not that, it's not that. But if it's her...she can verify that I wasn't hallucinating. That I was not having delusions. She's my only witness." With the receiver crimped to her shoulder, Laura paced the kitchen floor washing vegetables, cutting onions, stripping skin off chicken as the spiral phone cord stretched like an accordion. Every so often she peeked through the door to make sure Paul was settled in. The subject of past traumas did not set well with him.

"So what of it, Laura. That was twenty-four years ago. You've got to let go."

"You don't understand the whole of it..." Laura had only shared a fraction of the story with her friend, always holding to the lie that she traveled abroad for three years after her divorce. Wilma knew nothing of her incarceration.

"So you had a rat husband who cheated. Laura, it's happened to a few million other women out there, you're not the..."

"There's more, Wilma. I'm sorry, but you don't know everything."

"Okay, he used his power to wrangle your child from you, I know how wrong that was, how poor Bowen..."

Like May of 1964 was yesterday, Laura began to weep, tears flowing, choking, she couldn't tell her. Not this. "Wilma, I can't talk to anyone, no one, not Paul, not anyone, but you."

"What's wrong, Laura? Poor child, why are you crying?"

There was a long pause as Wilma listened to her voice quiver.

"Laura? Are you all right?"

Laura was about to weaken then realized one vulnerable moment could end her career. Wilma was a dear friend, but she was obsessively honest and in this case, honesty could destroy her. The school owners would never accept it. As president, Wilma would be obligated to do what she must. So Laura regrouped, pulled a jar of mayonnaise from the refrigerator and said, "Uh, listen Wilma, Phil Hardin will be at the meeting tomorrow to present his program on..."

"You're changing the subject, Laura. Why?"

"...on computerized homework aid, which seems to work well in many other private venues."

"Did someone just walk into the kitchen?" Wilma asked, confused.

It was a good out. "Uh, yes. Uh huh. Say, we'll meet in the coffee shop before the meeting, is that okay?"

Thirty five minutes later, as Laura was preparing to serve dinner, the phone rang again.

"Laura, it's Wilma. Turn on the television. Channel seven."

"Why?"

"Just do it. You'll see."

chapter twenty

"Hooray! Hooray!"
  "Wheeeeee!"
  "Whomp! Whomp! Whomp!"
"Speech! Speech!"
The crowd of twelve hundred ardent supporters swelled into a frenzy of young and old, black and white, men and women carrying placards and banners, wearing buttons and hats, cheering, whistling, whooping as the band played *Hail To The Chief.* Then, the shrill of strident screams as the favorite son candidate took center stage at the microphone. A thousand shirts clung to clammy bodies as humid dusk gradually turned dark at the Palm Beach amphitheater. Atop the stage, a white banner with bold red letters stretched the width of the edifice. The message was the same as a hundred other bobbing placards in the park; *Mayor Ramsey For Governor.*

A toothy smile beamed across his face as he stood before throngs of citizens, hands out-stretched yearning for approval, listening to his name called over and over, feeling those awesome pangs of power. He was truly someone special, this wealthy lawyer who had served the city as Mayor for the last four years. He combed his fingers though his blond pompadour then smiled and pointed a knuckle toward a first row supporter as though he knew him. He was Robert Redford handsome, looking a decade younger than his fifty-two years. Marchers came from around the corner of the stage, all devotees of Lloyd B. Ramsey, cheering and bobbing as the music played. It seemed like more of a victory party than a political rally.

"Whomp! Whomp!"
"Ram-sey! Ram-sey! Ram-sey!"

The chant grew louder and louder as Lloyd stood there in his open collar shirt, waving, smiling, pointing knuckles. A string of flash cameras were blinding, but it didn't matter. His dream was only six weeks from reality.

"Ram-sey! Ram-sey! Ram-sey!"

Several notables took seats in a row of chairs behind the mayor. One was a brunette woman in a business suit. Everyone knew her as *Miss Barbara*, the mayor's wife. Beside her sat a tall young man named Chip McGill, her son by a prior marriage. Old Thurgood Ramsey sat puffing a pipe, holding his ears. Beside him sat Chief Judge Loxley B. Arch, a famous rock star named Johnny Sprockett, a black movie actress, a Cuban bank president and a mix of citizens waiting to convey their messages. Finally, Lloyd held up his arms in a vague, bashful gesture to quiet the crowd. There was an agenda, people to give speeches.

The distinguished host, campaign manager and former councilman for West Palm Beach, John Krysakowski took the microphone.

"Quiet down everyone. Quiet please." He waited a few moments as the noise dissipated then tapped the microphone. As he opened with usual plaudits of Lloyd Ramsey, shrieks of applause drowned him out, then he continued. "As we all know, this state needs a Governor who will act on his promises, to hold down taxes, lower crime, build more prisons and appoint nononsense judges who will not tolerate the scourge of drug abuse."

More cheers. More screams. He raised his hands again to quiet the crowd. "We have an open forum tonight, ladies and gentlemen, for all you wonderful supporters with comments to offer about our mayor and next governor of the State of Florida."

"Whomp! Whomp!"

"Ram-sey! Ram-sey! Ram-sey!"

The black actress took center stage, praising Lloyd Ramsey for bringing more cultural events and motion picture business to the city. The bank president spoke of Ramsey's philanthropic work with various charities. The rock star applauded the mayor's open-minded approach toward young people and for spearheading drug rehabilitation centers. The approbation mounted as one citizen after another was allotted five minutes before audience and cameras to tell of their positive experiences with the mayor. Finally, it was time for John Krysakowski to bring on the man of the hour. A broad-grinning Lloyd Ramsey sat with legs crossed, holding hands with his wife while Krysakowski began his introductory remarks.

"Ladies and gentlemen, it is now...uh...quiet please, quiet please. It is now time for..." From the front of the audience, the figure of a tall slovenly fellow emerged from stage left, catching his attention. The man was holding the hand of a small boy. Approaching the stage, he raised his hand and whistled.

"Excuse me? Sir?" said Krysakowski peering down. "Can I help you?"

He looked like a hippie from the sixties generation, tall and gangly with long, light brown hair framing his full-bearded face, wire rimmed-glasses, sunken eyes, tattered clothes and rubber thongs for shoes. The little boy seemed about four or five. "I've got a few words to offer," said the hippie. "May I?"

"Well, sir," answered the host. "We've just about used up our time for..."

The stranger's voice was hoarse and subdued, like he'd been yelling at a sporting event all night. "I have something really pertinent to offer about this campaign, sir."

"I'm sorry sir, but..." Krysakowski felt a tap on the shoulder. It was Lloyd Ramsey from behind telling him to let one more supporter say a few words. After all, he needed to sway a few liberals along the way.

"Well then, come on up there sir, and...uh, bring your boy with you."

Slowly, deliberately, he strolled to the side and up the stairs as though time stood still, holding the hand of his little boy who used two feet to climb each step. At ease before a crowd, the hippie took the microphone in his free hand and slowly scanned the audience without saying a word. He had their attention.

"I am a drug addict." He paused while the crowd digested the bold revelation. Lloyd Ramsey looked on attentively, holding hands with Barbara. "I'm a junkie. Name it, I've done it all, I do it all. My story is not much different from a million other stories, stories of wrecked lives, perfectly good human beings relegated to the gutter, to prison, starvation and, if they are lucky, death. I would be long gone by now if it weren't for this little fella here. Ya know, politicians always promise to make things better, to improve education of drugs, increase enforcement, develop programs to help addicts like me get clean. Some mean it, very few actually. Most get elected then forget." His voice blared through giant speakers as the crowd remained eerily silent. "We need people, I mean senators and governors, to keep those promises and hold them accountable, to show us the results of our trust. We don't need politicians just for passing laws and hiring cops. We need to reach out to the users, for without users, there would be no sellers. I'm talking about the fat cat users who donate their fair share to these election campaigns."

Clearly disturbed and seeing this was going in an undesired direction, Krysakowski cleared his throat and approached the hippie from behind, smiling. "I think that's about all the time…"

"Wait. Just another couple of words and I'll be finished."

"Uh, very well, only one more minute, please."

The hippie gazed at the spellbound audience one more time then held the mike close to his lips. "You never know what you're really getting when you enter that voting booth. They say one thing, then do another. Mayor Ramsey here, well he's different. Yes sir. He's real different. You see folks, I know Lloyd Ramsey." He turned from the audience, mike in hand and faced the aspiring mayor. "I know Mayor Ramsey real well. And I can tell you, that it was this man, Lloyd Ramsey…" Perplexed, Lloyd furrowed his brow as the hippie sucked a deep breath and continued, "… was the first to turn me on to drugs. You see, Mayor? This is your grandson." The crowd gasped as the hippie turned to the audience. "My name is Bowen Ramsey and this man is my father."

Eyes ablaze, Lloyd leaped to his feet. "My God! Get him out of here!" Krysakowski shrugged his shoulders. Astounded, Lloyd peered into the hippie's eyes, looking for that teenage kid he once knew. The audience stirred, buzzing with anticipation, watching the reaction of the mayor while the hippie calmly continued talking into the microphone.

"Remember the marijuana, Dad? Remember giving me a hit and telling me not to do it behind your back? Remember all the pot parties night after night? Remember the big garbage can in the garage? I used to take handfuls of your pot and sell it at school."

"Get this asshole...I mean, this man, out of here!" Lloyd exploded into a frenzy, pacing, pushing Krysakowski to action but to no avail. Everyone continued to listen. Dignitaries and guest speakers were standing now, milling around, some leaving, some stunned by the fiasco on stage. They saw that Lloyd Ramsey was nearly out of control and of a mind to get physical with the hippie, but that would be a total disaster. "He's a liar. An imposter!" shouted the Mayor.

No one dared interrupt the long-haired beatnik who called himself Bowen Ramsey. Microphone to lips, he looked directly into his father's eyes and asked, "Remember the last thing you ever said to me, Dad? Eight years ago?" Lloyd stood paralyzed. "Remember? You said I did not exist." Lloyd was trembling, his face turning bright pink. "Still think I don't exist?"

The hippie and the little child calmly left the stage, wandered in and then out from the crowd and disappeared into the darkness. The rally was dead silent.

* * *

"Mom, what's the matter with you?"

Eyes bulging, Laura dropped a spoon and covered her mouth with both hands. Her voice squealed beyond recognizable words as a flood of tears spurted from the pools of her eyes. She stood riveted to the television. From his easy chair, Paul lowered his head into one hand and murmured to himself, "Oh no."

The news recap on channel seven was showing clips of a political rally where a strange hippie and his child shocked the state by accusing the lead candidate for Governor of Florida of being a drug user himself. The attractive news woman was speaking as excerpts from the bizarre turn of events were being shown.

"It is still not verified if this was, in fact, the long lost son of Mayor Ramsey, but verified or not, it is sure to have a profound impact on this campaign. The accusor, shown here,...."

"Oh my God, my God, he's alive. My boy is alive....look at him, he's alive. I thought he was dead. Oh my God, Paul. Oh Paul...." Her voice trailed off. "Eight years, eight years...."

"Take it easy, Laura, you can't be sure."

Her face was now drenched in tears. "It is him. Look, Grace, it's your brother, it's your big brother honey, oh God, oh God."

"Mom, he looks , I mean, real grubby."

"Look, Paul, the little boy. That's my grandson. I'm a grand-mother. I can't believe it. I'm a grandmother. He's beautiful. He looks just like..."

"Efforts to reach Mayor Ramsey have failed thus far. His manager has informed us that he is not going to an-swer any questions on the matter. Meanwhile, the search is on for the long-haired man who called himself Bowen Ramsey."

"Oh Paul, where is he? How can I find him? My God, I thought he was..." She broke down sobbing as the news recap came to a close. Choking, she fell to her knees and collapsed onto the couch. Twelve-year-old Grace tried comforting her mother.

"It's okay, Mom. I'm here."

With the left side of his face sagging, Paul was unprepared for the sudden outburst. He well remembered the nightmare of Bowen Ramsey living under his roof. After seeing the adult image of him on television, he shuddered with what was to come.

Still on her sofa, Laura wiped her eyes and gathered her composure. "I wonder what his name is?"

"Who, Mom?"

"My grandson."

"Gee, that would make him...my nephew?"

Laura took her daughter into her arms as they sat on the floor embracing. Grace stroked the stiff, wiry hair standing out from her mother's head as the crying jag became infectious. Paul changed the channel.

* * *

Later, all the television networks, including CNN, ran the bizarre story as headline news.

"Hey Fergie, check this out."

Two off-duty Dade County detectives drew cynical grins as they watched the oddball hippie stand before a public microphone accusing the top gubernatorial candidate from Florida of being his pot-smoking father. The younger cop turned up the volume.

"Ha. The Palm Beach mayor's shittin' in his pants. Look at 'im. You'd think he'd seen a ghost."

Matt Ferguson laughed heartily. It was always fun seeing a sleazy politician caught with his ass in a crack.

"What a fuckin' dirt bag. If he was my kid, I'd deny it too."

"Look at that poor little boy. To have a scumbag like that for a father."

The camera followed the hippie and the boy as they made a nonchalant exit from the stage until they were absorbed into the darkness. In a few short minutes, he had become an enigma, a topic of network attention for days to come.

"I wonder," asked Matt Ferguson.

"Wonder what?"

"I don't know. Got a hunch. Let's boot up the computer a minute. What'd he say his name was? Bowen? Bowen Ramsey?"

chapter twenty-one

"I can't believe that little bastard," barked Lloyd Ramsey as he angrily paced the office floor. The eyes of his father, his wife, his campaign manager and a muscular bodyguard named Rudolfo followed him left and right like they were watching a tennis volley. "Little son of a bitch. What goddam hole did he crawl out of?"

"I told you, Lloyd, not to allow an open forum at a political rally. It was too dangerous."

"Shut up, John, godammit!"

"Maybe now you'll start listening to me."

"Okay. So one time you were right. Big fuckin' deal. Now, let's think what we're going to do to salvage this."

Krysakowski shrugged, opened his hand and suggested his only route. "Deny, deny, deny. Don't admit anything. He was an imposter, Lloyd. That's all. Someone hired by Henry Stallworth's campaign cronies to do you in. Stay calm, and just deny."

"What if he shows up again? We gotta find that kid and smooth this over before the media gets hold of him." Lloyd rambled on, gesticulating. "Geez, that's all we need is to see that asshole on Larry King or some shit like that." The pacing continued. "Shit, I know. I'll admit that I dabbled when I was very young, that's it...."

"And then what, Lloyd?" interrupted Krysakowski. "You didn't inhale?" Everyone snickered but Lloyd.

"No shit, lots of successful people dabbled in their youth, so..."

Krysakowski butted in again, "Yeah, Lloyd, but they didn't turn their own kids on."

"If that little bastard shows up again with that fucking story it'll be curtains. A disaster. I'll never recover, I'll be ruined."

Lloyd paced back and forth, spewing epithets, running fingers through his hair. "I wouldn't worry, my boy," said the elder Ramsey, chewing on his unlit pipe. "He won't show up again. He's not going to undergo the scrutiny."

"Then why the fuck did he do it in the first place? What the hell was he doing there?"

Thurgood clenched the pipe between his teeth and answered in a deep, dolorous tone, "Your kid hates you Lloyd. That's a good reason."

"Thanks Pop. I needed that."

"Let's see, if I remember right, he's the boy you wanted so much..."

"Enough, Pop."

"...wanted to raise him and guide him..."

"Father. Please!"

"...and then you finagled custody of him until he was too much for you to..."

"God dammit, will you leave me alone. My goddam career is just about ruined and all you do is live in the past."

It was Barbara's turn. Married for five years to the fiery politician, she was accustomed to slander and false accusations. This one seemed to hit a nerve. "Is it true, Lloyd?"

"Is what true?"

"Did you really turn your kid on to pot?"

"He's a fucking liar!" he spouted back.

"Okay, Lloyd. Okay. Just asking."

A fresh idea seemed to strike the mayor as he suddenly halted. "Hey, do me a favor guys. Get the fuck outa here. I gotta lot of thinking to do. I wanna be alone for a while. Okay?"

"You mean...me too?" asked Barbara.

"Yeah. You too. Go. I'll be home later tonight."

The threesome arose from their chairs and headed for the door. Just as everyone walked out, Lloyd summoned one back, whispering, "Pssst. Hey, Rudolfo. Come here a minute."

"What's up boss?"

"Close the door."

* * *

Night sounds of the inner city, neons flashing, sleazy bars and sex stores, faceless human beings milling about the streets like insects, some dealing, some using, all searching, yearning for a single moment of pleasure like there was no tomorrow, the netherworld for a haggard young man and his boy, nestled on a dilapidated mattress gazing up at the cracked ceiling, wincing from the odor of stale sweat, listening to sirens and men shouting from an open, curtainless window one story above a run-down billiard parlor.

"Daddy, I'm hungry."

"I know, Jamie. Me too. I'll get some food, I promise."

He had just turned five, but this year there was no birthday party. Wearing shorts, tee shirt and worn-out sneakers, he sat at the foot of the bed and crossed his legs. "When, Daddy?"

"Right now, I don't have any money but I'll get some tomorrow...in the morning."

"Well, why don't we go and panhandle?"

Bowen sucked a deep puff from a cigarette, exhaled slowly, thinking. "Can't, son."

"But why?"

"Daddy made a big mistake. Remember when we went on the stage last night? Well, now everyone knows us because we were on television and there are people out there looking for us."

"Why did we do that?"

He took another puff and exhaled. "I don't know, son. It was something I couldn't resist."

"Is that why you cut off your hair? And shaved your face?" Jamie reached and touched his father's bare chin. "It's so funny."

Bowen smiled and raised an eyebrow. "Well, do you like it?"

"I don't know, Daddy. I'm just so used to seeing you with all that hair, it's like you're not Daddy."

Tires squealed on the street below. Footsteps passed by along the wooden corridor. A door slammed. They could hear a woman laughing and moaning from the other side of the paper-thin wall. Then, rhythmic pounding.

"What are they doing, Daddy?"

"I don't know, Jamie."

A rare sense of guilt came over Bowen as his little boy flopped on the pillow, then held it to his stomach in a fetal position. He knew he had to do something, anything. "Jamie, listen, Daddy has some serious problems and right now, maybe you need a woman who can…"

At the sound, Jamie panicked, sat erect, shaking his head. "Not Mommy. Please."

"No. Not Mommy. I promise. But I'm going to have you meet a lady, a very nice lady who might help me take care of you a while."

"Is she pretty?"

"Well, honestly, I haven't seen her in a long time. But I know she is very nice and she can give you lots of things I can't give you."

"Where are you going, Daddy?"

"Well, there's something that happened a long time ago that I have to take care of, and…well, Daddy's a little bit sick, okay? I have to go and get well so I can take care of you better."

"Oh. What's wrong?"

"It's nothing, son. Listen, Daddy has to go to the bathroom, I'll be back in a few minutes. Lock the door and don't let anyone in until you hear it's me. Don't forget the password. Okay?"

"Okay, Daddy."

Jamie watched as his father grabbed the cloth pouch from his shopping bag then disappeared into the darkened hall. He slid the bolt.

A single bathroom at the far end of the darkened floor served six apartments, but it was private enough. Bowen locked the door behind him and sensed a rush of relief, a few precious moments of stark privacy to dwell in his own world without a pressures, at least for a few precious minutes. He glimpsed his weathered face in the mirror and touched his sallow skin, peering into his dull, sunken eyes. He opened a pouch, pulled out a spoon, matches, syringe, the surgical tie and his precious smack. In minutes, he'd be normal again, functional. He wondered where he could get his next fix, but for now it didn't matter. For the moment, Bowen's hunger was satisfied.

* * *

The mysterious appearance of her long lost son sparked a renewed obsession. For three days, Laura spent more time on her phone talking to investigators, Salvation Army, various missions and welfare organizations than working on school matters. Her search was on. The image of the bearded, long-haired hippie sauntering off stage with a little boy was imprinted in her mind. All other issues were assigned to the *To-Do* basket. Knowing Bowen was alive and that a grandchild was out there somewhere ignited an inexorable surge of determination. She had to find them.

No longer her close confidant and counselor, Paul had withered into frailty, unable to cope with stressful matters. So Laura was careful to handle everything behind the scenes while presenting a normal facade at home. She reassured Paul that Bowen was not returning to their home and would not be a presence in their otherwise tranquil family life. It was a juggling act indeed. Paul phoned her office six, seven and eight times a day purely out of loneliness and a need for reassurance.

It was the fourth day since the ghostly apparition of her derelict son on the television screen. As she gazed at the last school photo taken of Bowen, her secretary buzzed to announce the presence of Mrs. Von Brauten in the waiting room. As instructed, she had brought all the records and forms. "I told her you were busy, Dr. Rosenthal, and that I could handle it, but she insists on seeing you for one minute. Sorry."

Red toe nails, dangling.

"It's all right Maggie. Send her on in."

This time she wore a pair of chic Nikes and tennis shorts with her hair swept back into a pony tail by a red band. Laura checked out her long, tapered legs wondering if this was the second, not the first time she had seen them. "Hello, Mrs. Von Brauten. How are you?"

"Oh, Doctor Rosenthal, I'll only take up a moment. I just wanted to thank you so much for accepting Michelle. I know she'll do really well here."

Laura studied her closer while the face of the 1964 woman flashed through her brain. It all happened in a fraction of a second, but it was the second of a lifetime. After twenty-four years, she figured cosmetic surgery may have altered her, but not much. Perhaps it was that pointed nose or the lips, or the glint in the eye.

"May I offer you a coffee at our canteen?" Laura asked.

The woman was startled. She hadn't expected such a personal reception. "Why, uh, I suppose so. Thank you."

They walked to the small canteen which consisted mostly of vending machines and sat at a wobbly table exchanging small talk. Every so often, a teacher or student would amble in for a soda then leave. Otherwise they were alone. Laura continued to study her, wondering, unsure yet determined to know. If it was her, then what? After all this time, what good would it do to drag it all out? Again, the images of her hippie-like son and grandson haunted her, wandering the streets like gypsies, seeing him on that stage, microphone in hand, pointing to his father saying, "...*that it was this man, Lloyd Ramsey, was the first to turn me on to drugs.*"

"Merrilee? Um, you don't mind if I call you Merrilee, do you?"

"No, not at all."

"Do I look at all familiar to you?"

The blonde woman smiled and flipped a wave of the hand. "Well to be honest, yes, but then again, so do so many people. Why? Do you think we've met before?"

It was an eerie moment as Laura removed the bobby pins from the side of her head. Merrilee watched quizzically while Laura slowly and deliberately pulled at the ends of her stiff, wiry hair until it stood out from her head. Then she removed her glasses and rubbed her face until it reddened. "Now, do I look a little more familiar, Merrilee?"

The woman squinted wondering what it was all about. Then, a gasp. "Oh my Gosh! Oh my Gosh!" She raised the palm of her hand to her mouth and stared, unbelieving. A pool formed in her eyes, her face flushed. That's when Laura knew for sure.

"Does the name... Lloyd Ramsey... ring a bell?"

Merrilee's expression turned from snobbish aplomb to humble conciliation. Her jaw dropped, eyebrows raised, shocked beyond comprehension. "Oh, I...uh, Doctor Rosenthal...I didn't know. My God, that was ...was you?"

A staredown ensued until Laura gathered the courage to keep going, her eyes glistening with tears that had yet to flow. "Just so you know. I went through hell, Merrilee. So has my son."

"I don't know what to say. Perhaps I better go."

"Twenty-four years of hell, all over one lousy piece of tail. You don't know. You don't know. No Merrilee, please stay."

"I'm so embarrassed." One hand covered her mouth while the other laid against her cheek.

"Look. I'm sure it wasn't your fault. You were probably just another trophy on his wall. He turned me on back then too." Laura could see her reaction was sincere. Two women adversaries from a few unsuspecting moments of a time past who never spoke a word to one another until this week, yet those moments impacted the lives of so many, so profoundly.

"I was so young then. I didn't know..."

Laura interrupted and reached over to touch her hand. "I understand. It's all right. It wasn't you, Merrilee. It was what he did to me, and our child after."

"I'm sorry, Doctor. So sorry."

"Call me Laura."

"You might not believe this, but that was the only time I was ever with Lloyd Ramsey. The son of a bitch stood me up the next date and then would never return my calls."

"It was a good thing he didn't get you pregnant." Laura noticed some onlookers among the staff, stood and offered her hand in friendship. "Why don't we talk more in my office?"

Later at the office, Laura held the woman spellbound by her account of the aftermath from that terrible experience, the mental hospitals, losing her son, the struggle to maintain her role as a mother, the constant humiliation, Bowen's abandonment by a surrogate contract mother, his disappearance of eight long years and the ultimate scourge of drugs.

"Merrilee, I was wrongly accused of hallucinating that episode. And because of that, I never had my son, my son never had his mother and I spent three useless years in a nuthouse when I wasn't nuts. Meeting you is like being vindicated."

Merrilee went on to explain how she was just young law student back in 1964 enraptured by the young, handsome profes-

grades. She never even knew he was married. She vividly recalled the episode, apologizing profusely, wishing she could take
it all back and somehow repair the irreversible damage that it
caused. Then she recalled, "To be honest, and I know it's not
funny, but you scared the living pee out of me. I thought I was
having a heart attack."

"I can imagine."

"Is there anything I can do?" she asked.

Laura looked at her pensively, then posed a question. "If I
called on you, would you testify?"

"Well, of course. So long as my husband had no objection."
She mused a moment, then grinned. "He won't."

"Thank you, Merrilee. Thank you."

It was near dark at seven o'clock before Laura tidied her
office, dejected from another day of drawing blanks in her quest
to locate Bowen. But all was not lost. The encounter with the
strange trollop in her bed from twenty-four years back now glued
some of the mystery together while giving her the only true
evidence in existence that she was never insane. Ideas rambled
through her brain as she trotted out to her car, debating whether
to pursue it all or let it be. She did not want to be a vengeful
woman but the anger still seethed in the abyss of her soul, especially since the television appearance of her junkie son. She
started the ignition of her Lincoln Town car and pulled out
from the driveway, unaware of the white Crown Victoria starting its engine at one end of the block and an old blue Dodge
van following from the other.

chapter twenty-two

Under an overcast sky, little Jamie Ramsey sat on a concrete sidewalk at the corner of Federal Highway and Atlantic Boulevard in Pompano Beach at morning rush hour, holding a torn-off side panel of a corrugated box. Bold letters written in black marker spelled out the words:

Homeless. Hungry. Please help.

Next to him sat a slovenly woman about forty, her face soiled, clothes tattered, toes protruding through old shoes, holding another placard which read:

My son is in need of home. Hungry. Please help.

Jamie didn't even know her name.

A short, skinny tramp who looked like he just crawled out of a dumpster paced in front of his spurious family holding a weathered section of cardboard on which more words were printed:

Homeless. Will work for food. Family starving.

Jamie didn't know his name either.

From a phone booth near a busy Texaco service station, his brown lank hair now cut to shoulder length, Bowen looked on, hoping his son could garner enough change for a Big Mac and bus fare to Miami. He had met the bogus couple the night before in the hallway of the flea-bag hotel, after the clatter of rhythmic noises had ceased. "Kids bring good money," remarked the junkie hobo who called himself Rambo. "We'll rake it in with this little fella. Yeah."

And so, by noon, Bowen and Jamie had enough for a burger each, one order of fries, a large soda and a bus ticket. It was to be a good day, indeed.

* * *

There was only one way in and one way out of the exclusive gated community, so they waited at the end of the second block from the guard shack, binoculars in hand. The old van had heavy tinted windows and a magnetic sign on each side which read: "Andy's Carpet Cleaning Service." She'd have to turn right if she was going to the school. But if *he* had made contact, she might be turning left instead.

It had been a long night. Fabio and Pepe took turns dozing, as one kept an eye on the entrance to Gables By The Sea. Pepe opened a thermos and poured the tepid black Cuban coffee into two miniature cups, drank in sips then shared an American donut. Fabio was the lout, festooned in gold chains, standing over six foot four with arms the size of most men's thighs. Wearing wrap-around shades which concealed his beady eyes, Pepe was the wiry one, smaller, smarter, the inside man who arranged the job. They spoke only in Spanish.

"What if the guy never calls her?" asked Fabio, munching on a donut. "I mean, like, he might never call, right?"

"What difference does it make? We still get paid."

"Yeah, but it's peanuts unless we make the hit. I mean this is bullshit sitting here every day like...Jesus, Pepe, how do they know he'll ever make the contact?"

"Because she's his mother, stupid. And he probably needs help with that little kid."

"Yes but if he hasn't called in eight years, why would he call now?"

"Simple. He's back here in Miami, probably strung out. Stop worrying. Rudolfo will take care of us. There's plenty of money there. I trust him."

Fabio released a raucous belch, lit a wood-tipped cigar then turned up the volume of salsa music. Pepe immediately turned it down.

"I'll take them down with this rather than fucking around with him and that kid." Fabio patted his belt, site of a stolen .380 Baretta with an obliterated serial number. "Shit, the silencer is right here, no problem. Fast and sweet."

"Fabio, you just don't get it. If he's found it will be an easy trace. No one is to know he's dead. He has to vanish, disappear forever, comprende? Like he did for eight years. If anyone knows he's killed, it's big trouble. So knock off the shit, you goon."

"Hey, watch who you call..."

"Once we lure them into the van, you can have your fun. What's more important is making sure they are never found."

Fabio looked out the window and took a deep drag on his cigar. "I say out in the ocean for a long swim."

"No, that means getting a boat and all that. I have a better idea."

"Ah, I don't like doing a kid."

"We have no choice." Suddenly, Pepe's eyes alerted to the street, "Look, there." A white Crown Victoria with tinted windows cruised by at ten miles under the speed limit then disappeared around a corner. "I'm going to get a car like that, maybe next week. Good car."

A bright golden haze hung over the posh neighborhood to the east as they sat quietly for another hour waiting, puffing on cigars. Finally, Pepe spotted a tortoise-shell beige Lincoln approaching the guard house. "There. That's her. Let's go, amigo."

* * *

Amid a labyrinth of garden pathways leading to the sparkling bay behind The Stanton School, Laura ambled slowly, stopping every so often to acknowledge a student or to pluck a red hibiscus flower or to marvel the acrobatic prowess of grey squirrels foraging for nuts and seeds. After so many years, her mind was spinning again, wondering, hoping, calculating advantages versus disadvantages, if she should follow up and make use of this new found ammunition or leave it be. In truth, there were no advantages other than winning money she didn't need. More importantly, it was an opportunity to resurrect her dignity and yes, taste the vengeance she so deserved, vengeance for herself and for her son, and for her son's son, wherever they might be. But she had to consider Paul, who now relied on her strength as she had relied on his twenty years before. He could not undergo the stress. But there were ways to manage, keeping the nurses at home, being candid with Grace, securing her cooperation and playing out the role of a dutiful wife. Now, it was time to gamble with her best friend and her future at Stanton

School. Her decision was made.

A blazing sun framed by a field of pure azure hovered at high noon as Laura sat on the iron bench, peacefully watching a pair of sloops pass as though vying for the lead. In the distance, the fleet of gleaming cruise ships sat ominously at the Dodge Island port. She mused how they would never experience those good times again. The image of a bearded, long-haired Bowen holding the hand of the little boy flitted through her mind for the zillionth time that day when she heard a familiar voice from behind. "Well, Laura. It's not like you to be taking a break in mid day. This must be pretty heavy."

"Hello, Wilma."

The matronly woman smiled, replaced a windblown strand of white hair from her face, then looked over the bay toward Key Biscayne. "Calm out there today, Laura. Must be good time for fishing."

Laura smiled as her eyes reminisced. "Yeah. Fishing. Bowen would sure like to be out there fishing right now."

"I bet."

"He looked awful, Wilma. Poor Bowen."

There was another long pause. "I wonder if this is all a good thing, Laura."

"If what's a good thing?"

"Him. Suddenly appearing. It just upsets your life."

"It doesn't matter if it's good or not. It was inevitable. I'm just so glad to see that he's alive."

Another duo of speed boats raced by with skiers trailing behind. "Laura, you're doing so well. I just...well, I don't want to see you so troubled."

Laura looked out over the horizon and replied wistfully, "He's my son, Wilma. He will always be my son, and I love him."

"But does he love you?"

She pondered a moment, then offered a wispy reply. "Yes, of course he loves me. He's my son."

"But does he love you as his mother?"

"Does it matter?

"It would matter to me."

"It's hard to explain, Wilma. It's like, well, like I've been chasing after him all my life, begging for a morsel of time, a glint in his eye, a rare hug if I could ever get it. I crave to feel acceptance as his mother but I now know it's a craving that may never be satisfied. But that's okay. I love that boy and it is not his fault. Don't you understand? What he has become is not his fault."

"Well, I never had children..."

"His father kept him from me, deliberately, and I never knew why. To this day, I don't understand why. I could accept being hated, but I couldn't accept him destroying Bowen's relationship with me, his own mother. He set out to destroy me, but in the end, he destroyed our son." Laura looked to the bay again and tasted a drop of perspiration. "You'll never understand the pain. The yearning to love my baby, to give and to act upon those instincts which could only have nurtured him and helped him to grow healthy and happy. Bowen was not a happy child and by the time he finally came to me, well..." She sighed, then continued. "It was too late. At thirteen, he was whatever he was going to be. The cracks in his foundation were fixed.

"It's amazing, how a single incident can pave the course of an entire life, then affect the lives of so many others. Just one single incident... a moment in time, a fleeting moment that I can never take back. I can't redo it. I can't fix it. It's just there, haunting my life and my son's life, and it touched so many others in the periphery, like Paul, Grace, and now Bowen's child." A cynical smile crossed her face. "Even Yvonne Rappaport.

"There were times, Wilma, that Lloyd deliberately concocted reasons I could not pick up my son. I would go weeks, even months between visits. Visits. Oh, how I hated ...*visits.* Imagine, being relegated to *visits* with your own child at the whim of an egomaniacal asshole who exercised total power over you.

"I'd go to the house to pick him up and he'd be gone. 'To the doctors', he'd tell me. When they moved to West Palm Beach, I had to hire a detective to find him. The courts? Forget it. He and his father knew every judge in Florida. Then Lloyd married an office bimbo to baby sit Bowen. It was an arrangement, a ten-year deal. Who knows how much that cost him. When the ten years was up, she split. Gone!

"Bowen always called her *Mommy.* There was something about her... I don't know, that he felt loved. I guess she was good to him. I'm thankful for that, but it really makes me angry inside. There has always been a hole in my heart, knowing my child loved another woman as his mother. You know, throughout his formative years, I had to teach him I was his mother. He was petrified of addressing me as *Mother* in fear that his father would hear him. So I was Miss Laura. *Miss Laura.* Not Mom, or Mommy. No, that was Yvonne. So cheated. When he was in the hospital waiting for his operation, I stood there like an outsider while Lloyd introduced he and Yvonne to the operating surgeon as his *parents.* Then he smirked. The bastard!

"I would have been a good mother. I know Bowen would be different today if I had him. He would be a college graduate, a happy human being with a future and a family. You see, Wilma, three months after he was born, I lost him to Lloyd. I never ever saw him at all again until he was four years old."

"What?"

"I almost died. I tried to kill myself."

"Oh, my dear Laura. Poor dear."

She took a deep breath then peered deep into Wilma's bespectacled eyes. "There's something I never told you, something about me."

"Go ahead. I'm listening." Wilma rested her hand upon Laura's.

"It will probably cost me my job."

"What? After twenty years? I doubt that, honey. Unless you were in on the JFK assassination." Without answering, Laura stared into her friend's eyes until Wilma looked back with utter confusion. "You weren't, were you?"

"Wilma, I never did go to Europe after I graduated college. I lied."

"So?"

"The reason I didn't work..." Laura started to weep and then composed herself. "The reason I never saw my boy, was... well, I was in a mental institution for three years."

"Oh my Lord."

Wilma listened as Laura embarked on her soul-cleansing confession. She narrated the horrible chain of events during those dark years only now, she could produce the exculpatory evidence of her innocence, her absolute sanity and of the malicious and unjustified assault on her integrity by the iniquitous father of her child. "The woman, Mrs. Von Brauten, remembers everything. I have to do it, Wilma."

"Do what?"

"I was never crazy, Wilma. Never. Three and a half years of my life was utterly wasted and then I was deprived from my own baby, a baby who's now grown to be a fractured soul, a baby with whom I can never recapture the years of estrangement, barriers I didn't deserve and neither did he. The anger has never stopped boiling inside of me and it never will until I can put it to rest. I'm going all the way. I'm going to use this ammunition. I've talked to a lawyer. Wilma, I'm suing for everything he has, to expose him for everything he's done to me and to his son, and I'll make sure he loses everything he owns on this planet, including his dignity." There was a long gaze into each other's eyes. "I want him ruined for life, just as he ruined the lives of others."

"Whew!" Wilma looked out toward the bay without saying a word, digesting what her best friend had just told her, then turned back to Laura. "I don't know. You better think it over very carefully. I see big trouble. Lloyd is a powerful man."

"Right," she countered. "And I've knuckled under over and over. Now the power has shifted. Why shouldn't I, Wilma? Why shouldn't I? There's not a remorseful bone in his body."

"I'm worried. I don't know. I just don't feel...well, you could get hurt. I don't want to see anything happen."

"Nothing will happen. I've got to do this, don't you see?"

"Think of all the publicity. What about Paul?"

"I'll do the best I can with Paul, shielding him. But after seeing my boy, Wilma, and what he's been through and what I've endured for no good reason..." Her eyes welled as Wilma placed a sympathetic hand upon hers. "...that son of a bitch..."

"Easy, honey."

"Paul is a wonderful man, Wilma, but there's always been something lacking, long before the stroke." Wilma listened, patiently. "I mean, we've all joked a lot and all, but the truth is, we haven't slept together in nine years."

"Well, I'll be...and I thought Hubert and I had a problem."

Then came the question only Wilma could answer. Laura

wiped a tear from her eye. "Look, because he's such a big shot and all, this is going to make news, big news. I don't want to embarrass the school, or you, so if you think I should resign, I'll understand."

"Resign?"

"Yes, Wilma. You know the Stantons will never tolerate a blight on their precious faculty record."

"The only blight I see, Laura, is the travesty you had to live with for all these years. I just don't understand why you didn't tell me sooner."

"You mean, you think I'll still stay on?"

"If they fire you my dear, they fire me in the same breath."

Laura smiled and wiped another tear, then embraced her friend as two female students passed by. "I love you, Wilma."

"I love you too, you nut."

* * *

It was nearing five o'clock when Maggie opened the door to Laura's office with a lump in her throat and an apprehensive expression on her face. Laura was placing a second call to John A. Spiegal, one of the most prominent family lawyers in all of Miami. She looked up, impatiently. "Yes, Maggie?"

"Um, there's a call for you on line three."

"Well, take a message. Can't you see I'm..."

"Um, Doctor Rosenthal, I think you should pick this up. He's at a pay phone and...uh, can't hold on very long."

Her heart skipped a beat. She knew instantly who it was. Eight long years deserved a deep breath, a quiver of her lips and a slow lifting of the receiver. For a moment, she thought of uttering her customary... *Doctor Rosenthal here*...but she thought again. She imagined him as he was on television that night, long hair, bearded, hardly recognizable, holding the hand of a little boy who looked so much like his father as a child. She raised the receiver slowly. "H...Hel...Hello?"

"Hello, Mother."

She cupped her hand over the receiver to muffle the sounds of her choking as a geyser of tears exploded from her eyes.

"Mother? Are you there?"

Nary a sound could pass her lips. Afraid that he would hang up, she composed herself and finally squeaked out a single word. "Bowen?"

"How are you, Mother?"

"Oh...Bowen. I saw you...on the television..."

"Mother I can't talk long 'cause I have no more change. I'm sorry that I... well, I need help, with my boy here."

"Of course, what...?"

"Could you come up to Greynold's Park? I can meet you at the boat docks."

"Now?"

"Now. Yes."

"Give me thirty, forty minutes."

"Okay. Thanks."

"Wait, Bowen. One more question. What's his name?"

"The little one here..."

Squeal. "Please deposit one dollar and ten cents for three more minutes."

Dial tone.

* * *

"I'm sorry Paul, I have some last minute business to take care of. I'll be another couple hours, at the most. Ask Consuella if she could stay on until I get there, okay?"

"You're going to see Bowen, aren't you?"

He always knew. There was no sense lying. "Yes, Paul."

A long hesitation followed as she listened to his breathing, knowing how he felt. But she had no choices. Finally, he murmured, "Yeah. I figured."

chapter twenty-three

"Jesus Christ, Pepe, where in the hell is she going?"

"Drive stupid, what does it matter. Just don't lose her. Look, she's turning into that... that gate over there. She must be meeting someone. Let's hope it's him."

"This is a park. The sign says two pesos. Pepe, give me two."

They carefully remained three to five cars back all the way from Coral Gables, up the interstate, then on Federal Highway, paying no mind to the white Crown Victoria which alternated with a grey Mustang to stay directly in back of Laura. "We got to get him alone. Maybe he'll give her the kid."

"Hey Pepe, I don't want to kill no kid."

"Shut up."

Jostled by speed bumps, they slowly snaked their way through the narrow tree-lined road, avoiding joggers and bikers and admiring the placid lake off to their right where half dozen paddle boats and canoes drifting lazily in the lush, humid forest.

"You talk to him, Fabio. Offer him two hundred dollars to run an errand."

The Lincoln turned a slow right next to the boat house. The white car behind her turned to the left, passing the stone observation tower.

"Yeah. If we get him alone...wait! Look. She's parking."

"Hold up."

* * *

She rehearsed it a thousand times during the forty minute ride north. *Hello Bowen. Are you all right? Why did you vanish for eight years? Tell me about the baby's mother. Are you mar-*

ried? Don't you want to see Grace, your sister? Where have you lived? I missed you, son. I missed you so much, I've been so worried. How about a hug for your....? No Laura, don't break down, stay composed, learn about the little boy, what about Bowen's addiction. What did he mean about needing help?

She stepped through the open boathouse and saw him sitting on an old wooden bench facing the lake, his head leaning back as though studying the universe. Nearby, a youngster in shorts and ragged sneakers chased a pair of ducks, laughing, tripping, then laughing more. She trembled nervously and smiled at the child, knowing it was her grandson. The little boy noticed the strange woman staring at him and seemed afraid. Bowen saw this, stood quickly and turned to face his mother.

She remained several feet back, studying his dark sunken eyes and the gaunt narrow face, wondering for a brief moment if this really was her son. He wore rubber thongs, a pair of oversized tattered jeans and a loose fitting long-sleeved shirt worn outside the belt. "My, you're, ...you're so tall. And you shaved. On the TV, you..." She wanted to embrace, to share this moment as a union renewed, but it was not to be. Not now. He seemed cautious, so customarily distant. She expected nothing else.

"Uh, yes Mother. First time in a couple years, actually," he answered, patting his jaw.

The urge to bring him close was near impossible to resist. She wanted to offer him safety and make him feel everything was going to be all right. But she knew better. "Bowen, you're so, ...so thin. You look sick." She was hesitant, nervous.

The boy ran to his father and clutched his leg, staring up at the woman. Bowen gestured toward her. "Jamie, this is your grandmother. Remember. The nice lady I told you about?"

She smiled and stooped to hold his little hands. "So, your name is Jamie? You are so... soooo beautiful."

He reminded her so much of Bowen as a child, with blond hair so pale it nearly looked white. "My daddy's taking me to the Keys," he said with enthusiasm.

"Oh? Really?"

"Uh huh. We're goin' fishin, in Islamorada.'

She looked up to Bowen with a *"sounds familiar"* expression. He shrugged and smiled. "I did promise him."

"Maybe we'll all go..."

"Mother, listen, um, I've got some problems, I'm not too well right now, and little Jamie here..."

"What's wrong, Bowen? Tell me."

"I have to take care of something, Mother. I've been, uh..." An embarrassed grin crossed his face. "...sort of a bad boy. I might be a little sick. You really don't want to hear about it."

"Where have you been? Oh, Bowen, I have so many questions."

"All over. All over hell, actually. I'm tired, Mother. Very tired. Can you take Jamie? For a while? He needs someone who can..."

As Bowen spoke, Laura noticed two men wearing suits and ties emerging from the parking area and thought it was strange being dressed that way in a casual park. Then, from the row of azalea bushes, two more men in suits and ties. She interrupted. "Bowen, who are those men? Do you know?"

He looked over his shoulder and then quickly handed his boy a small pouch. "Keep this, Jamie. Don't lose it." He turned to her. "Mother, if anything happens to me, please take care of Jamie. Whatever you do, don't ever give him back to his mother. Please!"

"Well, of course, Bowen, but who is his mother? What's happening?"

A helicopter whirled above as four men in suits approached from two sides. Bowen saw the inevitable and handed his son's arms over to Laura. "You were followed, Mother. I'm sorry."

"What is going on?" she pleaded.

From behind, an authoritative male voice barked, "Bowen Ramsey? Metro-Dade Police! Fugitive Squad. Put your hands on your head. You are under arrest!"

She stepped toward the concession stand, aghast to see guns pointed at her sallow-faced son. It was all so confusing. Bowen cowered acquiescently, as though he welcomed the end of an arduous journey across the netherworld. Like a swarm of television cops, they rushed over to grab his arms. He shouted, "Please Mother, help Jamie." He was shoved against a support beam and cuffed.

A row of boaters stopped near the docks to gawk at the unfolding scenario. "Oh my God," she murmured, holding Jamie's hand. Staring at the arrest scene, the child stood confused, looking up to Laura. The short stocky cop who identified himself as

Detective Matthew Ferguson approached, displayed his I.D. and asked to see the pouch Bowen had handed to his son. "Why, I guess so. I don't know..."

"It's just a seashell," remarked the small boy, holding it up to the agent.

The detective inspected the small blue and orange conical shell while Laura wondered why it seemed so familiar, why it was passed to Jamie the moment Bowen saw the arrest was imminent. Ferguson then checked inside the bag and handed it back to the child.

"What is going on? Please tell me," she pleaded to the officer.

"Trafficking, ma'am. Drug trafficking. Alias Capias from California, issued two years ago for bond jumping. Your son has been a fugitive from justice."

"Oh no."

Within microseconds, the history of his aloof and arrogant behavior flashed through her mind, the stealing, lying, disruptions, chronic truancy, running away and finally, the revelation that his father actually introduced him to drugs. She watched grievously as the crew of plain clothes cops marched Bowen into the back seat of a large white car. Little Jamie held her hand tightly, confused, not saying a word until he asked, "Does this mean we're not going to Islamorada?" It was then that she realized she was taking a five year-old child into her home.

My God. Paul. What will I say to Paul?"

* * *

The blue Dodge van with a carpet cleaning sign on its side drove off quietly from the gate. The passenger wearing wrap around shades puffed a wood tipped cigar and listened to his prodigious friend ramble on. "Shit! Rudolfo isn't going to like this."

"Yeah, well you mean Rudolfo's client isn't going to like this."

"Maybe he'll get out, on bond, maybe?"

"Fabio, there were four cops and a helicopter. Don't bet on it."

"*Mierda!* Fifty thousand, down the toilet."

"Well, look at it this way. You won't have to kill the kid."

Fabio gazed at the shopping plaza passing by and flipped a cigar to the gutter. "Fifty thousand. Down the toilet. I don't believe it."

chapter twenty-four

"Our special guests today on *Florida Backtalk* are gubernatorial candidate and mayor of West Palm Beach, Lloyd B. Ramsey and his opponent from the democratic ticket, the Lieutenant Governor of Florida, Henry Stallworth. Before posing questions about such issues as the state lottery, taxes, education and street crime, our viewers will naturally be interested in a response from Mayor Ramsey regarding the appearance of a young man claiming to be a son he hadn't seen in eight years, a man who said that the mayor not only used drugs, but also introduced him to drugs as a child. Our panel of interviewers will begin the questioning with Mayor Ramsey."

Bright lamps brought an instant bead of sweat to his temples. Lloyd adjusted his paisley tie and whipped up his infectious smile which had him ahead in the polls by almost two to one, until the past Friday night. It was a calculated risk coming on the show, but his only chance to overcome the devastating crush to his campaign. There was only one thing to do.

"....Categorically deny these absurd allegations and furthermore assert that the dirtbag, I mean...the person who showed up at that rally last Friday night was an imposter... Yes, I have a son named Bowen somewhere out there, but that young man was not Bowen Ramsey. Period! I know my son, and that was not him! I cannot imagine who would stoop so low to pull off such a sham. I have never turned anyone on to drugs, yet my own son, nor have I ever used drugs except for a brief experiment with marijuana some thirty-five years ago in my youth."

The female interviewer raised her head from her notes and posed the next question.

"Mayor Ramsey, could you tell us a little more about your son Bowen? I mean, when was the last time you saw him and what were the circumstances of his disappearance?"

"Yes. Of course. My poor son was the unfortunate product of a broken home. His stepmother ran out on all of us when he was eleven and he never got over it. Psychiatrists diagnosed him as a manic depressive. We did all we could, gave him the world at his fingertips, but he always managed to gravitate to the sleazy side. It's a tragedy to be sure. When Bowen was thirteen, I allowed him to go and live with his natural mother. He was terribly unhappy with her and I have always regretted that decision, especially after he ran away three years later. We've not heard from him since."

The interview carried on another twenty minutes with Lloyd artfully fielding the slew of questions about his veracity, his early years with drugs and the relationship with Bowen. His opponent sat smug, enjoying his new edge in the polls, barely noticed among interviewers as all the attention focused on the West Palm Beach mayor.

As commercial time was about to close out the first half, the news director motioned to the panel moderator that a bulletin was being announced. The anchor read from a prompter.

"...announce the arrest of Bowen Arthur Ramsey by Metro-Dade Police this afternoon on a fugitive warrant from California. Details are unclear but sources tell us that it stems from drug trafficking charges from which he jumped bond. Ramsey is the son of gubernatorial candidate Lloyd Ramsey whose campaign felt a sharp setback Friday night after the appearance of young Bowen before a microphone claiming the mayor had been his drug mentor. Ramsey was apprehended in a North Dade park with his five year old son who is now in temporary custody of his grandmother. The arrest photo shown here depicts a clean shaven Bowen Ramsey but it can clearly be seen that he is the same person who appeared at the rally. No bond has been set."

When the cameras were turned back on and the panel resumed interviewing the two candidates, there was one empty chair.

* * *

With his good hand, Paul Rosenthal clicked off the television, changed the channels of his mind and reached over to the CD player to put on a recording of Mozart arias, turning up the volume so he might immerse himself in the one human pleasure still within reach for his crippled body. He needed to shut out the new intrusion into their lives and hope that the miserable, wretched son of his wife would stay in jail or anywhere else far from Paul's world. He knew there was far more going on than Laura let on and he was satisfied, as well, to know as little as possible. For the first time in eons, she was coming home late, leaving him in the care of private nurses and tending to young Grace who had many more things on her mind than a decrepit old man. How he wished he could be whole again, to dress himself, work with his tools, play a tune on his baby grand and solve the complex problems of others rather than being one to the woman he loved. A smile crossed his lips as the rapture of Mozart's haunting aria *L'amero, saro costante* and the gentle voice of Beverly Sills captured his soul. Nothing else in the world existed for those few moments. His good hand waved like a symphony conductor, pointing, thrusting to the crescendos, his weak voice trying desperately to warble a duet with the soprano, deep in the musical abyss, apart from the universe until, a nudge.

"Honey?" she said with a smile. He opened his eyes and saw a small boy standing near his chair, a boy who looked too much like Bowen Ramsey twenty years before, a boy with bright eyes and soft blond hair. "Honey, this is Jamie," she said with reserved glee.

He peered at the child and scowled, wondering what he was doing there, what impact this would have on the little serenity there was left in his world. As he looked over with his half-drooped face, he glanced to his daughter, then his wife, both smiling. "What's going on, Laura?" he asked, drooling from the corner of his mouth.

She knelt by his chair and took a tissue to his mouth. "Paul, little Jamie doesn't have a home right now."

"Oh?"

"Jamie is going to stay with us a while but he knows you are
not well and we will make sure that nothing bothers you. Nothing will change for you, darling. All right? Isn't he beautiful?"

"I suppose so." *Go away, child, and leave us be. Go away. Go
away.*

* * *

Wracked with a melange of emotions, Laura managed to
avoid disrupting what was left of Paul's wretched existence.
Though he would not accept Bowen, there was a new mission
now, one which Paul would likely reject, one in which she was
compelled to consider the life of a five-year-old grandson over
her aging spouse. A foster home was out of the question. Once
again she was riding the crest of love, an opportunity revisited,
a new Bowen with whom she could play a significant role in
molding this child into a happy and secure human being. Now
she could fill the huge void created in 1964 and become what
she was never permitted to be for years past, a mother to a little
boy. But first there were questions, much to catch up on. She
needed to know about his mother. Who was she? Why the ad-
monishment to keep Jamie from her? What was to come of
Bowen? What of his drug problem? After eight years of absence,
she finally enjoyed a three-minute rendezvous before he was
jailed. Through it all, she still had to remain considerate to her
ailing husband, now wrought with anxiety over these new developments. Grace was a wonderful daughter whose only wish
was to be permitted her friends and activities and not be burdened with the care of her father. And now, a new grandchild
in her bosom. All that, plus a titillated attorney in waiting, ready
for her to give the green light which would make him rich.
Should she or shouldn't she?

"Grace, pass me the colander please," she asked as she
pranced about the kitchen, stopping every so often to watch the
little sprite following her.

His eyes widened with every step, looking up at copper cookware hanging from the ceiling, the counter-top television and a
virtual smorgasbord of gadgetry and appliances, the automatic

dishwasher, a garbage disposal, bread maker. Then with deep fascination, he stopped to gaze at the refrigerator's ice dispenser. "I want more ice," he said.

"Dinner will be ready in twenty minutes. Jamie, do you like spaghetti?"

"Yes. It's okay."

"Jamie, I have a big surprise for you. How would you like to go to the zoo?"

"Sure. But can we go fishin' in Islamorada first?"

She smiled and touched his cheek. "Why sure we can." Then she looked up to Grace. "Honey, how would you like to go fishin' in the Keys with Jamie and I?"

"Well, I guess so."

With the child near, Laura lifted her arms to open a cabinet. Jamie flinched, ducked his head and buried his face in his hands, guarding. Laura studied the boy, kneeled and looked deep into his eyes. "Oh, my poor baby. What's the matter Jamie?"

"Oh, nothing."

"Nothing eh?" She knew. "Who hit you, Jamie?"

The boy grew somber, looking straight at the floor, hesitant.

"Don't be afraid, Jamie. Who?"

"My mommy."

"Well, you listen to me, Jamie. No one will ever hit you here. You understand that? No one will ever hit you."

"Okay. I'm hungry."

Moments later, they all convened at the dinner table where a starving five-year-old boy dug into the plate of spaghetti with his fingers.

* * *

"That little bastard!"

Lloyd Ramsey was in a rage, throwing perfume bottles across the room, breaking mirrors, smashing lamps and screaming at the top of his lungs as Barbara lay petrified in her evening gown curled up with a bed pillow. "Please Lloyd, please, you're scaring me."

"Six weeks. He couldn't wait six fucking weeks! That miserable little fuck!" He continued to pace, sucking tumblers of pure scotch, his perfectly styled hair flinging beads of sweat, eyes blazing with pure anger. "I'm fucking ruined. I don't believe it, that bastard ruined me. I was locked in for Governor, now it's....."

"Lloyd, it'll be all right. You still have your practice. Please, stop this. I'm scared."

"You're what? Scared? You're scared? You stupid bitch! Who gives a rats ass if you're scared. Oh, poor little Barbara, yeah. She's all frightened while my career has just been harpooned, a direct hit into the heart and what do you give a shit about? How scared you are. Poor baby. Why don't you just get the fuck outa here. Go on, get the fuck out!"

"Lloyd, stop it!"

"You heard what I said!"

"Why? What did I do?"

"You? You're no better than all the other female pond scum. You're here for nothing else but the money and the prestige and you know it. Well, you can kiss both goodbye."

"What do you mean?"

"I mean, get - the - fuck - out! Is that simple English enough for you?"

She sat up defiantly and saw that she was married to a stranger after all. "You really did that, didn't you?" He took a long swallow from a glass of scotch, then tossed it against the door. "You turned him on to drugs, didn't you? Your own son."

"I said, outa here. I don't need you or your high falutin social status any more. Take your woman's rights and mother's groups and shove them all up your ass. You're history, bitch!"

"Why, you low down, filthy son of a..." The back of his hand slammed her cheek before she could spit out another word. A trickle of blood formed at the corner of her mouth. She had often warned him never to lay an angry hand on her. He knew he had crossed the line, but was out of control. She cringed, guarding her face. He stood over her and began slapping the back of her head until she screamed for mercy, "Please! Lloyd! Stop!"

"Get the fuck outa here, cunt!" He hollered, swinging maniacally, whacking her again and again. His arm was halted abruptly on the upswing by a powerful grip. Her son, Chip McGill, stood six-foot four and played varsity basketball in college. He'd heard the argument from his room across the house. In a second, Lloyd's arm was half-way up his back as Chip motorized him across the room, head first into a mirrored door shattering shards of glass in all directions.

Lloyd lay bewildered in a crumpled heap, his head streaming blood as Chip stood over him. "Don't ever hurt my mother. I'll kill you." He turned to Barbara, "Get your stuff, Mom. Let's go."

The phone rang. Lloyd leaped from the floor and snatched the receiver. "Hello!" he barked, panting.

Barbara hurriedly gathered her jewelry and clothes, stuffing suitcases while Lloyd paced the floor, phone to his ear, blood oozing on his forehead, drunk. "Yeah. What is it?" he blurted into the receiver. Lloyd pulled the antenna from the cordless. "Fuck you John. Fuck everything. It's all lost." As they were about to exit the room, Barbara turned back and removed the diamond studded Cartier watch from atop the dresser. "Hey, bitch! That's mine!"

"Not any more," she retorted. "Remember, I bought it."

Into the phone, Lloyd barked, "Look here, my money grubbing old lady is walking out on me. Get that? Ain't that a kicker, after all I done for that piece of shit, abandoning me like this? I'm now relegated to a mere mortal so she wants nothing to do with me. The bitch."

She checked her purse for the keys to the Jaguar.

"No, no, forget it John, I'm finished. It can't be repaired and you know it. My own son fucked me. God damn ingrate. Hey, I gotta go. I'll call you later."

Without another word, Barbara and her son carried suitcases from the bedroom and down the stairs to the front door. Lloyd stood at the rail, unkempt, bleeding, teetering. "Hey, bitch, where the fuck do you think you're going?"

She looked up at the pathetic excuse for a public figure and asked, "What did you ever marry me for anyway, Lloyd?"

"You really wanna know?"

"Yeah. I want to know. I'm sure it had nothing to do with love."

"You really are pretty stupid, ain't ya. Nobody gets elected these days unless they're an Ozzie and Harriet. You were Harriet. And that string bean mama's boy with you was Ricky. Now you're both shit."

Chip's neck turned pink as he stood with his back to Lloyd. Raising an eyebrow, she replied, "That might be true, Mr. Mayor, but we will becoming very rich little turds." Stunned, Lloyd instantly calculated his fortune, glaring down at his third wife. "Seems you told me to get the fuck out of here. Well, I'm getting the fuck out of here with great pleasure, you self-ingratiating asshole!" Then she added, "Start clipping your discount coupons. You'll be needing them."

She reached for the door. He shouted, "You ain't getting a fuckin' cent. You hear me, you cunt? Not a fuckin' cent."

She rubbed her bruised face and replied tersely, "We'll see about that." She stormed out.

"CUNT!"

As the door closed, Chip slammed it open and stormed up the stairs to the first landing, startling Lloyd who smartly backed away. In a moment he found himself looking up to the twenty-two year-old whose eyes blazed with contempt. "Listen punk, get the fuck..."

Before he uttering another sound, Lloyd's shirt collar turned into a noose as Chip lifted him from the floor. Lloyd tried pulling at those powerful hands to no avail, gurgling, his face turning bright red. As his head was slammed against the wall, Chip's face was nose to nose, gritting teeth, screaming into his ear, "My mother is not a cunt! You hear me, bastard? You ever lay a hand on her again, I'll kill you!" Chip released his collar, dropping Lloyd like a sack of potatoes.

Lloyd stumbled up the stairs, poured a scotch, paced the floor for another hour, mind racing, angered at the unexpected valor from Chip, thinking of his precious wealth. For a man who spent a lifetime in control, it was a dilemma indeed, feeling it all about to slip through his fingers. First Bowen's appearance, the dead political campaign and now his wife threatening him. Chaos was unfamiliar territory. Normally he would simply whip off one of his charismatic speeches, call an aide to have it fixed or promise money. But that was no longer an option.

Screening the answer machine, he waited through several incoming calls refusing to talk with the media he had courted so cleverly. Alone, drunk and angry, he dialed a number and waited through several unanswered rings. As he was about to hang up, a voice answered, "Ola?"

For a moment, he considered hanging up. Then he changed his mind. "Rudolfo, that you?"

chapter twenty-five

She phoned incessantly for five days but each time she was told that Bowen was in detox and unavailable. Authorities would release limited information, that he was charged with being a fugitive from justice stemming from a Bakersfield drug bust in 1985. Fugitive status kicked in when he jumped a ten thousand dollar bond, ergo, no bond in Florida. An extradition hearing would be scheduled whenever Bowen was physically capable of attending.

Without Paul's knowledge, she retained a defense attorney and former prosecutor, who managed to glean some background information for Laura. While living in Southern California, Bowen Ramsey, alias Bobby Matthews, alias "Bow Man", had been recruited by a low level smuggling operation to act as a mule, a transporter of illegal drugs throughout the state for which he was well paid and provided all the cocaine he and his wife could possibly need. The bottom fell out when he delivered a kilo of coke at a local dry cleaners, unaware that state and local police were working a reverse sting. Bowen was a mere minnow trapped in a shark's net. At the time, Bowen lived with his exotic dancer wife and small child in a rented house in east L.A. After a fellow crony put up the thousand dollars to a bondsman, Bowen took his two year-old boy and slipped out his back door into virtual obscurity, never heard from again until the phantasmic appearance at his father's rally. In the interim, unable to care for his son as a fugitive, Bowen ruefully returned Jamie to his mother for two years while he vanished within the underworld of drugs and crime. Paternal instinct drew him back to the nest for a clandestine visit. That's when he witnessed Zena's horrible treatment of Jamie, the utter absence of love and the constant physical abuse. The boy endured ridiculous punishments for committing simple childish acts, like dropping a dish or losing a toy. He was whipped and beaten, starved, refused permission to use the bathroom then got punished for soiling his shorts. Bowen could not ever leave his boy with her again.

All this was new to Laura, who had never been exposed to the criminal justice system other than the brief scuffle when Bowen was a juvenile. Not only was she embroiled in his criminal case, she was now caring for his child in a home where tension was rising and her relationship with an aging husband was as delicate as a house of cards. In light of everything, Wilma tried to discourage Laura from filing the suit against Lloyd, but the Pavlovish taste of final retribution for all the years of degradation was too alluring to pass up. She wanted...no, she needed revenge.

Jamie was enrolled in the kindergarten program at the Stanton School where she kept tabs on him daily and showered him with affection he had never known. He instantly became the center of her life. With the help of Grace and hired nurses, his presence had little effect on the fractured but tranquil world of Paul Rosenthal. Laura knew very little about the boy's mother other than her name, Zena, and that she must have beat him often in the face and on the legs.

It was a soggy day at Miami's civic center complex, the second Sunday since Bowen's arrest in Greynold's Park. She parked, opened her umbrella and looked up at the tall sandstone building which housed all the inmates awaiting trials or other legal process in Dade County. Sadly, her son was one of those. Just as it was twenty years earlier, she struggled to see him, to be a part of his life, hurdling barriers, always in compliance with a primary authority.

Steel doors, body searches, report forms, voices echoing in despair, drab grey walls, men and women in blue uniforms and sour faces walking, jangling keys, long strides down concrete corridors into another grey room with a row of semi-private partitions and chairs each facing a glass window. Beside each window, a black wall phone. No frills. *"No Smoking"* signs adorned the room. A black woman sat at the booth on the far end whispering into the phone to someone on the other side of the glass. Moments later, Laura would be doing the same. It was alien, this house of cages, surrounded by evil and desperation and the pervasive yearning to be free.

"Sit over there," said the female guard. "It'll be a few minutes."

Through a thick pane of glass, she watched his stick-like figure emerge through the door then led to a chair by a guard. His ashen face paled against the grey-blue jail shirt, but he seemed more fit and healthy than the gaunt, sickly figure she had met in the park. She sensed a warm glow from her son as he peered through the pane. Always a *barrier*. He motioned for her to pick up the phone.

"Hello Bowen."

"Hello Mother."

"How are you feeling, son?"

"Listen, Mother, uh, I'm really sorry about this, I..."

"I just want to know how you are feeling, Bowen."

He hesitated and peered through the window with a snicker and a grin, "Embarrassed."

"I see."

"Actually, I'm just great. Had a little bout with the flu this past week, but otherwise..."

"They told me you were in detox."

"They did, eh? Well, then, I guess I was in detox." He shrugged.

"Are you all right now?"

"Yeah, sure. For now."

There was a long pause as Laura reflected on eight years of absence. He wouldn't even ask the question, *How are you? How is Grace?* "Bowen, they are only giving me thirty minutes and there are some things I need to talk about."

"Go on."

"What about Jamie's health, his history, his mother?"

The question evoked the first sign of emotion from her son. "Whatever you do, Mother, do not give him back to Zena. If you can't take care of him, then put him in a foster home first. Please, believe what I'm saying."

"I know she hit him. It's obvious."

"Zena is a sick broad. It's drugs, her looks and her sex. Her kids come in last, behind everything else."

"Kids?"

"She's got another boy, fourteen. She had him when she was

fifteen. He's gone, out there somewhere, a male prostitute."

"My Lord."

"The only reason she would ever want Jamie back is to collect the welfare money and food stamps. She lives off the system."

"Where is she?"

"The last I heard, she was in Bakersfield, California, but I doubt she's there now. Just look out for her, please. She's cunning, smart and she's ballsy."

"Did you marry her?"

"We got married during a toot, Mother. She was already pregnant. After she had the baby, I had to stay with her. We were both, well...kinda strung out, if you know what I mean. Sorry if this causes you any embarrassment."

"What does she look like? I mean, you know, she is my daughter-in-law."

"She looks like a bitch."

"Okay, what does a bitch look like?"

"She's kinda chunky, long blonde hair dyed, a pretty face and huge tits with tattoos of butterflies on each one, plus tattoos of eagles on her ankles. She rode with a gang of bikers before she met me."

She checked her watch and changed the subject. "Bowen, I've got you an attorney, a good one. His name's Woodard. He'll be representing you..."

He interrupted, "Mother, don't waste your money. I need a lawyer in L.A., not Miami. I've already waived the extradition hearings here and they're transporting me this week sometime."

"Oh dear."

Shrouded in shame, he gazed into his mother's eyes, then looked away. "I'll probably be gone a long time, Mother."

"Is it true, son? I mean the drug charges and...?"

He pulled the receiver from his ear, looked over his shoulder then back to his her. "I can't talk about it. Not here."

"Maybe,...well, you know,... too bad,... your father knows a lot of important people..."

"My father? Please, Mother. After what I just did to him? Besides, I hate my father. I wouldn't ask my father for a morsel of food if I was starving to death."

"Oh, Bowen, I'm so sorry..."

"What is there for you to feel sorry about? Nothing is your fault."

"I'm just...just sorry that it couldn't have been different for you. So sorry. I love you Bowen, with all my heart."

"I know, Mother."

She didn't mean to stare, but her glass-eyed gaze gave Bowen a sense of uneasiness. Lost for words, she removed a tissue from her purse and blew her nose. Bowen looked everywhere in the room but at her. Then she remembered the incident of eleven years past and tried asking a question that always had preyed on her mind. "Remember, Bowen, a long time ago when we were taking a flight to the Virgin Islands to go fishing? It was for your twelfth birthday."

"Oh yeah, sure. I remember."

"Remember when you started chasing after that woman...?"

"Yeah, I remember."

"I was wondering..." She hesitated, still pondering, still doubting, afraid of his answer. "I was wondering, you know, if it was reversed, and..." *Bowen, if you were with Yvonne and it was me you spotted, would you have charged after me like you did her?* She looked into his eyes and saw it was not something he wished to answer. "Never mind."

He shrugged.

"What's with that little shell you gave Jamie? I remember you had that years ago."

"Yeah, well, I got it in the Keys, a long time ago."

"Must mean a lot to you."

"Uh huh."

Then she dared ask. "Ever hear from Yvonne?"

His eyes alerted, startled by her sudden aplomb, embarrassed that she could read through his thoughts. "Nope. Never. I was going to ask you."

There was another long pause. She hesitated a moment and asked, "Why, Bowen?"

"Why what?"

"Why did you run off? Eight years, disappeared. Why?"

A guard tapped Bowen on the shoulder as she looked up at the wall clock. Time was up. Bowen raised a finger to ask for one more minute, then brought the phone back to his ear, peered through the glass and said, "Mother. I didn't kill that store clerk. I had nothing to do with it. The other kid surprised me when he pulled out a gun and then, well, I was just so scared. I..."

"That's it? That's why you ran off?"

"I knew the police were on to me, and..."

"Bowen. There was no murder."

The guard tapped him again on the shoulder, but he sat stunned at what he'd just heard. "Yes there was, Mother, I was there."

"That store clerk never died, Bowen. The police said they only wanted your statement as a witness against the shooter. The clerk knew you were not involved, that you tried to stop the other kid. He gave statements in your behalf."

He gawked in disbelief as the guard laid a firm hand on his shoulder. Without saying another word, he hung the receiver, shuffled off and disappeared behind a door just as he had each time she dropped him off at his father's house.

"Oh, my son, my son."

* * *

Stuffed inside a small trash can next to the mini-bar, the lead story of the Palm Beach Post read:

MAYOR RESIGNS, CONCEDES GOVERNOR'S RACE

In an uncustomarily terse message, Lloyd B. Ramsey resigned as Mayor of West Palm Beach effective twelve noon this date, then sent a similar memo to the Secretary of State saying he was pulling out of the gubernatorial campaign for "personal reasons."

It appears that Mr. Ramsey has gone into some kind of self-imposed exile as he cannot be reached at home nor through any of his usual contacts. Sources also tell us that Barbara Ramsey, the wife of the mayor, is no longer residing with Mr. Ramsey, but she could not be located either. Thus, in a bizarre twist of events starting from the moment young Bowen Ramsey appeared at the now-in-famous pep rally for the mayor, the governor's mansion appears to be a sure thing for Lieutenant Governor Henry Stallworth.

From an Embassy Suites room in upstate Florida where he registered under the name *Robert Jenkins,* Lloyd Ramsey fumbled through a pocket full of crumpled notes trying to organize his thoughts and keep a lid on his gradually eroding sanity. He was uncustomarily alone, no support staff, no servants, no woman, no entourage, just his scotch and a body twisted with nerves. One week had passed dodging media, a week in which no one heard from Barbara, not her friends or family, not even the hit men. Finally, his trusted henchman spotted her returning from a trip to the Bahamas with a strange gentleman. She would remain under surveillance until the time was right. The mission would surely be complete by the next morning. He needed a strategy. How could he handle this and portray himself a grieving husband whose wife disappeared into obscurity, nowhere to be found? Ah, yes, Stan...the police chief, Stan Heller...*where is that number?*

"Hey there, Stan, uh,... Lloyd Ramsey here."

"Mr. Mayor, what a surprise. Boy, are people looking for you."

"Look, Stan..."

"Are you all right sir?"

"Yeah, yeah. Look, uh, Stan, I haven't got too much time...don't believe everything you read, okay? I need you to do me a favor...."

"Well, sir, that depends on what the favor is."

"Look, Stan..."

"The way the political climate is at the moment, I'd be crazy not to let everyone know your position."

"My position? How can you know my position?"

"Caller I.D. sir."

Shit! "Look, Stan, whatever you do, don't tell anyone where I'm at, you hear? Godammit, I gave you that fucking job, so show me a little loyalty, okay?"

"What's the favor, Mr. Mayor?"

"I'm worried sick about my wife, Barbara. Haven't seen hide nor hair of her since she walked out on me a week ago Tuesday. How 'bout you take a missing persons report?"

"Missing Person? Barbara? What makes you think she's missing?"

"Cause she is, dammit. No one's heard from her, and ...well,

she's my wife. You know I can't come to the station like any
ordinary citizen so do me a favor and take this fucking report.
And that's an order."

"Order? Uh, the last I heard, you aren't a mayor any longer."

"Sorry, Stan. You're right. I'm just asking, like an old friend.
Please do it. Please?"

There was a long wait as Lloyd jiggled the ice in his glass.
"All right," replied the exasperated chief. "Give me the information. I don't know how I'll handle this, but...go ahead."

Thirty minutes later, Lloyd was on the phone with his private office secretary screening the barrage of incoming calls,
mostly from the media which he refused to answer. He figured
he would lay low a few more days, then travel to Maui until
media intensity calmed down. He trusted Sally McGowan, a loyal
employee and sex servant for ten years, more than any other
human on the earth.

"Who?" Lloyd asked, inquisitive.

"A Mr. John Spiegal, an attorney from Miami. Wants to talk
to you. Says it has nothing to do with the media mess."

"John? No shit? We just had dinner last week. Give me
his number."

As he laid back on the bed in his underwear sucking a scotch
and soda, Lloyd called his old chum and occasional adversary,
and exchanged some cordial remarks. John Spiegal and Lloyd
had served on the same state citizen review panel years past and
became good friends and fellow members of the same country
club in Ft. Lauderdale. "What's up John?" he asked, tersely.

"Well, Lloyd, you know we're good buddies and all. My office sent in a thousand bucks to your campaign."

"Godammit John, will you get to the point?"

"Well, I know you're going through a lotta shit, Lloyd and I
hate to add to your problems..."

"Hell, what's one more. Let's have it."

"Normally, I'd just have the papers filed and then served..."

"Well...?"

"But, you and I, well we go back a long way, Lloyd, and I
thought I'd be up front from the get go."

"What is it, godammit?"

"I have this new client, Lloyd. It's a suit, naming you as

defendant."

Lloyd sat up on the edge of the bed and flung his arm in a tirade. "Me? You're kidding? Now, what the fuck..."

"It's a woman with a slew of allegations...mainly alienation of affections, fraud, causing pain and suffering...and so on...."

"Jesus Christ, John, I need this like a hole in the head. Who's your client?"

"Laura Rosenthal."

Lloyd lowered the receiver and reflected on the image of his hippie son appearing at the political rally, accusing him, destroying his political career, then his untimely arrest before *the boys* could get to him first. He took a long breath until he heard John Spiegal speak again. "Lloyd, are you there?"

Lloyd sighed. "What does she want?"

"Twenty million and to see you ruined for life."

"What? Jesus Kee Reist! I don't fucking believe this! You're not taking the case, are you?"

"Lloyd. Does a bear shit in the woods? I hate to tell you old buddy, but this is a lawyer's dream case."

"What is she accusing me of?"

"Oh well, you'll get it all at discovery anyway. She says you had her wrongly confined to a mental institution when you claimed she was hallucinating about catching you in bed with another woman, and that you wrongfully withheld her child from her for a number of years, that your behavior led the child into drug abuse, and so forth. Frankly, Lloyd, there's a ton of allegations here. If you want, I'll send you..."

"Bullshit, John! She was fucking crazy, a crazy hillbilly who wanted my money..."

"Lloyd..."

"...She never caught me with another woman...she was certifiably nuts, and that's provable..."

"Lloyd..."

"That bitch was nothing but a college whore who I unfortunately knocked up... she oughta be glad I married her, for Christ's..."

"Lloyd..."

"Well, godammit, John, what is it?"

"Lloyd, she has proof."

There was a lull. He looked at the receiver, then asked, "Proof, what proof?"

"The woman she caught you with, she's alive a ready to testify as her witness."

That little bitch. That fucking bitch.

chapter twenty-six

"When will I get to see my daddy, Grandma?"

"Well, Jamie, it's hard to say. Right now, he's got some important problems and he had to go back to California."

"That's where my mommy lives. California."

"I know."

From the back seat of the speeding Lincoln Town car, twelve-year-old Grace gazed at the sea of mangroves lining Highway One, wondering when they would ever arrive at the first bridge into Key Largo. It was another perfect warm and sunny day. "Mom, how much longer?"

"We'll be in Islamorada in another half hour. Be patient, okay Grace? Hey, kids, look up there. An eagle's nest atop the pole."

"Wow, it's big," exclaimed the boy.

Laura was in a mild state of euphoria, perennially smiling as she headed for those treasured Florida Keys, her daughter and grandson now forming the nucleus of her family. It seemed the clock had turned back to 1969 when Bowen was a five-year-old, so distant, so unreachable. Now, she had his son with her, loving her, sharing. Though Bowen might be facing prison, she figured it was a blessing in disguise, God's way of giving her a second chance to prove herself a worthy mother to a little boy. Three fishing poles extended from the open rear window creating a whoosh of air throughout the car. Little Jamie's blond hair blew violently. Grace wore a Florida Gator baseball hat.

"Mom, are we going to fish from a bridge, like those people over there?" asked Grace.

"Well, I think it's better from a pier. A long time ago, Bowen showed me a nice pier. I'll try to find it." Often, Laura glanced to Jamie and saw how engrossed he was in the journey, gazing from the window fascinated with the bridges, boats and the expanse of oceans on both sides of the islands.

As she crossed over into Tavernier Key, Laura remarked, "This is so familiar. I remember being here with some police officer, a detective. Let's see, his name was, it was..." Stopped in traffic, she wracked her brain trying to remember the name of the Monroe County investigator who entertained her for dinner with his family the night she found Bowen. "Grady. That's it."

"So?" asked Grace.

"I betcha I can find his house. It's on stilts."

"A house on stilts? Wow!" exclaimed the excited boy.

She made several turns on and off the highway, snaking through the labyrinth of residential streets until... "There is it. The one with the Real Estate sign out front. I wonder."

It seemed newly painted, white with blue trim with a mailbox in the shape of a dolphin. In front of the garage, a bright red Chevy Blazer was backed in. The southeast breezes whipped her hair as she trotted off toward the door. "Stay here a minute, kids." She remembered his strong, tree-trunk arms, the awe-shucks drawl, the loving family, his deep devotion to his job. She figured he had retired by now.

Suddenly, the door flung open. "Hello, may I..."

He was barefoot, wearing cut-off jeans and a tank top. It was as though time stood still, like she was standing in his presence the day Bowen was a runaway pre-teen. Twelve years hadn't aged him beyond the loss of a few strands of hair. She looked into his Sean Connery eyes and smiled. "Hello, Sergeant. Remember me?"

"Well, I'll be, of course I remember, it's...Laura...Laura...?"

"Laura Rosenthal," she replied, extending her hand.

"What a great surprise, won't you come in?"

"Well, I've got my daughter and grandson in the car."

"Grandson? You're a grandmother? My, you don't look like a grandmother. Please, have them come in too. I've got a litter of Shepard puppies they'd like to play with. Well...I'll be..."

It was a delightful encounter. While the kids remained in the garage with the pups and their docile mother, Laura and Grady sat in the screened-in Florida room sipping lemonade and looking out over the channel, watching boats pass, listening to the squawk of seagulls, smelling the salt air, reminiscing the search for young Bowen, catching up on the tragic life of the boy who ran away in 1976. Grady listened intently seemingly thrilled with the unexpected company. Laura realized she was talking only about herself, so she asked, "And how is your lovely wife? And the kids. Will she be home soon?" She saw that the question brought sadness to his eyes. "Oh goodness. I'm sorry. Is anything wrong?"

"Ovarian cancer. Ali's been gone three years now."

"I'm so sorry."

"She was a brave lady, but it was too far gone. I retired last year, after marrying off both daughters, so I figured it's time to sell the house, stop living in the past and start a new life. Living here, well...it's like waiting for Ali to come in the door any moment."

As he spoke. so relaxed, confident, so inexorably masculine, she caught herself fantasizing his embrace, his breath next to hers, imagining the unbridled passion, how it might really feel, passion she hadn't experienced since she was twenty-one years old. His lips were honest and sensuous as he proudly talked about his boat, his new grandson in San Diego, life as a widower. She listened and drifted off. Passion, she mused, and love. She'd had both in her life, but never at the same time. Entranced, she continued listening until Jamie broke in exuberantly, "Grandma, when are we going fishing?"

Grady leaped to his feet, laughing, "Fishing? You want to go fishing?" Jamie nodded excitedly. Grace was amused by his animation. "You kids see that boat there? Well...by golly, just before you got here, I was about to go fishing. But, doggonit, I didn't have a first mate or anyone to steer the ship. How 'bout you be my first mate? Okay?" Jamie pranced like a happy poodle, nodding, laughing. "And you, young lady, you can be by helmsman, whadaya say?"

"Sure, I guess so. You're funny."

And so it went. Laura made a call to Miami and assured Paul they would all be home before nine that night. Strains of a Mozart opera blared in the background. She hadn't experienced such feelings of excitement since the day she graduated college, a day that burned in infamy, a day which forever impaled her heart with a mistrust of happy feelings. But for now, she would seize the moment. For these few hours, there would be no drug addicted Bowen in jail, or an invalid husband, no wretched Lloyd Ramsey, no Stanton School, only she and the two children she loved and an old friend. That's all he could be, a friend. For the fleeting thoughts of desire shrouded her with guilt. She was a married woman with a devoted but crippled husband waiting at home, needing her. How could she feel these things? She dared not to fantasize. Not Laura.

Then again, why not? Why not savor this one oasis in her arid life? Who would know? Her imagination was running wild, wondering what life's bounty may have yielded if she could only turn back the clock. She embraced herself, smiling as she watched the children open to him like flower petals to the morning sun. She saw him enjoying this as well and it gave her a sense of well-being she hadn't felt in eons. But it wasn't the chit chat over lemonade, or his inexorable masculinity, or his sense of humor with the kids. It was when she stumbled into his arms stepping on to the thirty-two foot Chris Craft that she realized she was still capable of falling in love.

* * *

When Laura pulled into her driveway at ten that night, she roused both kids from a deep sleep and shuttled them into the house. She was surprised to see that Paul was still up watching a local news program. Consuella was sitting on the sofa nearby knitting a baby garment. As Laura leaned over to give her husband a forehead kiss, he remarked in a low, slurring voice, "How come you're so red? Look at you. And you smell like you've been sweating."

"How are you feeling, darling?" she asked, dismissing his question.

"How am I feeling. How am I feeling. How do you think I'm feeling? I'm a half man sitting here waiting for my family to join my life..." His eyes remained fixed to the television.

Consuella shrugged her shoulders, gathered her things and departed for the evening. Laura smiled and took Paul's good hand, sat near him and gave him comfort. "I'm here now, Paul. I'm here for you. I'm sorry I'm late."

"Where have you been? It's after ten." Drool formed at the left side of his sagging mouth. Laura used a tissue to dab.

"We all went out on a boat, fishing. The kids had a great time."

"Oh?"

"Grace was so excited, she caught two dolphins. Look, I have the filets here, for dinner tomorrow. Jamie caught a bonita, but I kinda helped."

"Uh huh."

"We took lots of photos. Can I get you a brandy?"

"Already had a brandy. Two actually. Isn't he supposed to be in bed now?"

Wearing pajamas, Jamie wandered into the den for a goodnight kiss, rubbed his eyes, crawled upon her lap and put his loving arms around Laura's neck. "Sweet dreams, little darlin," she said, embracing him. Paul glued his eyes to the television.

"Grandma, it was so fun. I wanna go again."

"We will, Jamie. Now go on to bed, hear?"

"Thank you. I love you." It was a moment for which she could have gladly died and gone to heaven. "And thank Mr. Culpepper too."

"Go on now, Jamie. I love you."

After Jamie disappeared into the hall, Paul turned toward Laura and asked, "Who's Mr. Culpepper?"

"Oh? He was the captain of the boat." *Please Paul, don't ask any more questions.*

"What boat?"

"The boat we chartered, you know, to go fishing." It was the first lie she ever told him.

Paul turned back to the television where a breaking news story caught his attention and turned up the volume.

"*...now on the scene where a police officer has been shot. Two suspects are in custody after a harrowing chase through the farm regions of Dade County. Two more officers were injured after they collided head-on into each other. The suspects are identified as Pepe Hernandez and Fabio Vasquez. Hernandez is an Ecuadorian immigrant who came to the United States one year ago. Little is known about Vasquez. Neither have a police record in* *the U.S. We are still trying to learn what precipitated..."*

* * *

At nine-twenty that night, a Metro-Dade cop named Danny Cook and his rookie partner, Linda Meyer, were returning from a back-up call to the Mikkosukee Police deep in the remote Everglades region of the county. He was in his nineteenth year. She, her third week. They were under pressure to avoid overtime so they sped up along the Tamiami Trail in hopes of getting back to their station before ten. It was an overcast night, the sky infinitely black with nary a star to be seen.

Cook was telling cop stories when they spotted a vehicle several hundred feet ahead with only its parking lights on emerging from a dirt road. As it turned east toward Miami, the headlights came on. "Strange," remarked Cook. "What's he doing way out here this time of night? There's nothing out there but alligators and it ain't huntin' season."

"Looks like a van," answered the female cop.

Cook accelerated, caught up quickly and turned on the overheads illuminating the sprawling sawgrass and rows of Australian Pine in a spectacular array of rotating blue and red lights. The dilapidated blue van pulled to the side and stopped. A magnetic sign was attached to each side which read, "Andy's Carpet Cleaning Service."

Following procedure, Officer Cook pulled the cruiser to the rear and right of the suspect vehicle, thus giving the driver a poor visual position. Still following procedure, Officer Cook ordered his rookie to call in the tag and give their location to the dispatcher. No one emerged from the vehicle so Officer Cook followed procedure by having his partner stand back by the police car while he approached the driver. However, Officer Cook failed to follow procedure this day by not wearing his bullet proof vest. The moment he came within view of the driver, a *pop pop pop* sounded from a nine millimeter, then a squealing of tires, a pillar of dust and a blue van fishtailing in the darkness speeding toward Miami. Stunned, rookie Linda Meyer found herself standing alone on the side of a darkened road with her wounded partner lying in a crumpled mass on the pavement, moaning. It was surreal, as if a dream, all so sudden, a simple vehicle stop altering the lives of so many at the blink of an eye. The humid air was silent again as she stood in the dark wilderness with her bleeding partner. Her heart raced, pulse pounding her head. It could have been her as well, alive and happy one moment then dead in an instant. The squawk of the police dispatcher bit into the silent wilderness, snapping her into consciousness. Not following procedure, she lifted her radio, depressed the mike button and screamed like an untrained civilian. "Help, please! Help! My partner's been shot! Can you hear me? Oh God, please, help!"

Minutes later, after involving eight police units on a wild chase through south Dade County, the blue van ended nose down in a watery ditch. Two Spanish aliens fled from the rear door but were captured, resisted arrest and earned themselves a set of swollen eyes and bleeding mouths. Once cuffed, they were taken to the county jail for processing and interrogation. No gun was found. Blood smears of blood were found on the floor of the van.

At the scene, Officer Linda Meyer went catatonic, was relieved of duty and taken to Jackson Memorial Hospital's psychiatric unit for evaluation. It would be an abrupt end to a very short police career. Officer Cook was shipped to Baptist Hospital Emergency Care Center with two slugs in his liver and one in his shoulder.

The next morning, homicide investigator Charles Harbolt organized a search of the dirt road where the van was first seen emerging from the vast sea of grass. A police academy class was mustered plus a dozen detectives, uniformed officers and a K-9 unit. The deployment worked. Two hours into the search and a half mile into the wilderness, the partly decomposed body of a Caucasian woman was found in a watery clump of sawgrass, her right arm ripped from its socket by an alligator. One full day under the Florida sun and there would have been nothing left, no trace, the obvious intent. The woman had been shot five times with a nine millimeter. The bullets recovered at autopsy would later match up with the three taken from Officer Cook. The victim's name was Barbara Ramsey.

chapter twenty-seven

Dear Bowen,

I hope this letter finds you in good health if not in spirits. I think of you every day, languishing in that horrible place with nothing to look forward to but endless confinement. I cannot imagine the horror. But we must try to find some good in this for you are still young, and there is a future for you, I know it. If you are sent to the penitentiary, think of it as a chance to start over, to be clean of drugs and to get an education to help you in later years. There is still time for happiness for you, Bowen. God knows how much I want for you to be happy. You will, someday, I know it.

Once you have secured the attorney of your choice, have him call me and be sure to let him know, or her, that money is not an issue here. I will pay all your legal fees. If it means he can get you a more lenient sentence, it will be worth it.

I will try to come out to L.A. for at least one visit before your trial. If I could, I'd be there every day. But it is not so easy, especially with Paul and his condition, then Grace, my job and of course, the love of my life, your little Jamie. Bowen, he is such a wonderful child. Thank you for allowing me the privilege of caring for him in these troubled times. You should know that Zena has called long distance asking to talk to Jamie. I assume she knew about your arrest here in Miami and that Jamie would be with me. She said she had heard good things about me, so for that, I thank you. Of course, Jamie was very hesitant. She sounded nice on the phone and quite unthreatening. She told me she was glad to know that Jamie was in good hands. But I'll still remember what you said, and I'm being cautious.

You might be happy to know that your father is in serious

trouble on a number of fronts. For certain, his political career is over, (thanks to you) and his wealth may be nearing an end as well. There's a big surprise in store for him. According to the news, he has been in hiding ever since you were arrested. He can't lie any more. The snake.

If there is anything you need which is permissible under the circumstances, please let me know. If there is nothing to write about but the pain in your heart, I'd be happy to get any mail from you. You can tell me anything, Bowen. I am your mother. I'll always be your mother.

I love you son.

Mother

Bowen folded the yellow legal paper and placed it under his mattress. He looked up to the ceiling toward the naked light bulb, then to the stainless steel toilet in the corner being shared by his cell mate, a prodigious black man named Richie, waiting to stand trial for three counts of house robbery. If convicted, it would send him up for life in California as a three time loser. Richie didn't talk much. He much preferred a brother for a cell mate.

It didn't take long to adjust to the stench of body sweat pervading the thick, musty air, the resounding echoes of metal against metal across dimly lit catwalks, voices shouting, pleading, demanding, voices unanswered. It was a virtual hell on earth. Bowen had been in jail twice since his first arrest in L.A., once in Arizona and another in Nevada, both times for misdemeanors, both times bonding out under an alias before they could identify him as a fugitive. He felt resigned now, like this was a place he belonged after all, a place that would protect him from his own self, no longer panhandling, no longer craving a fix so desperately he would kill, no longer trudging his little boy through the gutters of America. He pondered his life and thought how stupid he was to have run off at sixteen, thinking he was in trouble for a murder that didn't exist. He pictured Bedrosian again, the friendly store clerk, happy to know he was still alive twelve years later. If he could only take it all back. It seemed nothing mattered any more, that his pathetic life was over before it ever got started. If he only had a different father. If only he could have had his mother. And he wondered about *Mommy*, where she was, if she was still alive and how ashamed she would be of him now.

Richie stood up from his lower bunk, gave Bowen an egregious glance, turned to face the bars and unabashedly pulled his shorts to his ankles baring an enormous set of black genitals. No sooner than he sat upon the commode, he unleashed a rancid bowel movement causing Bowen to nearly vomit. Moments later, the guard rapped a stick on the bars and called out, "Ramsey, come on, it's shower time boy. You too, asshole."

Four unadorned shower heads served four bathers at a time. They were required to bring their own soap, no rags, no sponges. Bowen unwrapped his towel, turned on the hot water and stood facing the wall oblivious to three shower mates watching his every move. He savored the fresh feeling of water beating upon his head, thinking, picturing his son, his future living like an animal in a cage.

"Ain't she pretty now?" Echoed a soft male voice.

Bowen turned. They were in a semi-circle, facing him in touching distance. The tall white man with gaping teeth grinned while the two blacks, including Richie, peered lecherously at his body then glanced over their shoulders to check on the guard. The white man smiled again and leaned near to Bowen's face. "Take a good look, sweetie. Ain't they just about the most magnificent cocks you've ever seen?"

Instantly, he knew. He had heard about such things but never once imagined himself like this, trapped, frightened. No, petrified. Bowen backed away toward the wall, looking for any avenue of escape. He could scream his lungs out but they would surely kill him. So he decided to make a run for it. It was to no avail. In what seemed like a flash, one had him in a choke hold so tight he could not speak. Then a deep voice.

"Be nice to Richie now."

chapter twenty-eight

Laura was working on an education grant when Maggie unceremoniously opened the office door holding a bouquet of mums, carnations and daisies with a single white rose in the center. "Doctor, um...I think you have a secret admirer."

"What the...?"

"I'm sorry, Doctor, but...uh, where should I put them?"

Laura knew, but asked anyway. "Who sent them?"

"There's a card, right in there."

Slightly embarrassed, she took the arrangement, excused her secretary and examined the note.

Thank you for a wonderful day. Grady.

She felt her cheeks burning as visions of his ruggedness swirled through her mind, the placid ocean, long talks at the helm while children played and fished, and the wonderful laughter, as though they were all a family the way families ought to be, the way *it* ought to have been. Jamie gravitated to him like a moth to the flame and he in return seemed to love her children. It was pure fun, real fun. Grady was a fun man, a sincere man, and so damned sexy. Just as her imagination crossed the fantasy bridge, her conscience awakened and doused her with a sense of shame. An hour later there was an unexpected call.

"Hi. Did you get the flowers?" asked the husky, awe-shucks voice.

"Oh, Grady, they're beautiful, but why..."

"Just my way of saying thanks."

"Really, I can't accept, ...well, you know, ...it was very thoughtful but...."

"I'm coming up to Miami next week to take care of some business. I thought, if you weren't doing anything, we could do lunch. Just an innocent lunch. I understand your position."

Oh yes, yes, I would have lunch with you at the top of Mount Everest, I'll meet you in Venice, at the Fountainbleu, anywhere, anytime, you fill my heart with such passion like I've never felt before... "I'm afraid not, Grady. I mean, thank you for asking, but it wouldn't be right."

"I have, um, some arrangements to make for my grandchild's future schooling. Perhaps that would make it strictly business?"

She smiled and blushed, and pulled the receiver from her ear. "Well..."

"Well?"

"I'd really love to Grady, but ...maybe some other time. I just wouldn't feel right."

"I understand." There was a long pause as they each listened to their breathing. His voice sunk deeper. "I really enjoyed our time together, Laura. I've thought about you every moment of every day since."

Oh dear. "I enjoyed it too, Grady. Too much, I'm afraid. Thank you again, but I must go."

* * *

Clad in Bermuda shorts, a Bahama hat and Armani shades, a far cry from the dapper politician people would recognize, Lloyd Ramsey stepped aboard the *Cuba Libra*, a thirty-four foot fishing boat moored at a remote marina along a tributary to Ft. Lauderdale's New River. It was three in the afternoon, hot and humid. Paranoid, like a thief, he looked furtively left then right, making sure he went unnoticed then entered the cabin where the muscular Cuban extended his hand.

"Forget it, Rudolfo! Is anyone else here?"

"No señor, we are alone."

A naturalized American born in Havana, Rudolfo Munoz was raised fatherless along Miami's Calle Ocho where the Spanish culture had long displaced any remnants of the old southern city. After quitting high school, jobs were easy to find for a young, handsome Latino with almost no accent, especially further north into Broward and Palm Beach Counties. It was through Lloyd's boat captain, Quincy Eiland, that he met Rudolfo seven years prior. He had no police record and willing to do anything as long as the price was right, a perfect bodyguard for someone of Lloyd's gregarious nature, strong, dependable and passionately loyal.

"What in the fuck went wrong, Rudolfo?"

"It was a fluke, boss. Bad luck, what can I say? They did everything right, but who knew that a cop car would come down the road at that very moment. One day was all we needed."

"What do you mean?"

"One full day out in those glades and she would never have been nothing but alligator shit, never found."

"If the cops connect them bastards to you...."

Rudolfo waved his hands, then poured two glasses of vodka. The aroma of stale black beans and onions pervaded the little cabin. "Not to worry, Mr. Mayor. I only speak to those guys by phone, we are never seen together. No one can connect us."

"Godammit, they better not, 'cause if they connect you, they connect me and I've got enough goddam problems right now."

"Don't worry, don't worry, they made it look like a robbery. They're not stupid." Rudolfo threw some food scraps overboard, then changed the subject. "Are you here to pay?"

The question stunned Lloyd. "What? Pay you?"

"Mission is accomplished, Mr. Mayor."

"What do you mean? The mission was all fucked up."

"You asked, I delivered. Your wife is dead, your fortune is intact. I expect my fifty thousand. And their fifty thousand will go toward their attorney's fees. Right now, you should consider that a good investment."

"All right, all right. I'll have it for you at the end of the week. Right now I have another mission for you."

"A similar mission?"

"Yeah, you can say that."

Rudolfo paused, lit a wood-tipped cigar and faced his boss. "Excuse me, sir, but are you fucking crazy or what? I don't think you realize how hot we are right now. Go shopping elsewhere and don't come around here again until things calm down. Either that or do it yourself."

"Look, she's..."

Rudolfo raised his finger to lips, hushing the distraught lawyer. "No no, don't even tell me. I don't want to know."

"But...look Rudolfo..."

"No, you look, Mr. Lloyd Ramsey. You better pull your brain
out of your ass. You are a public figure and in case you forgot,
your wife has been found murdered, sir. Got that? *Your* wife
who you love and cherish, right? So you better come out of hiding and get back to that fucking pink fortress of yours, forget
your political losses and act like a grieving husband. The cops
gotta be looking for you to ask questions and if you don't put on
an academy award performance, you'll be a suspect, then your
Cuban bodyguard will be a suspect." Rudolfo leaned into Lloyd's
eyes, without blinking. "Then I'll have to kill you."

Lloyd removed his wide-brimmed straw hat and wiped his
brow.

"I go down? You go down. Got that?"

"Yeah, yeah, yeah."

"More vodka, Mr. Mayor?"

chapter twenty-nine

She had moved a chair next to the recliner to be near, to offer a display of love and loyalty. He deserved no less. It had been too long. Her presence was like a warm bath on a cold night and she knew that. It was rare that they did this any more, sit together, chat, hold hands, watch intellectual channels on television, discuss issues and solve the world's problems. Usually, he was asleep early or she was tending to Jamie or Grace, or whatever consumed her for the moment. But tonight was special, an anniversary of sorts, celebrating the day he timidly asked her on their first date. It was a day they celebrated more than their wedding anniversary.

Jamie was in bed. Grace was upstairs watching her own television. The telephone was quiet. Paul had his precious Laura all to himself.

He wiped the drool from the corner of his mouth and mumbled. "Dukakis oughta concede. Unless they catch Bush molesting kids, he don't stand a chance." Paul aimed the remote toward the forty-five inch television. "They don't make Democrats like they used to, Laura. Now it's all media glitz, sound bites, hairdos. It's all crap!"

"Bush had to know about the Iran-contra deal, don't you think Paul?"

"Who gives a damn. They're all crooked one way or another. We just get all worked up over who gets caught because it's big news." Paul started waving his good arm,

They watched quietly for another half an hour, sipping brandy until, out of the blue, Paul murmured something inaudible.

"What was that dear?" she asked.

Staring at the television, Paul mumbled again.

"Sorry, darling. I can't make out what you're saying."

His eyes seemed to glaze, unfocused. Then he said, a bit more clearly, "If you want, uh... a divorce, it's okay."

She could hardly believe her ears. "What?"

"I'll understand."

With sadness, she leaned to the husband who had looked after her in her darkest moments. Here he was still loving her, at whatever cost. She placed a tender hand upon his arm saying, "Oh, Paul. How could you say that. You know I..."

"I could go to a nursing home. I'll be fine."

"You're not going to any nursing home my darling. I'll always be here for you, you know that. How could I possibly want a divorce from a husband who I love and who has taken care of me like you have?"

"I'm a burden."

"Paul, I'll tell you when you're a burden. I think you know better."

"You're still a young woman. How can you love..." Paul began shaking his good arm, then patted his chest. "....this!"

A lull followed as Laura wrapped her arm around his neck and laid her head upon his shoulder. "Remember, Paul, when we were in San Juan? How beautiful the water, so clear. We walked along the beach with shoes in our hands, talking for hours until the sun set. Remember how we felt then like we had arrived at utopia and all those past nightmares were behind us. We were only married a couple years then but I felt like I'd been with you all my life. You were so worried that I only saw you as a father image. You said I was needy, that I was impressionable and too trusting, too honest. You thought I would get on my independent haunches one day and find some handsome tennis pro or something and run off. And I said to you, `Paul, I will never leave you, no matter what troubles would befall us. Never!' Remember, you're the one who said I was so honest. Well, I'm certainly not going back on my word because you got sick."

He nodded without expression, glanced at her a moment, squeezed her hand, then aimed the remote at the television. "Look, there he is again," he mumbled, changing the subject.

The nightly news showed a host of reporters at the driveway of the well-lit Ramsey mansion in Palm Beach with the former mayor himself standing before a grouping of microphones and an attorney by his side. Lloyd Ramsey was reciting a prepared statement.

"... this horrible crime. Please bear with me in this moment of grief. Barbara was a wonderful and loving woman, and I intend on seeing that the killers are brought to justice. I returned home as soon as I heard the tragic news, and have been helping detectives with as much information as I can. Thank you..."

Laura whispered, "He's such a liar."

They watched as a disheveled Lloyd Ramsey turned around to walk back to his mansion when suddenly, from his right side, a brawl erupted. It appeared that Lloyd was pushing, then punching a man in a suit. From there it disintegrated into a slugfest with men hitting and punching, wrestling, screaming epithets. Still on camera and totally confused, the well groomed news commentator tried desperately to discern the origin of the fight, but ended up taking an errant punch to the right jaw. When it was all over, a commentator from another station boasted the scoop.

"...reliable sources that it was a process server who approached Mr. Ramsey with a notice of a law suit. We don't know the nature of the suit as yet nor the allegations, but as soon as we have it, we'll pass it on. The saga of this former mayor and gubernatorial hopeful continues to make big news. We'll keep you posted."

chapter thirty

One Week Later

Dear Mother,
   This place can only be described as hell on earth. I am
at the point now that I want my lawyers to offer a plea
so I can get out of here and up to the state prison. With a trial,
I'm looking at another six to nine months in the county jail. I'll
never make it. I figure I'll be convicted anyway, so I may as well
get it over with. I really can't go into it all in a letter, but believe
me when I tell you, I'd rather be dead than in this place. If you
could send a few dollars for my jail account for cigarettes and
other personal items, I'd appreciate it. Don't worry too much,
I'll be all right. Please give Jamie a hug and kiss for me. I do
miss him, very much, but I know he's in good hands. Sorry for
any trouble I've caused you.

Love,
Bowen

* * *

Her watch read ten-fifty. A staff meeting was in fifteen minutes so she called Maggie in to have her arrange a Friday plane
reservation to L.A. So long as Consuella could stay at the house
for two days, Paul would be fine. Consuella was a friend as well
as a nurse, unwaveringly reliable and so good for Jamie. But
Bowen was needy and it was a chance for her to be there for
him, to show he was truly loved and to offer the brightness of a
mother's smile in the midst of his despair. It would be the first

time she'd see him since he was taken to jail in Los Angeles.

Next, she phoned John Spiegal who told her that the wheels were in motion and her first steps toward bringing Lloyd Ramsey to his knees were under way. No hearings were scheduled in the next few days and he saw no reason for her not to travel.

The staff meeting was held at the conference room and lasted its usual hour. Laura was efficient, holding to a strict agenda and watching the clock. Every so often, Wilma caught her day dreaming and snapped her back into the milieu with a gentle nudge. She mulled over Bowen's letter, wondering what he meant... "...*this place can only be described as hell on earth.*" She knew that jail was no picnic, but why this?. *Why would he forgo a trial? His lawyers cost him nothing. If there's any chance at all at a lesser sentence...*

Laura declined lunch with Wilma and returned to her office so she could call the California attorney. As she arrived, Maggie bared a curious expression, rolled her eyes and nodded toward the office door. "Uh, someone's waiting in there for you, Doctor Rosenthal."

"Oh really?"

She flung open the door, and stopped. Her face turned a hot pink. He stood up from the leather chair, smiled sheepishly and shrugged his shoulders with his hands in his pockets. "Um...I was just passing by, so I thought I'd..."

"Grady, well, uh, how nice. Such a surprise. What are you doing here?" Concealing her anxiety only made her more nervous. He looked marvelously casual in white cotton pants, a blue open collared shirt and white loafers with no socks, like he was ready to take her for another voyage n the high seas.

"My, I'm impressed," he said gesturing toward the decor. "Didn't realize you were such an intellectual." She stood to the side of her desk and watched him scan her array of framed photos. "Hey look, there's Jamie. And there's Grace. Sweet girl. Those pictures must be of Bowen. Am I right?" She nodded. "Must be a long time ago. He looks about sixteen there."

"I don't have a recent picture of him. Grady, you didn't answer my question."

"Ah, and Paul. A nice looking man. A good man."

"Yes, he is. He's a wonderful man. Grady, I have so much

work to do..."

Oh, I was passing through the Grove and thought I'd just stop in and say hello. Wanted to see your school and all. I was thinking about, um, arranging private school for my grandchild's future. Perhaps we could talk about tuition and such, over lunch?"

She felt herself blush, then she glanced at Paul's picture. "Oh, I don't think so Grady. Thank you."

"Strictly business, okay? We'll just go down the street here."

"Well..."

"So it's a go?"

"Well..." *Okay Laura, you know how you feel about this guy, so don't be a fool. Put a stop to it now. Tell him no, no way. You're married. This business thing is merely a sham. Forget it. You cannot do this.* "Well, all right. But only because it's about business." It was a dangerously warm feeling to see how happy he was. "But separate cars, okay? Just tell me where, I'll meet you there in, say, twenty minutes. That all right?"

"The Taurus. It's on the left as you enter the Grove. Great. See you there."

* * *

Just a few miles away, a slick homicide detective named Charles Harbolt had assembled a dossier on two South American immigrants charged with the murder of Barbara Ramsey. It was airtight, weapons recovered, matching bullets, robbery motive, fleeing the scene of the crime, gunpowder residue on their hands, a smoking gun case if there ever was one. The only thing missing was a confession. They wouldn't talk.

Something gnawed at the investigator. His lieutenant said to move on and take other cases, but there was more underlying in this one that needed clearing up. It was all too coincidental. The crumbling career of a frantic Lloyd Ramsey followed by rumors of a split between the victim and the former mayor made him all too curious. If it were a simple robbery, why kill her? And why go through the trouble of dumping her out in the glades? Getting these guys to talk was fruitless, so he did the next best thing and researched every soul in Dade County that either might be related to. Sure enough, they both had relatives who were illegal, Colombians and Ecuadoreans smuggled into the country on fishing boats that moored in the remote docks of the Florida Keys. One of these was Pepe's father, an escapee from a Quito jail.

So on this sunny Thursday afternoon, Harbolt located an elder Spaniard named Felipi Hernandez, who happened to be Pepe's father, at a coin laundry in downtown Miami and had him brought to the homicide office for a little chat. Harbolt was not at liberty to question Pepe without an attorney present unless, of course, it was at Pepe's expressed desire. So the next best thing was to allow Pepe a visit with Dad. No harm in that. They were left alone in a small interrogation room for a half an hour until Pepe knocked on the door, asking to speak to Harbolt.

"I can't talk to you without an attorney, Pepe, unless you insist," said the detective.

"Please, I don't want to see my father sent back to Ecuador. They will put him in prison."

Figuring he was buried under mounds of evidence and that cooperating might save him from the electric chair, Pepe Hernandez gave Charles Harbolt a full statement about the murder, saying it was not spawned from a simple robbery. Rather, it was a contract hit and the primary contact was a Cuban named Rudolfo Munoz, bodyguard for Lloyd Ramsey.

There was much yet to be done.

* * *

It was a delightful tryst. The Taurus was a landmark steakhouse a block from the Coconut Grove Playhouse and a staple for regulars who enjoyed finer tastes the district had to offer. As usual, Grady was lighthearted, funny and comfortable to be with. The topic of his grandchildren's schooling barely lasted thirty seconds as she sipped a glass of Merlot and he a bottle of Budweiser. For lunch, they had hors d'ourves, oysters Rockefeller, escargot and cold shrimp. Time passed rapidly, like an hour was ten minutes, laughing and talking about everything from family, politics, fishing and what was most on his mind, the future. He knew there were boundaries and he dared not step beyond his limits. He also knew there was a chemistry between them and somehow, neither one wanted to lose that, even if it went no further.

"The weather looks great for fishing this weekend, Laura, if you'd like to bring the kids."

"Sorry, Grady, I'm visiting Bowen in L.A. Maybe some other time."

"Sure. I understand. Well then, perhaps another weekend."

"Yes. Perhaps." She felt so transparent as he peered deep into her eyes. They shared the same unspoken desires, but they had to be left unfulfilled, unquenched, for there were higher priorities. As always, higher priorities. Always, *barriers.* It was best to be candid, so she asked, "Grady, I hope I'm not giving you...you know, wrong impressions, am I?"

He thought a moment and smiled. "No Laura, you're not giving me wrong impressions. I think my impressions are quite true. We just can't act upon them."

"Then why...?"

"I don't know. I just have a sense, a feeling, like it would be a mistake to walk away. A sixth sense, you might say. Honestly, I want nothing from you, nothing you can give me."

"I can't give you anything."

"I know. But when I saw you on my doorstep with those two kids, it was like a rebirth to me. I haven't felt those kinds of feelings, well, since a long time. I guess I'm afraid to let go."

She looked at here watch again. "My God, Grady, I do have to get back to work."

"Yes, well, um...perhaps we can discuss my grandson's education a little more in detail next week, say, on Wednesday? Same time, same place?"

"Grady, please..."

"Strictly business..."

"We'll see. Okay. I had a wonderful time. Thank you."

"I'll walk you to your car."

Her Lincoln was parked in the rear under a ficus tree. As she buckled her seat belt, Grady caught her completely off guard, leaned into the window and pressed his lips to hers. At first, she pushed at his shoulder in a meager attempt to resist, then succumbed to a gush of passion she hadn't felt in a lifetime. Her heart raced as she grabbed his head, breathing so deeply that she caught herself gasping on his mouth, pleading for more, never wanting to let go, sensing her dormant sexuality rise like a volcanic eruption. She imagined his body next to hers as the fantasies ran wild. Then, a moment of sanity rushed over and she pushed him away. Flushed, disheveled, she could not look into his eyes though he remained looking into hers.

"I'm sorry, Grady," she said, smoothing her hair into place, panting.

"Hey, it's me that should be apologizing."

"Uh, maybe it's best, uh, that you don't come around. I mean, I like you and all but I can't do this. I really can't do this." Still, she wouldn't look at him.

"Yeah. I understand. I'm really sorry. I shouldn't have..."

She started the engine, glanced up at his wonderful face for a fast second then drove off, leaving him standing on the macadam alone, hands in his pockets.

*   *   *

Wrought with guilt, Laura came home early that afternoon and dismissed Consuella until the following morning. Paul was in his recliner with the mute button engaged on the television so he could listen to Mozart arias. Grace was in her room mired in a school project while little Jamie romped about the house playing with toys. She sensed Paul burning a hole through her brain as though he could see Grady's reflection in her eyes. She sat close and held his hand, asking questions about his day, then told him she was flying out to visit Bowen the next day.

Jamie toddled up to the both of them and asked for a drink of juice. "Sure, honey. I'll get it for you," she replied.

Jamie remained at Paul's side, twiddling with a small top while Laura fetched the glass and returned with a broad smile. "Grandma, are we going fishing again in the Keys?" he asked bluntly. Paul stared straight ahead.

"Well sure, I suppose someday, Jamie."

"Is that why Mr. Culpepper came to the school today?"

The question jolted her. For a moment, her heart raced until she gathered herself. She stiffened, then looked toward Paul, hoping he wouldn't remember the name.

Jamie continued on. "I saw him leaving in that red car."

"Uh...Jamie, sure, we'll talk about it another time. Okay? Go on now."

She smiled nervously and took hold of Paul's good hand once more but he pulled it away. He glanced briefly up to Laura and mumbled, "Charter boat. Right?"

"Very good, Paul. Um, he's trying to pre-pay an enrollment for his grandchild. I guess he was impressed with the school."

"Uh huh."

chapter thirty-one

It was a bright and sunny Friday morning as children of all ages began arriving at the rear playground for another day of school. With her suitcase in the car, Laura arrived at the office early to prepare her agenda and write letters before the day's interruptions began. Jamie was playing with a group of pre-schoolers while teachers and counselors tended to the surge of students into the park. Jamie broke from the ring of children to fetch an errant ball when suddenly, a distant voice caught his attention.

"*Jaaaamieeeee.*"

Jamie looked around, saw no one and started back toward the circle of kids playing dodge ball.

"*Jaaaamieeeee.*"

He looked around once more. Amid a snarl of parked cars, he noticed an old brown sedan parked near the gate and a woman standing with the driver's door open. She wore white pants, high heels and very red lipstick. For a second, he thought he recognized her but her hair had always been yellow, not black.

"Jaaaamieeeee?" she called, waving her arms. That's when he knew her for sure. "Come along, Jaaaamieeeee."

Jamie looked back and saw the teachers busy shuffling children into the building where he was supposed to be. Then he looked back again at the familiar lady with black hair next to the brown car.

"Jaaaamieeeee."

Jamie was a good boy, always taught never to disobey.

* * *

"Oh my God, oh no!"

"I'm sorry, Doctor Rosenthal."

"This is terrible, terrible. It can't be. Hurry, we have to go look for him."

"It happened just a few minutes ago."

"Maggie, call the police. Now! Oh my God. My God!"

"Yes ma'am." As Maggie turned, Wilma rushed into the office.

"Who was supervising out there? Wilma, did anyone see...?" Trembling now, Laura paced frantically, her eyes darted wildly.

"Yes, Laura. Miss Turnbright spotted an old brown car near the back gate with a woman driving. Before she could do anything, it was too late."

"She can't be far. It's got to be his mother. Her name is Zena. Zena Ramsey. I'm going out there to look for her."

"Please, Laura, you can't. He's gone at least ten minutes already. It would be like looking for a needle in a haystack. We don't even know which way she turned."

"Wilma! That's my grandson!" Then she lost it. "Why didn't Turnbright do something for Christ's sake?"

"Take it easy Laura, we'll find him."

"That's Jamie! My grandson! We've got to find him! She's a child abuser! Oh no...poor Jamie!" Laura exploded in a fit of crying, gasping, screaming pathetically. "Jamie, my baby. Oh no, not again, not again, please!"

"Please, Laura," Wilma snapped, trying to calm her friend.

Laura darted out the door and raced to the parking lot toward her car. An entourage of teachers led by Wilma followed. As she entered her Lincoln fumbling for her keys, a Miami police cruiser pulled in. Laura leaped from her car screaming, "Officer, my grandson has been kidnapped. Please, it just happened!"

The officer held her arms to settle her. The crowd swelled. "Please ma'am, be calm and talk to me."

Hyperventilating, Laura sputtered information about the old brown car and the missing child, pleading all the while to hurry. Time was passing. "Who has legal custody?" asked the cop.

"Well, uh, my son Bowen, but he's in an L.A. jail right now."

"Oh," remarked the young cop. "Oh yeah, I know who that is. On TV. That's Lloyd Ramsey's son. Then the missing child is the same kid that was on the news..."

"That's right! Please, officer, put out a bulletin or something."

"But I need to know if the mother has custodial rights?"

asked the officer. "It makes all the difference in the world."

"Why?"

"Because if she has custody, she can't be arrested for kid-naping her own kid."

"Zena and I share equal guardianship. We never were divorced."

Laura's brain went into high gear. "Look, officer, at this point we don't know for sure who took him. He's just missing, okay?" Please, find him!"

"I'll take the report, ma'am."

Visions of blank walls and wailing echoes in the night rushed through her mind like the day her son was torn from her life. Just as Bowen disappeared in 1964, the horrible scenario was repeating itself like a nightmare coming true. Her chance at redemption was riding somewhere in the seat of an old brown car up a Florida highway like a phantom in the night. Now Jamie was doomed unless she could rescue him.

It portended a bad day. Secretary Maggie came running out to the parking lot, shouting, "Doctor Rosenthal, please, come to the office..."

"Maggie, can't you see...?"

"It's your husband, please. It sounds important."

"Maggie, he's always calling. Right now we've got a crisis here."

"I think you have another one, ma'am."

While everyone remained with the police officer outside, Laura rushed back to her office gasping for breath and took the call. "What's the matter Paul?"she asked, frazzled.

His voice was strained and slurred as always, but this time there an air of panic. He spoke slow and painfully hesitant. "Lloyd Ramsey called here, Laura."

"What? What did he want?"

"Something about pictures, Laura. I don't understand."

Laura looked out the window and saw another police car arriving and thought about the precious time that was being lost. Now this. "Pictures? What the hell is he talking about? And why is he calling you?"

"Pictures, in some car. Taurus restaurant?"

Her eyes widened, her chest pounding. *Oh my God! No. No! I was followed. He was there? He hired a...* It all came together, memories of that incredible kiss, caught in her single moment of passion in twenty-five years. She felt like the blood had drained from her head. "Paul, tell me, what pictures? What did he say?"

"What's going on Laura? Tell me."

Oh please God, not Paul. Don't make him a victim. "That's what I want to know. What did he say about pictures?"

"Very strange. Wants me to tell you he's got them. What is that rat up to, Laura?"

I knew it. I knew it. I should never have gone to lunch. She checked the window again where a detective car was arriving and felt compelled to be there yet torn between two crises at the same time. Paul's body may have been paralyzed, but his mind was not. "Paul, it's nothing. Everything's all right. Look, there is a problem here with Jamie...."

"Well, why is he calling me?"

"Because he wants to hurt me, Paul, and he can do that through you. I'm sorry. I should have known what a bastard he would be."

"Are you still going to L.A.?" he asked, slurring.

She checked her watch, then Bowen's letter which still lay atop her desk, then out the window once more at all the hubbub. "No, Paul. I'll, uh, I'll be home. Please rest, and don't worry."

That dirty rotten son-of-a-bitch!

Laura rushed outside and to the officer who was issuing a bulletin over police radio with the full description of Jamie, the woman and the brown car. "She'll be heading for California," she exclaimed, nudging at the officer. "I know it. Can't the High-way Patrol find her?"

"We're doing all we can ma'am," replied the starched of-ficer.

As thoughts of little Jamie being tortured and beaten raced through her mind, a Federal Express van pulled into the lot and stopped several spaces from the police car. A heavy-set woman emerged with a large white envelope, approached the crowd and asked for Laura Rosenthal.

"That's me," answered Laura, dismissingly. "Please, drop it off with my secretary inside."

"Sorry, I need for you to sign."

Frustrated, Laura snatched the envelope and saw the return

address was from L. Ramsey in West Palm Beach. *Oh no, oh no.* Stepping away, she excused herself and opened the package. Two copies of eight by ten inch photographs were taken at a perfect angle, the first showing them leaving the restaurant together and the other a zoomed shot with his head inside her driver's window, Grady's lips to hers, her eyes closed, fingers combing his hair. Laura's heart dropped to a new abyss. A small note was attached, typewritten: *"Is it worth it?"*

She wondered if Federal Express might be on the way to Paul as well. Without uttering another word, she raced back to the office to phone Consuella, instructing her to hold all mail from Paul. It was a close call.

"Did he open it yet?" Laura asked, raising her voice in a near panic.

"It just arrived, Mrs. Rosenthal. I signed for it."

"Do not give it to Paul, Consuela! You hear me? Do not give it to him!"

"Yes. Please settle down, I won't give it to him. I promise. Are you all right ma'am?"

Laura was trembling now as she fumbled for John Spiegal's phone number. Once again, Lloyd had emerged the victor, she thought to herself. She had to stop the litigation before it went any further. Control was rapidly eluding her as she screamed at the top of her lungs, "Maggie godammit, where is John Spiegal's number?"

The door burst open as the secretary rushed in trembling, rocked at being yelled at. She saw Laura's hair standing out from her head, her eyes ablaze. "Here it is, Doctor," she answered frantically.

"Call him! Call him right now godammit! I can't see the numbers on the phone without my glasses, so call him now!"

Wilma overheard Laura's screeching voice from outside, darted in and grabbed her by the shoulders, pleading, "Laura, please calm down. We'll find him. They will find Jamie."

Laura screamed at Maggie once more, "Get that fucking bastard on the phone now!"

"Uh, who, what fucking bastard, Doctor?"

"Mayor Lloyd B. Ramsey! That's who! Get him on this phone!"

"Yes, Doctor."

The office was now filled with curious staff members as Wilma chased Laura pacing frenetically, babbling, hers arms flailing in a vituperative tirade. "Laura, stop it, you're working yourself into a...well, Laura, you seem psychotic. You have to calm down!"

Psychotic? Psychotic? How familiar. Who would she go to now? There is no psychiatrist like Paul Rosenthal. There is no husband to confide in. No parents. They were dead. Jamie was gone. Bowen, gone. Always, Bowen was gone. The walls seemed blank again as they grew closer, narrower, blank faces and night howls echoing in her brain. The air was thick and musty, like that horrible closet, barely able to suck a single breath. She didn't understand why they all were staring at her, those bug-eyed people in her office standing in a circle.

"Let me alone," she demanded, recoiling, sputtering saliva, grimacing, pulling at her hair.

Maggie stepped inside once more, frightened, then exclaimed, "Sorry, Doctor, um I can't seem to reach anyone."

"Get away! Get away!" she hollered, extending her arms, visualizing men in white coats approaching her, one holding a straitjacket, the other grinning. "Get away! Get away! No...please...no!"

Wilma watched pathetically then knelt down as Laura collapsed to the floor, wailing. She motioned for everyone to clear the office and close the door while she cradled sobbing Laura to her bosom and rocked her like a baby. "It's all right, Laura. It's going to be all right."

"Please! Please," she cried over and over. "Don't let them take me. Please."

"Don't worry Laura, I won't let anyone take you."

"Bowen needs me. I want my baby."

"I know, Laura. I know."

"He needs me. I'm his mother. Please, please, don't let them take me."

"I'm here, Laura. I won't let anyone take you."

"I love my baby."

"I know, Laura. He loves you too."

Laura wept until she could hardly breathe as Wilma sat on the floor near the desk, holding her head to her bosom, rocking, stroking her hair and letting her know she was truly loved.

chapter thirty-two

The Following Week

Lloyd Ramsey paid no attention to the speedometer as he topped his Mercedes over ninety miles per hour north bound on the Florida Turnpike. The buxom redhead to his side puffed a cigarette and let the smoke escape through the crack in her window. Opal was a divorce client in need of money and unable to pay her legal fees any other way but to entertain her lawyer at a weekend rental cottage in the Ocala National Forest. For Lloyd, she was heaven sent, tall, voluptuous, uninhibited, half his age and most important, amoral. It was certainly better than hiding like a hermit in his mansion as he had done for the last ten days.

The turmoil seemed to be settling down. As expected, the private investigator's photos of Laura's tryst with Grady Culpepper paid off and the civil complaint died an early death, much to the chagrin of John Spiegal. The media was focusing more on current issues and no longer stalked him for daily headlines. And the two Latinos charged with the murder of his wife were safely tucked away in the jail. His ruined political career notwithstanding, all else was back under control. He had his wealth and his women. What more could he want?

His fantasies raced as fast as his Mercedes as he reached over and gently took her hand. "Come on, Opal " he said, grinning lecherously. "Touch it." She extended her hand, grabbed his crotch and saw that he was already hard. "Take it out," he said. "And kiss it."

"While you're driving?" she asked.

"Yeah, cool. I like that."

Opal accommodated, performing her specialty, paying no attention to truckers beeping horns each time Lloyd passed a semi. Suddenly, as though awakened from a trance, Lloyd alerted to the sound of a siren blaring from behind. He checked the rear view mirror and saw blue lights flashing. "Get up," he ordered. "Sit up, godammit. I'm being pulled over."

"Okay, okay, take it easy."

It was quite a task slowing to a stop, driving with one hand while tucking his love tool away with the other. After he stopped, Lloyd stepped briskly out toward the trooper who was radioing in the tag number. The paunchy middle-aged cop donned his Stetson, emerged from the cruiser and asked to see a driver's license. The officer hesitated and peered curiously at Lloyd, looked at his license and then into his eyes once more and asked, "Aren't you...?"

"Yeah, Officer that's me. I'm sorry. I know I was speeding. I promise to slow it down."

"Well, I'll be," he chuckled. "Uh, that's all right, sir. It's a pleasure to meet you."

"Thank you, Officer, if you need to write a..."

"Hey, Mr. Mayor, sorry about all those problems I read about, I was goin' to vote for you."

"Well, thank you, Officer."

"And that poor Mrs. Ramsey, so tragic, I'm so sorry. You've had it pretty rough."

"Thank you, thank you." *Just leave me the fuck alone and go away.*

The cop leaned closer. "At least they caught them spics. I hope they fry all three of them motherfuckers, I surely do. No mercy."

"Thank you, Officer. May I go now? Or are you going to write me a ticket?"

"Naw, no ticket, sir. Just take it easy, heah? Here's your license. Have a good day."

As Lloyd started back to his car, the trooper's words replayed in his head. "*I hope they fry all three of them motherfuckers.*" What? He ran back and caught the cop before he entered his cruiser. "Hey, Officer."

"Yes sir?"

"What was that you said? About, you know, three motherfuckers?"

"I said I hoped they fry all three of 'em."

"Did you say three?"

"Well, yeah, why?"

"I thought they had only arrested two men."

"Oh, you ain't heard? Just came out in the news this morning how they picked up another fella, a Cuban. I'm surprised you didn't know about that?"

"No, uh, I've been busy. What did they say?"

"Well, it was just on the hourly broadcast. Big news around these parts. A Cuban, what else? Some guy named Rudolf, or somethin' like that. Charged with first degree, just like the others."

Oh shit!

"Well, I'm sure you have plenty on your mind, sir. You have a good day, and good luck."

"Right, Officer. Yeah, right."

Opal saw an instant change as he ignored her like she no longer existed. Without uttering a word, he hung a two-wheel u-turn at the next exit and headed back south, peering intensely out the window, chewing fingernails, eyes darting, wondering how Rudolfo could have been nailed with the killing. *One of those rotten little Spaniards must have talked.* And if they talked, Rudolfo surely wasn't going down alone. He made that very clear. Thoughts of a prison cell caused his heart to pound like a sledgehammer, his mouth dry, palms wet. He was oblivious to his nubile friend sitting nearby as she reached over and grabbed his crotch, startling him.

"Leave me alone, godammit! Keep your fucking hands to yourself."

"Geez, sorry. I was just tryin' to... What the hell got into you all of a sudden?"

"Shut-up. Can't you see I'm in a problem here?"

"Over speeding? And why are we turned around?"

"Shut up."

"Okay, okay. Just get me home, all right? Geez. You crazy or somethin'?"

Lloyd snatched a cell phone from the glove box and punched a set of numbers. He checked his speed, making sure there was no reason to be pulled over again. "Hello, Sally?... Yeah, I heard all about it... What? What was that? Who...?... What did they want?... Oh no. Shit!... No, I'm, not coming back to the office... Don't tell them anything. Don't even say you talked to me, you hear? ... Yeah, I know it sounds serious... No, godammit, Sally I didn't do it, I swear... Look, I need you to book me a plane reservation... Today, now, as soon as..." Lloyd checked Opal once more and figured it was time to talk privately. "Hold on a minute, Sally." He laid the phone atop the dash then pulled the car to the shoulder and stopped.

"What are you doing now?" asked Opal.

"Get the fuck out."

"What?"

"I said get the fuck out. Now!"

"Are you crazy? We're in the middle of nowhere."

Lloyd then reached across the buxom redhead, opened her car door and shoved her shoulder.

"Out, I said!"

"My God, you are serious. I don't believe it!"

Each time he shoved, she slapped him frenetically, screamed and scratched at his face. He exited, walked around to her side, grabbed her hair with both hands and pulled violently until she lay on the macadam crying. Quickly, he tossed her purse and overnight bag out the window and squealed off.

"Sally, you still there?"

"I'm here Lloyd."

"What detectives? What do they want?"

"Harbolt. Says he needs to talk to you to ask some more questions."

"No way. Not now. Look, get hold of Jerry Blumenthal. He's a friend, and a good criminal lawyer. Have him find out what's going on then call me on my cell phone. Book me on a flight to Maui under my other name. I gotta get away, to think. If you can't get me out of West Palm book me in Ft. Lauderdale or Miami if you have to, but get me the fuck out of here. Today!"

"Which other name, Lloyd?"

"It's the only other I.D. I've got. Harcourt. Wendell Harcourt. Just like at the hotel in New Orleans. You remember that, don't you, Mrs. Harcourt?"

He knew he had caused her an embarrassing grin. "I'll come

with you if you want, Lloyd."

He ignored her. "And send me my passport, overnight mail, to my Maui address. Look Sally, I need you right where you are. Listen to me. Except for Jerry Blumenthal, tell nobody anything! You got that? You have not spoken to me., you don't know where I am, just play dumb. That should be easy enough. Let me know as soon as you have reservations made."

"Sure, Lloyd. Sure. But these detectives, they seemed pretty serious. Said they would check back with me later today."

"Fuck 'em!" he said, just as he pressed the off button.

An hour passed. Lloyd had just walked out of a costume boutique in Boca Raton and heading to his car when the cell phone rang.

"Hey, Lloyd, Jerry Blumenthal here."

"Jerry. Did Sally tell you...?"

"Lloyd, I've spoken with the state attorney. I'm sorry, but you have to turn yourself in."

"What? Turn myself in? For what?"

"They have warrants. Murder one. The Cuban rolled over and has accused you of master-minding Barbara's killing. They're looking for you."

"Oh my God."

"Lloyd, right now I don't know anything about the case. I'll try and get you bond but for now, I can only urge you to come to my office. Use the back entrance. I'll make sure there's no press, nice and quiet like. I'll do all I can to..."

"Right. Yeah. Right. Just hold on there Jerry. I gotta think. I don't know. I'll call you back in a few."

"Don't do anything foolish, Lloyd."

"Right. Right. Bye Jerry. See ya later."

Shit!

* * *

Hours became days and the long days eventually turned into a week without any trace of Jamie. Investigators worked around the clock putting out notices, following leads, searching, interacting with California police but without any luck. The boy remained on the missing list.

It was the first time she had taken off from work in two years and staying home was becoming painfully dull, plagued with agony thinking about the fate of poor Jamie. Though Paul appreciated the gush of attention, Laura felt idle and unproductive and constantly worried about her grandson as well as the state of affairs at the Stanton School. But Wilma had insisted.

Grady Culpepper had called her office at least once a day, leaving messages with Maggie. "I think that man really likes you, Doctor Rosenthal," she said. But Laura resisted, knowing a relationship with another man would only complicate matters more. He was an untouchable fantasy and for that, she was thankful for it awakened the dormant woman within her. She dared not return his calls. It wasn't Grady she didn't trust, it was herself.

On the home front, it was as though there had been a death. Things were not the same without Jamie's big brown eyes lighting up the home every morning and every night. Though he lived there barely a month, he had brought a spark to an otherwise depressing household. Every so often, she would alert to the sound of a car door outside or catch herself checking the clock to see if it were time for his vitamins or his bath. How reminiscent these feelings were, a child ripped from her life, feeling helpless, knowing the boy was now worse off than ever. Each hour of every day, she wondered where he was, how he was being cared for, if he were being beaten, fed properly, nurtured and loved. Bowen's words echoed in her mind. *Zena just wants him for the welfare money. She beat him almost every day, just for drill. She never wanted a boy. She never showed him any love.*

It was a cool and breezy October morning as Laura took Paul for the daily walk along the shoreline at Matheson Hammock Park. He was customarily quiet and pensive as she casually pushed the wheelchair toward the small marina where a dozen small boats were moored. She smiled at the sounds of children, then looked over to see a woman lifting her boy into a fishing boat. She thought about Jamie and Grace and the outing with Grady Culpepper. As her thoughts digressed, she felt another pang of guilt, then stopped to sit on a bench. They chatted a moment until she felt the vibration from the air pager.

The digital displayed her home number.

"What is it, Consuella?" she asked from the pay telephone at the dockmasters building.

"Oh Mrs. Rosenthal, they found Jamie."

"What?"

"Yes ma'am."

"Oh, that's wonderful. Thank God. Is he all right?"

" He's fine. The officer just called. He's with his mother, back at her place in Bakersfield."

"Oh thank goodness. That's wonderful. I'm so relieved. Have they arrested her?"

"Uh..." A long silence followed Laura's question.

"Consuella, tell me, did they say what they were doing? The police?"

"Well, uh, they say there is nothing they can do. She is the mother. They say Jamie is fine, that he belongs with her."

Laura glanced at Paul in his wheelchair gazing ahead, paying no attention to the pelicans pandering for handouts from behind a docking boat. In her heart she knew the law was on Zena Ramsey's side, but she could not accept that. Not again. She knew what she had to do. "Consuella, can you stay with Paul for this weekend?"

"Of course, whatever you need."

"Good. Call and book me on a flight to L.A., as soon as possible. Any flight. I'm going out there to rescue Jamie. Somehow."

"Yes ma'am."

"Don't say anything to anyone. I'll also see Bowen while I'm out there too."

Laura returned to the bench next to Paul and acted casual and attentive though her mind was consumed with the abuse Jamie was enduring. Paul noticed her checking her watch every two or three minutes. Finally, he dribbled and waved his good hand, "Come, Laura. Let's go home."

"Are you sure, Paul?"

"What was that all about? Did Bowen escape from jail?"

She chuckled, "No no. Jamie's been found. He's fine. His mother has him back in California." He looked away, a tacit sign he knew what was to come. She placed her hands upon his.

"I have to go there. You understand, don't you Paul?"

He looked off to the distant horizon, hesitating, trying to collect his shattered thoughts. He took a long breath, then, "Well, you better get going then. Don't worry about me."

"Thank you, Paul."

He remained quiet throughout the fifteen minute drive home. As they arrived in the driveway, Paul pointed a finger in the air and sputtered the words, "She won't let you have him."

She smiled, happy to know that his inner most thoughts were of her. "I'll get him back, Paul. Somehow, I'll get him. I promise."

"You'll need money. You'll need lots of money."

"We'll see."

As she helped him from the car, he tapped her purse. "Bring a pocket tape recorder. You never know."

"You're always thinking, aren't you Paul?"

"Well, that's all I got that functions."

chapter thirty-three

Just before dusk and long after Laura was on her way to California, Grace and two school chums were in the yard practicing a cheerleading routine while Consuella watched from a lawn chair. Paul had earlier retired to the bedroom to listen to CDs using his earphones. He was not feeling well. Not uncommon.

When they finished, the girls charged into the kitchen for sodas and snacks, then into the family room for idle chatter, laughing, fun and games. Consuella enjoyed being accepted within the young coterie of females more than half her age.

After they all settled, Grace sat on the edge of the sofa with an announcement. "I'll tell you all something if you promise not to say anything," she said, blushing.

"Sure. Come on, come on."

"We won't tell, honest," replied the other.

Consuella smiled.

"Well," Grace said, "You won't believe this. Dave Markham asked me to be his date at the junior prom."

The two friends screamed then leaped from their chairs holding their cheeks, laughing. "Are you kidding?" one asked.

"Grace ...you mean *The* Dave Markham, the middle school track star, eighth grader, voted best looking...*that* Dave Markham?"

Grace nodded. "I just have to ask Dad. He said I couldn't date until I was older."

"Well, like it's not really a go-out date or nothin', I mean, you guys won't be alone like in a car. Maybe your mother could convince him, after all, it is a prom. And you're only a few months from thirteen."

"I don't know. I have to be so careful with Dad and all. I'll see what Mom says."

"Gee, just that he asked you, is Wow! Boy, won't you be the envy..."

"I bet if you ask your Dad right, he'll make an exception."

The familiar jingle of a small bell sounded from across the house. Before anyone had a chance to respond, another jingle. Consuella strode dutifully to the master bedroom but stayed only a few moments. When she reappeared into the family room, she motioned to Grace. "Your Dad wants to see you."

"Me?"

Consuella shrugged.

Grace skipped across the living room, anxious to get back to her friends before they had to leave. It was depressing entering the darkened chamber where her father lay half paralyzed, like going from bright sunshine into a dismal fog. When she stepped through the door, he was wearing his head phones propped against a pillow, waving his good hand in the air. "Come, Grace," he mumbled, removing the equipment from his ears. "Mozart," he said informatively. As though Grace cared.

She neared the bed. "Yes, Dad. Are you all right?"

"Not too good honey. Here." He pulled his hand from under the covers and handed a brown padded envelope to his daughter. His speech was slurred and labored. "Do me a favor honey. Put this in the mailbox."

Paying no attention to the envelope, she looked at him quizzically, wondering why he didn't just give it to Consuella. "Sure Dad. Is there anything I can get you?"

"No, thanks."

She studied him a moment, then figured it was a good time. "Uh, Dad, can I ask a favor?"

He waved, a signal to keep talking.

She took a breath. *Here goes.* "I know it's something that, well, you're probably going to say no, but...can I go to the junior prom?

He didn't hesitate. "Yeah, sure. You go. Have fun."

She couldn't believe her ears. "A boy named Dave Markham wants me to be his date. He's fourteen."

He waved again. "You have fun. Go."

"You mean it?"

He waved again.

"Oh, Daddy, thank you."

There was a pause while neither spoke a word. Feeling awkward, Grace turned to walk off when he called out, his voice straining, "Hey, aren't you going to give your Dad a kiss?"

She bent over to press her lips gently on his forehead. "Sure, Daddy."

He touched her face. "My daughter. My sweet daughter. I love you."

"I love you too, Dad. Uh, my friends are waiting. Is it okay...?"

"Go on. Mail that. Do it today," he said. "Help me put this contraption back on my head."

"Sure." The faint sounds of music emanated from the headphones. He started to mutter but she interrupted. "I know, Dad. Mozart."

"Go."

Grace rushed exuberantly back to her friends to relate the good news. They all screamed and laughed and jumped like little children until Consuella reminded her it was getting late. Grace asked her friends to walk with her to the mailbox, then they burst into a sprint. They all laughed and frolicked as Grace quickly inserted the envelope without ever checking to see the name of the addressee.

chapter thirty-four

Departures were a half hour late due to heavy rains from one of those South Florida squall lines. Exasperated travelers moaned and groaned but the Delta agents at the gate were powerless to do anything. Laura decided to pass the time with a glass of Chablis at the Flight Deck Bar where she brought pen and pad to organize her thoughts in preparation for Jamie's mother. This was a desperate journey, one that would impact the life of that little child forever. She had to convince Zena it was in her best interest to let Jamie come back with her. If that didn't work, she would call social service authorities and initiate an investigation. Surely, if they checked thoroughly enough, they'd turn Jamie over to her. Perhaps Paul was right. It could all be handled with money. She could offer her whatever welfare paid her now. It didn't matter so long as she had her grandson back.

She was anxious, as well, to see Bowen and wondered how he was holding up. It would be the first time since his transfer to the Los Angeles jail. Bowen, Jamie, Zena, Lloyd, Paul, Grady, Wilma, so much to deal with, so many players complicating her life and all she ever wanted was peace and love.

Suddenly, her ears alerted to the television sets surrounding the lounge. The female news anchor was mentioning that name, *Lloyd B. Ramsey*. At first she thought she wouldn't care, that he wasn't worth a second of her attention, but she couldn't resist.

"....are combing the area for any signs of the former mayor and gubernatorial candidate, Lloyd Ramsey. The arrest of his bodyguard, Rudolfo Munoz, in connection to the murder of Mrs. Ramsey has sparked speculation that the former mayor may have had additional information. While investigators are not committing themselves officially, inside sources tell channel seven news that a warrant has indeed been issued for the arrest of Lloyd Ramsey for first degree murder. According to these sources, one of the three suspects arrested has implicated him. Stay tuned, Mr. Ramsey continues to make big news."

Well, well. Look at that. The son-of-a-bitch has finally hung himself. Poor Barbara. She should have known better.

Two hours later her head was resting on a small pillow in seat 35C of the giant L1011, daydreaming, nodding off to the droning hum of the engines. Visions of little Jamie floated through her mind, then Bowen as a little boy, then Grace and Paul and Grady Culpepper. At thirty-one thousand feet over the Gulf of Mexico she felt at liberty to let fantasies roam wherever they took her, so she wondered how it would feel to be embraced by a man or to ever make love again, or to make love ever, for she wasn't sure if she had in her entire life. His arms, so strong yet so gentle, his voice deep yet soft, his eyes so sincere, such a man, *such a man*. But there had to be closure. She had to stop it before it went any further. She had to tell him in no uncertain terms there was no chance for them, ever. Her platter was full.

A pilot's announcement jarred her from a light sleep as passengers were watching the in-flight movie, *A Fish Called Wanda*. Her bladder dictated an emergency recess so she stepped to the front and waited impatiently outside an occupied lavatory. As she started toward the opposite aisle, the occupied switch turned to vacant. The door opened and a tall blond man quickly emerged with his head lowered. He was wearing glasses, a baseball hat and a thick mustache. Lights were low. As he turned toward first class, Laura glimpsed a triangle of small moles to the front of his right ear. She watched his gait curiously as he returned to his seat, then entered the lavatory. She sat on the commode wracking her mind. Something was hauntingly familiar about the arrangement of those moles. Then it struck her. He had the height, build, the shoulders, the gait. *Lloyd!*

My God! He's in disguise, on this plane. Wanted for murder. Lloyd Ramsey. Oh my gosh. What do I do? Where is he heading? I don't believe it. Oh Lord, what do I do? Did he rec-

ognize me? Then it occurred to her. *I've got him. He's trapped, and I've got him. I don't believe this. He's got nowhere to go. I've got Lloyd Ramsey. I've got him!.*

She exited the small compartment, stepped to the far right aisle and into the forward cabin to catch another glimpse. The back of the baseball hat could be seen at the second row, window seat. The aisle seat was vacant. He seemed to be staring out the window. A male flight attendant approached, asking if he could help her with anything. She thought quickly. "Oh, uh, yes," she replied in a whisper. "I have a bit of a headache. Wonder if you might have an aspirin."

"Certainly ma'am. Where is your seat? I'll bring it to you."

"35C." With her eyes steeled to the baseball hat, she ambled slowly back toward coach. The man shifted and turned his head slightly, enough for Laura to catch his profile. It was him! There was no doubt. Afraid he would recognize her, she raised a hand to her face and hurried back to her seat. *What do I do? What do I do?*

She checked her watch. There was another four hours remaining on the flight, no hurry. *Don't rush into this Laura. Think. Think.* She had to think. She could ignore him and take the easy road out, not get involved. No, that was out of the question. She had to do something. She was the only person on the flight who knew who he was. If she confronted him, there could be a scene. She couldn't trust her own emotions.

An idea hit. *Yes!* She removed a pen and slip of paper from her purse, wrote a brief note and folded it. When the attendant approached with two aspirins, she handed him the note saying, "That man down there, second row first class, left side by the window, wearing a baseball hat, well, he's an old friend. We haven't seen each other in many years. He doesn't know I'm on this flight and I'd like to surprise him. Please give him this, but don't tell him who it's from. Okay?"

"Yes ma'am. Certainly."

"And do you have a blanket please?"

"Of course ma'am."

* * *

His head wrought with migraine, engines droning, ignoring the laughter around him from movie watchers, Lloyd laid his forehead against the window, tilting the bill of his cap. He glanced at his watch every five minutes, praying to get this trek over with. For the first time ever, his life was totally out of control, a wanted man being hunted like a common criminal. *That rotten Cuban. I'd like to get my hands on him.* Petrified of spending one night in jail, he had no options other than running as far as he could and disappearing somewhere in the world. Others had done it. He could change his identity and live a comfortable life in anonymity. Money would do him no good now other than to sustain his self-imposed exile. Once he reached Hawaii, he'd continue on to another country, perhaps New Zealand where he had friends, people who he helped years ago. They owed him. There were other friends in the Phillippines. He had friends all over Europe, but he was going the wrong direction. Switzerland would be ideal. *Damn! Should have gone the other way.* Wilfried owed him a favor ever since he bailed him out of money laundering charges in Miami. Besides, he had a reservoir of cash there which the IRS and police knew nothing about. Yes. He had to find a way over to Switzerland.

The good life was behind him, at least for now. The mansion in Palm Beach would probably be taken over by his father and sold. His cars too. Ah, Father. What shame he must be feeling, the family name stained for eternity. Bah. Too late now. The mere thought of a stinking jail cell cloaked him with horror. He'd been in cells before visiting clients for a few minutes then out as fast as his legs could carry him.

He noticed movement in the aisle near him and figured it was time for another offering from the crew. Concerned he'd be recognized, he lowered his head and barked, "Another Dewars."

"Yes sir," replied the young man. "And I have this for you."

Lloyd looked curiously at the folded slip of paper being handed to him, careful not to glance up. "What's this?" he asked.

"I don't know, sir. It's from an admirer."

My God! Someone recognized me! Oh no. "There must be some mistake. Who is it from?"

"The party asked not to be identified," he replied, smiling.

Lloyd snatched the note and waved him off. He looked furtively around the first class cabin then sat back in his seat. His
hands started to tremble as he unfolded the paper. Written with
blue ball point pen, in printed capital letters, it read:

"YOU'RE TRAPPED - BASTARD"

His heart suddenly pounded like a jackhammer. He looked
at the note once more, wondering *who? Who? WHO? Could it
be a mistake?* His hands vibrated out of control, his entire body
trembled. There was nowhere to go, nowhere to run. Jail awaited
him once the plane landed unless he did something, fast. He
thought of pretending to brandish a hidden gun and try skyjacking the plane to Mexico, but that was risky. He might beat
murder charges, but he'd never overcome skyjacking. *Who sent
that fucking note? I've got to know!*

With the hat pulled low over his eyes, he rose, stood in the
aisle and searched for the young attendant who gave him the
note, but he was not around. Slowly, frantically, Lloyd made his
way toward the coach cabin, cruising the aisles, scanning left
and right, looking for anyone who might be familiar. Window
shades were pulled down to darken the cabin for the movie.
Nearly three hundred passengers were aboard, many children,
families, a pair of nuns, a congregation of black ministers, many
Hispanics, many watching the film giggling and laughing, some
sleeping under blue blankets. Three passengers were curled up
and completely covered. He was tempted to lift one end to see
their heads, but he dared not. He recognized no one. Finally he
spotted the flight attendant. His first thought was to intimidate
him and demand the author's identity. No. That would be a
mistake. *Can't show panic here. Can't draw attention to myself.*

"Say, young man..." said Lloyd, now standing in the forward
galley which separated first class from coach.

"Yes sir?"

"You know, I'm really very, very curious. It's quite important to know who sent that note."

"I'm sorry sir, but I made a promise."

Lloyd scowled and nearly blurted an expletive. "Please, it
is really important."

"I said I can't, sir. Later, if you wish, I will relay your concern."

Okay, I'll watch where you go.

"But not now. I'm busy. I suggest you take your seat."

Several minutes passed when the same flight attendant came over. He thought, surely, he was going to reveal the passenger's identity. Instead, he handed another note. "I'm sorry sir. I was asked not to reveal the party's name."

He opened it:

"GOT YOU BY THE BALLS, LLOYD"

His heartbeat surged once more, head pounding, face burning, body trembling out of control. Beads of perspiration dripped down his temples. *Godammit, who is it? It's got to be some citizen who just recognized me. I've got to change seats, gotta hide, somewhere. I can't stand a jail, no way, I'll go crazy. No, No! No! No!.*

He roamed the cabins once more searching, to no avail. An idea struck. He returned to his seat, tore a page from the in-flight magazine, wrote a note along the border then folded it.

" *Whoever you are, I'll make you a millionaire. Let's talk"*

"Please, give this to the party," he asked the flight attendant.

"Yes sir, but this is the last one. I'm quite busy."

Thirty minutes seemed like thirty hours as he awaited a reply from the anonymous antagonist. He turned periodically to see where the steward had been, where he was going, but it was useless. Finally, the young man returned with one more note and stated quite firmly, "Unless it is an emergency, this is the last time."

"Yeah, yeah, sure." He opened the third note hoping, praying.

"GO TO HELL"

Shit! He crumpled the note and threw it to the floor. *Okay. Stay calm. Don't panic. I gotta hide. I gotta hide. Where?*

Lloyd checked his watch one more time and estimated the arrival time in Los Angeles at 4:15, one and a half hours to go. One and a half hours to steel handcuffs and jail cells unless he could devise a plan. There was one chance. Planes usually begin their descent about thirty minutes before touchdown. That's when the pilot orders everyone seated with their belts fastened. That's also when the lavatories are all vacant. He'd time it to about thirty-five minutes before landing, enter one of the aft lavatories then wait it out until the plane landed and everyone deboarded. It was his only chance. Hopefully, no one would miss him.

At 5:02, forty three minutes before landing, the captain announced there were squalls over Los Angeles and the approach to the airport would likely be met with some turbulence. Lloyd didn't care. He had to hide. Before reaching the storm, he'd better scramble to the rear and vanish. He'd just wait it out. Minutes later, as he sat on the cramped commode with his pants on, another announcement blared from the female flight attendant.

"Ladies and gentlemen, we are beginning our descent into Los Angeles, please be sure to buckle your seat belts. We are anticipating some rough air ahead."

Lloyd elected to stay put until the plane was at the terminal then wait until everyone was gone. He figured he could hold on. Turbulence increased. The plane wobbled. He grabbed the hand grip. It was all anticipated. Until...

WHAM!

The plane took a sudden dive. His stomach rose into his throat. In a split second, all seemed upside down. Lloyd's head struck the ceiling and turned a somersault in mid-air. "Yeow Ouch!" The storm jostled the plane around like a kite without a tail. He tried holding the hand grip as he caromed left, right, whacking his ribs, his head, then his face against the small mirror, feeling like an giant ice cube in a tiny cocktail shaker. "My God!" he exclaimed. "We're going to crash. We're going to crash!" While he lay in a crumpled heap, a gust of violent weather whipped the plane into another sudden drop. Again, Lloyd's head hit the ceiling, ricocheting off the bulkhead and down against the rim of the commode. "Ow! Yeow! Arrrggghhh." Thrashed side to side, left, right, up, down, Lloyd vomited over his pants, barely able to breathe when the plane took another plunge. "Help! Ouch!" He thought, surely, it was time to die. How bittersweet, death instead of jail.

The aircraft touched down. Reverse engines roared as Lloyd's face rammed against the cabinet. "*Oh nooo, nooo, ohhh the pain, uggghhh*". The odor was nauseating. He felt like vomiting again. As the plane taxied, he tried to lift himself from the floor but he was wedged, wincing from excruciating pain in his ribs. He figured no one knew he was there, still a chance of escape once the plane emptied out. But how would he get himself up?

The plane arrived at the terminal followed by an announcement by a female flight attendant.

"All passengers are asked to remain in their seats until further notice. Please do not stand up or begin deboarding until we have completed a special inspection. Thank you."

What's that all about? Shit! Ouch! Damn, the pain."

The plane's cabin remained silent for what seemed an eternity until he heard footsteps, men's voices, then a woman's voice. A small commotion seemed to erupt next to the door. Finally, a strong male voice blared, "Mr. Ramsey, this is Sergeant John Larcey, L.A. P. D., Homicide. Open the door. We know you are in there."

Oh no, no, no....My God, how did they...? Ohhhh, the pain. He tried to speak, but only grunted. "Uggghhhhh... help... pain... ughhhh..."

The latch opened from the outside. The bi-fold door suddenly pressed inward jabbing his ribs. "YEOW!" He screamed. "DON'T! ...uggghhhh."

Excruciating time passed, listening to sounds of tools against metal as they disassembled the door from the outside. It was all over. Sure enough, as the door came off and he lay in a crumpled heap, two sets of powerful hands lifted him by the armpits. "Ugghhhhh. Ouch!" Grimacing from sore ribs, reeking of vomit, his false mustache dangling from one corner of his mouth, bruised and bleeding, he looked like he'd been in a street fight with George Foreman.

Surrounded by an army of cops, the cop named Larcey stood him against the bulkhead, attached the handcuffs and read him the Miranda warnings from a card. He could barely breathe. It was horribly humiliating. As they were about to escort him down the long aisle toward the exit, he saw all the passengers still seated, watching. All except one. Directly behind John Larcey, a lone woman stood glaring at him with loathing eyes he hadn't seen in twenty years.

"YOU?"

*   *   *

For the last two hours of the flight she kept herself buried, feigning sleep, peeking every so often to monitor his actions, praying he would not lift the blanket as he walked by. She had a perfect view of the left aisle from her seat all the way into first class so she could see him come and go. Her stomach was tied in knots with the thought of confronting him. It might be her long awaited chance to dispense all the hate stored inside of her, but it would be a foolish thing to do. No telling what demons would take control of her emotions.

She had sent him three notes portending a certain end to his precious freedom. The mere idea that it was driving him insane gave her a sense of pleasure. But it wasn't enough. She needed something more.

After the captain announced the possibility of a turbulent approach to Los Angeles, she spotted him step lively out of first class and down the aisle toward the rear lavatories, cap on, head low. A smile crossed her face. *So, he thinks he's going to hide in there.*

A woman flight attendant approached her, kneeled and spoke softly. "Mrs. Rosenthal, the authorities are going to board first and seek you out. They want to interview you briefly before they take the man off the plane. You understand?"

"Of course." She was tempted to tell the stewardess where Lloyd was hiding, then remembered the cautionary announcement about the pending turbulence. *Why tell? Why not let him suffer in there, the bastard.*

It was at that moment the plane took a sharp dive. A cynical smile crossed her face as she held on to the arm rest, pondering the years of waiting for this one precious moment.

Forty minutes of turbulence passed and the plane landed safely. As instructed, everyone remained in their seats after arriving at the gate. Several police officers boarded led by a young, dark-haired detective. A flight attendant asked her to come forward and meet with them. "Mrs. Rosenthal, I presume," he asked.

"Yes sir. I'm the one who notified the crew. Lloyd Ramsey in one of the rear bathrooms, hiding. I doubt he's feeling too well right now."

Pathetic moans emanated from the aft lavatory as crew members worked on the doors. Once removed, they looked down in amazement. Like a circus contortionist twisted on the floor, his face was pressed against the cabinet, bleeding, reeking a nauseating odor. After he was lifted, he spotted her behind the detective. And it made her feel good. It made her feel very good.

"YOU?" he screamed out, wincing in pain.

Yes, me, you bastard. Payback is hell, isn't it?

"Would you follow us to our police cars ma'am, we'd like to get a statement downtown?" asked the detective, holding Lloyd upright like a boneless puppet.

"Yes, of course sergeant. But before you take him, may I say one thing to him?"

"Yes ma'am. Go right ahead."

As two officers propped him by his armpits, his face swollen and bleeding from a dozen tiny cuts, Laura seized the moment she had dreamt of for eons. She was safe now. Nothing to fear. She walked closer to him, ignoring the stench, and peered into his eyes with hate, inches away, glaring for several long seconds. She wanted him to know the repugnance she was feeling. The entire plane was eerily silent as she sucked deep into her sinuses and spat directly into his eyes, then spat again and again until the officers restrained her.

"I'm sorry," she exclaimed. "It was something I had to do."

Minutes later, she stood on a curbside outside the terminal as they loaded the shackled Lloyd Ramsey into the rear seat of an white unmarked Crown Victoria. How well she remembered, like it was yesterday, men in white, the Nash Rambler in 1964, she in a straitjacket looking out the rear window seeing Lloyd Ramsey standing there smiling and waving, the cop nearby.

The Crown Victoria drove off.

Look back, you son of a bitch. Look back to me!

As though he had actually heard her, Lloyd Ramsey suddenly turned his battered head and peered out the rear window for a brief second.

Laura forced an ugly smile, baring her teeth and waved, "Bye bye".

Thank you, Lord.

chapter thirty-five

I t is a humbling experience indeed when a wealthy fifty-two year-old man who has had the world at his beck and call all his life is suddenly plunged into the bowels of an urban county jail. No more world travel, fine brandy, sports cars, Armani suits, French restaurants and voluptuous women. No more respect and admiration. No more power. Jailers seemed to enjoy bullying the bully, bringing the lofty down to eye level and seeing the rich beg for morsels of food and cigarettes like any ordinary junkie.

From the moment Lloyd Ramsey felt the cold steel shackled to his wrists at the L.A. Airport, he sobbed uncontrollably until his juices dried. News photographers and television cameramen reveled in capturing the bedraggled, near-Governor of Florida being hauled off like a common criminal, shielding his face, dragged and dumped into the back of a police car like a sack of feed.

First stop, the county hospital where he received swift treatment for cuts and bruises sustained inside that minuscule aircraft compartment. He had hoped the injuries were serious enough to secure a bed in the hospital but, alas, nothing was broken. From there, well bandaged, he was introduced to the infamous Los Angeles Men's County Jail, largest jail in the world holding sixty-eight hundred inmates.

He had read about it and seen movies and television, but they never captured the horror of true life nor the smells and sounds and the air of depression which pervaded every room, hall and cell. The clamor and stench of pungent odors was like nothing he had ever experienced. Steel doors slamming, voices screaming from all directions, key-rattling guards ordering him around like a child. "Everything out of your pockets, stand there, stand up, sit down, turn right, turn left, bend over, spread your cheeks...Asshole! I said, Spread-Your-Cheeks! I don't give a fuck who you are or how much you hurt, you're Asshole to me. Got that? Asshole?"

It seemed like every guard dehumanized him, manhandled him, pushed and screamed at him until he broke into fits of weeping. His stomach tightened in knots, nauseous, feeling the vomit breeching. He complained about his medical conditions until a fat guard bellowed, "Yeah. Right. That's what they all say. Suffer, Asshole!"

"But I do have headaches. And my ribs, please..."

"You're going to really have headaches before this is over, Asshole!"

"I have lots of money, I can help you out." Lloyd said, begging. "Just put me in a cell by myself, okay?"

The guard laughed. "Heh heh heh, I love it."

"Love what?"

"I love tacking on bribery charges. You rich assholes are all alike."

"I have to sleep in a cell with twelve men?"

"Consider yourself lucky, Mayor. Because you are who you are, you'll be quartered in a two-man cell. They're reserved for celebrities, informants and cops, and some of their relatives."

It took nearly two hours to book the former mayor of West Palm Beach. Before embarking to his cell, he made his one phone call to Jerry Blumenthal in Miami who promised to fly the next morning and secure a criminal attorney in Southern California. For now, there was no bond, no way out. Not for murder one. Lloyd was there for the duration, a common inmate until, at the very earliest, a bond hearing.

The clock said half past eleven. Only thirty minutes to midnight before spending his first night sleeping on a fetid, urine-stained bunk mattress. Once led away from the central guard station, steel corridors were cold, dark and bleak. Frightened, subservient, carrying a blanket, clothing and soap, Lloyd shuffled behind the young black guard, shivering, glancing into dark, bleak cells along the way, dreading what lied ahead. Some inmates stood at cell doors, some lay on bunks, others paced. All idle. All stank of body sweat. One man sat on a toilet. Another was naked on his bunk unabashedly playing with himself. They passed by a larger cell where several inmates sat around a television situated just outside the bars. It seemed the long, arduous stroll to his cell would never end. Finally the guard said, "Stop right there." Lloyd halted abruptly and began weeping pathetically. The guard opened the barred door. "Inside," he ordered. Then he wept harder, louder, sniveling like a baby.

In the darkness, he saw a man lying on the upper bunk so Lloyd placed his gear on the bare mattress below. Chills exploded over his entire body at the sound of the steel door, *WHAM .. CLUNK,* the turn of the lock, rattling keys, the fading footsteps of the guard, cold silence. Alone now in the first black moments of his new and eternal abyss, trembling, Lloyd glanced at the stainless steel toilet and the small sink and wept, holding his ribs. The space was barely larger than the aircraft lavatory, three concrete walls and one set of bars. A grunt sounded from the prisoner on the upper bunk and he wondered, no, he hoped he was white. Forget the political facade. In truth, he was a die-hard, first class bigot. Blacks made him feel uncomfortable. Especially criminals who were black. His heart began racing, fearful of what kind of scumbag he was caged with. He stood there frozen, shivering, trying not to weep or make any noise. From the dark shadows, he watched his cellmate stir from above, turn slowly, then drop his legs over the side, cough and slowly crawl off where he stood face to face. Lloyd gasped, blinked his eyes, squinted and nearly fainted. *I don't believe it.*

"Bowen?"

"Father?"

* * *

Rather than groping her way around a strange city in a rental car, Laura hailed a taxi from her Bakersfield hotel and handed the driver the address she had for Zena Ramsey. The day was bright and the California sun had risen boldly over the eastern range, no better time for a confrontation. She had all the angles, she figured, butter her up, appeal to her maternal instincts, plead for Jamie's sake, match her welfare money, offer more or simply threaten her with a child abuse investigation. She thought about kidnapping Jamie herself, just as Zena had but there was one major difference. Zena had rights to the child. For Laura, it was a felony.

As she sped through the city, her mind drifted to Lloyd's arrest the evening before and the wonderful image of seeing him hauled away like a common criminal. She had yet to make arrangements to visit Bowen in the L.A. County Jail before her return to Miami. And when her confrontation with Zena was over, she had to call home and check on Paul. Laura should have been exhausted, but adrenaline surged through her body, giving her the energy of a stallion. She hoped to see Jamie and wondered how he would react if he was there, if he would run to her loving arms as he did every day after school or if he would feel suppressed and frightened.

The taxi turned a corner into a mixed race neighborhood where small children of all nationalities and colors played in the streets, mostly half naked. Tiny pill-box houses, all pale yellow or white, many scarred with graffiti, sat in rows amid yards of mostly sand and rock. In the driveway of every second house, derelict cars without hoods and wheels were perched atop cinder blocks. Finally, after several turns, they reached a corner where an old brown Chevrolet Caprice was parked in front.

"This is it ma'am," said the driver.

Laura sucked a deep breath, paid the driver and asked him to stay around, "I'll pay for your time," she promised. "I have no other way back."

The muted sounds of heavy metal rock music was audible from inside the jalousie door. She knocked, but there was no response. She looked back to the taxi driver and signaled for him to keep waiting. She knocked again, harder this time. It seemed dark inside with no curtains on the windows. She tried peering in, but saw nothing except sparse furnishings and the flicker of a television set. Then a baby's cry cut through the music. "Hello?" she said, raising her voice slightly. "Hello?" No answer.

Laura turned the knob, opened the door and stepped into the kitchen area where the pungent odor of cannabis pervaded the house. The small, dim apartment was in disarray, cookware and dishes piled in the sink, clothes crumpled everywhere, lamp shades atilt, open cereal boxes laying atop a coffee table, ash trays mounded with cigarette butts, marijuana roach clips laying on the table. From one of the back rooms, a baby cried, louder this time, wailing. It sounded like a newborn. A television set with rabbit ears antennae was tuned to a talk show, no sound. Laura stepped onto the filthy shag carpet which had once been a gold color and saw a hallway leading to rooms on each side. The music played on. The baby wailed on. Laura's caring instincts led her to the child. The first door on the left, where the music was coming from, was closed. Memories flashed, *knocking on windows, music, closed doors.* To the right, a small bedroom with bunk beds against the crayoned wall and a crib in the corner where a small baby was lying face up, kicking its little legs. There was a bare cot against the wall. She figured this was where Jamie slept. Clad only in a plastic diaper, the baby coughed and wailed louder. As Laura reached to pick it up, she was startled by a door slamming open, the thump of footsteps and a female voice shouting, "You little brat! Shut the fuck..."

She was naked and fleshy with huge tattooed breasts hanging over a paunchy girth. Her face was flushed and angry, her auburn-red hair in disarray, standing there astonished.

Stunned, Laura's heart skipped a beat as she stood face to face with the nude trollop. Unabashed, Zena Ramsey charged like a rhino, "Who the fuck are you?" Laura winced. The baby wailed on.

A male voice in the background asked, "Who's there baby doll?" Zena shoved Laura angrily, her breath reeking of stale tobacco.

Laura stepped away, suppressing the urge to run. "I, I...I'm sorry. I heard the baby..."

"Wait just a minute!" Zena screamed, then turned toward the bedroom. "Sammy, bring me the shotgun!"

Laura's heart dropped to her knees. It was just what she didn't want. A thin, naked black man with gaping teeth emerged, holding a long barreled gun which was quickly snatched by Zena. Laura had to think fast. With hands raised, trembling, thinking of Jamie, she muttered, "Listen please, I'm Laura Rosenthal and I've come to offer you a deal."

"Yeah, sure. And I'm Madonna. You're nothing but a fucking burglar and I'm going to blow your brains all over the ceiling."

"I am, really. I can prove it. I want to make an offer."

"You're Bowen's mother? You don't look anything like he described you. She's got blonde curly hair. 'Bouncy curls,' he always said. Yours looks like a oversized fucking Brillo pad."

"Bowen had, well, sorta like, two mothers. That was his step-mother, the one with the blonde hair. Please, put down that gun. I'm a wreck here."

"Lemme see your I.D."

Laura pulled a wallet from her shoulder purse and produced a driver's license from Florida. Zena lowered the weapon. "Sammy?" she barked to the nude man standing behind her, her eyes glued to Laura.

"Yeh? Whah?"

"Go home. I'll see ya later. And leave the money on the dresser."

Laura breathed deeply. The baby cried until Zena laid the gun aside, picked him up and cradled his lips to her nipple. Finally, the crying stopped. "Wait in there. I'll be out in a minute," she barked as she disappeared into her bedroom. "I gotta get dressed."

Long after Sammy had left, Zena returned wearing a bright orange dress, her long, auburn-red hair combed neatly, carrying her baby. She was quite pretty, Laura mused, despite being overweight, but her eyes were cold. "You're here to take Jamie back, ain't ya?" she asked, opening a can of Coors from the fridge. "You think I'm going to hand him over?"

"Well..."

"Want one?" she asked Laura, raising a beer can.

Laura waved her off. "No thanks. Where is he now? Jamie?"

"Out. Day school. Where do you think?"

"I'd love to see him."

Zena glared at her mother-in-law, then growled, "Look, Bowen snatched Jamie from me eighteen months ago. Eighteen months, I didn't know where my own child was. Now, Jamie is fine, in case you want to know. And if have any other ideas, he ain't goin' anywhere, but right here. Now, does that shorten your little visit? Laura?"

Ignoring the question, Laura glanced at the baby being cradled in one arm, "Is that a boy or a girl?" she asked.

"Boy. Bad luck. I always try for a girl, but end up with little dickheads instead."

My gosh, that would be Jamie's brother. "If you don't want him then why...?"

"He stays. He's my kid, I'll take care of him. Okay? Sorry you wasted your time."

Laura had to stay calm and focus on her mission. "Can I show you some pictures?" asked Laura reaching into her purse.

"Pictures? What pictures?"

"Pictures of my home."

"I know you got a big fucking house. Frankly, I don't give a shit."

Laura removed a stack of color photos of her spacious Miami home showing Jamie's room with all the toys, the pool, his school and pictures of him frolicking about the house. "See, Zena. This is all at Jamie's disposal. We can give him so much more. His opportunities with us are endless. And I love him so, he's such a good..."

"Forget it. He's *my* son. He is supposed to be with his mother and that's where's he's staying. Anything else, Laura?" Zena smirked impudently, puffing a cigarette.

Laura fanned smoke from her face. It was obvious the *"for his own good"* ploy would not work. "Look," she said, "This place is, is ..."

"A mess? Is that what you're trying to say?"

"You haven't the means..."

"I have means, Laura. I don't have *your* money, but Jamie belongs here. Is that all? Look, your taxi is waiting."

"I smelled drugs..."

"Yeah. So? I smoke a little pot now and then. What's the big deal. Twenty million people in this country smoke a little pot."

"Don't you see, Zena, that's how Bowen got started, his father..."

"I know all about that shit and his asshole father. And I don't give a shit."

Laura knew it was time to play hard ball. "Look, Zena, All

right! I know that you beat him! All right? You're always hitting that poor little boy. I know it, and I'm going to..."

"Ha haaa haaa. Do what? Have me arrested? And who told you that? Jamie? Did Jamie tell you I beat him?"

Laura corralled her emotions. If she repeated Jamie's tale of horror, the child would surely pay consequences. "No, no. I just figured it."

"Then you have no evidence, so fuck off, bitch! Maybe you better go. I got appointments."

"Can you tell me where Jamie is now? May I see him?"

"He won't be home until later. I think it best that you leave, Laura..."

"Look, Zena." As Laura's blood started to boil, the harsh reality that Jamie would not be joining her back to Miami was setting in. It was worse than she ever dreamed, Jamie living amid such filth, drugs, neglect and open iniquity. It made her all the more determined. "I want that child! He needs me! Don't you see, he needs me." It all flashed back, it always flashed, *I want my baby, please Lloyd, where is my baby? I want my baby.*

Zena laughed, stepped to the door and opened it. "Good bye, Laura."

"No. You don't understand! You can't let that poor boy grow up like this. I'll call the authorities. I'll have you investigated." Laura's voice started rising to a higher pitch.

Zena laughed again. "Look, bitch. I've been investigated plenty. Ain't no social service agency gonna take any kid away from me unless they can prove abuse or neglect. And they can't. Wanna see my fridge? It's loaded with food. Ain't no lobster, but it's food. Nothin' wrong with Cheerios and Spam. The kids have clothes. Jamie goes to school and he ain't got no bruises on his precious little body. So, fuck off and get outa my house!"

As Zena held the door puffing a cigarette, Laura looked to her side where a small, shadeless brass table lamp was all too inviting. It would take but a second, one swift blow, *now, do it, grab the base!* No one would see... *No, no, no don't, don't lose your cool Laura.* She pictured Zena dead, her head bashed and feeling good about it because it was all for Jamie. Then, the memory of night howls, locked away, crazy people. *No Laura, don't do it.*

"Are you leaving? Or do I call the cops?"

Laura looked down at the lamp again.

"You wanna hit me, don't ya? Well, come on Laura, come on. Take your best shot."

"No. I'm leaving. But I have one other proposal."

"Yeah? What?"

"I'll give you an income, the same as the welfare money you get now."

Zena broke out into a fit of laughter. "Haaa Haaa. Are you shitting me? Bribing me? Money? You want to give me money?"

"Yes. I'll give you money, if it means saving Jamie's life."

"Okay," she replied, grinning arrogantly, her head within a waft of smoke. She chuckled, "Make it a million bucks."

Laura looked in amazement. "I don't have a million dollars."

"Well then, tough shit. Goodbye, Laura."

"I can give you some money, but not a million dollars. My husband's been very ill and it's drained our..."

"How much? Come on, Laura, how much?"

Okay Laura, there's room to haggle. It's a matter of price. God, please help me. "I don't know. I have to see, uh, maybe twenty-five thousand? I can give you twenty...."

"Goodbye, Laura. Nice knowin' ya."

"Fifty?"

"Get the fuck out of my house! Did you hear that?"

Her eyes welled up as she started toward the taxi. Then Laura turned to face Zena one more time. "If I had anywhere near a million dollars, I'd pay it. Because Jamie is worth it. I'll be back. You can count on that."

"Goodbye, Laura."

"Just like my son," she whimpered, dabbing her eyes with a hanky. "Jamie's doomed, no opportunity, no love, all because of..."

The door slammed in her face.

Barriers. Always barriers.

* * *

Her mind wracked with horrible visions of Jamie's life and shaken from her foiled confrontation, Laura returned to her hotel room, reminding herself to remain calm and organized. She'd yet to check on Grace and Paul and needed to find her way to the L.A. County Jail for the long awaited visit with her son. When she dialed the jail for instructions, the desk officer dropped a bomb. "I'm sorry ma'am, that's impossible right now."

But, I thought it was all right...."

"Ma'am, I'm sorry. There's been some added charges. I cannot release any other information. Right now, Bowen Ramsey is in solitary. Sorry."

"Solitary?"

Barriers

Her heart sunk to her feet. Always negotiating, she thought, always barred, always trying but failing. For twenty-four years it has been like this, shut out, meaningless to someone who means so much. Nothing had changed. The California trip had been a colossal failure, returning home without Jamie and never seeing her ever-so-elusive son. *He needs me now, I know it. Bowen needs me now. Oh, if I could only show him my love.*

She checked her watch and calculated the three hour time difference. It was time to check on things at home.

"Hello, Consuella. This is Laura. How is...?"

"Oh, Mrs. Rosenthal. We've been trying to no reach you."

"Why? What is it?"

"We called hotels in Los Angeles and Bakersfield, and tried to find Zena Ramsey's number..."

"Consuella, is Grace all right? Paul?"

"Oh, Mrs. Rosenthal. I'm so sorry. So sorry."

"Oh my God, what are you talking about, Consuella?"

"Your husband, he had another stroke. Sometime during the night."

Oh my Lord. She paused and took a deep breath before asking, "Stroke? Consuella, is he...?"

"I'm sorry, Mrs. Rosenthal. It happened in his sleep. I'll stay here until you get back. Grace is fine, I'll be with her."

"Paul? Paul... is dead?"

chapter thirty-six

The stench of urine, sweat and smoke pervaded the steel darkness as distant echoes of harsh voices, rattling keys and metal slamming against metal rang out by the minute. By three in the morning, Lloyd had not slept as he paced the tiny space like a captured tiger, occasionally sitting on the edge of the mattress then rising to pace again, mumbling to himself, sobbing. He tried talking to Bowen but he would have none of it. At first, Bowen summoned a guard demanding he be moved to another cell. It was to no avail. "They figured you guys were perfect cell mates," said the officer. "Ask the sergeant in the morning. Now get some sleep."

Bowen lay with his back turned, ignoring his father. Lloyd's mind raced frenetically, thinking about the destruction of his life, his public stature and those stupid mistakes that got him where he was. He paced on and on, his mumbling more audible, cursing Barbara and Laura and the "stupid Cuban" in Miami, unaware of the hatred seething on the upper bunk inches away. As always, Lloyd was consumed with Lloyd, with no concerns about anyone else. Little did he realize that Bowen was struggling to contain himself, loathing the one person most responsible for his lot in life.

It was past four a.m. He had to break the ice. "You started all this," said Lloyd, pacing and pointing a menacing finger at Bowen. He was ignored. "After eight fucking years, you show up like a goddam ghost and hand me up in front of thousands of people. I would have been governor now!" Faster, he paced, but three steps in each direction.

"That was a fucking lie, Bowen. It was a lie and you know it. I never turned you on to drugs. Letting you try one hit ain't turning you on and you know it. You ruined my fucking life."

A voice rang out from another cell, " Hey man, cool it in there..."

Then another, "Yeah, we're trying to get some sleep..."

"Shut the fuck up, asshole!"

Running fingers through his hair, Lloyd lowered his voice, paced again, sniveled and babbled on blaming the world for his troubles while Bowen harnessed his emotions, wishing for him to shut up. Finally, the elder Ramsey struck a nerve. "If that miserable cunt hadn't taken off on me, that money-grubbing bitch, stupid bitch."

Bowen turned his head to ask one question. "Who? Barbara?"

"No, not Barbara. That cunt who ran out on me and left me stuck taking care of you. I wasn't in any position..."

"You mean, my mom? Mommy?"

"Mommy your ass. Yvonne wasn't your mother. Bitch!" Bowen alerted and sat up. Lloyd was glad, for now he had an audience.

"Tell me about the deal, Father," he asked in a soft voice.

"What deal?"

"You know. The deal she wrote about in the note. "Remember? *A deal is a deal.*"

Lloyd looked up into the darkness where he could see the whites of his son's eyes glaring at him from the upper bunk. "The bitch ripped me off for a half million, but I paid it anyway to make sure someone took care of you."

"So why did she leave?"

"She held me to a ten year contract. I never figured she'd take off, leaving me hung out to dry like that, the cunt!"

Cunt?

"That *cunt,* Father, was my mom. At least to me she was, and she's not a *cunt.*"

Lloyd halted and began flailing his arms like a madman. "She's a goddam cunt! You hear? A no good, money grubbin', miserable..."

"At least she took me fishing!"

"Who gives a shit?"

"She loved me!" A chorus of angry voices exploded from

nearby cells demanding quiet. A symphony of metal cups grated against steel bars as the clamor intensified, louder and louder, deafening. Wrought with anger, hating the man from the pit of his stomach, Bowen shouted, "No one else loved me!"

"Bullshit!"

"God damn you!" As though driven by an outside force, Bowen charged from his bunk and plowed his fist into the center of Lloyd's face, propelling him against the wall near to the toilet. Bowen swung wildly, whipping both fists against his head until the elder man cowered to the floor pleading for him to stop. Lloyd wailed in pain, holding his chest, shielding his face. A raucous cacophony of shouting and clanging cell bars echoed across the floor. Bowen had lost control, screaming at his father, "I fucking hate you, you bastard! That was my mommy! You hear me? You never call her a cunt again!"

"Okay, okay, please, no more, ugghhhhhh, no more, get off me."

Angry inmates continued shouting expletives, calling for guards. Bowen was on the concrete deck holding Lloyd's head in a choke hold, gritting his teeth, whispering contemptuously into his father's ear. "How's it feel having the shit beat out of ya by someone that doesn't exist? Huh? Daddy? Say it. Come on, say it, motherfucker!"

"Say wha," he choked, barely able to speak, grabbing fruitlessly on to Bowen's arm.

"Say I don't exist. Say it."

As Lloyd began gurgling, a second away from bursting like a red melon, footsteps were heard running closer, followed by the rattling of keys, the slip of the lock and the opening of the cell door. Powerful hands pried Bowen's arm from his father's neck and carried him out the door. Lloyd Ramsey lay next to the commode, moaning, gasping, massaging his neck, grabbing his chest. It was the last time this father and son would ever face each other.

chapter thirty-seven

The non-sectarian service was held in the rear patio of his house near the garden he loved so much, his ashes atop a velvet shrouded table in a porcelain urn while friends offered eulogies, just as Paul Rosenthal would *not* have wanted it. But for Laura and his daughters, it was a means of closure and so long as there was no reference to God, she figured he would forgive this single act of benevolent defiance. Amid the background of subdued Mozart arias, Doctor Harry Ashenbrenner reminded the small select gathering of Paul's contributions to the science of psychiatry, the books, the research and the hundreds who he guided toward a saner, happier world. Though grief-stricken, Laura was dry of tears as she held Grace close to her with one arm and Cynthia, now married and twenty-six, with the other. Her lips curved into a faint smile, somehow gladdened he was no longer suffering, always faulting himself for the unfortunate plight of others when in fact, he had been a guiding light for those in darkness, especially Laura.

Two hours later, aboard a chartered, thirty-two foot Bertram oscillating to the motion of the Atlantic seas, she released his ashes to infinity just as he had ordered in his will. As with his body, so went the urn as well.

After she dropped off the girls, she excused herself, saying she needed time alone to reflect on life with him. It was the least she could offer, a heart and mind dedicated for this one day to the man who truly loved her and restored her dignity at a time when she was in the pits of despair. She felt so indebted, so unable to repay as he should have been repaid. It had been almost a week since she'd set foot on the property of The Stanton School. It was Sunday and no one was there, so she would have the iron bench to herself to gaze over the glistening waters of Biscayne Bay, pondering the future, trying to confine her memories to Paul and Paul alone. But that was impossible as images of little Jamie flashed through her brain, the squalid apartment, the wretched mother, Bowen rotting in a jail cell, the years of struggle with her son, trying desperately to be a mother, *his* mother.

It was wonderful, the serenity, the peace, moments to herself without an agenda, knowing no time of day, nor caring. Even in death his therapy was comforting, this man who showed little physical love, but was filled with it. Despite choppy waters, boat traffic was dense in the bay this afternoon as an armada of schooners headed for the ocean channel. Soft breezes touched her cheek making her breathe full and deep, her nostrils flaring with each exhale. Perspiration beaded from her forehead which she wiped with a finger then tasted the salt. She looked around, happy to be alone, just she and the bay waters and the warm breezes. Grady Culpepper's masculine image passed through her mind, and the kiss. *That* kiss. Then, the pangs of guilt. Wouldn't it be terrible, she thought, if Paul was up there watching her, invading her thoughts.

She pondered life without Paul, reflecting on his wisdom, wishing she could ask his for his guidance as she always asked. She caught herself speaking aloud as though he were sitting next to her and she felt foolish. She was free now to pursue her son and her grandson like never before, without restraints, without worrying each day how to care for her invalid husband. How terrible he would feel if he knew she harbored those selfish feelings.

Two hours passed like it were two minutes. Grey skies were turning black as an afternoon squall rumbled over South Florida, certain to drench Miami streets with one of those brief but voluminous deluges. Laura gave thought to remaining on the bench and letting God shower her at will, happy to feel the cool water soak her body. But she realized she had no change of clothes, that it was stupid and impractical.

As rain began falling in giant drops, she darted toward the portico for shelter, then used the key to her office so she could relax until the squall passed. She spotted a week's worth of mail stacked in the in-basket. It was something to do. A temporary diversion. She couldn't resist. She perused a few reports, then spotted a brown package envelope with a bump in its center lying in the center of the heap, addressed to her with a familiar, scrawled handwriting and postmarked: Coconut Grove. Hair rose on the back of her neck.

Oh my Gosh, it's from Paul. What's this?

Quickly, she used a scissors to cut it open, reached inside and pulled out an empty vial of pills wrapped in a torn sheet of paper, labeled as *Inderol.* His medication. His *lethal* heart medication. The hand written note read:

I free you once more, Laura my dear. Take good care of that little boy. Don't forget I loved you.

chapter thirty-eight

For Lloyd, the thrashing by Bowen was a blessing in disguise as it granted his wish; a bed in the infirmary. While the aircraft lavatory left him bruised from head to foot, Bowen exacerbated the rib damage, fully breaking two of them, then shutting one eye completely with a pounding fist until guards pulled him off. When he was wheel-chaired into the lawyers conference room two days later, he looked like he'd been run over by a stampeding buffalo.

"Lloyd, my God, what happened to you?" asked the portly lawyer from Miami.

"You don't wanna know, Jerry. Just get me out of this hell hole." Lloyd grimaced with each word. The second gentleman was younger and thinner with slick black hair, reminding Lloyd of actor Al Pacino. "Who's your friend?"

"Lloyd, this is Augie Petrocelli. Formerly the Assistant D.A. in charge of major felonies here in L.A. Augie's considered the number one defense lawyer on the west coast."

"Nice to make your acquaintance, Mr. Ramsey. I've heard..." The attorney extended his hand.

Lloyd barked, "Lawyers are lawyers. I pay, you get me out. We're not friends. Just get me the fuck outa here."

The three sat around a rectangular table inside a tiny room with a window overlooking the exercise yard. Walls were grey and bare with a telephone situated next to the door. Lloyd's body listed to one side in deference to the excruciating pain in his chest.

Jerry Blumenthal opened a set of folders and shuffled papers. "Lloyd, I think we have a chance of getting you a bond," he said in a near whisper, winking one eye. Then he lowered his voice even further. "This is supposed to be a private room for attorneys and clients. But I don't trust these bastards." Lloyd nodded. Augie Petrocelli sat quiet, still digesting the caustic retort by his new client. "It's a weak case, Lloyd. All they have is a single witness against you with a good reason to lie. Of course, fleeing the jurisdiction didn't help you any."

Lloyd interrupted, wincing, "Who says I was fleeing? I didn't know I was being charged, right Jerry? I was just getting out of town to rest."

"You knew. I told you."

"Yeah. But no one else knew that."

"Okay. Okay."

"Then how do you explain the phony name and the disguise?" asked Augie.

"I'm a celebrity, okay. I needed space. That's all. I've traveled like that before."

Augie shrugged. "Sounds plausible to me. I just hope it sounds plausible in court."

Lloyd grunted another question. "When's the bond hearing?"

"It's set for next Wednesday."

They convened for over an hour, discussing the particulars of law and the facts of the case until Jerry winked his eye one more time. "Uh, Lloyd, perhaps we should discuss fees?"

"Fees? I don't give a shit about fees, you know that. Get me...."

"I mean, Lloyd, uh, before we go to court, we gotta have some amount set."

Lloyd remained silent for a few seconds and curiously processed the dialogue. The lawyer winked. Then it struck him. "Oh yeah, sure."

Both lawyers leaned over and nodded affirmatively. As he continued talking, Jerry Blumenthal wrote a note; *One Million.* "Uh, as you know, we charge two hundred fifty dollars and hour, plus expenses, investigators, whatever. Just for the extradition hearing, your cost could run over a hundred grand."

"Sure, fellas. Whatever your fees are, I'll guarantee them. By the way, who's the judge?"

"Scheduled for Harold Rainess," replied Augie. "Good man. Used to be a defense lawyer."

Lloyd panned their eyes.

"We, uh, need some payment up front for our services, Lloyd, you understand."

"Sure. No problem. I'll arrange it."

And so, as always, wealth prevailed over justice. The fix was in.

Wednesday could not come soon enough. Lloyd convalesced another day in the infirmary before being returned to a regular cell where he languished four more days and nights with a tattooed cell mate who refused to talk. It allowed enough time for his wounds to heal.

Flanked by his attorneys, Lloyd Ramsey stood before Judge Harold Rainess wearing a grey Armani suit as the prematurely balding man returned to the bench from recess where he had purportedly studied the issues at hand. Lloyd refused to waive extradition, thus setting legal arguments in motion whether or not enough probable cause existed to compel the State of California to release Lloyd Ramsey to the State of Florida. This set the stage for a full extradition hearing which could not be scheduled for two to three weeks. Meanwhile, the second issue was whether Ramsey would be permitted bail.

The courtroom hummed with media and celebrity watchers anxiously waiting for the jurist to decide. The defense team claimed the Florida case was based solely on the testimony of one self-serving informant with no other corroborating evidence to tie Lloyd Ramsey to the murder of his wife. In addition, Lloyd Ramsey had been a *"pillar of integrity"* within his West Palm Beach community where he served as mayor for four years. He certainly could be trusted to remain within jurisdiction. The lawyers pleaded Ramsey be permitted a bond.

Attorneys for the State of California argued it was not within their purview to render judgement of the merits of the case, that Lloyd Ramsey had demonstrated a proclivity toward fleeing the jurisdiction and should be remanded to authorities and transported to Miami forthwith.

"I have studied this matter with great care," announced the judge, reading through granny glasses. "And based on the information presented here, I have reached an opinion that the Florida indictment charging the former West Palm Beach mayor with murder is flimsy as an overcooked noodle and I cannot in all good conscience require this man to languish in a jail cell pending the extradition hearing unless there is more evidence to support the claim of one questionable accuser. Further, I am not convinced that Mr. Ramsey will flee jurisdiction despite his use of disguises in the public arena. Considering his notoriety, it is perfectly understandable. An extradition hearing is hereby set for November twenty-third. I hope to hear a stronger case from Florida prosecutors at that time. Meanwhile, bond is set at two hundred thousand dollars."

The courtroom burst into a chorus of gasps and murmurs as the judge rapped his gavel, demanding order. Lloyd swallowed and nearly fainted as the exuberant attorneys shook his hand. Moments later, Lloyd met with the clerk of the court where his attorneys helped to guarantee his bond, thus setting him free from the horrors of jail after two miserable weeks of incarceration. At the top of the courthouse steps, a huge gaggle of reporters and cameras nearly attacked the ailing politician demanding a statement, asking ridiculous, inane questions.

"Did you have your wife killed?"

"Are you happy to be released?"

For ten minutes under a bright noon sky, Lloyd and his attorneys politely accommodated reporters by fielding questions with evasive answers before heading for a waiting limousine at the curb. Just as Lloyd leaned to enter the rear seat, *Pop Pop Pop,* three shots were fired in rapid succession, felling Lloyd Ramsey who grimaced as he clutched his stomach. Pandemonium erupted as the crowd ducked and hit the sidewalk. One lawyer grabbed the arm of a tall young man holding a thirty-eight caliber nickel-plated Colt revolver. As he wrestled him to the street, the boy shouted, "Scumbag! I warned you, you bastard!"

Police hurried to the scene and slammed the youngster against the vehicle, cuffing his hands behind and whisking him away from the maddening crowd. Chip McGill, son of Barbara Ramsey, was charged with Attempted Murder in the First Degree.

* * *

A concert of trucks and autos, sirens and horns echoed over

the twelve foot razor-wired walls as Bowen languidly strolled to and fro, hands in pockets. His mind regressed, as usual, to a fishing pier somewhere in Islamorada, wondering how it might have been if his Mommy was still alive somewhere, if she ever thought about him or really ever cared at all. Evil abounded around him, horrible men who had committed atrocious acts against innocent people without blinking an eye, prepared to do it again if they could only free themselves. Every third or fourth step within the exercise yard, he stepped aside allowing them to pass, careful not to arouse the anger that seethed inside of them. Some dribbled basketballs, yelling profanities. Others walked solo, like him, happy to be out from the stinking six by nine cell for one precious hour.

Above the crowd, a familiar voice rang out, "Bowen Ramsey, get your ass in here!"

It was the tall, broad-shouldered, crew-cut shift sergeant standing in the door like a Roman soldier, the boss of guards, the one who enjoyed humiliating him, the one he hated more than any other. *What the hell did I do now?* As he reached the entrance, he was made to assume the position, hands behind his back and then cuffed.

Moments later, Bowen was sitting in a small conference room waiting for someone unknown. Strange, he thought. No glass barrier, no phone. Perhaps it would be his mother, though she normally would have written before coming. His lawyer? Doubtful. Zena? No way, she hated him, wished him dead. Maybe it was something to do with Jamie?

A small man, dark-haired man wearing a sharkskin suit entered hurriedly, sat, stared at Bowen a moment and spoke in a New York accent. "You're Bowen Ramsey?" asked the gentleman.

"Yeah. So?"

"My name is Augie Petrocelli. I'm your father's attorney. I need to talk to you, Bowen. There's been a..."

Bowen glanced to the ceiling, stood up and, to the amazement of the attorney, walked back toward the exit door and knocked. His expression left no doubts about his sentiments. When the door opened, the waiting sergeant turned Bowen's shoulders around and ushered him back to the table. "Sit down

Ramsey," barked the guard. "Listen to the man. That's an order. There's no time here to fuck around."

Bowen remained standing and glared into the eyes of Augie Petrocelli. "I want nothing to do with my father. My father is a piece of shit. As far as I'm concerned, he doesn't exist."

"Your father's been shot..."

"Good."

"He's critical...."

"That's good too."

"He needs blood desperately...."

"So, find a pig. That should be quite compatible."

"He needs your blood, Bowen, and he needs it now."

"You got any more jokes?"

"Bowen, he's AB negative. You're jail records show AB negative. Less than one percent of the population has AB negative and there's not enough in the bank at the facility where's he's..."

"He can go fuck himself. Besides, I don't have a father."

"He's going to die."

As Bowen turned, he saw the hefty Sergeant still in the room by the door, obviously privy to the conversation. Suddenly, he grabbed Bowen by the shirt collar and backed him against the wall. The attorney looked on, passively. "You're giving blood, you hear that, Ramsey?" barked the guard.

"No way. Let me go."

"You don't give, you're back in the cell with big Richie."

That stunned him. The mere thought was mortifying. Instantly, he reflected on that horrible first week in the county jail, the pain, the fear, his disgusting breath, panting, humping, plunging, groping as he lay helpless, over and over again, mornings, nights, any time at the man's pleasure, knowing he was sure to die if he uttered a word to anyone. Bowen's eyes watered and flipped to the ceiling. His back to the wall, he smiled cynically at the guard. "They got to you, didn't they? How much did it cost? Huh? My father paid..."

"Shut up, Ramsey. There's no time for bullshit. You giving blood? Or are you getting remarried?"

Bowen glared into the guard's eyes. "Bastard!"

chapter thirty-nine

Two Weeks Later

Sunday morning was the worst day of the week for inmate visitors. She was warned about the Men's County Jail, that it would be long hours of frustration waiting behind hundreds of other visitors just to have her hour per week, or half an hour if she wanted to divide it up for another day. For Laura that was impossible.

Sounds of steel doors, voices, keys, hurried footsteps everywhere as she wondered if Bowen had become inured to it all. After two hours, her turn arrived and was permitted entry in the booth where rows of visitors chatted with inmates with a receiver to their ears. Wearing a flowered print dress, heels and a new shade of lipstick, Laura looked anxiously through the glass pane as Bowen was led into the room. She lifted the receiver, brightened her eyes and offered a loving smile.

"Hello, darling."

"Hello, Mother."

"How are you feeling, son?"

He snickered. "What can you expect? Pretty lousy, actually."

"You look tired."

"Yeah. I'm tired of living." She was disappointed at his answer. "How was the trip, Mother?"

"Fine," she replied, still managing a forced smile.

"I heard about Mr. Rosenthal. Sorry."

"He's finally at peace, Bowen. I'm happy for him, actually."

"Yeah, well, so am I, I guess."

"Bowen, you really do look washed out. You sure you're all right?"

"I'll feel better when I finally get over to Chino, the state prison. Doc says it's not uncommon when you give a pint of blood."

"I'm still puzzled why you gave that rat a pint of your blood."

"I had reasons, Mother," he replied, looking away from her eyes.

"Reasons?"

"Well, it sure the hell wasn't out of love. Someday, maybe, I'll tell you about it. How's he doing? Have you heard?"

"Still alive, unfortunately. Looks like he'll survive until he goes to prison. Then they can execute him."

"What prison? They had so little evidence, they let him out for Christ's sake."

"The state attorney from Miami says he's got a stronger case. The last time Lloyd was with Barbara, they argued violently. Barbara threatened to suck his fortune. Barbara's son heard it all. Also, the South Americans are turning state's evidence. Seems they were going after you as well, until you were arrested."

"No shit?"

"The judge revoked the bond and remanded him back to Florida as soon as he's fit to travel."

"All right. That makes my day."

"I've got some more news that will make your day." Laura saw a glimmer in her son's eyes. She was about to make him happy, for the moment.

"What is it?"

"Paul left me a considerable amount of money, Bowen. There were mutual funds from years back that I never even knew about, all left to me as the beneficiary. Plus a half million dollars in life insurance."

"Wow. Good for you."

"No, it's good for Jamie."

"What do you mean?"

"I've come to take custody of your son, Bowen. Zena put him up for sale, for a considerable price. At least I give her credit for that. I have all she's asked for. Hopefully, Jamie will be with me when I travel back to Florida."

"Wow. That's great. I'm so happy." For the first time since she could remember, a tinge of emotion come over her son. His eyes welled up, his voice cracked, glancing off, embarrassed that he was on the verge of crying. "That's really great, Mother."

"I want you to sign papers, Bowen, giving me all rights to the child, full unconditional guardianship. It's necessary."

"What about Zena?"

"She has to do the same. Don't worry. She will. I've got a cashier's check in my purse, in her name."

"How much....?"

"One million."

"Oh my God."

"I love that little boy, Bowen."

"I do too."

"I love that little boy, just like I loved you."

There was a brief, strained hesitation before Bowen answered, "Yeah. I know, Mother."

Tears formed in her eyes. "There was nothing I wouldn't have done for you, if, you know, your father hadn't..."

"I know, Mother. I know."

Mother.

She looked away, then back to the dullness in her son's eyes. "Okay, I'm sorry." Time to change the subject. "So, what's happening with your case? What do the lawyers say?"

"I'm testifying, Mother. Then pleading guilty. The judge might consider..."

"Bowen, why? Why plead guilty? The lawyer told me you have a chance at winning, that the evidence against you is flimsy. You've got the best lawyers."

"Mother, please listen."

"You can beat this thing. You just have to be patient."

"Mother, that would mean staying in this shit house another six months to a year." His eyes intensified. "I can't stand it. I'd rather do six years in the joint than six months in this hell hole."

"But..."

"No buts, Mother. You don't know. You don't know what I've been through here."

She paused a moment, pondering. "What, Bowen? What's happened to you?"

He began trembling, looking in all directions around the room, but seeing nothing. He couldn't tell her, she realized that now. "Look, they could be listening in, they read my mail, they're everywhere. Just, let it go, Mother. Please."

She lowered her voice to a whisper. "Do they beat you?"

"No Mother it's, look, never mind."

Then it occurred to her. With one hand on the receiver and the other across her mouth, she posed the question although fearful of the answer. "Have you, have you..." Her voice quivered, below a whisper now, barely audible. "....been....?"

He stood and glared at her with dark, sunken eyes then hung the receiver on its carriage, walked off and banged on the door.

"Oh Bowen, my boy. Bowen."

* * *

Public address announcements at the TWA terminal gate seemed relentless, one after another as Laura covered her ears. With a roll-about suitcase at her feet, she waited anxiously at the designated coffee shop, her heart pounding, imagination running rampant, wondering how the child would react seeing her after two months living with his mother. She checked her watch then looked up at the airport clock. It read seven twenty-two, five minutes slower than hers. *He should be showing up any minute now.* She looked once more through the legal papers, hoping she had not left out any details and reflecting on the instructions she had given Zena over the phone. *"Don't forget the record of his shots, his social security number, the school where he's attending and his birth certificate. Bring a notary. I don't care how much it costs. I'll pay."*

"No money, no kid. And I ain't kidding."

"Don't worry Zena. I pay my debts."

"He ain't got much in the way of clothing."

"Leave the rags there. He'll have clothes."

Thoughts rambled as Laura recalled the first day she laid eyes on her own son, four years after that fateful day in May of 1964. How history repeats itself, she mused, only this time she would not be leaving the child at the end of the day, wondering when she would see him again. This time she would not be relegated to utter insignificance. This time she had the upper hand, paid for, destined to make a difference in Jamie's life before it was too late. She thought about Paul and thanked him again under her breath for all he did for her in his lifetime. When she checked her watch, her heart skipped a beat for it was past seven-thirty. She remembered twenty years past when the gate guard refused her passage into Star Island because Lloyd hadn't made the notification and her sense of panic when the deadline passed, those desperate, horrible feelings. She looked toward the clock once more, then heard a child's voice cry out from amid the crowd, "Grandma! Grandma!"

Zena gripped his hand as they stood in the center of the concourse. He wore a torn tee shirt, dirty shorts and sneakers without socks. "Oh, Jamie, how are you?" Laura leaped from her seat and started toward him when Zena held her arms out.

"Hold it, Laura. Let's see the money."

Laura was amazed at how attractive she looked in a peasant's skirt, her hair pulled back in a long pony tail. Beside her, an older woman held a pouch with a disinterested expression on her face. Laura figured she was the notary. With eyes steeled to Jamie, Laura removed the cashier's check from her purse and handed it over. Zena looked it over, then unceremoniously re-leased Jamie into Laura's waiting arms without even a parting gesture. A broad smile crossed Laura's face as she showered the child with kisses. His tiny arms were hugged her neck like he would never let go. "Grandma, Grandma, I'm going home with you."

"I know, Jamie. I know. You're going to be fine." She could hardly choke the words, "I love you."

"I love you too, Grandma."

After papers were signed and notarized, Zena turned and walked off into oblivion, a millionaire. She never even said goodbye to her son.

The barriers were gone. Laura was bringing home her little boy.

chapter forty

March 1989 - Four Months Later

Except for a bouquet of flowers sent to the services, Grady Culpepper had waited more than six weeks after the passing of Paul Rosenthal before trying any contact with Laura. She appreciated that. Not only was it a sign of respect, it was acknowledgment that Laura had a deep devotion to her husband and he knew she would feel uncomfortable, even disloyal, entering into a relationship so soon after.

When he called, she knew his intent, that he wanted her, that he would be there to love and comfort her. He was what she had always fantasized in a man. But it wasn't right. So she politely put him off again and again, hoping inwardly he would not surrender. His tenacity prevailed and she finally agreed to meet with him in a public place, wary of her own weaknesses, afraid she would succumb to the passion he brought out in her if they were alone.

"Okay, Grady. How about the same place we had lunch? The Taurus, for dinner. Tomorrow, at seven. Please, don't come to the house. I'll meet you there."

She arrived early but he was already waiting at a table in the second dining room which was less crowded than the first. He stood, smiling ear to ear. She reached her hand, businesslike. He smelled of a musk-like cologne. "You look well, Grady. So good to see you."

"You look, well, you look wonderful, Laura."

"Thanks. I put on a few pounds. My, you didn't have to get all dressed up."

"Well," he tugged at the edges of his sports jacket, "You're worth it."

Dinner was cordial but strained. Here were two human beings, desperately attracted to one another, boiling with passion,
yearning for love, with opportunity at their disposal, yet so restrained. What was it, she wondered, that was holding her back?
Months ago, she dreamt of the day she would melt in his arms,
making love the way love was supposed to be made, letting herself go. He was a good man, caring, masculine and so attractive.
There was no reason to deny herself, yet it could not be. They
talked about Jamie, Grace and Bowen and of his own married
daughters. Then the subject of Lloyd Ramsey came up.

"I couldn't imagine what went through your mind when you
saw him on that plane," he said, sipping from his glass of beer.
"When you sent that first note, he must have had a coronary."

"I didn't know what else to do."

"You handled it perfectly, Laura. I'm proud of you."

"I hear the trial's being postponed indefinitely," she said.
"News reports say that Lloyd has contracted pneumonia in the
Miami jail."

"Well, maybe he'll kick off and save everyone the money of a
trial."

"That would suit me just fine."

"And how is Bowen? Have you seen him lately?"

She sighed, looked into space a moment then touched the
rim of her wine glass. "I'm flying to L.A. once a month to visit.
He's at Chino state prison now. At least there, we won't have to
talk through a pane of glass." She drew a wry grin and reflected.
"Visits. I was always relegated to visits with my son. Still visits.
Anyway, he doesn't look good at all, Grady. I'm very worried.
He's gaunt, weak, always a cold or something."

"What happened with his case?"

"Fifteen years. Might get out in seven or eight with good
behavior. He cooperated, then pled guilty. I didn't want him to
but..."

"Probably the smart thing to do, Laura. Otherwise, he might
have faced three times that sentence."

"Perhaps." Then she redirected the subject back to Grady.
"Look, we didn't come here to talk about that. *Him.* Tell me
Grady, what's going on in your life? Your boat and the house?

The kids still talk about going fishing with you."

"Anytime, Laura. Tell Jamie I still need a first mate. I've got the boat docked at a marina in Key Largo."

"Oh? Why Key Largo?"

"I sold the house."

"The one on stilts? So, where are you living now?"

"Oh, here and there. Renting right now. Thinking about buying a condo maybe. Trying to decide between living in the Keys or moving to Miami. What do you think?" That was her cue, a question asking if there was a future between them, a question she was there to confront.

She placed her hands upon his and looked endearingly into his eyes. "Not now, Grady. Maybe someday, but not now."

"I'll make you happy, Laura. You know that."

"I know you'd make me happy. And I you. But it's hard to explain, I just..."

"I'll be a good step-grandfather to the boy."

"Is that a proposal?" she asked, smiling.

He offered a smile in return. "No. It's a prophesy."

"My my, such confidence. I'm flattered."

"It's only a matter of time, you and I. My preference is sooner. But I can wait."

Their eyes fixed upon one another until Laura pulled her hands way gently. "Grady, it's, it's Paul. Somehow, I would feel wrong. He deserves my grief. I need to stay a widow to him, at least for now. Maybe, in the future, a year or so, whatever..."

"Is that what he would have wanted?"

The question stunned her. Paul's hand-written note flashed through her mind. *"I free you again."* What would Paul have wanted for her? What would he be saying, right this minute?

Her happiness meant everything to him and she knew that.

"I'm not sure, Grady. I'm really not sure."

* * *

Bowen had finally achieved his wish. The L.A. County Jail was behind him. Ten of twelve counts of drug trafficking were dropped in exchange for his testimony against other traffickers, paving the way for his attorneys to work out a deal for a reduced sentence in a minimum security facility in Northern California once processed through Chino. Fifteen years was far better than consecutive life terms and with points for good conduct, he would be out in less than six. Laura sent letters almost daily telling him how wonderful Jamie was doing, sending money for cigarettes, stamps, stationary and basic supplies, imploring him to learn a trade, to get clean and stay clean, to look forward to being a full-time father to his son someday and assuring him of her undying love, as always.

The exchange of letters was mostly in one direction. Laura checked her mailbox daily in hopes of a letter from Bowen but it was rare. And when he did write, he always asked for one favor or another. But that didn't matter to Laura. She valued anything he would send.

It had been a long, arduous Friday at the office, one which left her unusually tired. No longer in need of money and weary from life's tribulations, she gave thought to retiring and paying full attention to raising Jamie. For the first time in twenty years, she felt her career had evolved into a mere job. After arriving home, she laid the large stack of mail on the kitchen table and used a steak knife as a letter opener. Buried in the pack was a grey envelope. Grace saw her eyes light up. "What is it Mom?"

"It's from Bowen."

"Oh."

The very mention of Bowen as a half brother embarrassed her. Grace shrugged and strolled up to her bedroom while Laura sat at the kitchen table and opened the envelope.

Dear Mother,

Could you send me some books? They've put me in isolation and I have nothing to read. Anything you have about animals and fish would be great. Even if it's about sports, I don't care. I'm bored crazy here. I've been losing weight and feeling very weak, and these bruises are showing up on my arms for no reason. So they gave me a bunch of tests and put me in isolation to play safe. I probably have a virus or something.

When are you coming out again to visit? At least, in this place, visitors aren't separated by a glass window. I know I don't write much, but that's because there's nothing to write about. But I

*like your letters, Jamie's too. I'm sorry Grace feels so distant
from me, but that's my fault, not hers. Anyway, give my love to
Jamie and send some pictures if you can.*
    Love, Bowen

The worst of thoughts consumed her. She had read about it,
seen it and smelled it during hospital visits. It was the subject of
television news and documentaries almost nightly. One former
student died of it three years after graduation. She knew symptoms, she knew causes. Bowen had been a hard core drug addict, including the use of hypodermic needles. He was also a
young inmate, jail fodder amid a zoo of rapists. Under her
breath, she whispered, "No, please God. No more. He's had
enough. Hasn't he been through enough? Please, don't let it
be."

Jamie scampered into the kitchen for a Yoo Hoo when he
noticed his grandmother clutching the letter, her head bowed
as though praying. "Are you okay, Grandma?" he asked.

"Yes love. I'm fine. Your Daddy says to tell you..." She could
barely choke out the sentence. "...that he loves you."

* * *

Later, Laura sat upon the sofa reading aloud from a fairy
tale book while pajama-clad Jamie leaned back on her lap, head
resting on her shoulder. Every so often she would stop and savor the moment, then resume her narration. All was quiet in
the Rosenthal house. Television was off. Mozart arias were an
echo of the past, no longer a backdrop of sound. Grace was at a
friend's for the weekend. The oxygen tanks and all the other
medical paraphernalia were long gone. The only remnants of
Paul were a few photos atop the mantel and the old chair which
had been his roost the last six years of his life.

She held the book with one hand and stroked his hair with
the other, contented, basking in the love of a little boy as though
drinking from the well after twenty years of thirst. She switched
to a poem which her father recited to her as a child, and he
chuckled. She loved to hear his chuckle. "This is the house that
Jack built. This is the malt that lay in the house that Jack built.

This is the rat that ate the malt, that lay..."

"Grandma, that's funny. I bet I can say that."

"This is the maiden all forlorn, who milked the cow with the crumpled horn, who tossed the dog that worried the cat, that killed the rat, that ate the malt..."

"Ha ha, he he, that lay in the house that Jack built."

"This is the man all tattered and torn, who kissed the maiden all forlorn..."

"Ha ha ha ha, haaaaa."

"This is the priest all shaven and shorn who married the man all tattered and torn who kissed the maiden..."

"Hee heee, all forlorn who milked the cow with the clumpered horn..."

"Crumpled, Jamie, not clumpered."

"Hee heee, crumpled horn, that tossed the dog, worried the cat, he heee..."

"Oh Jamie, you're so silly."

"Was my daddy silly when he was a little boy?"

The question came from nowhere. She wondered why a five year old child would think about the personality of his own father at his age. She stroked his hair again and replied, "You know, Jamie, I don't know. I honestly don't know. I'm sure he was."

"You mean you don't remember?"

"Yeah. I guess I don't remember. But I'll always remember you, don't you worry about that."

There was a long silence as they nestled amid their affections, each starved for love, each sating that hunger. Out of the blue, Jamie remarked, "I hope I never see my mommy again. She was a meanie."

Jamie was never asked to talk about her, so Laura saw it as a breakthrough. "You want to tell me about it, Jamie?"

"She hit me. I was always a bad boy and she hit me. She made me afraid."

"You'll never have to worry about that ever again, Jamie."

"She said she never wanted a boy. She didn't want me."

"Your mother was a sick woman, Jamie. But think how lucky you are that you can live here with me, and Grace."

"She's not my mommy any more."

"Well..."

"You're my mommy now."

"Well, not exactly, Jamie, but I'm kinda like your mother."

"Can I call you Mommy?"

Her heart skipped a beat. The sound of him uttering those words ravaged her soul. *Oh Yes! My little boy, call me Mommy, come to me, be mine, love me as your mother, let me care for you. I shall give you all that your Daddy was denied, a mother devoted to you, who would give her life for you, I love you so. Oh yes, I would love for you to call me Mommy. Please, yes!* She took a long, nervous breath, thought deeply, then replied, "No, darlin'. It's important that we live the truth. I'm your grandma. If I was your mother, I would love for you to...

"It's okay, Grandma. You act like my mommy, even though you're not really."

"This is the cock that crowed in the morn that waked the priest all shaven and shorn, who married the man all tattered and torn, who kissed the maiden all forlorn, who milked the cow..."

PART III

chapter forty-one

He died at the Central Florida Prison Reception Center in an infirmary the last day of July, 1991, after whimpering day and night for three years, never once seeing the light of freedom since suffering two gunshot wounds at the foot of the Los Angeles courthouse. He thought it was all fixed back in '88 but it only took a lunch hour for the jury to return a guilty verdict for first degree murder and a recommendation for life. Though they went for naught, his appeals ground slowly and were aborted by his demise before reaching the decision stage. He did his time miserably, working in a prison laundry, cowering to guards, cooped up with hard-core criminals in a tiny cage until it became evident that he was seriously ill. Then he was transferred to the medical facility at Lake Butler and later to Orlando where he regressed until his final days.

By the end of 1990, the AIDS virus swept through his body like a swarm of piranha, rejecting all available medication, rendering him a frail human skeleton for the final six months, hopelessly relegated to a slow, humbling, tormented death. He was buried in a Miami cemetery where no one except a handful of reporters and a former secretary attended his funeral. The story was a classic tale of irony. For all his life of sin and crime, this man received the ultimate sentence, awarded not by the state, but inadvertently by his own son. In the desperate pursuit of life in 1988, Lloyd Ramsey received the tainted blood of a donor who had contracted the virus so recently, it was not yet detectable through testing. In essence, Bowen had killed his father.

For Laura, it was another insurmountable hurdle in the quest for peace with her boy. Bowen was originally serving his time at the California Institute for Men at Chino but was later transferred upstate to the state prison's medical facility in Vacaville. There he was treated with a barrage of drugs for the AIDS virus, but it was all futile as his frail body slowly deteriorated, rallying times, offering hope that he might live long enough to receive parole and be with his nine-year-old Jamie before his inevitable passing. For three years after contracting HIV, Bowen seemed more resilient than most victims, responding to medication and looking forward to a cure before it consumed him into eternity. But it was short lived as the regression set in shortly after hearing about the death of his father.

Ever the eternal optimist, Laura flew into San Francisco's airport at the beginning of each month for a Sunday trek to Vacaville where she had become a familiar face among guards and medical staff. Required to wear a surgical mask at his bedside, she was often afforded special privileges, staying with her son for hours at a time. Armed, as always, with stacks of photographs, tapes, books and her undying love, Laura relished this time for it was more than they ever had together since he was a boy. Yet, her heart hung low with the thought of what lay ahead.

Bowen often rallied during her visits, happy to view pictures of his little boy, wishing he could have shared more and been a significant person in his life. Laura reassured him that he truly made a difference, for giving Jamie to her paved the road for his future stability.

By January of 1993, after weeks of failing eyesight, Bowen went completely blind. Letters from Laura waned and eventually stopped altogether as prison staff could not be responsible for reading aloud. She began flying to California every two weeks to be with him more often, to demonstrate her love until his final moments, so he would not feel cold, so there was someone to hold his hand.

The smell of antiseptics pervaded the floor as Bowen remained constantly bed-ridden, too weak to walk, barely able to lift his bony arms. His six foot frame was reduced to one hundred and twenty pounds and declining. His gaunt face and sunken cheeks reminded Laura of those skeletal-like images from

Nazi concentration camps. During these visits, she would sit at the edge of the bed holding his bony hand, telling stories about Jamie. Her heart gladdened each time a smile formed from his lips. His speech was slurred now, often unintelligible, mouth agape, seemingly unable to close his lips, uttering vowel sounds as he rambled on about imaginary journeys, fishing and sunsets. She understood most everything he said. His eyes had dulled, agaze at the ceiling, moaning, no longer able to see the photos that his mother brought.

It was the second week in May, another routine trip to the Vacaville Prison Medical Facility. As usual, she signed in, *Mrs. Laura Culpepper.* After arriving at the hospice center, she was greeted by one of the regular nurses, a heavy-set, brown-haired woman named Carla who had a tendency to chatter, but she was caring and thoughtful. "He's been delirious, Mrs. Culpepper," she said. "I don't think it will be long now. Three or four weeks, maybe less. I'm sorry."

From the nurses station across the floor, Laura could see into the private room where Bowen was asleep, his mouth agape, eyes sunken in a blank gaze. The eerie silence was interrupted by the perpetual sounds of hospital equipment, *beep.....beep..... hsssss......beep ......beep....hsssss...*, gentle footsteps, soft voices, antiseptic odors, white colors. Laura had hoped for a few moments with Bowen's during his conscious moments before she had to leave. The nurse chattered on. "Poor thing, he asks for you all the time," she said.

"Oh? Really?"

"Oh yes. Yes. Poor thing. Keeps repeating, *'Mommy, Mommy,'* over and over, when he's awake. Like he dreams of being with you. He really must love you, Mrs. Culpepper."

Laura sighed and swallowed hard as she looked to her dying son. Softly, she muttered, barely audible, "So, he wants his Mommy. Is that it?"

The nurse shrugged. "Sometimes he blurts it out and wakes the other patients. He just shouts, *'MOMMY'!* Out of nowhere. It's wonderful that you come all this way to be with him."

Laura remained mute, unable to speak. Then, she mused aloud, "Mommy. Hmm. How flattering. Yeah, very flattering." Carla was dumbfounded as Laura paused, staring at her boy.

"Huh. I wish it were me."

"Excuse me?" asked the nurse, confused by Laura's odd response.

"Oh. Nothing."

* * *

Aside from the pending tragedy with Bowen, Laura's life had reached a level of fulfillment like she had never known. Now fifty-one and married to Grady Culpepper for three blissful years, she retired from her position at Stanton School, sold the Rosenthal mansion in Coconut Grove and moved to Marathon Key where they bought a thirty-four foot fishing boat and built a giant house on stilts. With the love money left to her by Paul, they opened a small marina and cafe where she and the kids enjoyed the good life, fishing on weekends, skin diving and enjoying scores of friends from around the nation. Nine year-old Jamie was a natural in the water and had already won his first deep sea fishing tournament by landing a forty-seven pound sailfish off the coast of Islamorada. Zena was never heard from again. Jamie mentioned his father from time to time but the memory of him was fading.

Now in her mid-teens, Grace maintained a straight A average at her high school, excelling in math and science and certain to follow in her father's footsteps in the medical profession. Grady Culpepper was a blessing indeed, sent from heaven to a woman who had struggled all her life to find love. He was a perfect step-father to two beautiful kids, a wonderful role model and a natural at managing a marina, his life long dream. All that was missing for Laura, all that was ever missing, was Bowen.

Laura often wondered how it might have been had it not been for that one fateful day, losing her composure and allowing another human being to take control over her life and the life of her son. One day, one act, one mistake charted the crooked path for his entire future. She wondered how Bowen might have turned out had *she* raised him, if he would have played sports, graduated college, become a professional, or simply been a loving person. She wondered if genetics influenced Bowen's personality, if he was truly doomed at birth with a deceitful mind, without conscience. She rejected the thought, certain that his environment made the difference. Though time rewarded her with Grace and then Jamie, she still wondered how it might have been to enjoy those same feelings from Bowen. Envy gnawed deep within her, knowing he had accepted another woman as his mother. So unfair. Still, Yvonne's memory lingered deep in his heart as he lay at death's doorstep at age twenty-nine.

* * *

From her Los Angeles hotel room, Laura phoned home and asked her husband, "Grady, I need to hire a detective. Right away. Someone we have to find. Her name was Yvonne Ramsey, maiden name Rappaport. Haven't heard hide nor hair of her in eighteen years. She's about my age, blonde, always wore her hair in curls, a former secretary who came into money when she married Lloyd. I think she was from Brooklyn. New York."

"Why? What's the urgency, Laura?'

"It's Bowen. He's slipping. She meant a lot to him, and I want to find her."

"You're quite a woman."

"No. I just want to do it for Bowen."

"Sure, Laura. You got it. I know just who to call. When will you be home?"

"I'm staying. Please Grady, I hope you understand. I want to find that woman, and...well, I have to be here when...."

"Say no more sweetheart. Take as long as you need. The kids will be fine. I'll call as soon as I have any information."

"Thanks, darling. You're wonderful."

"No, you're wonderful. I'm just in love."

* * *

Yvonne had seemingly vanished from the face of the earth. But her father, now a lonely widower, was located in a seniors-only condominium complex in Naples, Florida. Two days after hiring the detective, Laura was knocking at the door.

"Who is it?" barked the graveled voice from inside.

"My name is Laura. Laura Culpepper. I want to ask you something about your daughter."

"What are you? A bill collector?"

"No no. I'm...well, an old acquaintance. Please, this is very important."

"Ain't seen my daughter in over twenty years. Can't help you."

"Please, may I come in. I just want to talk."

"Door's open."

Laura stepped inside to find Herman Rappaport sitting in the darkened living room in a wheel chair against the wall facing a television set, puffing a cigar. The stench of stale smoke made her bring a handkerchief to her nose. Sunshine beamed through sheer curtains, offering a dim ray of light while a ceiling fan spun slowly above. "Mr. Rappaport, I'm sorry to bother you, but this is very important."

"What's she done?"

"It's not what's she's done sir, it's what she can do for a dying man with AIDS."

"Huh?"

After Laura explained the circumstances, Herman Rappaport relented. "I ain't seen her, but she sends money every month. Helps with the expenses here and all. She's a good woman, like her mother."

"Where is she, please sir?"

"In London. Managing editor of some publishing company. Married into the company.

Look in my desk over there, in all that mess. You'll find her envelopes. Maybe there's a return address."

"Oh, thank you Mr. Rappaport. Thank you so much."

chapter forty-two

Each time Laura identified herself to the London publishing firm, a secretary placed her on hold then said that Mrs. Southersby was not in. Finally, after the fourth call, the secretary was more honest. "Sorry, Mrs. Culpepper, Mrs. Southersby does not wish to talk with you."

Forty-eight hours later, bedraggled from red-eye flights across two continents, Laura presented herself at the front office of Ivy Publications located on the fourth floor of an office building not far from Piccadilly Circus in downtown London. After being directed to the Chief Editor, a matronly woman intercepted her from barging through the office door. "One moment, Madam. Where do you think you are going?" Laura recognized the voice from the telephone.

"I must see Yvonne Southersby. Please, it is urgent."

"Mrs. Southersby is in a meeting. Leave me your card and I'll..."

"Miss, this is a matter of life and death. I'm not an agent, it's a personal thing. I've traveled from California to be here. Please."

In condescending fashion, she looked Laura up and down, pursed her lips and replied, "What is your name, Madam?"

"Formerly Laura Rosenthal, now Laura Culpepper. She knows who I am."

"Oh. It's you. I told you Mrs. Southersby didn't..."

"Look, lady, I've traveled halfway across this world from California. If it wasn't urgent, I wouldn't be here."

"Wait here."

The woman wrote her name on a slip of paper and disappeared through the large, mahogany door for what seemed like an eternity. Laura anxiously sat on a stiff leather sofa, then paced the floor, stopping once to scan the array of photographs adorning the wall. One large frame featured a collage of old snapshots which she glanced at casually and turned away, her eyes remaining steeled to the door. But something caught the corner of her eye. *That picture.* She stepped to the collage once more where she scanned photos of various office staff, men and women in business attire, smiling, shaking hands. She bent closer to the smallest photo at the lower right corner, incongruent with the others. A note written with blue ball-point pen was scrawled along the bottom edge, taken in 1975. They were somewhere on a fishing pier in the Florida Keys. *My God, that's Bowen.*

"Madam?" Laura was startled by the woman's reentry into the room.

"Yes?"

"Mrs. Southersby cannot be disturbed at this moment. She said to give you this note."

Laura took the slip of paper. In red ball-point ink, it read:

Trafalgar Square. I'll meet you there in one hour. Yvonne

* * *

Traffic was heavy at the famous landmark as caravans of red, double-deck buses passed by, intermingled with miniature cars and black Austin taxis creating a chorus of shifting gears, blaring horns and a noxious odor of fumes pervading the air. Laura was nearly killed when a small car approached, screeching its brakes from the right as she crossed the street. She had mistakenly looked to her left.

Yvonne may have put on twenty pounds over the years but she looked strikingly unchanged from the last time Laura saw her in person, the day five-year-old Bowen was being readied for surgery.

"*Hello Doctor, we're Bowen's father and mother.*"

"*And you are...?*"

"*Oh, I'm ...I'm Laura Rosenthal. And this little fella, well, he's pretty special to me.*"

"*I see.*"

She strutted confidently amid a fluttering flock of pigeons, her hair still atop her head in a bouncing cluster of blonde curls.

Clad in a chic business suit and four-inch heels, she passed the towering monument to Lord Horatio Nelson and walked directly up to Laura in a challenging pose. Laura stood from her bench.

"Hello Yvonne," she said sensing hostility in the woman's carriage, her eyes intense. "You're looking well."

"What do you want?" the woman asked, disregarding customary greetings. Laura was taken aback. Before she could reply, Yvonne continued on, "I expected this would happen one day."

"I don't understand. I think you're mistaken."

"This will never escape me, will it?"

"I don't know what you're talking about."

"How much? Just tell me how much."

"How much what?" Stunned, Laura shrugged, unable to penetrate.

"Money. That's what you're here for. Just tell me...."

"I don't want your money, Yvonne."

Yvonne studied Laura's face a moment, then asked, "You mean, this isn't blackmail?"

"Blackmail? Huh?"

"What is it then?"

"It's Bowen."

Yvonne paused and lifted her chin, showing no emotion. "Bobo? What about Bobo? Let's see. He's got to be almost thirty now."

Laura was startled at hearing the sobriquet. "Bobo?" she asked

"Yes. Well, I mean Bowen. What's this all about?"

"Was that your pet name for him?"

"Yeah. That's what I called him. So, tell me, what's up?"

Bobo? I never knew. "Yvonne, uh,....." Her lips quivered trying to spit out those horrible words. "I'm here because, well, he's dying."

Yvonne suddenly gasped, her eyes opened wide. "Oh, my God." Laura could see the blood drain from her face as her hands crossed her chest, her knees weakened. She took a seat on the bench where pigeons gathered around her feet. "Dying? What do you mean?"

It was a breakthrough for Laura to see an emotional reaction. "Bowen has AIDS. He's had it for five years and there's little time left."

"Oh my God, poor Bo, that's terrible. I don't know what to say."

"You can say, well, that you'll go out to see him. To be with him before he dies."

"Is that what you're doing? You came all the way to England to get me to visit with Bowen?"

"Yes."

"Why me?"

Laura paused, then placed her hand upon Yvonne's. "Because he loves you. He's never stopped thinking about you. Even in his delirium, he asks for you."

Yvonne sighed deeply, lit a cigarette nervously, sucked long and hard, then exhaled. She looked up to the sky as a giant Boeing 747 passed over. "I'm sorry to hear of it. I mean, I'm truly sorry. But I must be honest, he doesn't mean anything to me. Until now, I haven't given Bobo, uh Bowen a thought since I walked out of Lloyd's life eighteen years ago. And that's the way I want to keep it."

"I don't believe you."

"Don't believe all you want, I'm telling you, he means nothing to me."

"Is that why you still have his picture on your office wall?"

Caught in a lie, Yvonne took another puff and exhaled once more. "You have a good eye," she said with a wry grin. Laura remained silent, allowing Yvonne to gather her thoughts. She looked around the square then continued, "Okay. You're right. Maybe that's not true. I often think about that boy like some old dream. I had to close that chapter in my life. You may think all you want about money and stuff, but for me it was a ten year prison sentence. You don't know what hell I went through living with that miserable son of a bitch. The only thing that made it all worthwhile, was Bo. So when the time came, I had to walk away and never look back. You understand?"

"I understand."

"Contact with Bowen meant, well, staying linked with that asshole. I couldn't allow that. Besides, Bo had his mother."

Yvonne looked Laura in the eye. "You're a good mother, Laura. I never held anything against you. It was wrong, very wrong, what was done to you. I had no control over..."

"Yvonne, you don't have to explain."

Another long puff, another exhale. Laura waited patiently. "So, how is Lloyd these days?"

"Dead. From AIDS."

Yvonne burst into laughter, coughing from a puff of cigarette smoke. "You're kidding? Well, that's one bright note."

"He got it from Bowen, in a transfusion."

"Holy shit. That's one for the books. I oughta find an author to write this one up."

Laura remained somber. "Yvonne, please come. He has little time left."

Yvonne panned the square, looking up at the pedestrians passing by. She shook her head directly at Laura. "I'm sorry."

"Yvonne, don't say you're sorry, please. Bowen's final wish is to be with you."

She looked deep into Laura's desperate eyes and asked, "This must be terribly hard for you. I mean, here you are his mother, begging his long forgotten step-mother. I mean I was like, the competition." A tear trickled down Laura's cheek. Yvonne continued, "I don't think I've ever known anyone who loved another person so much. Look here, I..."

"It's not as hard on me as it is on Bowen. Come. See the little boy who loved you so much."

Yvonne sighed and leaned back, reminiscing. "We went on a fishing trip to Islamorada. His father never would, so I took him. I never saw a kid so happy, so content, so excited."

"That's when that picture was taken? The one in your office."

"Yeah. I'd just given him a little seashell I found on the shoreline. You'd think I gave him a million bucks."

Laura reflected on the conical relic Bowen gave to Jamie the day of his arrest. "Was it kinda blue, and orange?"

"Yeah. Pointy kind, like a cone, ya know? I think that's the last time I was ever on a beach."

"He kept it, gave it to his son to keep."

"No shit? Bobo's got a kid?"

Laura smiled. "Jamie. He's nine and he's wonderful. He lives with me."

"I see." Yvonne lit another cigarette, then stood abruptly. It seemed another person had just slipped into her skin as she turned hard and cold, checked her watch, cleared her throat and said, tersely, "Look, I'm very sorry, Laura. I have to get back to work."

Laura stood with her. "You're not...?"

"I'm sorry. You can think what you want of me, I simply can't do it. I must be getting back." Laura peered deep into Yvonne's eyes, hoping she would see the desperation, praying she would acquiesce, but it was not to be. It was time to hurry back to Vacaville without Yvonne. "Can I ask you something?" Laura asked.

"Sure," replied Yvonne, checking her watch again.

"Was that you? That day at the Miami airport?" The woman turned her head away, no reply. Laura had stunned her. "About a year or two after you disappeared, Bowen thought he spotted you in the airport and he went berserk running after, calling for you," Yvonne listened as Laura spoke on. The expression in her face was all the answer she needed. "... and you just kept walking off. Like you said, not looking back."

"I really have to get back. Give Bobo a kiss for me."

Ruefully, she sighed, "Good bye, Yvonne."

She strutted off amid the sea of pigeons when a final thought came to Laura. "Oh, Yvonne?" As she walked away, she stopped and looked indifferently over her shoulder. "What kind of perfume have you got on?" Laura asked.

A quizzical expression crossed Yvonne's face. She hollered, "Chanel Number 5. Why?"

"Have you always worn that?"

Without answering, she turned away toward the traffic, scattering the pigeons around her.

chapter forty-three

She called the Vacaville Medical Facility no less than three times daily, checking on Bowen. Carla said there was little change in his condition, that he was in and out of consciousness, moaning and rambling and pining for *Mommy*.

Billowing with emotion, Laura was preparing for those dreaded final moments, moments approaching too soon, moments inescapable. Her head swam with ideas, anything to please her son, to draw one last smile from his lips, to experience that ever-so-elusive feeling of nearness. Yvonne's refusal to grant her son's dying fantasy left her bitter. How awful, she thought, how terribly frigid. Here she was, the natural mother swallowing her pride, craving the very love he felt toward a surrogate, yet she was out there seeking Bowen's final wish.

Time was short. Laura was feeling pressed to get back to Bowen's bedside. She made an exhausting one day detour to Miami, not so much to visit with family but as a mission, pursuing three important objectives before returning to California. Her calls to Vacaville were every two to three hours now, desperately afraid she would be too late, that she would miss those final seconds together. Fearing her family was feeling neglected during the crisis, she spent a few hurried hours enjoying their attention and asking for forgiveness until the ordeal passed. Grady was a gem, truly understanding. "The kids will be here, they're fine. I'll be here for you always, Laura. I just wish I could be with you, to hold you when you need holding."

"I love you, Grady."

"Go, sweetheart. Do what you must. I'll pray for him, and for you."

Her visit at home completed one objective. From there, she

stopped at a department store before spending four long hours at a beauty salon. Now it was time to be with her boy.

* * *

By morning, Laura had everything she needed. She boarded another plane for California knowing this would be her journey of closure. It was her destiny to be with Bowen during his death moment, compelled by love to do anything to bring a ray of gladness into his heart before his final exhale. There was an odd sense of comfort knowing he would now be with her for all eternity, that he would probably be joining her on her return flight, in a box.

The noon sun blazed high in the hazy California sky when she arrived at the prison gates. It was Wednesday morning, May 27th, oddly enough the twenty-ninth anniversary of that fateful day in Golden Beach when her life, and her son's life turned inside out. As usual, she was provided a visitor's pass which she wore clipped to her blouse. She offered her customary greetings and addressed the sallyport guards by their first names as they conducted their perfunctory searches. This day, the guard saw her carrying a plastic shopping bag which required an inspection. "Please," she asked. "There's no contraband, it's nothing harmful."

As Laura waited, the tall uniformed guard carried the sack behind the glass enclosure and showed the contents to a supervisor. They looked at her quizzically, then shook their heads. Laura motioned for them to come out so she could make her appeal.

"Sorry ma'am. Prison rules. You can't carry anything in that is unauthorized. That means, you can bring..."

"I know what I can bring, Sam. I've been here a hundred times. This time Bowen's dying, and you know..."

"Sorry ma'am. You can leave the bag here."

"Hold on a minute," she said, snatching the bag from their hands. To the amazement of both guards, she removed a curly blonde wig, shook it out and then placed it over her own head, changing her appearance immediately. "Now it's part of my apparel. Any problem with that?"

The guard named Sam smiled and waved his hand permissively. Before turning over her purse, she removed a small glass container and poured a half bottle of Chanel Number Five perfume into her hands, dripping some upon the concrete floor. She reeked of sweet fragrance. "Any problem with that Sam?" she asked, handing him her purse.

"No ma'am."

"Now let me see my son."

Carla was taken aback when Laura entered the hushed infirmary, shocked to see a nest of blonde curls atop her head. Laura looked to the far corner where Bowen lay emaciated in his bed, head moving side to side, mouth agape, sightless eyes in a blank stare toward the ceiling. Laura stared briefly, happy she made it back before it was too late.

"May I?" she asked the nurse, motioning.

"Whew. What'd you do Mrs. Culpepper? Sit in a tub of perfume? Sure, you can go on in," she replied. "But what's with that get-up?"

"It's time for my boy to be with his Mommy."

"Oh. Huh? Wha...?" Carla was clearly stunned, yet dared not ask another question. "Uh, don't forget, Mrs. Culpepper, put on the mask."

"Not today, Carla."

"But Mrs. Culpepper."

"Not today. Just, just let me be with him. Okay?"

The slow walk across the room seemed an eternity as she passed other rooms where inmates lay ill, paying them no mind, her eyes steeled to her dying boy in the corner, wondering if he would react, if this was all a futile, wasted effort, if she was making a fool of herself, if he was too far gone into oblivion to feel, to smell, to smile once more.

She stood at his side and gazed, wondering, hoping. He remained unresponsive, as though asleep with his eyes open. They were together now, the two of them as she took his bony hand into hers. She pulled the sheet down slightly and touched his chest, then spoke in a whisper.

"Hello, Bobo."

There was no response. His breathing was so shallow that she glanced fearfully at the heart monitor. She leaned to his

sallow face and touched both sunken cheeks, wincing from his
acrid breath. "Bobo?" she said once more, reeking of perfume.

He sniffed, then alerted. His head turned to her, eyes fixed,
lips barely moving, obviously conscious but confused. His right
hand clutched hers. Then he moved his left hand impaled with
an IV needle, skeletal thin, waving, uttering nothing but grunting sounds. Bowen was answering.

Her heart felt like it pounded from her chest. "Hello Bobo,"
she whispered once more, straining to keep from crying. Now
was not the time.

He sniffed again and squeezed her hand slightly. For the
first time in weeks, he pressed his lips together, for a moment.

"Mahhmmy?"

Tears welled in her eyes, but she couldn't break down now,
not now, it was too essential that she carry on the ruse. "Yes,
Bobo. I'm here, my love."

"Mahhmmy?"

"I love you Bowen," she said, whispering near to his face.

"Mahhmmy?" His brow raised broadening his eyes as though
he could suddenly see again.

"Oh yes, son. I'm here, with you."

"Mahhhhmmieeee?"

Bowen relaxed his grip and as a warm glow came over his
face. Laura had finally achieved her wish, the wish of her lifetime. As she gazed into happy eyes that could not see, she took
his right hand, leaned her head down and had him touch her
hair. He patted.

This time his response was not a question. "Mahhmmieeee,"
he grunted, feeling the curls. "Mahhhhmmieeee."

"I love you, Bobo."

"Mahhhhmmieeee."

The hint of a smile crossed his face. She saw he was no longer
in pain, happy now that he had *Mommy's* love, the love he
sought since he was eleven years old. He could no longer press
his lips together as his grunts faded, barely audible. But to Laura,
it was fresh air and music, vivid colors, the smell of roses and
everything wonderful, a love like she had never known before,
that she would never know again. It was time to savor it all for
eternity. She continued to hold his hand as he settled in, so still,

happy now, and unafraid. She was so glad.

Hssss....Beep....Beep....Hssss....Beep....Beep....Hssss.......

There had been another long silence. Too long. Bowen lay quiet and still. Laura combed his hair with her fingers, kissed his forehead once more then placed her hand on the side of his face.

"Bobo?" No response.

"Bobo?"

An explosion of tears gushed from her eyes, her face grimaced uncontrollably. Twenty-nine years of broken hearts, pain and degradation had just come to an end, for both of them.

"Come on, son " she sobbed, whispering, holding tight. "One more time, honey. Call me Mommy."

Then she heard the seashell strike the floor.